Traitor to the Crown

A Young Adult Historical Novel

by

C. E. Ravenschlag

Book & cover design by R. Gary Raham, Wellington, CO
Email:rgaryraham@gmail.com

Library of Congress Control Number: 2021918861
ISBN: 0-9729421-1-9

Fort Collins, CO 80549

Dedication

This story is told in honor of my forbearers who through hard work, strong will, compromise, and religious faith somehow survived all the invaders of Briton from Vikings, Romans, Saxons, and Normans and came out the other side of these occupations with their culture and customs still dominant.

Acknowledgments

Without the previous generations of my family who preserved legends through the centuries, the impetus for this story may never have evolved. These legends sparked my own research into Saxon culture, William the Conqueror, Old Briton, clothing, weapons, armor, history of the eleventh century in Wessex where my ancestors experienced the brunt of the invasion of Britain in 1066 and much more.

For all the people who have assisted with this story, thanks go to the Penpointer's writing group, and Barbara Fleming and Sylvia Falconer of my other writing group. Hours of their critiques have made the story so much stronger. Historian Jack Steele was instrumental in attesting to the factual accuracy of the events of the eleventh century and giving suggestions for the Welsh parts of the story. Without Gary Raham, who shepherded this story through the publishing process, this tale would never have reached print.

Scotland
Hadrian's Wall
North Sea
Northumbria
York
Isle of
Anglesea
Mercia
Hillmen
Merane's Village
Bleddyn's
Caernervon
Chester
Gwynedd
Kadeg's
Oswestry
Bala
Shrewsbury
England
Powys
Severn R.
Hereford
Wales
Gloucester
Wessex
Dyfed
London
Odo's Castle
Winchester
Herstmonceux
Odo's
Village
Exeter
Cornwall
English Channel

Chapter One

14 October 1066

Streamers of fog lifted and evaporated over the valley. From where they stood in the edge of the wood, Edan and Fergus looked down to the land below.

"*By gwdihu's* eyes*, I can't see a thing!" Edan whispered. Puffs of steam punctuated his words in the chill air.

A lance throw away, the English army, led by King Harold Godwineson, set their line of battle near an ancient apple tree at the Hastings crossroads. Edan could see his father's white and gold banner fluttering next to the king's big Dragon of Wessex and grimaced rebelliously at his broad back.

"Of course you can," Fergus whispered back. "You lackwit."

"Aye, the backsides of our soldiers and the bums of the horses. As soon as the troops move off the hill to fight Duke William, we'll see nothing of our first battle."

"It be too dangerous to go closer," Fergus argued.

"We can get a better view over there." Edan pointed to a grassy hillock, dotted with a few solitary shrubs.

"Have off, that lookout is on open ground." Fergus balked. A look of mulish stubbornness crept over his freckled face.

"Come on." Circling the gathered soldiers, Edan knelt and crawled through frosty, knee high grasses into the open. Near the hillock crest, he dropped to his belly and propelled himself by his elbows. Fergus followed, despite his protests. Though Edan was Fergus's junior by a year, his birthright as son of the village thane gave

** gwdihu--pronounced "goody hoo"; in Welsh, an owl*

him the right to command. With the luck of the ignorant they eluded roving scouts of the two armies.

Shivering with excitement and cold, Edan's breath caught when he parted the coarse blades to look upon the probable meeting point of the two forces, a valley between two hills. This little rise contained treacherous boggy spots but provided a better view as he had hoped. Since Father forbade him to fight, now he must lie here out of sight while his eager heart ached to be a part of it.

The rumble of thousands of voices, the clank of weaponry grew.

Fergus gave a low whistle, "How many are they? Are they more than King Harold has?"

"There must be thousands and thousands, all the way to the Narrow Sea." Edan's voice strained over the mounting noise.

As they talked, trumpets blew and Norman archers loosed an opening volley. Arrows clattered onto the tight-packed wall of oblong shields like a hailstorm. Duke William's lines of infantry and horsed knights flooded across the valley and surged up the bramble-covered hill toward the English army like a great wave from the sea. At its crest two banners fluttered, one William's blue and gold, the other, red and white, unknown to Edan. The nearness of his friend, his calloused hand upon his arm, reassured him, kept his pounding heart in his chest.

King Harold's troops waited in tight formation atop their hill, sun glinting on metal, red and white pennant rippling.

Then the forces met with a thunderous roar that split the air. Fergus yelled above the din of battle when King Harold's forces took early advantage, "Harold has them on the run." Edan clenched his fists until his nails cut his palms, while his heart skittered in his chest like a scalded snake.

During the opening charge, combat boiled to where he and Fergus hid. After a flurry of lance, broadsword and battleax, a man rolled toward them, his mouth open in a silent scream. Edan clutched the earth with his fingers, frozen in horror.

The ground trembled under his hands. Behind him came the clatter of lances and the thud of hooves. He twisted to see. He jerked his head around to Fergus, whose widened brown eyes mirrored those of a rabbit hearing a falcon's wings stooping to the kill. They flattened themselves.

Would the Norman knights ride right over them?

Edan's heart beat so, he feared it would be heard. The earthquake of hooves drew closer, passed on their left, and on their right. He tensed his body against a crushing blow from a trencher-sized hoof. The line of Norman cavalry passed without seeing them and made a flanking move around the end of the battle line to strike at the English rear. Fear for the home forces clutched his heart. He wanted to warn them. He started to rise, but Fergus grabbed his arm and yanked him down.

Another noise behind him. Edan turned. *What now?* A lagging knight, his horse mired to the knees in a boggy place, cursed and whipped the animal. He dismounted and tugged at the horse's reins, his companions unaware of his plight.

The knight glanced up. His gaze followed his advancing troop and must have caught a flash of foreign color. He dropped the reins and moved toward Fergus and Edan, drawing his broadsword from its scabbard as he came.

Edan leaped to his feet. "I'll not lie still, stuck here in the grass squealing like a pig at slaughter."

Fergus stood trembling at his side. "A plague on him before he reaches us," he murmured.

Edan made a small movement of his left hand. "Mock fight," he mouthed. The two split away to each side of the advancing warrior, drawing the daggers at their belts.

Close enough now to see the nosepiece of the Norman's helmet, the burning fierceness of the eyes, and to hear the whine of the sword as it slashed air, Edan was mindful only of sweat trickling down his ribs. His legs shook. They had no real weapons, only their tiny hand daggers.

"You be up," Edan said. "You're bigger."

Fergus nodded, then circled to get behind the warrior, while Edan kept the man's attention forward as boys so often did mock-fighting in the village. One would ride his partner's back, while trying to knock another rider off an opposing pair. Only this time it would be different. The warrior would have no partner. He looked from the tall boy to the shorter one. The boys circled back toward the mired horse. Edan spotted a battle axe hung from the saddle.

Edan feinted toward the smiling knight, who swung his sword. Edan retreated three steps. When the warrior's arm extended, sure of its unskilled target, Fergus leaped for his back. Clinging there, Fergus got a forearm around the warrior's neck. Edan's breath caught at the terror on his friend's face. The man clutched Fergus's arm with his free hand, his face a mask of surprise.

Edan dashed to the horse, grabbed the axe and turned back to the warrior. He must help. Fergus had done his part. Edan had practiced with such a weapon, but could he get close enough to do any damage without having an arm or his head lopped off? His arms felt as limp as pottage in stew.

The warrior staggered, one foot in a boggy place. The sword hand dropped as he tried to balance. Fergus clung with desperation and threw his weight to the unbalanced side. Seeing an opening, Edan lunged forward and swung the battle axe with all his might against the knight's mail-covered ribs. A satisfying thud, a grunt. The man went to his knees.

Fergus leaped off, grabbed at the knight's sword hand. Edan swung again at the man's head. A clang. A jolt ran up his arm. The helmet rolled free. The man slumped to his haunches, disbelief in his eyes. Edan swung again. A mushy thud. Blood sprang from the wound in his head. Edan's arm tingled to the point of numbness. The knight fell forward to his face like a tree under the axe.

Fergus grabbed at Edan's sleeve. "Is he dead?"

"I don't know," Edan replied before jerking around to the battlefield to see the flankers, who had nearly ridden over them, join other Normans and surge forward. After fierce hand-to-hand battle, a contingent of English troops flowed down the slope in pursuit of Norman troops and cut off the flankers.

"Look," Fergus called out. "Harold has them on the run."

"Harold has routed the attackers," he yelled back.

Throwing themselves prone again on their hilltop, Edan watched Norman knights on horseback ride forward, isolate their pursuers and in a flurry of lance, broadsword and battleaxe, cut them down. The fallback was a trap. Breathless with horror and anger, Edan heard a groan of anguish, then realized it came from his own throat. Fergus dropped his head onto his arms.

The screams of men, pierced with a lance or crushed by war-horses trained to kill, stabbed Edan's brain. He pressed his mouth hard against his sleeve to quell his stomach's revolt. The troop lines wavered forward and back as the advantage swung like a great tide, crested by the pennants. How long had he been watching? A night-mare of days? He wanted to look away but could not. The noise of weaponry and shouts, even smells of blood and sweat swirled onto their hiding place. Edan's head swam with the assaults on his senses. The superior mobility of the mounted Norman knights against the warriors who pursued them on foot became painfully obvious.

Out of the bedlam, a segment of Duke William's troops made another run at the hill with combined infantry and cavalry. Edan's breaths grew rapid as the Normans clamored like hounds on fox scent. Why did King Harold remain atop the hill, his surrounding troops with oblong shields locked? A downward surge could sweep the Normans backward.

In another part of the field, Duke William removed his helmet, proving to his men he still lived after his wounded horse fell. A knight dismounted and gave William his own. The Duke rode beside a mace-swinging noble astride a gray stallion, and they continued the strong assault, achieving the hillcrest where Harold's housecarls held rank around their king in a desperate last stand.

King Harold's banner fell, followed by banners of supporting nobles as Norman knights pressed their stallions into the Saxons. Edan's eyes sought Father's white and gold banner in the twilight. It had been next to the king's Dragon of Wessex; now it was nowhere to be seen. The hilltop swarmed with Normans. The main body of Harold's army had never moved from that hill. Again he asked himself, why? His mind denied what his eyes told him. A chill crept from his toes to the top of his head. Father must be dead.

He heard Fergus exclaim, “They run. Our soldiers flee the battlefield, our leaders are dead. What will happen to us?”

Splinter groups of Normans flooded from the field, bent on looting. *The village!*

He turned and sprinted for the ponies.

Chapter Two

The pounding of hooves and the ringing of steel against steel had ceased. Screams and moans of the wounded and dying waned. The bloody hills of Sussex hid in the dark of a moonless night, while fog rose in wisps from the marsh, eerie grave markers over the bodies of the dead.

Bereaved families' torches weaved everywhere as they searched for loved ones, until the valley breathed smoke and sparked with star-like points of light. Among them, Edan and Fergus searched the battlefield with their borrowed cart, Cecil's cart, a torch of rushes fastened to its side. Only Cecil the forester lived outside the village, escaping notice of the Normans who had taken Herstmonceux after the battle.

Edan determined to do something right today, a day that had been a shambles from the time he disobeyed until the defeat of the English army. Enduring one grotesque sight after another, disemboweled men, the earth slippery with blood, hearing the groans of impaled horses, and the death rattles in men's throats, at last he found the body of his father near where his banner fell, so close to the encamped Normans he could barely force himself to be there. Father's body sprawled, arms flung wide with his sword grasped in his fist, a sneer of defiance on his lips. His cross still on its leather thong lay blood-smeared upon his chest.

Edan trembled when he looked upon the horrible sword slash. So much blood. He could not bring himself to touch Father's body. The sights and sounds around him blurred. Reality was replaced by a hollowness. His vision ran red with blood, trickles, splotches, puddles. His knees buckled. Fergus caught him under the arms.

"Are you all right, man?"

Edan's voice sounded far away to his own ears. "I feel..."

As he spoke, he felt sour bile rise in the back of his throat. He fell forward, retching into the bloody mud. He knelt, shuddering and shaking with shock. Only when he felt Fergus's strong hands seize him under the armpits once more did he come to his senses. He staggered to his feet and took a step toward his father's body.

Fergus drove the cart as close as he could. He and Fergus half-carried, half-dragged his father's body. So heavy. His muscles strained. Something popped in his back. Spear length by spear length they moved until they reached the cart and hoisted Father onto its strawed floor, his sword alongside.

Amid the littered battlefield Edan pushed with all the strength left in him to move the cart carrying his dead father. Trampled mud sucked hard at the wheels and threatened to pull the very boots from their feet. Coal, the carthorse, bunched his body, leaning into the harness. Fergus pulled at his bridle, muscles straining to help the struggling horse.

With the boys' effort combined, the little horse broke the cart free. Neither spoke. What surrounded them remained beyond words. Merciful shadows masked some of the horrors, but Edan gagged on the reeking stench around him, a stench worse than ten pigstyes.

Edan's foot slipped, and he fell face first into the mud. Sputtering and spitting he wiped an arm across his mouth to rid himself of the muck. Finding his voice, Edan cursed, "Duke William, you blood-sucking butcher, you bag of sheep's entrails,... Then he whispered, "You greedy, luck-blessed oaf."

Fergus stopped and turned haunted eyes upon him.

Edan put his shoulder to the wheel once more. Tears slid down his cheeks and dropped into the black mud. What would he do without Father's big blunt fingers on the chess piece across the board, the musky smell of him after a hunt in the wood with Toby and the rest of the hounds, the sound of his deep voice, his fierce protection? He could not imagine an existence without this towering figure at its center. He forced himself to think of Fergus, who worried about his own father, but said nothing. He drew a sleeve across the tears on his muddy cheeks.

"Just a bit more and we'll be on high ground," panted Fergus from his position at Coal's head. Torchlight revealed his familiar freckled face streaked with mud. "A league and we'll be back safe at the outskirts of the village."

"We can stay by Cecil in the woods all night. We still have our ponies to get away if need be. The Normans dare not catch us," Edan said, terrified at the thought of a rope about his neck, of being kicked and pummeled into whatever task the conquerors desired.

With one last push the cart slid onto dry ground. Behind them, a strange honor system existed, Edan thought, after a battle when the women and children of the dead could mingle with the remaining enemy and not fear for their lives. Here and there in dark areas away from torchlight, Norman armorers searched among the already heaped bodies retrieving weapons and armor. Ragpickers scurried in, then hurried off with some weapon or amulet they'd taken from a body amid the carnage.

Edan imagined the swish of ravens' wings at dawn. He clenched his jaw. The birds would not peck at his father's eyeballs.

Loud words nearby caught Edan's attention. A woman in a rich cloak with some surviving thanes searched among the stripped and stacked bodies. She looked for King Harold she said. He could not see her face.

Two rats scuttled under the cart almost between Edan's feet. More attackers of the dead. He shuddered. Time to leave this gruesome place.

Edan and Fergus slogged along next to the cart, tired beyond talk, enduring the distance to Herstmonceux.

At last Fergus led the horse near Cecil the forester's hut where they enlisted his help to hide Thane Selwyn's body from prying Norman eyes.

"There now, our Thane will lodge safe with the larks until the priest can bury him proper," observed Cecil. His tear-filled eyes shone in the torchlight. His big shoulders slumped, he stepped back from the rock pile which sealed the thane's hiding place.

Edan remained by the rocks, Father's sword filling his thoughts. A wave of hate swept through him. Someday he would wield that weapon and be a brave warrior as his father had been. He would avenge. He would be merciless. In one hand he clutched the cross on its leather thong. He stared down at it, then looped the thong over his head and stuffed it inside the neck of his tunic.

"Now I must take word to Mother. I am afraid for her," said Edan, striding behind Cecil, energized by his new resolve.

"What in the name of five fiends would make you take such a risk as seeing your mum with all those soldiers about?" Cecil exclaimed, turned to Edan and fixed him with a glare.

"I must know how she does." Edan's jaw took on a stubborn set.

"Must be a halfwit or a full fool to take such a chance," Fergus added glumly.

"Aye, but I must go. They'll be drunk by now and less than alert. There is no need to put you in danger as well."

When they returned to the cottage, Fergus stood, legs apart, frowning, watching Edan go.

The juices of hunger and fear and grief skittered in his stomach as Edan approached the village. The gate remained open, and no one challenged him as he crossed the bridge over the moat. In torchlight he studied the fallen men heaped there for Fergus's father, Dugal. He did not lie among the dead. Passing across the common, he saw big Norman battle horses crowded English ponies and carthorses in the stalls of his father's stable.

Sliding forward from shadow to shadow toward the kitchen, Edan no longer heard the crash of pillaging. Bawdy song and laughter rang out from his father's hall. If only celebration would keep the Normans occupied. Hidden behind a rain barrel next to the kitchen he waited for someone he knew to appear. Hours seemed to pass before he heard a sound. In the quiet, tears came again and again, sliding warm down his cold cheeks, dripping onto his tunic. A hollowness grew in his gut.

He felt a muscle twitch in his jaw. His legs cramped. With loud footsteps, Maddie, Fergus's older sister, emerged with a wooden bucket and emptied it. Long brown hair disheveled, her gaze swept from side to side. Her kirtle and gown hung from one shoulder, the other side ripped apart.

"Hist," Edan signaled.

Maddie's gaze jerked to the side. She hurried to the barrel to scoop up a bucket of clean water. A fierce whisper came from the darkness. "You clodpole, get out of here. Your mother has been beaten senseless by the filthy Normans."

"Get a message to Mother for me when she wakes. Tell her Father is dead."

The kitchen door burst open spilling light into the yard.

Tears sprang to her eyes. Pale-faced, Maddie scurried back toward the kitchen. As she reached the doorway, a tall Norman emerged and grabbed her about the waist. Edan flattened against the wall, helpless to do anything, thankful he had not moved after Maddie. He must get back to Fergus and Cecil. Together they could make a plan.

When the struggling Maddie disappeared from view, he slithered from kitchen to stable. He passed the dark stalls where horses stood munching and darted around a pile of hay.

His legs thrashed air. Plucked from the ground like a pup by its dam, he hung suspended by the scruff of his neck.

A coarse laugh burst into his left ear. "Step outside to wet the English sod and what do I discover but a heathen cur!" a voice said in accented Saxon dialect.

Edan's stomach turned. His heart beat like a blacksmith's hammer. He shouted, "I be no heathen!"

"One more to brand on the morrow." The Norman's voice rose in a bellow of drunken laughter. He lowered Edan to the ground, grabbed his long, red-blond hair in one fist, and slung him toward the lighted kitchen doorway.

Chapter Three

15 October 1066

Wood coals burned low in the hall's great fireplace. Trussed tight and roped to a line of men and boys, Edan shivered and itched in at least fifty places. Lying upon the flea-ridden, rush-covered floor, he chafed at his ropes. While he squirmed, he felt something hard beneath his leg. Straining his hands against the ropes, his fingers closed on a small chunk of wood among the dried stems. He felt its shape. A game-piece from Father's chess board. He worked his hands to one side and slid the piece into his scrip. He clenched his jaw and closed his eyes against the ache that grabbed his throat.

A familiar whine made him open his eyes. His father's hunting dogs chained in the same dark corner with the prisoners had been subdued with kicks and curses from the Normans. His favorite, Toby, cowered behind the others, whining. Toby could not understand such cruelty. Edan wanted to scratch behind the dog's ears, comfort him--have the dog lick his hand.

Around him were the rude noises of Normans as they slept and snored on tables where they had recently gorged on his father's food. Torches guttered, throwing shadows upon oiled skins stretched over the window slits.

Exhausted yet sleepless, Edan watched his mother's huddled shape at the feet of the clean-shaven Norman, who seemed to be in charge here, and mouthed a short prayer to St. Leonard, patron saint of prisoners. She had not moved. Her feet remained hobbled together, and a rope trailed from her neck to the Norman's wrist.

Edan shook his head. Not only had he disobeyed his father but also he had failed his mother by getting caught. Now he could do nothing to help. He glanced once more at the Norman who slept, slouched in his father, Selwyn's chair. Edan longed to burn it stick by stick in the great fireplace rather than see it used by the Norman.

A whispered sound made Edan turn to the man roped next to him. He recognized Wulfan, a farmer from the village. Someone else lay awake this night.

Leaning toward him, Wulfan muttered into Edan's ear, telling him what the Normans had done to his mother, "Aye, your mum didn't serve a horn of ale quick enough to one of the sergeants. The one snoring on the table there." Wulfan inclined his head toward the fireplace. "He laid a heavy hand to her. When she came to, trays of food and drink were shoved into her hands. Men seemed determined to step on her hobbles every chance they got." He glanced at Edan with a sidelong white-eyed look. "Then they laughed when she fell upon the floor time after time. For your skin's sake, be silent and keep out of their way."

Edan felt the skin fair shift on his bones as if it already creased under the keen edge of a Norman knife.

The sergeant snorted awake, snarled, and threw half a cup of ale at them to signal quiet, then resumed his snoring. Not wanting to endanger Wulfan further, Edan turned away, still trembling, the sticky liquid trickling down his cheeks. Outwardly he quieted; inside, his anger smoldered. If he had been here earlier, he would have been unable to bear the sight of his mother so abused. He would have given her attackers short shrift if he once laid hands on them. *Aye, in your dreams. You'd have been killed*, said a little voice in his head.

His sister, Moira, disappeared soon after he had been dragged into the hall. He did not want to think about what had happened to her. Where were his little sisters, Regan and Cara? Hopefully with village women somewhere.

Someone stirred next to Edan. One of the Normans rolled from the table and stumbled outside, returning moments later. The captives in the corner had no such luxury. What would happen to them in the morning? The threat of being branded sat fresh on his mind. If he kept his mouth shut about his identity, he would be branded and sent back to the fields to farm with the rest of the crofters. If he revealed himself, for certain he would be held hostage or even be killed as heir to Thane Selwyn.

What should he do? Where was Fergus? Had he heard of Edan's capture through the servants' gossip? He had to escape while his captors snored in drunken sleep. How? The Normans' swords lay on the tables next to them, yet Edan could not reach even one. Shafts of pale light from the oilskinned windows fell across the floor. Soon the sun would rise. Fergus must hurry if he thought to free him.

Edan's gaze roved once more to the shadowed form of his mother. Did she move? His breath came faster. Yes. She tried to sit up. But had her senses been scattered? If she jerked the Norman's wrist or stumbled and fell, she would wake her captor.

He watched in agonized silence as his mother sat up and removed the tether over her head. She reached to her belt and dug into her pouch for the dagger he knew she kept there. Had the Norman confiscated it? No, he had likely dismissed Mother as harmless. She leaned over, loosening the ropes around her ankles with the point of the dagger. She rose onto her knees and crawled away from her captor, careful to make no noise. She came toward Edan.

His heart beat faster. Did she know he lay roped in the corner? Or did she think to try her luck at freeing all the village men? He watched her move around the sleeping Normans, ever closer. He could not see her face in the dim light. Her dark hair hung in straggles. Glad he could not see the marks of her beating upon her face, he trembled under her touch moments later. Her arms clung to his shoulders, her lips brushed his hair. She lowered her mouth next to his ear.

"Edan, I am so glad you are alive. I have lain awake a long time but pretended otherwise." She studied the prisoners who continued to sleep, even Wulfan. "I heard them bring you in. I know enough French to understand much of what they say. You must escape or they will kill you if they suspect you as heir to the thane. Go to Cecil, the forester, and he will tell you the way to my brother in Cymru. Get Fergus to go with you. I'll tell his mother. Two on the road in these troubled times will be safer..."

"Mother, I cannot leave you, Moira, Regan and Cara. And what of Father's burial by the priest?" Edan protested.

"Shh." She put a finger on Edan's lips. "You must go. We will be safe as long as we obey. I will take care of Father. Where have you hidden him?"

She had gotten his message after all. "Cecil knows."

"Good. I will make arrangements with the priest. So far, they have left him alone. I have a plan which you may not understand now, but you will later." She glanced at the sleeping forms. "The man who has been given our land arrives in hours. You must leave very soon. I love you dearly. I'll send messages. Until some tomorrow..." She dropped to his ropes with her dagger and picked them loose as she had with her own. He started to protest how much time it took to untie knots when he realized that a cut rope would point to someone as guilty of freeing a prisoner.

Edan tried to speak, to argue. No other plan came to mind. He prayed the Norman oafs would be eaten by wolves, drown in a bog or have their horses go lame before they arrived. If only something would happen to them. He leaned forward to kiss her cheek. She squeezed his shoulder one more time and turned away. Massaging his ankles where the ropes had cut into the flesh, Edan watched as she moved past her captor and ascended the stair up to the living quarters, mayhap to find Moira.

Crouching, he crept to the door. He stopped and returned to the corner. The snoring sergeant snorted and moved on his table. Edan knelt and froze. The Norman's even snoring resumed. In moments Edan's fumbling fingers freed Toby. He moved soundlessly from the hall, through the detached kitchen, to postpone being in the open common, the lean hound padding at his heels. How could he get out of the fortified village? The gate had closed after the last horse patrol came in last night. Before long morning patrols would leave.

He walked with caution across the common to the first of the village houses, keeping a close eye on the privy for early users. Not likely would there be too many early risers among the Normans--most would be suffering severe ale head. If anyone were watching, his slow pace might make him seem one of them.

A stack of hay between the privy and the stable caught his attention. A guttering torch wedged near the privy door gave him an idea. As he stopped, Toby regarded him, head cocked to one side. Edan tossed the torch into the hay. Soon the stack smoked, then smoldered. A spark flew to the privy. He smiled with satisfaction. Let the Norman swine wet the mud in the pigyard when they awoke from their stupor. And the curse of the Old Ones on their Norman nags. They would not eat his father's hay.

He hurried on, Toby at heel. A vision of himself mounting one of the big Norman destriers and galloping from the village crossed his mind. But he had never ridden one of these huge, specially trained war horses. Nor could the stable be entered with all the sleeping soldiers. The beginning of an idea came into his head. What if he could persuade one of the village women to give him a girl's gown to cover his tunic and hose? She could pull his hair back like a girl.

At the third house a woman opened her door, basket over her wrist, and walked to her chicken shed rubbing her hands together against the chill. Round and cheery Gildas, wife of the tinker. Edan hurried toward her. She jumped and stopped when she saw him.

"God's blood, Edan, what do you here?" she demanded looking about for Normans. "You scared me half to death."

"I just escaped the hall. Mother helped me. I did not see your husband, Wat, there. Did he escape?"

"Yes," she breathed and nodded. "He took our sons and went to the forest with several others. Seven died at the gate. The rest were taken prisoner. What of the thane?" When she saw Edan's eyes, she waited no longer for a reply. "I'm sorry for you and yours."

Edan nodded. "Can you help me? I need clothes to get through the gate and back to the forest. Mayhap you have an old gown and could help me look like a girl?"

"Come to the henhouse with me, while I feed and gather eggs."

Edan made Toby sit by the door and hurried after her. Inside the shed, the sleepy hens still sat on their nests. Gildas poured feed and gathered eggs, the hens clucking, indignant over their loss. When he heard shouts from the stable yard, he couldn't stifle a grin. Gildas gave him a puzzled look. By the time they emerged, she had promised to help. Edan glanced toward the stable to see a line of Normans with buckets dousing water on the privy and haystack. Gildas clucked her tongue at the sight, then said,"Your little sisters are safe. They are with Fergus's mother. Fergus's father is with Wat and the others in the forest."

Grateful for the news, Edan would now be able to reassure Fergus if…no, when he escaped the village.

Back in the warm kitchen Edan smelled bread baking, as he waited for Gildas to scurry to a storeroom for a gown which needed mending. Absently, he patted Toby's head, while his belly growled with hunger. She returned and put the gown over his head. When it dropped to the floor, she saw it hung overlong. She removed his belt and cinched it over the gown, drawing it up, then stood away to see her handiwork. She giggled behind her hand. Edan felt his cheeks grow warm.

"You have no bosom," she stated. She hurried back to the storeroom for something else.

Edan glanced down at the flat expanse of his chest. Gildas returned with old hose that needed mending. She stuffed them down the neck of the gown and adjusted them several times, shook her head. She disappeared, reappearing with a long band of linen. She removed the gown, wrapped the wadded hose to his chest with the band and replaced the gown.

"What errand can I do that will take me through the gate into the forest?" Edan asked as she cinched the belt, plucked at the cloth to get his look just right.

She pulled his hair back with a hairband, pulled a curly strand free to hang over each eye to disguise his strong brows. Looking him up and down, she nodded approval.

Next Gildas took a wooden paddle and removed three loaves

from the hearth. "You may take two of these loaves to Cecil. I'll wrap them in a cloth for you. But first, sit down and wet your throat and take a bit. I have enough and you most likely have had nothing."

Edan sank onto a stool at her table and bit into warm bread with cheese, washed down with milk. Two bites and he stopped. His stomach tight, he could not swallow any more. He could not linger. It would be wise to leave before the Norman mounted patrol. What about Toby? When he freed the dog, he hadn't thought what he would do with him.

"Thank you, Gildas. May God shower graces upon you."

Gildas reached out to pinch his cheeks, giving them the bloom of a sweet maid. She gave an encouraging smile and squeezed his shoulder. "On with you."

Edan left the warmth of the house, Toby trotting behind, leaving Gildas sweeping the earthen floor. He knew she would sprinkle and tamp it next as she and the other village women did every day.

In a hushed voice Gildas called after him, "Take smaller steps."

Edan made a face and walked down the narrow street of houses to the outer gate of the village concentrating on small steps. He clutched Gildas's mantle around his shoulders against the autumn air and tried to keep the folds of the gown free from his legs.

While he had eaten and dressed, daily activity had begun. A cluster of women sat in a yard picking burs from the weaving wool. Small children sat close, hushed by worried mothers. The odor of baking bread wafted out of kitchens. As he neared the gate, he heard the thunder of hooves behind him. He turned his head to see the Norman patrol bearing down on him.

Two guards manned the gate. Somehow he had gotten caught in the middle. Who would question him? He slowed. Toby lowered his head and slunk along by his side. A Norman voice yelled at him. He darted to one side. The patrol galloped on by and over the bridge. He found himself shaking.

Would the guards at the gate believe his disguise? What if they treated him like the soldier in the kitchen treated Maddie? They would soon discover he wasn't a girl, but he couldn't go back.

Walking with small steps, Edan approached the guards. One stepped forward into his path. "What is your errand, wench?" he questioned in Saxon dialect. Edan was startled to hear his own tongue spoken by another Norman soldier.

In a soft, husky voice which he hoped didn't sound shaky, Edan replied, "I go to an old widow's in the woods with fresh loaves. She has been ill." Surely God would forgive such a small lie.

"Open your cloth that I may see," the man demanded. His red nose dripped in the chill morning. His dark bushy brows drew down close to his eyes as he awaited Edan's reply. The stink of him made Edan's nose wrinkle as he held out the bundle and lifted one corner of the cloth to reveal the loaves. He could scarcely breathe.

A crafty look came into the man's eyes. "The old woman needs broth not bread. We'll take these." He reached for the loaves and held one to his nose. Dried blood stuck to his face, speckled down his front. English blood.

"Yon maid is a comely one," put in the other man. "Perchance she needs company to the widow's hut." He reached out.

Edan's breath caught and he turned a shoulder forward. What would his sister, Moira, say? "Your lord may have something to say about that as he favors my company," he flung at the guard. What if he just bluffed his way through, flouncing haughtily with his chin held high like Moira could do so well before the man could grab at him. He feared the thud of his heart made his ribs rattle aloud. If only Toby would mind his manners.

He moved around the first guard and started to pass the second. A hand reached out to pinch his bum. Edan squelched an urge to spit in the guard's face and took small mincing steps, chin high, looking straight ahead to the wood, Toby trotting by his side. Raucous laughter followed him. Lackwits! The plague take them!

Edan's footsteps echoed over the moat bridge. At the sound, he looked down at his feet, at the leather brogues. The men had not noticed his shoes and he had not thought of needing to wear a girl's slippers. He could have been caught by this alone. He hoped he had not betrayed Cecil to the Normans.

The gauzy, gray dawn sharpened intensity to blue. The sun rose above the forest top. After the horrors of yesterday, how could God allow such a beautiful day?

Ahead, lay the safety of Cecil's hut in the wood. Edan's stride lengthened the further he got from the village into the trees. Free again. Minutes later, he pounded on Cecil's stout wooden door. A dog barked within the hut. A deep voice answered. Toby's ears pricked, but he stayed silent.

"Patience, I'm coming." The door creaked open on leather hinges. Cecil, his large chest straining his drab tunic, gaped at him. His gray, springy hair stuck up in tufts. A large, shaggy dog at his side whined and wagged its tail.

Edan curtsied, "Good Keeper of the forest, your humble servant has brought you fresh loaves from the tinker's wife," he said in a sweet falsetto, even though he no longer had those loaves.

"Yon face is not a familiar one," Cecil replied looking sharply at him.

Still, Cecil stepped back allowing him to enter. Edan spotted Fergus's appraising eyes from the loft above. He allowed himself to glance up and pout prettily before saying to Cecil, "I am Gildas's niece come to stay from Eastbourne." He made the mistake of looking up at Fergus again and laughed for the first time in two long, cruel days. Reaching up, he removed the headband allowing his hair to fall into its normal path. He undid the mantle and slung it off, then stepped out of the gown.

"Edan?" exclaimed Cecil. He clasped Edan's shoulder in one meaty hand. "Come out, Fergus, it is not one of the Norman swine, but Edan."

For a moment Fergus knelt at the lofthole. His cowlick stood straight up adding to his astounded expression. A grin took over his face. "You escaped after all! I thought you'd be skewered by now." He grabbed the edge and swung down to the floor. "Have you heard any news of mum and pap?"

"Yes, all your family is safe. Your father ran to the forest with other men of the village. Seven were killed defending at the gate, the sawyer, the miller, the smith, and four crofters. Some were captured and are being held in the manor hall. The Lord who won our land arrives today. Mother says I must be off from here before he arrives, and she ordered you to come with me." He stopped for a breath and looked hard at Fergus. "She'll tell your mother."

He paused and his voice lowered. "Cecil, you are to tell us the way to my Uncle Kadeg in Cymru. Then she will come to you about burying Father."

The two boys scooted rough-hewn stools over the hard-packed floor to the hearth. Toby lay between them, seeming loath to stray from Edan. Cecil pulled his crude chair from the table and drew it to where the boys sat. He told Edan the Normans had found the boys' ponies and taken them.

"Oh zuggers," Edan sputtered. This news deflated both Fergus and him. The journey would have to be made on foot. "What haven't they taken or destroyed?"

"At least they have not found me yet," Cecil said.

Edan's anger faded with this fact, and he urged Cecil on with his directions. The forester had accompanied Edan's mother to Kadeg's twice so had advice about places to go and places to avoid.

Within the hour, laden with cloth sacks of nuts, apples, dried fish and venison, a hunk of cheese, and a promise from Cecil to somehow return the borrowed gown, the boys were ready to set off through the wood. Since Cecil was sure William would march on London, they would keep out of sight until they cleared the area around the village. Their path would return to the track that ran into an old Roman road which would skirt to the south of London to avoid Duke William's troops before taking them west to the Cotswold Hills.

They would then turn north to Gloucester, to the Severn River, continuing to Oswestry where they would go west again into northern Cymru. Uncle Kadeg had a stronghold there. If all went as planned, they should arrive in little more than a fortnight.

Edan had never been further from home than the four leagues to the nearest large village, Lewes, for the fair. He chewed his bottom lip as he concentrated on all the directions. His head crammed with enough directions and advice to confuse even his own tutor, a weight of responsibility descended upon him, crushing, numbing. Would he be able to remember all these directions? His life and Fergus's depended upon it.

Cecil went into his hut and returned with two long crude sticks, higher than their heads, and a firebox with hot coals. "Keep these cudgels in hand. They will help you along your journey. If beasts or outlaws be about, they be good to crack them on the pate. God speed your journey. Send a message to your good mother when you arrive at Kadeg's."

Edan slung the firebox from the end of his cudgel and carried it over his shoulder. Toby clung by his knee as if sensing Edan meant to leave.

"Lad, leave the beast with me. You be having enough weighing on your mind."

Edan studied Cecil's sincere gaze. "Aye, you're right. He'll have Bear for company here."

Bear wagged his tail at mention of his name. Cecil reached down to hold Toby.

"Be gone with you now."

Edan looked back once when he knew they would soon be out of sight. Cecil stood in his doorway, flanked by his shaggy Bear and Toby. Edan could not look again or he could not go. He could still hear Toby's whines.

Chapter Four

15 October 1066

Later that morning, even in the protection of the forest, chill winds gnawed into every crevice of their clothing. The blue skies of early day had given way to menacing, wind-driven clouds. Edan moved parallel to the track, Fergus at his side. They dared not stray far, as the narrow track served as their map to the next village.

They had to hide three times after taking leave of Cecil when mounted Norman patrols passed. Seeing the strong, mobile knights armed with bows, light swords and lances, added further chill to the day. The first time, Edan's heart beat furiously against his ribs. After that, they dove for cover at the first unfamiliar sound and praised Cecil's good sense in keeping Toby.

Around midday, Edan and Fergus sliced off a hunk of cheese, ate a handful of nuts and washed it all down with a drink from a small stream. Then they were underway again.

At the moment all seemed safe about them. But even common forest sounds, the creak of deadfall rubbing or the rustle of dry leaves, made Edan edgy. A sudden gust caused him to pull the woolen mantle more closely about his neck. Winter must be at hand, his cheeks and ears tingled so with the icy bite of the wind. Warmed by his rapid strides, nearly two to every one of Fergus, his legs were the most comfortable part of him.

They could keep Cecil's schedule if they turned to in earnest to make seven leagues a day. With the bone-chilling winds they endured today, the faster they traveled, the better.

"We must be near the old Roman road to London. I wonder, will that road be more dangerous?" Fergus asked.

Edan scowled. "If we only knew where Duke William and his main army have gone. Cecil guessed they would go straight north to London to secure his power."

Fergus said, "It would seem he wants to secure Harold's own lands first, then worry about the rest."

"Where does that leave us..."

A shout sounded ahead. Edan's gut spasmed. He stopped and raised his hand. Fergus slipped behind a large oak, while Edan crouched low in nearby bushes. Hooves thundered from both directions along the track, which had opened to a long green sward. Through the dense copsewood alongside, they saw two armored forces of similar size appear. One group carried the Norman banners they had seen in the battle, the other, a banner from Sevenoaks. Both groups kept swords and lances at the ready and displayed their shields. The English ranged themselves wide to meet the Normans.

"Are these Normans Duke William's army or just a small band of his men like the one which took Herstmonceux?" whispered Fergus, his eyes wide. His knuckles turned white around his cudgel.

Edan shrugged a response, concentrating on the action playing out before them.

A Norman voice shouted in a commanding tone. Fluent only in a dialect of Saxon, the language of England, Edan picked up but few words of the French dialect--enough to know the Norman group flung a challenge. The English leader faced the patrol head on whether he understood the words or not. "I am Alric of Sevenoaks and I do not abide this Norman, Duke William," he responded. "I have sworn my arms to King Harold and his heirs and with God's help we will send Norman invaders from our lands. We will have no king but that which we choose."

The Norman may not have understood Anglo-Saxon either, but the defiant tone needed no explanation. He gestured toward his men who readied arms. He whirled his destrier and rode back several paces. He gripped his lance tightly and with a shout spurred his black warhorse forward. The animal's huge hooves pounded the turf, its muscles rippling with effort, snorting with each ponderous stride. The ground shook beneath Edan's feet.

Dismounting, the English men leaned into their lances and ran forward. The two forces met with a thundering crash. One Norman was unhorsed. The rest whirled and set toward each other again. Edan clenched both fists, willing his countrymen to triumph. This time the greater skill of one of the mounted Norman fighters made itself felt, his lance turning the shield of the opposing knight. Watching them fight, Edan saw the French rode with leather straps for the feet. He had never seen this among the English. These gave them balance for fighting. He pointed, "Look Fergus, at the Normans' feet!" Edan whispered.

Fergus peered through the roiling figures, then turned back to Edan. "By the strength of Woden, their feet hang in leather. They have a surer seat in the saddle," he replied in a hushed whisper.

Startled by Fergus's words, Edan noticed Fergus's curses had veered away from Christian ones and taken a pagan turn. Edan could not remember when.

Another Englishman's lance hurled aside, but the warrior held his place. His lance arm dangled useless. With the opposite hand he drew his broadsword. Blades met and rang, the men thrust and parried. Grunts of the straining horses accompanied the ringing blades. A Norman destrier thrust its chest into an English swordsman. The Norman rider's sword clashed upon the opposition shield. Another blow rained down. With the Englishman upon his knees, the Norman blade swung down onto the rider's shoulder full force, wounding him despite his mail shirt.

Through Edan's mind flashed a picture of a hill strewn with bodies and another sword slash upon a shoulder. He pushed the image to the back of his mind.

The five Englishmen left yielded the day by laying down their arms. They were stripped of arms and shields, no longer bound by oath to King Harold, but prisoners.

While the men had their attention focused on each other, Edan motioned Fergus forward. The two slipped away, dejected but unnoticed. The prisoners would be forced to fight for the Normans now. A part of Edan cried out for them, but there was nothing he could do to help them. He drew a slow, deep breath and fought back the waves of sorrow that washed over him. He jutted his chin and cleared his mind once more.

The gray skies lowered, turned black with rain. Edan and Fergus moved closer to the track for fear of losing it, confident now they could hide if necessary.

Pointing backward, Fergus said, “How many soldiers does England have left?”

“Before the battle, I heard Father say as many soldiers as were in the annual callup of the fyrd could be called up against an invasion. What were you thinking?” Edan replied. He watched a small red fox slink under a holly in front of them.

“If there’s that many left, why couldn’t they gather and fight the Normans again? Back there, the little band of soldiers had no chance against the Normans. Yet if our knights gathered in bigger groups...” He left the words hang.

This lack of one large force bothered Edan, too. English soldiers were brave men. Why couldn’t King Harold’s remaining earls and thanes gather another army? He could not change events himself. He knew he must continue on to Uncle Kadeg. He must grow big enough to wield a broadsword longer than a few minutes.

A depressing drizzle sifted down that clung to hair and clothing, obscuring the gnarled arms of ancient oaks which had overflung the rest of the forest. If only peace could rain down as easily as the drizzle from the skies.

During the day Edan and Fergus had passed one village giving it wide berth, knowing Normans were within. They saw many displaced villagers fleeing from the invaders like winnowed chaff in the wind. Now they neared another village. They stopped at the edge of the woods to scan the village. Burned houses and warhorses in the common told the story.

Icy wetness seeped down Edan's neck and dampened his spirits even more. He and Fergus trudged on in silence. He went through the mechanics of walking but paid little attention. He was nearly asleep on his feet, yet his mind overflowed with unrelenting images of blood, severed limbs, mortally wounded men and horses, more blood. Recent events whirled through his head as he put one tired foot in front of the other. Only three weeks ago a large part of the annual fyrd callup, or national army, had waited here in Wessex to defend the south coast. Their yearly duty expired and with no threat imminent, they had returned to their villages. Then the attack at Stamford, where King Godwineson defeated Harold Hardraada and his outlaw brother, Tostig Godwineson, had changed everything. New troops were gathered along the way south to Hastings by King Harold and his housecarls. Meanwhile Edan knew Duke William had landed on English soil and had begun looting the countryside. King Harold's army had marched double-time for Wessex to meet the new challenge without waiting for more fyrd troops to assemble.

In the early hours of the day of the battle at Hastings, his father, neighboring knights and thanes, returned with King Harold. After three hours' rest, Father and the others had mounted to fight again. During this, a courier had ridden into the assembled soldiers and delivered a message to King Harold from Duke William. Everyone had watched in silence. Among all the thoughts whirling through his head, Edan remembered standing next to Father's horse and seeing the tall king sag in his saddle, his face go pale above his blond beard. No reply was given and the courier departed. *What had been in the shocking message?*

When the day grew late and his feet were icy, his senses returned to the present. If only they could find a place to spend the night out of the wetness. Trees turned to black shadows, Norman knights reaching out with long gnarled arms. Dripping water became whispered hoofbeats approaching. A sudden burst of leaves swirling down through oaks and beeches hissed like evil spirits. Edan jumped at every noise and thought Fergus looked uneasy as well, his eyes darting about.

Despite their search, no dry refuge appeared. They ate some dried venison and apples while they walked, chewing slowly to make the taste of it last, then huddled together under the branches of a low growing tree. Night arrived early.

As Edan spread one mantle for them to sleep upon, an eerie yelp sounded nearby. Another answered, then another. Edan's head jerked up. Fergus's frightened eyes stared into his.

"Black Dogs or wolves?" Fergus asked, his eyes wide. "By the dog, where's the coals Cecil gave you? We've got to start a fire."

"Everything's too wet," Edan replied. Fergus's tone of voice told him there was more to the question than which animal. He wished he could root through Fergus's thoughts like pigs rooted for acorns. Maybe Fergus knew of more danger than he shared.

"Here, under the tree, close to the trunk, dig beneath the wet leaves. There might be dry ones. I'll dig over there by the log. Hurry! If they get us, they'll tear us apart no matter they be Black Dogs or wolves."

Edan scrambled about in the leaves, at last cradling a few dry ones in the bottom of his tunic. Fergus found some in a hollow log and some dry moss. Between them they found enough to get a fire started in an open spot with the embers from the firebox. Flames soon allowed them to put on damper, larger pieces of fuel. A mound of dead branches lay stacked by the fire. They clutched their cudgels in readiness. Finally, they spread the second mantle over their shoulders and sat by the fire, shivering, tossing branches on whenever the flames wavered.

Edan needed to know more about Fergus's question. "Fergus, what does it matter if the animals are Black Dogs or wolves?" Wolves he knew about. Their howls could bode death. They could rip you apart. If you believed in old myth, they could be shapeshifters, a man cast in wolf form by a single slap of a witch's wolfskin glove. If anything made him fear darkness, it was wolves.

"Black Dogs be vicious," Fergus began. "They roam lonely tracks, ancient roads, bridges. Enormous, shaggy black creatures with glowing fiery red eyes they be. Sometimes they can wound a body most horrible, then vanish. Sometimes they kill. Some say they be guardians of ancient burial places of the Old People or guardians of a lost treasure belonging to an ancient Celtic chieftain. They have frightful powers. The sight of them can foretell death."

Edan shuddered. It did not matter to him. Both were fearful. However, he knew that Fergus was more afraid of these mythical beasts than real ones. They seemed to conjure unnatural fears of spirits and witches and curses out of the dark. He focused his eyes on the darkness beyond. For awhile all was quiet. They waited, their weapons held ready, and stared out into the night. Edan looked beyond where the yellow light of the flames cast its circle. The flickering firelight played tricks on his eyes, for he thought he saw a ghostly shape glide silent through the shadowed reaches beyond the light.

All at once Fergus gripped his arm, and he knew he had seen it also. "There. I see them," Edan exclaimed. "Their eyes glow in the light of the fire."

"Red or yellow?" Fergus asked in a shaky whisper.

"Yellow," Edan replied. Beside him Fergus shivered and tightened his grip on the sling shot.

"How many?"

"Four, no five."

One crept forward, slinking low to the ground. Edan hurled a firebrand at it. The eyes disappeared.

To the left, two pairs of eyes moved in. To the right, two pairs. Was there another? Fergus took out his slingshot. He gathered rocks, chunks of wood. Placing a rock in the leather thong, he whirled the sling above his head and loosed the missle toward the nearest wolf. A yelp and the animal whirled away. Another came, and another, passing in swift menace before them, then disappearing into shadow once more. Fergus repeated this many times, while Edan chucked rocks at the wolves whenever they ventured too close and tossed another log on the fire to keep it blazing. The flames lit the ghostly gray hides, turning the menacing eyes to brilliant yellow fire.

Fergus whispered, "They gather their courage. They smell our flesh and crave our blood."

"The darkness makes them bold," Edan replied. "Throw another log on the fire."

Once, all the wolves came forward together and stopped in full glare of the firelight. Edan threw two firebrands, and Fergus kept his slingshot busy. One big male opened his jaws and they saw the ivory fangs gleam. It yelped excitedly. Edan could feel the breath on his face. It smelt of carrion and things rotten. Then it lunged toward them. Edan grabbed up a firebrand and whacked at the fangs. A yelp and the beast leaped through the fire and out the opposite side.

Fergus screamed and staggered back, keeping his slingshot lined up on the other shadows. He let several rocks fly and was rewarded by three whining yelps. The wolves, repelled, slunk back to the shadows beyond the firelight.

All the stories they had heard about wolves and spirits in the forest tortured Fergus in the long hours of the night as they fought to keep awake should the wolves advance again. Thoughts of his warm bed at home tugged Edan's eyelids down as he fought to stay awake.

"They could be shapeshifters after our souls," Fergus moaned.

"Or they could be waelwulfs," Edan said. "That's just old wives' tales. There's other thoughts on wolves. Have you heard of the bounty on wolf hearts in the west country? We should kill one and give ourselves power."

Fergus fingered his amulet, a holed stone worn on a thong about his neck. "This is my protection. I have no spells or gifts to placate the evil spirits."

Edan tried again. "Look at King Harold's brother, Wulfnoth. He is named for the wolf to gain its power. Let's have no more talk of evil." Absently, his fingers found their way to his chest and touched the cross hidden beneath his tunic.

As it happened, toward dawn, fatigue caught up with them. They sagged against each other and slept, their fire only embers. The wolves had gone.

16 October 1066

The next morning they awoke to continued rain. The wolf tracks had been washed away and seemed but a vivid nightmare. After eating venison and cheese, they set out again. The aches in their muscles from sleeping on cold, hard ground eased after an hour of travel. Midmorning found them at the juncture with the Roman road. A glance in both directions down its grass-grown, cobbled length revealed no one. If they dared travel the road, they would be able to travel faster. Besides, they would not be on it long before they cut west again.

Taking a risk, Edan overrode Fergus's protests to walk the road. Time passed quickly with the faster pace. They had passed no one when they arrived at the sign pointing to the Tonbridge track.

"Show me the letters, Edan."

Edan had just begun to teach Fergus the alphabet, so he could write his name. Glancing both ways down the road, Edan stepped to the sign and traced the letters, saying each aloud. He wanted to teach his friend how to read. Fergus proved to be an eager pupil, so Edan wanted to continue.

Back on the dirt track to Tonbridge, open and used, Edan looked over his shoulder less. Rain had turned the packed dirt to a slippery mire. Mud clung to their shoes in heavy clumps. Before long they heard the rush of a stream ahead. The sounds of angry curses came from that direction. Fergus put his finger to his lips and slipped off the track into the trees. Edan followed. "Soft, have we more Normans? The blessing of St. Withold upon us," he muttered and spat at the ground.

"May Thor's hammer fall upon them," growled Fergus in return.

They crept closer until they heard the murmur of several voices. Edan mouthed a short prayer to the patron saint of travelers, St. Christopher, to cover all the possibilities of divine help. They dropped onto their stomachs, inching forward through the mud.

Chapter Five

16 October 1066

A swollen stream appeared through crouching clusters of bushes where it crossed the track. In dry times, it would have no more than wet the hooves of a horse, but now the waters created a mire at least two rods across. This small crossing boasted no paved ford. In midstream sat a wagon holding two women and several children. Two men in leather jerkins stood in the water straining at the muddy wheels, while one of the women slapped reins on the backs of a pair of tired draft horses.

Fergus turned to Edan, a question in his eyes. Edan nodded. They got to their feet and hurried forward.

"Can we help?" Edan asked.

The older of the two men jerked around at the sound of a voice. His hand flew to the sheathed knife at his waist. The hunted look on his face betrayed his fear. Once he took their measure, the knife went back in its sheath.

"Aye, we'd be thankful."

Edan and Fergus laid their cudgels on the bank, strode forward, and put their shoulders to the back of the wagon. The extra force changed the grip of mud upon the wheels. With a loud sucking sound, the wagon broke free. The weary horses lunged up the incline from the mire. Edan pushed the image from his mind of the cart carrying his father's body that Fergus and he had freed from mud only two nights ago. The men stood panting at mud's edge, while the boys retrieved their cudgels.

When they returned, the older woman looked down at the boys, her eyes filled with gratitude. Edan eyed the horses whose heads hung with exhaustion. They wouldn't get much further today.

The elder man turned to Edan and asked, "Who be you and where are you bound?"

"I be Edan of Herstmonceux. My father, Selwyn, was thane. He died under King Harold's banner fighting the Norman duke. This lad is come with me from my village. We flee the bonds of slavery."

The elder man continued to speak for his group. "I be Brant, smith of Sevenoaks. I, too, fought with Harold, but against Harold Hardraada and Tostig at Stamford." He turned and gestured to the woman driving the wagon. "That one is my wife. This other is my sister and her husband. Normans burned our village, and we are bound to search for a new home since they have taken ours."

Sevenoaks. That lay south of London. The fighting Saxons yesterday had been from there. "Have you heard if Duke William's army pressed on to London?" Edan asked, anxious for the answer.

"Nay, nary a sign except the small band that took our village."

Edan relaxed and for the first time noticed the soot streaks on the travellers' clothes, the wagon which held but little, mostly smithy tools, and the glazed looks in the eyes of the children. They hadn't been able to save much before they fled.

"Where do you go?" Edan inquired.

"We would find a place north or west where we can know our own home again. Every village hereabout is already taken by William's men."

Edan saw fear and uncertainty gain the upper hand in the men's faces as rain trickled down their cheeks. At least he and Fergus had a destination.

"We go to northern Cymru," Edan said, wishing he could invite them along, knowing he could not.

"God be with you," said the gray-faced woman driving the wagon.

"Best of luck to you as well," Edan replied.

The men touched their fingers to their foreheads in farewell. "Godspeed your journey."

As soon as they were out of sight, Fergus exclaimed, "I thought we would join forces with them and travel in numbers."

"We will travel faster alone." Edan prayed such a judgment would prove true. "What if Normans come along and want these men as slaves? They can't easily hide with their wagons, horses and families."

As darkness approached, the steady rain which had plagued them since yesterday slowed to a drizzle. Confident they had made the goal of seven leagues for the day, Edan spotted a huge uprooted oak. Beneath its large, slanted trunk would be dry shelter for the night.

He and Fergus swept aside wet leaves to reveal dry soil and spread one damp mantle. Edan sank onto the woolen cloth, placing his food sack in its center, as did Fergus. They ate some cheese and apples in exhausted silence. The food sack grew light. As they moved further from the Norman ravages, food might be available at some of the villages. What they had would not last more than two or three days.

They had met no one else on the track after the two families. No Norman patrols either. Would there be wolves tonight? Or would wolves curl up in a dry den themselves?

"Fergus, think we should gather sticks for a fire against wolves?"

"What dimwit wolf would come in this rain?"

"My thought also." Edan pulled one knee up. First, he must tend his feet. His mud-crusted shoes were stiff and had rubbed blisters on his heels. Each limping step had become more painful at day's end. He grimaced as he removed the shoes and hose. He wrung out the hose and examined his raw heels. If only he had dry hose to put on.

Fergus leaned over to look. "If I had some horse liniment, I could fix it up."

Edan snorted. "In a pig's eye. You fix everything with that. Mother would make a salve of valerian from her herbs."

"There's nothing to be done for it," Fergus pronounced. He arranged himself on their damp woolen bed. "I wonder how things are back at the village. If those Norman pigs have swilled all the ale and eaten all the food yet."

Edan grunted, "Aye, probably." Fergus said nothing of his father, no wondering aloud if he remained unharmed. No hint of homesickness. He lay down beside Fergus and pulled the other mantle over them. His heels stung and kept him awake. He looked up through the lofty oaks where here and there the blackness of the sky filled with stars. They flickered and pulsed, then a cloud scudded across, filming them gray. Occasionally, a breeze would rustle the brittle leaves still clinging to the oaks.

On through the night he watched the clouds and stars dance, seeing visions of his family in the great hall before a roaring fire drinking cider, playing chess with Toby lying at his feet, hearing Father's sudden bark of laughter as he made the winning move. His mother and Moira working on some piece of stitchery. His younger sisters telling simple riddles. Hounds scratching in the corner. An ache spread through his chest for all he had lost. Would he ever go home again? Wetness trickled down his left temple, soaked a strand of hair, disappeared into the wool next his cheek. Clutching the chess piece and missing these things, he slept at last.

17 October 1066

When he opened his eyes next morning, it was to thick fog. Fergus did not lie beside him.

Edan came full awake with a start and felt the woolen cloth next to him. Cold to the touch. His heart beat faster. Fergus had been gone a while already.

"Fergus?" he called softly.

Under him the ground seemed to vibrate, then he heard the sound of galloping horses. He squinted into the thick swirling mist. He couldn't remember how far off the track they had been when they spotted the uprooted oak. Scrambling to his feet, blisters forgotten, he grabbed the mantles, hose and shoes, food sacks, and cudgels, then slipped into the branches of the uprooted tree where it lay upon the ground.

The hoofbeats slowed. Bits rasped. Hard-ridden horses stamped and blew just outside his vision, but very close.

Had the Normans found Fergus and now come for me? Edan's

heart pounded.

A voice shouted something in the Norman tongue. "Halte! Aupres de…arrete…gant"…something about being close and finding a glove.

Edan wished he had paid more attention to his lessons. He had only a smattering of Latin and French. Moira, his sister, loved the French language, mayhap because of young Josse, who had been their tutor.

Another rider dismounted, picked something from the leaves and answered the first.

Edan caught a word here and there. They were looking for a man, not Fergus or himself, someone who had left a glove and a trail of blood.

He heard the impatient first voice say something about their quarry having to stay out of the forest, to take the easiest way. An irritable exchange ensued. The pace of conversation became too rapid for Edan to follow. He hoped wherever Fergus was he didn't blunder back right now.

The first voice shouted a command. A clank of bits and spurs. The horses grunted and struck into a gallop again, their hooves thudding hard on the wet turf. The voices receded. All Edan could hear were faint dripping sounds as moisture fell from the trees onto sodden leaves. He exhaled softly.

No sooner had the sounds of the riders faded than he heard an urgent whisper that jolted him back to full alert.

"Edan!"

"Fergus, is that you?" Now that Fergus appeared safe, Edan's anger flared. "By the holy oak, where have you been?"

The disembodied voice replied. "I got up to take a leak. I heard a noise and crept out to see."

"And left me there!" Edan exclaimed.

"I did not leave. Come here behind the oak and help me."

Edan dropped his bundle and crawled from the veiling branches. Carrying his shoes, he high-stepped over the rough, cold ground to a nearby tree where Fergus stood and gasped.

His unruly hair going in five directions, Fergus knelt over a man in battle dress who lay crumpled upon the ground. Even in the fog, Edan could see a dark stain across one shoulder of his hauberk. His coif along with helmet and shield were gone.

"This poor fellow must have heard the horses coming and stumbled off the track to hide. Just as I got up, leaves rustled. I couldn't see anything because of the fog, so I didn't know if beast or man approached. I crept round the tree and saw him lying here. His heart beat, so he must have fainted from his wound. Then I heard the horses."

"So that's who the troops are after. They talked of a glove and blood. I could only make out a few words of what they said." Edan knelt by the unconscious man. His face looked young, not much older than Fergus and he. Blood and dirt streaked his forehead and cheeks above the beginning of a thin mustache and beard. The facial hair and the make of his armor confirmed he was a Saxon not a Norman. The clean shaven Normans with their short hair looked almost girlish in comparison. Too bad they didn't fight like girls. Long brown hair, matted with blood and dirt, hung over one side of this man's face. Edan felt for a pulse in the dirt-caked neck. Warmth and a faint beat under his fingers confirmed life.

"What can we do for him?" Fergus asked.

"First, let's see the nature of his wound. There may be nothing we can do." Edan drew his dagger and sliced at the fastenings of the chain mail hauberk until he reached the quilted garment beneath. It, too, showed a large, fresh bloodstain. "Help me lift this shoulder."

The man groaned. Edan peered under the shoulder to see an exit wound. "Someone speared or lanced him through. The wound is above his vitals and should drain. Let's get the rest of this off, so I can see if it is festered." He tried to remember what he had seen Mother do when he went with her to tend an injured sick villager.

They removed the quilted fabric down to the last layer, the knight's shirt. The linen showed bright crimson. Edan slit it away and swallowed hard before looking at a dark well filled with blood, flesh jagged around it. The wound showed no sign of festering, but he needed to staunch the bleeding. The warrior had lost much blood.

Edan felt his forehead. No fever, yet. What did Mother do for bleeding? Then he remembered.

"Fergus, look for big spider webs. Maybe we can slow the bleeding."

Fergus hurried into the trees seeking the webs. Edan remained by the young man's side. Without his armor, he wasn't much taller or heavier than Fergus, about ten or eleven stone. Edan fingered a charm worn on a thin leather thong at the man's neck, a wolf's tooth. Had it saved him from death? Mayhap he had been wounded at Hastings. With a wound that severe he couldn't have come far unless by horse.

Fergus returned with a glob of sticky webs, minus their hosts. Edan carefully placed half on the front, the other half on the exit wound. He wondered how they would ever move him to safety. Wherever that might be.

The knight groaned again. His eyelids fluttered open. But the pain must have been too much for his struggling senses. He shut his eyes and lapsed back to merciful sleep.

In the distance came the thunder of hooves. Did the Norman patrol return? *Like the Cwningen*, we must bolt into a hole.*

*Welsh for rabbit

Chapter Six

17 October 1066

Edan looked at Fergus, holding him with his eyes. Each grabbed a leg of the knight and dragged him under the sheltering canopy of the great fallen tree. While Fergus covered him with wet leaves, Edan slid his own feet into stiff shoes, scooped up their belongings and scuffed leaves over the drag marks. His eyes sought tell-tale blood smears. Hammering hoofbeats grew nearer. The clatter of weaponry became distinct.

"A plague on their black hearts!" Fergus whispered.

"Come, Fergus," hissed Edan.

His eyes wide and fearful, Fergus stumbled from the tangle of branches, and they slipped away from the track into thick woods. Careful to avoid stepping on a stick or brushing clothing against a branch, they moved quickly. Thanks be for the mist and fog, Edan thought. Scarce had they reached a line of dense thicket, than the patrol arrived at the fallen oak amid stamping feet, snorts, and the clank of bits. Voices carried clearly, voices without flesh, belonging to the fog.

Edan motioned Fergus to stop. He strained to understand the French being spoken. He caught a word here and there. It seemed the patrol had followed the road in search of sign after they had seen blood and hoofprints. So the knight had a horse. He must have fallen from it. Edan wondered where it had gone.

The patrol dismounted and began to search the area again on foot. Edan took shallow breaths and prayed the knight did not move or groan in his hiding place. He heard boots swishing through the leaves. Edan looked around at Fergus, inclined his head. The sounds faded into the thick undergrowth as they retreated. Soon they could no longer hear voices. Edan continued until they reached a deep-cut rivulet where exposed tree roots lined one bank. They climbed down and wedged themselves in, Edan first as the smallest, beneath the twisted foundation of the giant above, smells of earth and mold strong in their noses.

For what seemed like hours but most likely was no more than one hour, they lay under the bank. At one point searchers approached close enough for them to hear bushes drag against breeches, the strident breaths of men in pursuit. Edan could scarcely breathe. Evidently, the knight had not been found if they still sought him.

"How long must we wait?" Fergus whispered after the searchers moved on.

As if in answer to Fergus's question, a distant hunting horn sounded one blast. "The leader recalls his soldiers," Edan replied. "Soon we can go back." Did that mean that the knight had been found or that the leader had given up the search?

They waited, then waited more. At last Edan said, "Let's go, a little at a time." He moved stiffly from his curled up position and crawled up the bank with his bundle. Fergus close behind, Edan stopped every few paces to listen, wary of the Normans, as they made their way back to the track and the fallen oak. He tried to control his unease. He had no reason to suspect they were in danger, Edan tried to assure himself. Better cautious than sorry.

Steaming manure and churned ground gave witness to the recent visit. Edan searched the track for the direction the patrol had taken, while Fergus checked on the knight. The patrol had gone back the way Fergus and he came yesterday. Was the knight still there or had he been found?

A grunt from Fergus as he walked to join Edan. "He's still out of his head."

"Fergus, let's look for signs of his horse. I heard the Norman speak of it. Without it, I don't know how we'll move him."

They returned the short distance to where Fergus had come upon the wounded man. Blood spotted leaves attested to where the man had lain. Edan shook his head. "I don't fathom how the Normans missed all this blood."

"Spirits of the forest must have saved him," Fergus muttered, giving nervous glances into the trees as if he might see one of the spritely, brown-clad spirits sitting there.

Edan and Fergus circled the tree making ever-wider casts until Fergus grunted again. "Here," he said. "Another spot."

Edan joined him, and they searched that area until another splotch appeared. By following the traces, they found themselves moving parallel to the track, following the patrol.

"How far do we go back?" Fergus asked, voicing the thought already in Edan's head.

"A bit further yet," Edan decided. For a few minutes more they trudged onward. Suddenly the splotches veered into thicker forest away from the track. Deep within a chestnut grove they found a place where the knight had lain. A patch of bloody leaves, stirred up ground, his discarded coif and helmet, then hoofprints told their vivid story.

Edan looked over at Fergus with raised brows. They took off at a trot, the hoofprints providing a clear trail. In a small clearing stood a bay stallion cropping grass. Edan let out a sigh.

At their appearance the horse threw his head up and stopped chewing, brown grasses hanging from his jaws. He sniffed the air, ready to bolt. He stood motionless for several minutes, then assured of his safety, he resumed eating.

Fergus walked toward the horse, a few steps at a time, speaking soft. When he stood next to it, he reached for the one remaining rein. He pulled the horse's head up, patted it and led it toward Edan. It limped a bit.

Edan noted the wooden saddle with blood stains, the sword in its scabbard and a shield which hung from the saddle. The stallion's coat had a whitened crust of dried sweat and lather. A wound on its haunch, a long cut, appeared to be a diverted blow from a lance. Though it stiffened the horse's gait, it apparently wasn't serious.

Anxious to make up lost time, they returned to the knight at a trot, while Edan's mind worked on the problem of getting the knight to horse. Much of the morning had been wasted, hiding. They needed to be underway. The stallion moved along beside them without resisting. Mayhap the horse could be made to help.

Back at the fallen oak, they dragged the wounded man from his leafy bower. The horse sniffed him and nickered in recognition. That triggered another thought. Edan removed his belt and fastened it below the horse's front fetlocks like a hobble. He pulled the horse's head low, grasped the horse's head around the cheek with one arm, grabbed an ear with the opposite hand and twisted. With its head to one side, the horse, unbalanced, leaned and staggered, then went to its knees. Edan strained to hold the head over, keep the horse down, ignoring the reek of dried sweat.

"Fergus, drag him--up--over the saddle," he panted.

Fergus turned the knight over onto his stomach and dragged him upward by the arms onto the horse's back, then shoved him up to the waist over the saddle.

"Hold him on--whilst I--let the horse up," Edan directed. In moments, the task complete, they were on their way.

"Aye, and that was a pretty piece of work," commented Fergus. "How'd you think of it?"

"Once the smith had trouble with one of Father's young horses. He did something like that to doctor a foot."

Feeling less on edge now that they were on the move again, Edan still pressed to cover ground quickly.

At dusk they came upon the outer fence of a large village, surrounded by at least two furlongs of fields in all direction. Skirting its perimeter, they stayed in the trees. Though invaded, this village had not been laid waste. They could see Norman soldiers within, yet smoke came from chimneys and crofters just now quit the fields for the night. Edan scanned over hedgerows and fields for Normans outside the moat, seeing none. Guards held the bridge.

The sharp approach of hooves along the track announced return of a patrol. Edan stepped backward into the grove. A clatter of hooves across the bridge, and the men were in the village.

"Do you think to enter?" Fergus asked into his ear.

Edan stayed silent for awhile. "I had thought to. Our knight needs the healing touch of the lady of this village."

Their hiding place grew cold and silent when the pale sun dropped, except for a wind that rattled leaves and tapped branches against solid trunks. It came from the north bringing the promise of more rain. Goosebumps rose on Edan's skin. The stallion grew restless, pawing the ground, then nipping at Edan with ears flattened. Instinctively, he bumped an elbow gently against the horse's nose.

Across the field a creaking sound carried on the wind--the village mill. "Follow me," Edan said. They circled the open space until they saw the dark bulk of the wooden structure. The soft liquid rush of water churning through the tail-race covered any noise they made or any sound of Norman guards, be there any near.

"What do you plan?" asked Fergus, surveying the steep-banked swirling river.

"The shortest swim is to the wheel. I ride it up into the millhouse like we do in summer at home. If no one is there, I sneak along hedgerows to the cottages and get help. Or if the miller is there, grinding flour, so much the better. When he goes home for the night, he can carry a message."

"How does the woman of the village get out to help?" Fergus asked, his eyes full of doubt.

Edan sat on the bank, removed his shoes and hose. "There must be a way," he replied through clenched teeth as he felt the chill of the river on his thin, bare legs.

Edan stroked downstream with the rain-swollen current, angling for the wheel. The gurgle of the water blotted out all other sound. He looked forward, almost there. When he reached the wheel, he grabbed for it. Slippery with moss, the wheel eluded the grasp of his cold-stiffened fingers. He grabbed again. Almost losing it a second time, his hand held, nails dug into the moisture-laden, soft wood. He swung around to grasp with his other hand. Getting one foot on a paddle, he rode the wheel up. At the top, he entered darkness within the mill. He leaped from the wheel and landed on boards near a noisy wood gear which creaked with each rotation. The air was pungent with the dusty fragrance of grain.

Water dripped into his eyes. Flinging his wet hair aside, he spotted a faint light coming through a hole in the floor. The top of a ladder stuck over the edge. Shuddering with cold, he moved toward it. In torchlight he saw sacks of grain piled on the floor below. He stiffened as he saw a man tying off a sack to add to the pile. Edan watched for a time and saw no one else. Deafening noise numbed his ears. The man tied a second sack, a third.

Edan waited until he moved to the grain chute with another, his back turned. He crawled to the ladder. When the man turned with the full sack, Edan crouched before him with his finger to his lips. The stocky, dust-covered man jerked in alarm and exclaimed, "'od's body." His small round eyes filled with fear then calmed at the sight of only a half-drowned lad.

Edan moved close. "Is anyone else here?" he mouthed against the din of the grinding wheel.

The man nodded.

"Norman guards?" he mouthed again.

The man nodded and pointed to the door. Edan pulled at the man's sleeve to draw him closer. In a few minutes he explained his need for medicines.

To Edan's relief, with the usual peasant sense of hospitality, the man agreed to help. He doused the torch, shut down the grinding, and accompanied by guards, went home for supper. His wife would get a message to the thane's wife, and someone would return with medicine for the injured knight.

Shivering, Edan grabbed an empty grain sack and dried himself the best he could, then wrapped himself in another. He peered out a window toward Fergus. Just at treeline he was sure he saw the stallion's white feet. Staring, he could just make out Fergus at his head, rein slack, letting the horse graze. Somehow that knowledge comforted him.

In a short space of time Edan heard someone opening the latch on the door. He shrank back among the sacks. For all he knew, a Norman might be there bent on filching a grain sack. Silhouetted in the doorway, a small boy stood. Edan moved toward him.

It seemed the mistress of the village had been among the cottages when his message arrived. She had sent a salve and poultice with instructions by the miller's son. Edan and Fergus would have to do their best.

The miller's wife had sent a fresh loaf in a waterproof packet for them as well. Edan could feel the juices gather in his mouth at the prospect of fresh bread. He thanked the boy, pocketed the pouch and left the mill. The bread he stuffed down the front of his jerkin. He walked upstream and steeled himself against the chill river for the return swim. With easy strokes, he floated and swam downstream with the current, the precious pouch gripped in his teeth.

He had taken no more than four or five strokes when something tangled in his feet, bore down upon him, threatened to shove him under. He kicked, but his feet were held. Wrenching himself over onto his back, he saw a dead tree floating next to him. His feet were still stuck, and his hands could not reach a branch to push off or hang on. He felt himself sinking below the surface.

He rolled back onto his stomach and stroked wildly. He tried to jerk one leg up to his chest. The sudden movement freed one leg, but the other remained imprisoned. Without kicking, his arms grew weak doing all the work to keep afloat. He panted like a windbroken horse. The cold rush threatened to fill his mouth and nose. His wet clothes weighted him down, dragged at his arms. His icy hands clawed at the water. The river curved around the village, toward the bridge over the moat. If he could not get free, he would float right past the Norman guards and be killed. Unless he drowned first.

He rolled onto his back again to catch his breath. He moved the imprisoned foot side to side, then up. A give in the pressure on the upward move. He tried again and felt it come free. Rolling over onto his stomach, he stroked for the bank, weakening with each pull of his arms. Ahead he could see a torch at the bridge.

Through the dark, Fergus's face appeared along the bank, his hand outstretched. He felt the fingers grip, tug his own outstretched hand, then his feet struck the bank. He grasped dirt, grass, a root with his other hand and pulled himself out.

"By the wolf's tooth, I thought you were drowned," Fergus growled, gruffness masking his worry.

On hands and knees they crawled away from the river until they reached cover. With one hand Edan squeezed water from his hair and shivered. Fergus wrapped his mantle around him. It reeked of wet wool, but its warmth was welcome. His body spasmed with shivers. Fergus led the way back to the tethered horse where Edan replaced his hose and shoes.

"Can they help?" Fergus asked when Edan remained silent.

Edan still had the pouch gripped in his teeth. He yanked it free. Emotion made him speak quickly. "They sent a salve and poultice in this pouch. That's all they can do." Edan could not see Fergus's face but imagined the disappointment there.

They needed to get back to the track and put distance between themselves and the village before settling for the night. They strode out briskly until Edan stopped shuddering and warmed somewhat.

"How far away did you leave the horse?" Edan asked.

"Just ahead. I was afraid to leave him close for fear he would greet the Norman nags and give us away."

When a league had fallen behind them, they stopped, left the track and went deep into a birch stand. Edan used the firebox and despite the gusting wind, got a fire going in the lee of a rocky outcropping. He had to finish drying himself and hoped no Normans were prowling the darkness to discover them.

They tethered the stallion and removed the knight. The spiderwebs had slowed the bleeding. After doctoring him the best they could with the salve and the poultices, a torn strip from the knight's linen undershirt fastened the poultice in place. They dribbled spring water into his mouth. He felt feverish now and mumbled in his stupor. Could they get him more help in time? Finally, covering him with one of the mantles, they ate the last of the dried apples and dried fish with hunks of fresh bread, before curling about the fire in the remaining mantle.

Long before dawn, Edan woke to pelting rain on his face. "Are you trying to drown me again?" he exclaimed, shaking a fist at the sky.

He got up to retrieve the knight's shield from the saddle and propped it over their faces with a stick. Teeth chattering again, he wiggled under the mantle, nestling against Fergus's back for warmth. A lump under his left hip caused him to roll away. He fished about and found the lump in his scrip, the game piece he'd picked out of the rushes the night of his captivity. He held it tight in one fist, and lay awake worrying over what happened at home. Had his mother gone back to the Norman that night and put the tether back onto her neck and replaced her hobbles? Had she and the priest buried Father? He forced his mind elsewhere to what could be done for the knight. Was there another village where they could find help?

How many villages were off limits to them because they had been taken by the Normans? On foot he and Fergus moved slower than the mounted patrols. Patrols, that's all they had seen.

"Fergus?" he said softly. "Are you awake?"

"Umhm."

"We're three days out and probably seventeen or eighteen leagues along on our journey. We are not moving as quickly as I had hoped with all our delays. I'm not sure Cecil's plan will work."

"Cecil must have been right--William's main army must have gone to London to wait for another attack of the fyrd, while these small bands of knights and their trained soldiers knack about Harold's lands taking villages for William. So far, we've been able to avoid them." Fergus repeated what they had thought to be true yesterday.

Today Edan had a different reason for asking. The villages were all along the main Roman roads or the biggest tracks. "What if we got off these main-travelled routes to smaller out-of-the-way villages? Might we find some not taken?"

"Mayhap, but what if we got lost?" Fergus said, his back stiffening against Edan.

"We need to leave Cecil's route to get help for the knight. We can't drag him all the way to Cymru. He'd surely die, or we'd be captured in the slow process. And, we can't get food from captured villages filled with hungry Normans."

Fergus, focused on his fear, was not listening.

"If we get lost, we can't help the knight. Who knows what unkind spirits are about in the forest?"

"So far the spirits seem to have been kind to the knight and to us," Edan replied reasonably.

"True enough." Fergus's tone still sounded reluctant. "And our food is getting low."

It was settled. They would take one of the faint paths from the track when it appeared.

Chapter Seven

18 Oct 1066

Edan opened his eyes a crack and saw a hint of dawn. In the gloom he could see silhouettes of tall, gray tree trunks. He had dreamt of the battle at Hastings and awakened panting as hard as Father's dog, Toby, after the hunt. The agonized screams and the din of weapons still rang in his ears. He again saw the blood, the endless streams of Norman warriors--and Father's corpse. His throat ached unbearably with the images.

He swallowed hard and tried to gather his thoughts, staring into the dawn. Somewhere near the rocky outcropping behind him, the knight moaned. Edan rose to check his patient. When he knelt to place his hand upon the knight's forehead, it was dry and hot. The young man moaned again at the touch. The poultice remained in place with no sign of festering in the wound. Edan studied the knight's face. He saw that his lips were dry and cracked from fever. His eyes traced a scar on the left cheek that bespoke of an old sword cut. He wished the young man would wake. He had questions for him, but the knight remained in another world.

Instead, Edan woke Fergus. They ate bread and some nuts and washed them down with spring water. With little talk, they gathered their few things, got the feverish knight aboard his stallion as they had the previous day and set off.

They passed stands of fir, barren birch, and oak. The weak morning sun laid bars of light and shadow across their path. Tension hung in the air, whether from the knight's feverish condition or something else. Both boys jumped at every sound. When a red deer broke cover at the side of the track and crashed away, Edan's heart raced. It was so close that he saw the liquid shine of its eye.

"That like to have scared the foof out of me!" exclaimed Fergus. "I imagined it a wild boar set to rip our innards out."

Ten rapid heartbeats later, the sound of hooves on damp ground filled Edan's ears. He thrust aside an overhanging branch and tugged the stallion into the copsewood along the track. He clamped his hand high and hard over the horse's nostrils to prevent a challenging whinny between rival stallions.

The leaves had barely stopped quaking from their passage when a Norman patrol bowled by, the largest they'd seen. Nearly a score of men, moving too fast to notice fresh hoofprints.

As the thunder of hooves receded, Edan's eyes fastened on the ground where they stood. It was bare and indented. He reached out to tug at Fergus's sleeve and pointed down. The overhanging branch concealed a path off the track. Just what he had been looking for. Without having to find sudden cover, he would have missed it. The small path snaked through dense forest.

Edan turned to Fergus, "Shall we take the path?"

Fergus hesitated. "By the whiskers of the Black Dogs, I would we were safe at our journey's end! Would we were out of the shade of these infernal trees that I might at least see any of the Old Ones before they spring out upon us."

Edan pushed forward through underbrush and low hanging branches. A startled woodcock burst from the foliage and flew deeper into a stand of oak.

"A piglet's sweet breath!" Fergus clasped a hand to his chest and ducked, sure this time he would be had by the spirits of the wood. Edan struggled to hold the stallion as it crabbed sideways, eyes rimmed white.

The pungent smell of damp juniper filled their senses as they followed the path. What was that on the tree trunk ahead?

"Look, Fergus. Someone has marked a tree."

"Aye, a notch--to mark the path."

Edan stepped over a protruding tree root to examine the exposed raw wood.

"Over there, another notch," directed Fergus. "Pap taught me of notched paths when we boys of the village took the pigs out to browse acorns. We could find our way home."

"We must be near a village then." Edan said.

Fergus looked over his shoulder. "The sooner we leave the shadowed hordes of the Old Ones, the better."

Notches to mark the way--the way to what, Edan wondered. A village, or something else?

According to the sun, which had burned through the mist and was now bright in a blue October sky, they were heading northeast. Edan stared into the sunlit expanse, grateful that for once they were dry.

They travelled steadily, following the muddy path into deep forest, the thick, gnarled trunks older than any yet. They skirted bogs, ducked branches, Fergus's head jerking to inspect every shadow or rustle of bush. When the sun filtered through directly overhead, they stopped to have the last of the dried venison. The knight began mumbling in a feverish way, the first hint he might be coming awake.

"Who are you?" Edan asked.

The knight replied, "Niland." After, he lapsed into jumbled talk of battle events, events Edan and Fergus recognized from Hastings.

"Oren? Oren, you were just here…Oh, I am pierced through… your horse? I must stay in the saddle…Normans everywhere…King Harold is falling…I must get away…overrun…can't leave without Oren. Shaftesbury…" He tried to raise his head, grimaced and his body went limp.

"Who be the Oren he's askin' after? A friend? His brother? His father?" asked Fergus.

Edan lifted his hands, palm up, and shrugged. "He seems worried about Oren's welfare in the Hastings battle over everyone else's."

"Aye, this person is close to him. The things he said...about Harold. He must have been right there when Harold received his fatal blow and saw the fight was done."

Fergus didn't say 'when your father was killed,' but Edan thought it. His mind traveled back to "Shaftesbury." Edan had heard of it, but it was much further southwest. Perhaps Niland and the mysterious Oren hailed from there. Edan and Fergus entertained themselves as they trudged on, speculating about the knight and his possible relationship to King Harold.

As they climbed a small hill in late afternoon shadow, they saw a dark smudge ahead. Drawing closer, the ruins of a small chapel appeared to them in the gloom. Chestnut leaves drifted silently to the grass, but the air was full of rustling from the oaks which still held their leaves. The shrine appeared far older than the Roman temples to Mithras scattered across England. Edan knew it would have a stone or spring dedicated to a Celtic god, who cared for the spirits of dead men.

On the leaf-strewn ground they picked their way through what looked to be foundations of ancient outbuildings. One end of a sagging gate leaned to the earth in a creeper-covered wall. The way was open, beckoning them in. They passed through into a small courtyard, and floored with flat stones.

A look of awe upon his face, Fergus whispered, "The Old Ones are everywhere." He made a protective finger sign against evil, then fingered the charm which hung from his neck.

Edan's gaze took in broken paving stones wearing pelts of moss. Old foundations told of other buildings that had once stood within these walls. The place must once have been impressive. Now the walls had caved in places, and buildings had tumbled to rubble except for the chapel.

The wooden door stood ajar. With a scrape of wood on stone, Edan pushed the door open and set foot inside. Fergus refused to enter, telling Edan with great zeal stories about the Old Ones who were seen lurking in the woods or who came slinking from the earth's depths on stormy nights to join the Dark King of the Otherworld.

With a burst of wings, an owl streaked past Edan out the open door. He ducked, while his stomach turned somersaults. An owl, evidence the place was deserted. Again he stood upright and peered into the dark interior. Only a shrine full of dust and cold air and yes, owl droppings. Were the Old Gods still here as Fergus insisted?

These beings of the very air?

Edan could hear Fergus still muttering outside, while he moved forward over uneven stones to the ancient altar. Goosebumps rose on his skin. Faint light shone down from the smoke hole overhead illuminating its ancient runes. Edan stood quite still, long enough for the owl to return on silent wings. He tried to imagine what must have taken place here, the smoking incense, the invocations, the sacrifices. However, he felt no presence as he did within the chapel at home and turned to leave the place.

Just as he passed through the door to see Fergus's anxious expression turn to relief, he smelled smoke. The smoke of an ordinary cook-fire and with it the faint smell of food. It came from somewhere beyond the walled courtyard and ruined buildings.

"Do you smell woodsmoke?" he asked of Fergus.

Again composed, Fergus replied, "Aye, I do and food cooking, too. Just the thought made him lick his lips."

Edan crossed the courtyard, Fergus and the stallion behind, clopping hollowly on the stones. He went through the gate, and guided by his nose, found the source of the smoke. A small hut sidled into the ancient trees near the outer walls. A dog barked. An old man in a long, shabby robe emerged from the hut and called the dog back.

Edan breathed a sigh. At last, a place without Normans.

"Come forth, travellers. I be Galt, keeper of the shrine." He motioned them in. His eyes riveted on the knight slung over the horse.

"Peace to you, good sir. I be Edan of Herstmonceux and this be Fergus. We have traveled far. Could we lodge here for the night?" Edan asked. Could this old man be trusted? If so, food might be offered as well.

As they drew closer, Edan saw the dog was old with a gray muzzle. It stood next to the hermit, growling. The man himself had long white hair and beard. Despite his apparent age, his eyes were keen and intelligent.

"Do you have someone wounded? Let me see him straight away," the old man said, walking toward the stallion.

"Do you know of medicines?" Edan asked, while the dog edged

forward to sniff his hand. Its tail trembled.

"Don't mind my Brieg. He sounds fierce, but he won't harm you. I have some herbs to help wounds. Now, let's get this poor fellow out of his upside-down position." The three of them dragged the knight from the horse and laid him flat next to the fire.

"Ye've got a good poultice here," Galt observed, pulling up an edge to examine the wound. "The wound is clean through, which is to his advantage, but the fever has hold of him. We must work on that." He disappeared into his hut and returned with a cup filled with herbs and spring water which he poured into a pot and heated into a tea over the fire. Meanwhile he applied fresh salve and a fresh poultice. When the tea was ready, he got a few sips down the knight's throat before he turned his head away.

He sat back. "We'll try more in a while. If I'm not mistaken, you would eat some of the stew I've prepared. There's plenty. I have a small garden in a clearing nearby, and my sister in the village sends bread and honey mead every week." His brow wrinkled. "No one has come this week yet."

"They may not," replied Edan. "Mayhap you have not heard, but England has been taken by the Norman Duke William. He defeated and killed King Harold at Hastings. My father, Thane Selwyn, was killed there, too. Now William's troops are all over this southern part of our country securing villages. If they took your sister's village..."

"Ah, that must be the truth of it. I am sorry for your loss," the old man interjected. His cheery demeanor vanished. "Are they wasting the villages? Have they gotten this far from the coast? My sister's village could be taken?"

"Those near the coast they wasted," Edan replied. "But inland they seem to just be taking them over. We don't know how far they've come."

"I think we be safe here. No roads lead here and no army could make its way through this forest." His brow furrowed, the old hermit grew silent for a moment. "It's time I mind my duties. Would you share my meal?" Some of his cheer returned along with his manners.

The three settled around the fire with bowls of stew and black bread and a cup of honey mead each. As soon as the boys' hunger slaked, the old hermit asked, "Where are you headed?"

"Fergus and I go to Cymru to my Uncle Kadeg, but we hoped to leave this wounded man here. We have no way to care for him, no extra food, nor do we know him. He mumbled something about the battle at Hastings, he mentioned Shaftesbury, his name, Niland, and a man's name, Oren. The rest was just mutterings. Tomorrow will see us on our way if you can take him in."

"As keeper of this shrine, it is my duty to care for anyone who seeks shelter here. I will gladly share what I have with him," Galt offered. "I can give you some vegetables along and some nuts I've gathered, but little else."

Now that the wounded man had been accepted, Edan asked Galt to tell them about the shrine he tended. He talked with pride of the great days of the shrine when the pagans had built it a century before the Romans came. All this time a servant of the old god had kept the shrine and passed the story down.

Galt grabbed up a firebrand and took them to a monolith just inside the wall and showed them the Runic inscriptions and the moss-covered libation bowl before the stone. The flickering flame made the bowl seem filled with blood. Edan shivered.

Fergus's head turned to look behind as if he expected to see the Black Dogs who guarded ancient Celtic shrines slavering at his heels, fangs snapping.

"According to the story," the old man began, "the altar was dedicated to Mabo-Mabona, god of youths. A battle took place on this hilltop, and many men of several tribes were slain. One youth who fought valiantly and won the day for the defending tribes, a youth who had seen his own father fall, grabbed up his sword. He wielded the sword with valor and strength, slaying many enemy. His name was Yoghan. This monolith stands at the spot Yoghan fought. In years after, the chapel was built and its altar and this libation bowl were used during initiation of youths of surrounding tribes."

A stout lad for sure, Edan thought. *If only I could have wielded Father's sword with Yoghan's strength to slay many Normans.*

“Now what will happen to our land?” the old hermit mused when they had returned to the fire. “With Normans taking over the land, people are run off and villages are burned. We’re in for hard times.”

Edan and Fergus nodded.

Our people need a Yoghan. Could I ever be such a hero to my people? Then Edan’s thoughts turned to the old hermit, who had lived most of his life on this secluded hilltop with but one focus to his days. What happened beyond the forest shrine did not usually concern him. The old hermit *would* be affected, especially if his sister had not survived. Could he survive without her aid and feed another as well?

If in truth, Duke William’s men secured the south first, and took London, mayhap Fergus and he could find villages yet untouched to the west and north. If his legs weren’t so weary and the forest so dark, they could move on yet tonight now that Galt had promised to take care of the knight. *That would be foolish in the darkness*, said that little voice in his head.

When talk finished, they bedded down by the fire. Galt disappeared into his hut with his grizzled dog to tend his patient.

“Edan, we best not accept the vegetables and nuts Galt offered. The old man will need them. I know how it is with winter coming on,” whispered Fergus.

Edan had not thought in terms of food. “Aye, you are right. He does not have much and now he has the knight to feed, too. His sister may not be able to help.” He was silent a moment. “If he doesn’t have a snare to catch rabbits or fowl, we could fix him one in the morning and show him how to set it.”

“We can hunt more nuts in the woods tomorrow,” Fergus suggested. “Or stay an extra day if we find no food along the way and set up a snare for ourselves.”

Why had he not thought of that? Edan chastised himself.

19 October 1066

Morning came with sunshine. The old hermit emerged from his hut with a pot in hand and made his way to a spring nearby. Edan could see polished offerings set on a stone over the trickling water. This must be the sacred spring of the Celtic god, Mabo-Mabona.

The old man brewed tea and offered them some.

Edan and Fergus accepted Galt's herb tea but no more.

"Can you give us direction to the village nearby where your sister dwells? Then maybe we will be able to get back on our journey to Cymru," Edan asked.

"Surely. The path you came on continues past my hut through a chestnut grove, around a bog, over two hills to the village. The path is clear, and the trees are notched."

Edan thought that sounded an easy trip. If only the village weren't taken, but...no one had brought the hermit food this week.

"Galt, do you have any means of catching game? A bow and arrows? A snare?" Edan asked.

"Na, I mostly eat vegetables unless my sister brings a meat pie."

Fergus offered, "We will set up a rabbit snare for you. I saw a rabbit warren near the old ruin. Come, we will show you."

When Edan and Fergus set out upon the path, frost still rimed the edges of fallen leaves, but the air warmed even as they walked. They had left Galt with Fergus's slingshot tucked in the belt of his robe and a rabbit snare.

"If only the old hermit can keep the knight alive," observed Fergus.

"Aye, and feed both of them and the horse. We've left Galt a task. At least he knows what's going on in the outside world so he won't blunder into his sister's village unaware."

By midmorning, even with stops to gather nuts where they found them, they reached the edge of the forest surrounding the hermit's sister's village. Norman guards stood at the bridge over the moat. The Normans had found even this out of the way small village. They circled the cultivated clearing around the village and picked up a northerly track. By afternoon, they had encountered four crossroads. Edan had no idea where they were other than north of where they were two nights ago. They weren't exactly lost, but he had no idea how to get back to Cecil's route.

In the late afternoon Edan and Fergus stood at yet another crossroad. Edan chose one that led west. Fergus had not questioned his choices, but Edan saw unease in his friend's eyes. He knew Fergus recognized his indecision. He recalled no familiar village name in any direction on the signposts. They had detoured around two more villages after the first, all taken by the Normans.

The only incident had been encountering a white-haired, bewildered man who wandered the road, crying out to whoever would listen. As he drew closer to them, Edan heard him lament that he lived, yet all the younger men of his family were dead. He wrung his hands and shouted, "All is wasta" over and over. His glazed eyes seemed unseeing. He appeared to have lost his mind.

Edan's thoughts drifted back to Herstmonceux. Had his own family suffered similar tragedy? Had his village been wasted? Was his mother still of sound mind after all that had happened? What of Moira? Thoughts of what might have happened made his skin crawl.

No Norman patrols had been on any of the tracks they traveled today, yet when they heard the clatter of wagon wheels in the distance, they instinctively dove for the underbrush. A wagon outside a village was indeed a rarity, unless it contained more fleeing villagers.

Crouching, they watched a curious apparition come into view. A two-horse draft team pulled an enclosed wagon hung with all sorts of objects village wives and mistresses of the manor might buy or barter for. As it clanked and clattered down the track with its load of tubs and pots, birds stilled.

Fergus exclaimed, "How in the name of King Arthur has the traveling pedlar avoided the Normans? His wagon can be heard half a league away! I never saw one who didn't load his wares on a mule."

"Mayhap he hasn't avoided them. He can sharpen knives and swords, mend harness, provide things they need." Edan stopped talking. An idea had occurred to him. "What if we stop him and ask to ride along for a day? He knows the villages."

Fergus opened his mouth to protest, then said, "By the wolf's tooth, he might have food. My stomach's been growling all afternoon."

By this time, the wagon drew close enough to see the dun horses and their colorful driver, a blend of pedlar and jester. Clean-shaven and clad in a red jester's cap with a bell and frizzy red hair peeking out each side of it, the man sang minstrel's songs as the team plodded along. Over his tunic lay a crimson mantle of strange design which hung down on each side of his wagon seat. His stockinged legs were encased in gaiters. He clutched a long alder switch in one hand, reins in both hands. Upon his face lay a half cunning, half-foolish expression, as he sang.

This personage arrested their attention to such a degree that Edan almost let him pass by before stepping out into the road with Fergus. The pedlar jerked the reins and stopped singing at their appearance.

"What ho?" he called out in the Saxon dialect, suddenly wary at the sight of two lads with stout cudgels.

"Peace to you. We be Edan and Fergus of Herstmonceux. We seek direction in our journey."

"A truce to battle," the pedlar replied, pointing his alder switch toward their cudgels. "In truth, your warlike appearance has frightened the way to the next village out of this nidering soul's head. Off with you."

He flicked the switch over the backs of the horses and sang out, "Hie up!" Startled, the team set off at a brisk trot, tubs and pots swinging, the jester's bell jingling.

Edan and Fergus stared at each other with a look of stunned surprise.

"What are we going to do now?" Fergus asked.

Chapter Eight

19 Oct 1066

Edan turned to watch the wagon sway off down the track. His stomach growled. The few nuts he'd eaten had not been nearly enough.

"By the hair in my grandfather's ears, he be unfriendly," Fergus exclaimed heatedly.

"He'll not leave us in his dust like rustics. Follow him!" Edan burst into a run after the wagon, Fergus close behind.

The pedlar's frizzy head appeared around the side of the wagon, checking to see if he had pursuers.

Edan and Fergus sprinted half the gap before they ran short of breath. Slowing to a jog, they kept after the wagon. Every few minutes the pedlar's face reappeared, his eyes measuring their distance.

Once while he looked behind, the right rear wagon wheel hit a large pothole. Within two rounds, the rear wheel came free and rolled to the side of the track. The wagon tilted and drug on the rear corner. The sudden change in weight startled the horses, giving the pedlar all he could handle to pull them to a halt.

"Now's our chance to catch up," Edan said.

They sprinted forward. When they closed on the wagon, Edan tossed his cudgel alongside the track. Fergus raised his eyebrows, then did the same.

"We mean you no harm," Edan panted.

The pedlar snubbed the horses' reins around a tree and turned to meet them, bell jingling, his own cudgel held in both hands across his body. The look of the amiable fool had evaporated, replaced by a look of confident cunning.

"All we want is direction toward the Cotswold Hills," Edan continued as he stopped by the rear of the wagon. He was not eager to feel the pedlar's cudgel alongside his head. "First, we'll help you fix your wheel to prove our good faith."

The hands holding the cudgel lowered a fraction. "How do I know you won't set upon me as soon as my back is turned?"

"Then tell us what to do to fix your wheel and you'll not have to turn your back," Edan replied.

"Well then," answered the pedlar, "kneel there and tell me what is broken, then we will set about repairs."

Edan knelt by the wheel. A quick glance told the problem. The wooden pin which held the wheel onto the axle had snapped in two. "You need a new lynch pin," Edan said. "Do you have one or must we whittle one?"

The pedlar answered by producing a huge knife from somewhere under his voluminous, bright crimson mantle, and cutting a good length of wood from a sapling by the track. He slit and removed the bark, measured it against the front pin, and cut it to size.

"You two lift the back of the wagon and I'll fit the wheel back on."

Fergus and Edan eyed the bulging wagon. "Aye, we'll try."

Each selected a handhold, bent their knees and lifted with all their might. Their faces reddened, the veins stood out in their necks. The corner continued to rest in the dirt.

"Enough. You." He pointed to Edan. "Move over." In a swirl of crimson, he removed his mantle, revealing a stout, muscular body, and took Edan's place. "If we get her up, you slide a log under the corner. We'll rest and lift higher for the wheel, using it as a lever."

Edan's cheeks burned with shame at his weakness as he scrambled into the trees for a sturdy piece of deadfall and dragged it back to the wagon.

"Ready?" asked the pedlar. "On three, heave up. One-two-three."

Wood creaked, pots shifted, the corner rose slowly, slowly until Edan could poke the log under. They rested, Edan got the wheel, and Fergus and the pedlar lifted again with the lever. When the axle was high enough, Edan slipped the wheel on and pounded the pin in with a rock.

"A job well done, lads," the pedlar exclaimed. "Now for directions. Hold this path until you come to the next crossroads. Take the track to the left."

"But what of the next crossroad and the next?" asked Edan.

"If you go our way yourself, could we ride along with you until we are back on track again?"

The pedlar stared into their eyes, as if boring into their minds. When they met his gaze unwavering, at last he seemed convinced they were not outlaws and let out a hearty guffaw, slapping his knee. This set his bell jangling. "With that silver tongue of yours, you might help me sell me wares. I do have some food I would share with you and you won't have to beat me senseless for it."

He untied the horses and mounted the wagon. "Hop on."

As soon as Edan and Fergus went back for their cudgels and clambered aboard alongside him, he slapped the reins on the backs of his team.

"My name be Ridley. What be yours again?"

"Edan, And this is Fergus, both of Herstmonceux."

"You speak a cultivated tongue, Edan. No farm lad are you."

Edan had never thought that he and Fergus spoke so differently. "Aye, my father, Selwyn, was thane."

"Was?"

"He was killed against Duke William."

"Ah..." Ridley paused in perception. "You have come far in four days. What path have you taken?"

Feeling awkward, as though he were divulging a secret, Edan said, "We followed the old Roman road, came through Tonbridge, Reigate, Guildford, and last night, strayed through an ancient wood and came out upon this track." He refrained from telling about their night at the shrine, its hermit keeper and the wounded knight.

Ridley nodded. "Good plan to avoid London."

As they talked, the wagon reached a crossroad and took the left track. The wood began to thin, and soon they were in open country upon the Downs.

Since this was a chance for news, Edan could not help but ask, "What have you heard of Duke William's army and its journey toward London?"

Ridley replied, "As you must know, patrols are on all the roads. The main army waits in Hastings for offers of submission."

"The main army has not gone to London? They haven't taken it yet?" Edan exclaimed. "What are they about?"

Ridley shrugged. "Mayhap they assume they've left no resistance, and it's only a matter of time before England realizes and surrenders to William."

"Have you heard of any countrymen who still oppose?" Edan asked, hope rekindling in him.

"I heard the Archbishop of York and others are taking steps to recognize Edgar Atheling as King."

Fergus looked over sharply at this news, but Edan asked, "How could Edgar become king?"

"I don't fathom how, but the young northern earls who survived the battle aren't enthusiastic to take on the problems of the south. I haven't heard of any nobleman who's gathering force to oppose who could help Edgar's cause." He drove, silent for awhile. "What do you lads know of royal succession in our land?"

Edan sat speechless for some time thinking. "Father told me it had to be someone of the royal family. I know both Edgar and Duke William and even Sweyn Estrithson are all related, so I guess all could have a claim to the throne."

Ridley nodded, "The right of jus sanguinis. Aye, and who has the closest relationship?"

"I don't know."

"Edgar is the closest of the eligible members, but there are two other qualifications."

Edan sat, eyebrows raised, thinking. If that were true, King Harold had no legal right to be king, except for the vote of the Witan, his popularity, and his military genius. It was hard to let go of the idea that the English king was not a rightful king. Why should a Norman have the right even if he was related?

Ridley continued, “The first of the two other qualifications is the expressed wish of the reigning king as to who should be his successor; second, the acceptance of the named successor by the magnates, or Witan, by oath. Old King Edward is said to have named William as his successor years ago, but the second condition has not yet been met. If Duke William can somehow be kept from that second qualification, Edgar could still be king.”

“How could Edgar, a thirteen-year old like me, be king?”

Ridley replied, “He would be advised by a regent until he reached his majority. With the disunity between north and south and the great loss of life that occurred at Hastings, his chance of success is small unless William can be defeated or ousted.”

Edan’s digested this, his mind plunging this way and that with kingship possibilities.

“Have you been in any villages since the battle?” Fergus asked.

“Aye, my business lies in every village. The murderous sons of Norman swine need weapons re-sharpened.” Ridley grimaced. “The villagers themselves can ask for nothing as they are treated as slaves. The Normans have no women with them, so need no pots and tubs.”

“They let you in with no threat on your life?” Fergus persisted.

“That they did, they were so eager for help sharpening all those weapons,” Ridley said, nodding self-importantly. “Not enough armorers to go around when they split off the main army.”

Edan wondered if Ridley enjoyed his role of newsmonger.

“Will we be safe with you if Normans come along?” Edan asked. “Or must we hide?” He looked about as they emerged onto open, rolling hills stretching away to the horizon.

“We’ll be able to see them coming,” said Ridley. “One of you could be explained as my son, us with our red hair.” He turned to give Edan a wink. “The other as my apprentice. Just keep your mouths as close as the coins in a Bishop’s purse.”

Fergus spotted a ram’s horn swinging from a leather attached to the wagon frame. “Is that the horn you blow to announce your arrival at a village?”

"Aye. We'll be needing it at Swindon in the morning."

Edan felt a shiver go down his spine. Go into a village with Ridley among Normans? Would they be safe?

When the team topped the next hill, a village lay nestled in the valley far to the right.

"Yon is the Vale of White Horse. Do ye know its legend?" When Ridley received blank stares, he continued. "In the white chalk hillside near the village of Uffington, a huge figure of a horse is cut. Some say it commemorates King Alfred's victory over the Danes, while others say it's far older, done by the Old People."

Edan piped in, "Do you know the legend of The Long Man of Wilmington, sometimes called Fighting Man because he holds clubs in both hands? It's in a village near mine. That figure, too, is cut into chalk. King Harold even used it as his personal emblem."

"Maybe it was done by the same people," observed Fergus.

Edan saw his friend make the finger sign against evil behind his back. Fergus still couldn't shake the idea the Old Ones magical powers reigned supreme.

Ridley grunted in agreement with Fergus. "We'll go down to the trees and camp for the night, then enter Swindon in the morning. You can go with me or hide in the chestnut grove till nightfall when I return."

Should they go to the village with him and lose a day of journey or get direction and go on? Edan wished he could get Fergus aside and talk it over.

The going was easy, and the wagon made fair speed. Edan grew drowsy in the lazy warmth of the late afternoon. When Ridley spoke again, Edan started.

"If you lads stick with me tomorrow and the next day, I'll get you across the Avon and the Severn Rivers on the ferry. Otherwise, you'll have to find your own way and pay the toll. Do you have any coin for a toll?"

A sinking feeling in the pit of his stomach gave Edan the answer to his question of what to do tomorrow. They would have to stick with Ridley to cross the rivers which they had not known about.

"We'd be grateful for the help. We could go into the village with you tomorrow and help earn our keep," Edan answered.

"If someone could turn the handle of my grinding stone, then I would not have to find some village lad." His mischievous eyes turned to each of the boys. "Now which of you would do that?"

"I will," volunteered Fergus.

"We both will," Edan chimed in, hoping he could keep up his share of work.

Edan's thoughts turned to food as the wagon drew near the grove of trees in the valley. What would Ridley have? Would the man dare build a fire? He felt hungry enough to eat a tough old boar complete with tusks and bristles.

Before they were close enough to the village to see if it had been overrun, they pulled into the grove out of sight of the road. Ridley unhitched the team with the boys' help and fed his horses. He inspected the new pin in the wheel to see if it held before getting his food from the wagon.

Edan felt the juices gather in his mouth at the sight of a fresh loaf, a skin of goats' milk, dried venison, and fresh apples. No fire would be needed.

"Do you lads have food?" Ridley asked.

"We are out of food."

"Have some venison then and an apple," Ridley offered.

To Edan his offer appeared somewhat grudgingly made. Remembering Galt's lack of food despite his hospitality, Edan protested, "You won't have enough."

Ridley replied, "I'll have more on the morrow."

When they finished, nothing remained.

Darkness fell, and Ridley disappeared into his wagon, leaving the boys to sleep on the ground mantle-wrapped as usual.

"While we're in the village, listen for any news, aye?" Edan murmured to Fergus as they settled.

"That, and I'll see if I can charm some food from the thane's kitchen--that is, if the Normans are there and have left them any," Fergus said.

"What do you make of Ridley?" Edan asked.

"He seems to blow with the wind as my Pap says," Fergus answered at length, "but I think we can trust him."

"I, too."

Edan stared up at the immensity of the heavens, watching the stars come out and listening to Fergus's soft snores. Outside the grove he heard the stirring of grasses as a frosty breeze sauntered their way. Overhead the boughs moved, and his ears filled with the rustling of dry chestnut leaves. He pulled the mantle closer around his chin. The land smelled ripe and fragrant, ready for squirrel-time against the coming cold. He watched the quarter moon and wondered idly whether Ridley wore his jingling cap to bed. His eyes drooped and closed, the night air kneading his back.

Hoofbeats pounded down the track. Edan rose on one elbow and peered into the dim light. He saw a horse under spur galloping toward the village, its rider's weapons clanking.

Ridley stuck his head from the wagon and announced, "Courier. Must be some important news. We'll get it in the morning."

Fergus continued snoring. Wide awake again, suddenly Edan was impatient to get to Cymru and begin his fostering. His mind swirled with thoughts of weaponry and tactics, tactics to avenge his father's death. Edan prayed Ridley could indeed help them.

Chapter Nine

20 Oct 1066

Edan did not wake until Ridley clattered out of his wagon, cap jingling in the stillness of the morning.

Breakfast was a hasty affair of bread, cheese and honey mead. No sun warmed the morning this day. Thick, slate-colored clouds hung low on the horizon creating a damp chill.

Ridley eyed the sky as they climbed on the wagon to ride to Swindon. "Something coming in from the north. By afternoon there'll be a blow."

Despite the cool morning, a fine film of sweat covered Edan's body by the time the pedlar's wagon approached the Norman-guarded bridge into Swindon. As if he were outside the present, looking on, he heard Ridley blow his ram's horn and call out in the Anglo-Saxon tongue his intent to sell his wares or sharpen edge tools. He dared glance to see the half-foolish expression in place on Ridley's face, the vacant eyes, the ridiculous frizzy hair creeping out from the jingling cap. Why would these Normans trust a fool with edge tools?

Thankful he did not have to converse with the soldiers, Edan rode the wagon seat, head down, avoiding eye contact with them. Someone understood Anglo-Saxon, as they lowered their weapons and waved the wagon forward. The hair on his neck prickled. Sweat trickled down his ribs. It was all he could do not to break and run from this smothered feeling. Being here scared the toenails off him.

Soldiers crowded around the wagon. The clank of mail and creak of leather surrounding their movements soon drowned in the noisy clamor of voices, as they thrust broadswords forward to be sharpened. Weapons glinted briefly under a weak sun that was soon swallowed again by cloud. Some were still bloody. Ridley held up a hand to stay them and selected a place to work under a tree. Fergus and Edan watched, frozen to one spot.

Ridley settled his team and jerked his head at Fergus. "You. Come and help me lift my stone," he ordered.

Surprised at first by Ridley's brusqueness, Edan decided the superior tone toward them lent realism to their presence.

Puffing and grunting with effort, Ridley and Fergus lifted the pedlar's sharpening stone from the back of the wagon. Edan eyed the large round stone. It must weigh as much as half a small ox. Ridley seated himself with a theatric swirl of crimson and a jangle of his bell before reaching for a proferred weapon.

Edan scrambled to the stone and began to turn the crank that moved the stone. Without a task, he could not stand to be in this circle of the enemy. Yet he wanted to hear the courier's news. Fergus wandered over to the team and fed them drop apples from a small orchard at village edge.

The air filled with the whining, abrasive noise of metal edges on stone. The clank and creak of soldiers' movements and their voices were overcome by the monotone of sound from the grinding stone. Edan's heart slowed to steady, hard strokes as he cranked. His arms moved in rhythm to the pace Ridley set for him.

From time to time Edan glanced round the ring of stubbled, grimy faces. No eyes met his. Attention was focused on Ridley's skill or on conversation with each other as the warriors waited. It came clear to him that no one cared who he was or that he was a conquered native. They just wanted their weapons sharpened.

At last the honing of the first sword met its bandy-legged owner's expectation. "Good enough to lop off a hand or a head, eh?" Ridley exclaimed. He giggled foolishly before beginning to sharpen the next sword.

Before the whine of wheel began, Edan could hear something was up outside the circle. He heard Gloucester mentioned. An air of excitement hung over the common as he saw knights saddle, soldiers gather gear and weapons. Others gathered in small groups waiting for Ridley's services. Soon a mounted Norman patrol departed—a dozen strong.

During the break between sharpenings, the soldiers talked freely of the courier's news. Ridley's guise must have freed their tongues. Edan discovered that the courier had related details of the first movement of Duke William's troops since Hastings. As the men talked, it became clear that William's troops had waited in vain five days for Saxon surrenders. None had come, so he gathered his army and moved toward Dover, then Canterbury meeting no resistance, now holding two major cities. Who was left to lead fyrd troops against the Normans—the earls of the north, boys only a few years older than himself?

Edan's mind worked the other tidbits of news he understood. It sounded as if Duke William would go to London now unopposed. If Ridley's rumor proved true, Edgar Atheling might be selected king by the Witan Gemot and crowned by the archbishop before William could get there. Could King Harold's former troops be gathered again to fight for Edgar?

Edan glanced over to see Fergus move closer to a crofter's cottage and speak with children playing there. If anyone in the village had news, they all had it—even the children. Edan saw a few women, tense and hollow-eyed, sitting by their doors, eyes fast on their children. The men would be prisoners as they were at his own village, Herstmonceux.

Would the Normans let the villagers go about their fall chores? The women needed to make ale and process grapes for wine, and the men should begin butchering of animals not to be wintered over. All the harvest produce needed to be processed. When Ridley'd entered the village, Edan saw the fields down to stubble. The villagers had threshed and winnowed their grain before being attacked. The big mill ground steadily at the edge of the village.

Edan spotted Fergus walking toward the circle of men around Ridley. *None too soon.* Edan grit his teeth and kept cranking, his arms aching and burning with fatigue. Ridley pulled the edge from the stone and tested it with his thumb. Edan stopped cranking. Pretending to cut himself, Ridley grabbed one hand with the other and mimed a serious wound to the delight of his onlookers. He nodded and handed the weapon to its owner.

"Be done with your dreaming and get to work," Ridley growled at Fergus who moved in and took Edan's place at the stone. Edan walked through the circle of men who gave him nary a glance. He considered where to go.

A sudden commotion attracted his attention. Shouts erupted from a cottager's shed across the common, accompanied by the bawl of an ox. A cluster of Normans emerged from the shed leading an ox, a woman protesting in loud shrieks. Shoved aside by two laughing soldiers, she fell to the ground. As Edan watched from under the tree, a Norman swung his mace down upon the ox's head, then thrust his sword into its jugular. It bawled noisily and struggled. By the dog, what did they think they were doing? Oxen were necessary to each family. Without them they couldn't farm. Plenty of other animals were available for eating. Didn't they have farms in Normandy? Didn't they understand?

Without thought of time he watched them hang the ox to bleed out, then start to butcher it and carry slabs of meat to the kitchen behind the thane's manorhouse.

What had happened to this thane and his family?

The air grew quiet. He realized the grinding stone had ceased. He hastened back to take his turn from a red-faced, glaring Fergus.

"Time you did a little work," snapped Ridley. Edan ducked his head submissively. On his next break he wanted to talk to the woman whose ox had been slaughtered.

When Edan's arms burned and grew limp with fatigue, Fergus returned as if to prove he looked out for Edan's length of time at the stone. As soon as he cleared the knot of men, Edan went to the woman's cottage. She sat in a yard with flowers, two small children playing near. Dust covered her gown from her fall. Her hair straggled from its stays.

"Would you have a chore I could do for a hunk of cheese?" he asked gently.

"Be you with the pedlar?" she replied, tight worry lines creasing the skin around her mouth.

"Aye."

"Whence have you come?" Her red-rimmed eyes studied him.

"We came along the track through Reigate."

She nodded. "Do you have news of how far north the Normans have gotten? I've a sister north of Gloucester and me husband has people in Banbury."

Edan repeated what the pedlar had told Fergus and him, then asked, "Where are the men being kept?"

Her eyes brimmed with tears. "In the manor hall. I haven't seen my man for two days. Every morning I pray this was but a bad dream…" Her emotion choked off the words. In a moment she continued. "If only they just let them work the fields…" Her voice broke again. The two children ran to their mother and tugged at her gown. She hugged and shushed them.

"Could I cut some kindling for your fire?" Edan reminded her of his request.

"You may." She looked up. "And I do have a hunk of cheese. I'll cut a piece for you. The wood is at the other end of the garden." She wiped at her cheeks with the hem of her apron and marched into the cottage, the children at her heels.

Edan finished splitting two days' worth of kindling before his arms protested. He collected the promised cheese and left. He hadn't been able to talk of the ox after all when he saw the woman's tears. Despite his outrage, he realized no one could stop the Normans from this behavior.

He returned to Fergus. The day dragged onward, their shifts growing shorter as they tired more easily with each turn at the stone.

In the heat of the afternoon, Edan could smell the sweet fragrances of fermenting apples and pears from the manor kitchen as he cranked. His parched throat craved the cool tang of a cup of cider. *Of course, the Norman swine would let the women continue with ale and mead making, cider and perry making, and food preservation as they would be drinking and eating it. How long would these whif-flebrains stay? Until the new owners came?* He prayed the French would not bring their own farmers and run these people out.

By late afternoon, with Fergus taking the last shift, Edan was free to roam. How far did he dare go? The thought of being captured was fresh in his mind. He headed to the village edge to the fields, look ing over his shoulder for Norman guards. Before he got out of the cottage lanes, he saw the imprisoned men of the village, tethered in a line in front of the blacksmith shop. A fire burned in the dirt. He left the lane to stand in the shadow of a cottage. Norman guards lounged as irons heated in the fire. The village blacksmith pounded a red-hot metal collar on his anvil, a small boy working the bellows at his fire in the shop. Entranced, Edan watched as one man stood, obviously the leader, and nodded to a guard. The man sprang up and grabbed a metal rod from the flames. Two others held the first prisoner, while the hot metal rested on the man's forehead. The dark-haired leader slouched against the edge of the building as if the proceedings were of no consequence.

Edan shuddered when he heard the man's screams from the branding. Instead of the acrid fumes of burned hoof, usual around a smithy, he smelled burned flesh. A collar was fastened about the man's throat by the smith. *Now who would brand and collar the smith?* Mesmerized by the spectacle, Edan watched as all were marked, collared and sent to the fields to clean and ditch. As he followed at a distance, he could almost feel the sting of pain from their burns. Norman guards stood at intervals along the moat to keep men from escaping.

Edan slipped into a berry patch next to a lad who worked a ditch, a bright red weal across his forehead, his posture drooping and spiritless. Upon his collar, Edan saw the boy's name, Ban, indicating he was a thrall of the Normans. If he had not escaped Herstmonceux, that could be Edan's name on a collar. Or Fergus's.

"Hsst," Edan hissed.

The boy looked up and registered surprise at seeing a boy free and unbranded. Without thinking, Edan pulled the food packet he had earned that day and tossed it to Ban. The boy looked around him as he caught it, before stuffing it down his jerkin. He touched his fingers to his forehead and returned to his ditching.

Edan could watch no longer. He turned and hurried back to the common, to what seemed like an island of safety around Ridley. Amazing. After knowing the man only a day, he felt as if he had known him much longer.

The circle of soldiers had not diminished, no matter how many swords Ridley sharpened. Light had faded, and Ridley could no longer see the sharpness of the edges when he called a halt. He had hardly spoken all day except to direct Fergus and him or make some clownish remark. While they helped hitch the team, Edan wondered if Ridley understood French and had picked up any more news of Norman movements. The grinding wheel was packed back into the wagon along with the foodstuffs, ale, and trinkets the soldiers had paid for his service. The three mounted the wagon and drove from the village toward the chestnut grove.

As soon as they were out of earshot, Edan's questions came tumbling out. "Are you going back tomorrow?"

"They've swords enough," Ridley snorted in derision, his eyes again full of life. "But no, weather is coming in. We must get across the Severn."

Ridley frowned as the wagon bumped along. "They killed the old thane and his wife. His sons had gone off to fight with Harold and taken the village garrison, so there was no defense when the Normans arrived two days ago."

So Ridley did understand French. Two days. They were that far behind the troops. Edan's spirits fell a notch further, thinking of the old thane and his wife. Everything would be taken ahead of them. Marauding Normans were everywhere.

Fergus, who listened avidly, shook his head. He asked, "Did you see them butcher the ox? The wind must whistle through their ears."

"I could scarce believe my eyes. Bloody cheese-headed oafs," Edan blurted. "What are they thinking?"

"Of themselves," Ridley put in. "If they keep on like that, before spring all the food will be gone and there will be no oxen to do the spring planting. But what do they care if the people starve? Now are you interested in what the courier had to say?"

Two eager glances gave him an answer.

He recapped the courier's news giving the boys the details Edan had not understood. Ridley glanced at them when he finished. Something in Edan's expression must have made him feel the need to say more about what the news meant.

After a pause, Ridley continued, "The war has happened to everyone. It's what men make of the situation that will determine how it affects them."

Edan thought this comment sounded cold. Why did he say that? What choice did non-soldiers have in what happened to them in war?

The three sat in silence the rest of the way to the grove, each immersed in his own thoughts.

With the boys' help, Ridley unharnessed the team, fed them and went to the back of the wagon. "We have many choices for our meal tonight—fresh bread, goose, barmcakes, porkpie, cheese…"

With each mention of foodstuffs, Edan's guilt took root. How could they eat this food that had been stolen from the villagers by the soldiers? But they must. The villagers wouldn't be able to get it back. He had to think of it as stealing from the soldiers.

Ridley chose pork and raisin pie with fresh plums and a cup of ale for each. Even so, Edan had to force down his supper, images of imprisoned villagers haunting his mind. The back of the wagon held an obscene mound of foodstuffs.

With an effort Edan pulled away from such thoughts. He realized Ridley had said something. Edan heard him explain about his disguise. He focused just as Ridley finished. "If you carry a trade or skill with you, men think about that, instead of looking closely at who you are."

Mayhap that explained why Ridley acted as he did, foolish one time, cunning the next. But why did he want to avoid being looked at closely?

The wind and cold that Ridley predicted arrived as they sat about the fire. Gust-driven ash coated the food they ate. Leaves swirled in the grove making the horses nervous.

Fergus appeared deep in thought as he wiped ash from a porkpie with a forefinger before biting into it. At last he spoke. "If they haven't ridden out to take Gloucester until today, we must be close to the frontier of attack."

"Aye," agreed Ridley.

"Would the River Severn stop them?" asked Edan.

"Aye, it would if no ferry lay in at the bank. The ferryman may have heard news of their coming and gone to the opposite side of the river to keep them on this side," Ridley replied between bites of his barmcake, picking a currant from his teeth with the edge of a ragged grubby fingernail.

"Good." Fergus nodded, stretching his hands out to take on the fire's warmth as a gust of wind surged through the grove.

"How will we cross then?" Edan inquired.

"I know of another crossing upriver if need be," Ridley said, tipping his horn for the last swig of ale. "Or if the Gloucester garrison did not go with Harold and remained at home, the Norman swine may have a surprise waiting. Then the regular ferry may be running its route."

Edan prayed this were true. "If they are beaten back, where will the Norman patrol go instead?"

Ridley made no answer to Edan's question. He shrugged and put the leftover food into the wagon.

Edan planned ahead. If the Severn stopped the Normans, Fergus and he would have faster traveling, no worries about food, and Englishmen to the north might have safe haven to mount a counter offensive against Duke William.

Edan and Fergus wrapped themselves in their mantles and lay close around the fire. Tomorrow they would move on. What would they find? Wide-awake, Edan watched the fire's glowing embers winking in the chill wind.

Chapter Ten

23 October 1066

Two days of wind and hard rain had turned the roads into a pigsty. Now on the third day, every few turns of the wheels required Edan and Fergus to push the wagon out of yet another pothole. Their clothes, leggings and shoes were wet and stiff with mud. Edan's skin protested the rough cloth and constant chafing wetness. He now had an idea why most merchants used pack mules and relied on lodging in woodcutter's huts or sheep shelters. He couldn't wait to reach the Severn and its ferry.

This beautiful hill country had turned into the most tortuous part of the journey yet, Ridley's jingling bell the only cheerful sound.

A jolt and sudden stop nearly knocked Edan from the wagon seat.

"God's sweet breath if we bog but again," Ridley cursed, signaling the boys to jump down. Wiping straggles of wet hair from his face, Edan put his shoulder to the back of the wagon alongside Fergus for what seemed the hundredth time this long day.

"Ready," Edan yelled to Ridley.

"Hie up," Ridley called out. The sharp crack of the long switch followed. The boys pushed, and the team lurched into their breast collars, the wagon jerking forward, freed from its pothole. Fergus staggered and kept his feet, but Edan slipped and fell face first into the mud.

"By heaven and St. Dunstan," he sputtered, wiping the slime from his face.

Ridley's mouth twitched with some hidden emotion as he stopped to let the muddy boys mount the wagon.

At the top of the next hill a lone soldier sat huddled over a small fire, warming his hands. His horse stood by him, saddled, its head down enduring the wetness.

"Good day to you," Ridley called.

"Aye, and the best thing about it is the Norman swine turned tail and fled when they saw the closed gate of Gloucester," he boasted.

"Why is he here?" Edan asked when they had passed. "He could do nothing if the Normans returned."

"He's a sentry. Any sign of Norman approach will send him scuttling down to the river to warn the ferryman," replied Ridley. "The rivermen are the best defense against the Normans moving north as fast as they've moved through the south."

Edan shivered and hoped they would get across the river before the sentry's warning was needed.

As they saw in passing, Gloucester itself remained closed tight to outsiders, weaponry bristling from its walls, its gate tightly shut. Edan wondered where that Norman patrol had gone.

No more potholes bogged the wagon before it topped the hill overlooking the Severn. Fergus joined Edan in surveying what lay below them. The estuary spread a league wide, red mud of tidal flats along the water the only color in the gray landscape. The smell of salt and the chatter of wild ducks carried on the stubborn, drifting mist.

As the team descended toward the river, mud sucked at the horses' hooves and the wagon wheels. Edan's eyes searched for the ferry among the black skeletons of alder trunks upstream from the wharves of Gloucester. This side of the river was high ground, while the other lay flat and marshy, lifting gradually to open woodland. On the far side Edan spotted small dots in the distance, cattle tended by herders and dogs.

They'd better hope the Normans didn't get across the river or their beef might wind up on a Norman spit as it had at Swindon.

Then he saw the ferry. It was tied to a small jutting wharf next the ferryman's hut across the river.

Ridley headed the horses down the road that ran straight to the shore. As they came closer, Edan saw the swollen, muddy waters roiling angrily toward the sea. This crossing would be far different than the Avon. When Ridley drew rein, the wagon stood on the damp shingle next to the ferryman's hut. The flame of an oil torch burned on its post at the end of the wharf, smoke streaming in the wind. Waves slapped high and ominous about the pilings until Edan's ears rang with the pounding.

Ridley dismounted and went into the hut. In moments he returned. "It looks as if the ferryman plans to return," he announced. "He's left a fire burning and food on the table."

Their feet sinking into the sand, Edan and Fergus walked along the river, while they waited for the return of the ferry. Edan eyed the swift-moving water, feeling his stomach churn.

Edan considered waiting for the river to subside. No. They would lose their guide and payment of custom.

In silence he watched a large dark object roll in the middle of the river, long projections reaching upward. A tree? No, legs. A drowned cow! Then another.

The movement of something at the far side of the river caught his gaze. The ferry. Watching its return progress, Edan grew more apprehensive. It could not make a direct course to the wharf, despite its double rudder and two oarsmen. It would land downriver. Edan and Fergus retraced their path to the hut.

At last the ferry's bottom grated on shingle well below the usual landing. Ridley had seen and proceeded to unhook his team with the boys' help. They led the horses downriver to tow the ferry up. Edan welcomed the delay before venturing onto the river.

When the ferry lay secured to its wharf, its crew disembarked. The ferryman was a short, broad-shouldered fellow with dark hair and a black, stubbly beard.

"By the Raven, Ridley, how came you through the Normans unscathed?" barked the ferryman as he came off the wharf.

"All soldiers' swords need sharpening and I acted as armorer," shrugged Ridley. "How be ye, Pieran?"

As the old friends greeted each other with hearty claps on the back, the two oarsmen, well muscled young men, stood by.

"Get some food and rest," Pieran directed them. "We'll go back across in an hour."

The oarsmen exchanged a look, but they had their orders. They moved toward the hut.

What was in that look, unrest or fear? Edan felt Fergus move closer. A half-glance at him showed the appraising look in his eyes. He, too, sensed tension in the oarsmen.

"Have a cup of ale with us. Mayhap your servants can gather some faggots for the fire whilst they wait," boomed Pieran.

They were getting used to their roles. Ridley would pump Pieran for news, while Edan and Fergus would spend the waiting time gathering a hefty bundle of firewood each.

At length, the ferry was loaded with Ridley's team and wagon, the horses blindfolded with strips of cloth and trembling on their swaying floor. Edan's hands shook as he and Fergus stepped aboard and took their places at the horse's heads to talk to them and hold tight to the reins. Ridley counted out halfpenny coins for custom, then joined them, taking charge of one horse himself.

"Cast off," Pieran shouted to one of the oarsmen, after dropping the coins into his pouch. The bigger of the two oarsmen slipped the rope from its piling and grabbed his oar. From the edge of his eye, Edan saw the look exchanged between the oarsmen, the set looks on their faces. The hair on the back of his neck roused like a guard dog's. He felt his blood run faster. Even *they* were afraid of the river.

The low freeboard of the flat ferry allowed water to lap onto the deck in a disturbing manner. The nervous horses lifted their feet in exaggerated high stepping and snorted at the swirling water around their legs. Edan held one horse low on the headstall, murmuring, "Steady, old boy," even as he felt his stomach churn.

Fergus stood on the other side holding tight and crooning calm words to the other horse whose ears flicked back and forth at the reassuring words.

Abruptly, the right oarsmen dropped his oar and rushed forward with a stout pole to push off a large dead tree buffeted in the current. The ferry turned aside momentarily, then caught by the current, swung downriver.

Edan's horse sensed the shifting motion, gave a shrill whinny and half-reared, dragging both Fergus and him off their feet. "Easy boy," Edan murmured to the distraught animal. Edan's feet hit the deck again, and he glanced warily at the tree that moved downstream. Ridley struggled to keep the other horse settled.

The oarsmen resumed their hard paddle across the flood current, breathing hard with their efforts. Now and then, the ferry lost momentum and swung in the current. Pieran shifted the rudders hard right to set the ferry back on its crosspath. Edan felt a sickness grow in the pit of his stomach.

"Row harder!" Pieran ordered.

The oarsmen picked up the cadence, but their red faces and strident breathing did not bode well with half the journey still ahead. Edan stared through the renewed curtain of rain pelting the tumbling waters, at the whirlpools, the uprooted trees floating by, trying to calm the anxiety that welled up in him.

When they were three-fourths of the way across and could see the approaching shore clearly, Edan felt a thump under his feet.

"A log jammed under," Pieran cried out. "Can anyone see an end poking out?"

The oarsmen, Edan, Fergus and Ridley all stared into the angry debris-filled waters.

The floor bulged beneath Ridley's feet. Any moment Edan expected to see water bubbling up between the boards. Cracks appeared in the flooring. Edan remembered the flood-borne tree that nearly killed him a few days ago.

As the log scraped underneath, a tremble of fear shivered along Ridley's horse's flanks. With the jolt, its hooves began a frenzied clawing at the ferry bottom. Ridley held tight to the headstall and murmured soothing words. The horse's haunches bunched as it prepared to leap.

"Whoa, now. Easy," Ridley exhorted.

With a terrorized snort, it swung its haunches to the side, knocking Ridley into the water. Fergus reached over to grab the horse's bridle, leaving Edan to control the other horse.

"Row on the left," screamed Pieran as he pulled the rudders left with all his weight.

Ridley splashed and struggled alongside, his mantle tangling his efforts to save himself.

Watching Ridley struggle, Pieran shouted, "He can't swim!"

"We can't let him drown!" Edan shouted back.

Pieran yelled, "Get off the oar, Dugald, and help Ridley!"

Edan saw the young man's face go white. Was the young man so frightened of the flood his hands were frozen to the oar? With no time to waste, he dropped his own mantle. "Hold this horse. I'll go in."

Dugald moved then to take the horse, and Edan climbed behind the wagon to the other side.

"Here, tie this rope around your waist so we can pull you in," directed Pieran.

As soon as the rope was secured, Edan dove in. He wasn't sure what he would do.

"Get behind him," Pieran yelled. "Grab his collar and pull him close to the ferry where we can help you haul him in."

The current pulled Ridley downstream, but the ferry was headed parallel under Pieran's rudders. Edan reached out for Ridley's collar. He sank and rose, sputtering and flailing.

Avoiding Ridley's threatening arms, Edan grabbed the collar from behind as Pieran directed. As broad as Ridley was, Edan managed to drag him with the buoyancy of the water. He kicked hard and stroked toward the ferry with one arm. His chest heaved as he drew deep breaths. It seemed he came no closer to the ferry. His lungs burned. His arms ached.

He felt Pieran pull on the rope about his waist. Edan gasped and nearly went under trying to keep Ridley afloat. Pieran pulled hand over hand drawing them nearer. Dugald and Pieran leaned out and pulled Ridley next to the freeboard. Edan grabbed the side and hung on, while the men dragged and lifted a sodden Ridley back aboard. At that moment, the dead tree under the ferry broke free with a jolt and floated out from under.

When Edan turned to look at the bobbing bulk of the huge tree, he spotted a blob of red floating in its branches. “Ridley’s hat,” Edan exclaimed. Before anyone could stop him, he shoved back into the current for the hat. He could hear Pieran yelling, “Leave it, come back to the ferry.”

Out of the lee of the ferry, the current tore at Edan, tossing him left and right, sloshing water down his throat. He stroked hard toward the branch and the soggy hat. At last he grasped it, plucked it from the branches. Stuffing it in his teeth, he turned to swim back. Three strokes and something yanked at the rope. He took the rope in his hand and pulled. It gave a bit but something heavy bore it down. Another tree or a dead animal? He yanked harder now as the weight threatened to bear him under. Untying the rope was the only choice left.

He tread water as his fingers tore at the waterlogged, looped knot. He undid the half-hitch and pulled the rope through the loop. He was free! He looked for the ferry. It could never catch up to him. He couldn’t swim upstream to it. What could he do? *Am I doomed to drown?*

He worked his way back along the tree, hand over hand, to its roots. He must not get tangled in branches as he had at the mill. Angling toward shore, he swam hard until his breath gave out. He rolled over on his back to catch his breath. The river curved, and the opposite shore bulged out toward him. He swam closer, his arms numb, his fingers clenched like claws. He coughed and spat, feeling sure he’d swallowed his body weight in river water.

Just when he thought he must sink like a stone, one stroking arm hit bottom. He could stand and staggered ashore like a drunk where he fell full length on the shingle clutching the hat. The bell jingled once as it hit ground.

Relief flooded Edan’s senses. His fingers dug into the sandy ground to reassure himself, *I’m alive after all.* In a daze he lay there until Fergus came searching.

“Edan, are you alive? By all the fishes and frogs in this river, say something! Let me know you still breathe.”

“Aye, I’m just so tired. I could sleep for a week.”

Fergus flung himself to his knees by Edan. "Let me help you up. Can you stand?" His voice broke.

Edan looked up at Fergus's tear-streaked cheeks. "I'll be alright. Just give me a hand."

"This time I thought I--lost you—-for sure. I wanted to put out a hand and grab you, but I was too far away…"

Getting onto his knees first, Edan stood with Fergus's help.

The ferry had landed some distance upstream. Edan and Fergus made their slow way along the marshy flat to join the others. Somehow the horses had calmed when the shore grew closer and stayed aboard the ferry. Pieran and the oarsmen helped Ridley get the horses and wagon off the ferry.

"Gods and fiends," Ridley exclaimed when he saw the boys approach. His frizzy hair ran wilder than ever without its cap. Other than that, he appeared none the worse for his dunk in the river. "You could have drowned saving me not to mention that piece of cloth." Then he grabbed Edan and clapped him on the shoulder. "But thank ye."

The rain ceased at last. Leaving the roar of the floodwaters behind, the horses threw their heads repeatedly, eyes still white-rimmed, and plunged away on the marsh road dragging the clanking wagon. The waters had laid claim to a rod or more of the local farmers' bottomland fields. Grazing cattle eyed them curiously as they hurried past, intent on gaining the light woodland above--escaping the stink and mire of the marshland, escaping the bog pools reflecting the twilight sky, escaping the noise of frogs.

By the time the road speared into the woodland, the last light faded. Ridley headed for three trees together and pulled the wagon under, preparing to unhitch and feed the horses.

"You rest, Edan," said Fergus. "I'll help Ridley do chores."

Grateful for the offer, Edan still could not sit and do nothing. He dug around the edge of the wood and found a few dry sticks for the fire. They'd need one to rid themselves of the shivers from their dunk in the river.

"Time to feed ourselves," Ridley called out after the work was done. "Dried venison," he said holding up some strips of meat at the back of the wagon. "Ale and black bread." He clattered among his utensils and emerged with his horn cups, a loaf and the venison.

He set the provisions on the back of the wagon and gave Fergus a canvas cover to put up. He built a fire under the leanto. They huddled about it, wet and cold, chewing the venison and bread. Ridley and Edan shed their leggings and shoes, warming their feet and drying the footwear on sticks held to the fire. Fergus foraged for more wood and threw it on the smoking flames.

The three lingered about the warmth, gazing over the wetland below. Marshlights flickered within the mist which hung low over the water. Fergus had been whittling a slingshot but laid it aside to stare. His hand flicked in a defensive way to ward off enchantment from marsh spirits.

Now was the time to ask Ridley questions and set Fergus thinking about something else. "Are we safe from the Normans on this side of the river?"

Wiping the back of his hand across his mouth, Ridley belched and shared what he'd learned from the ferryman. "Aye, the Normans have been kept to the other side so far. According to Pieran, they rode upstream and haven't been seen. If they go far enough, they'll find another crossing that isn't as well defended. But they'll lose two or three days. Meanwhile I can get on with my journey unhindered and perhaps stay ahead of them. Where do you lads go from here?"

Edan had wondered how far Ridley planned to go after crossing the rivers. Instead of answering Ridley, he asked, "Where do you go next on your journey?"

"Hereford, a market town. I should find sharpening work and perhaps sell a few pots. If you boys stick with me a while longer, I'll continue north to Ludlow, then on to Oswestry on the Cymru border. That should take four days. Then I will turn north and continue ahead of the Normans, if the gods so please."

Edan glanced at Fergus. He saw agreement in his friend's eyes. He wished to stay with Ridley as long as possible. "Aye, we would welcome your guidance to Oswestry. Then we turn west into Cymru to my Uncle Kadeg's home."

“You are nephew of Kadeg? I know of the man. I would be glad of your company these next days as it seems we travel the same road to the north.”

Ridley appeared done with talk and set about putting bread and the ale horns back into the wagon.

Half an hour later, the boys lay under the wagon in case the rain started anew. Above them, the boards creaked as Ridley turned over seeking a comfortable spot. Light from the fire flickered on the stick-supported leggings under the leanto.

Edan’s thoughts turned to Ridley and how they had nearly lost him. As close as they had been to the pedlar these last days, what did they really know of what he believed? Other than he despised the Normans. He seemed a religious man, but what gods did he believe in, Christian or pagan? Did he have allegiance to any man?

The steady dripping around them as trees shed their moisture created a sleepy rhythm. Life would be very different when they left Ridley’s company.

Chapter Eleven

27 October 1066

Flanked by long low hills, the broad plain of the Severn valley flowed on and on, pasture after pasture around Hereford filled by fat red cattle with white faces like so many red apples on a green orchard tapestry. Beside them the ever-present river glittered in the sun. Ridley remained in high spirits all the way, singing, selling his wares and gathering news, even strumming the strings of his lute in the evenings. They journeyed at ease in warmth and sunshine although a certain crispness hung in the air.

In the late afternoon four days later, Ridley paused the wagon on a hilltop, their destination at their feet. As Edan looked down on the village of Oswestry, it seemed a clean, pleasant settlement. He saw it not as a destination but as a halting place like all others on their northward journey.

Ridley's voice broke into his thoughts. "You lads are about to enter a territory where wild peaks challenge the sky and streams thunder through rocky chasms. The land called Cymry, means land of compatriots. The people are a mix of Celts and Old Britons with different gods and a fierce and gloomy blood. Edan, you say these are your mother's people, so you are part of this yourself whether you know it or not. The blood of kinship is thick in this region." Ridley nodded in a knowing manner before continuing.

"Villages are small and far between in the wild crags of the north, called Gwynedd, where Kadeg lives. When you cross the border, follow the big valley northwest to Bala."

Ridley clucked to the team, and the wagon lumbered toward the village. Edan's head swam with the unfamiliar names, the unfamiliar sounds of the words Ridley spoke. The thought of a foreign speech had not occurred to him as Mother never spoke the dialect of Cymru, except for a few epithets. Would anyone there speak the Anglo-Saxon dialect? As to that, how many dialects did Ridley speak?

He imagined Uncle Kadeg as pale-skinned and dark-haired like his mother. Were all the Welsh like this? The Saxons, who peopled most of southern England these last few hundred years, were fair, like his father, Ridley, Fergus and himself and all his sisters, save Cara, who was dark like her mother. For the first time Edan questioned how Fergus and he would be greeted. Surely, as his mother's son, Kadeg would be duty-bound to take him in. Mother seemed certain of it.

Before Edan knew it, the wagon came to the moat around the village. The gatekeeper exacted his toll, and they entered. Already Edan sensed a stronger clannishness here, even though they were still among the Saxons. When they stopped in the common, the people were hungry for news of Duke William as every village was, but here the resistance to the invaders seemed deeper, fiercer.

On this occasion, the villagers knew more than Ridley. According to a thin, stooped man, word had just come along the Roman road from London that Duke William had gone around the head of Rye Harbour on the east coast, through Ashford and then to Dover which he burned even after it surrendered.

Why hadn't Duke William gone to London? The conquerer pussyfooted around the most important city as if he were afraid to enter. Puzzled, Edan continued to listen to news.

"What good did it do those poor folk to surrender?" lamented the thin man. "They had just as well have fought the Norman swine."

A harrumph came from an older man with layers of jowls like a fatted sow. He crowded into the circle next to the thin fellow. "Even worse, he sent men further north to Romney where two of his own ships put in after they missed the landing at Hastings. The townsfolk put the ship crews to death for their mistake."

What a rogue of seven countries! Then William killed all the townsfolk for a mere mistake by his own men!

The men in the circle raised their fists. Shouts of "demon," "devil's own," "murderer" filled the air.

A plump young woman flanked by her tall but silent husband observed, "Mayhap the gods'll get even. The flea-bitten sods sit in Dover now, sick from bad water—afraid to stray far from their privies."

Serious faces dissolved into laughter.

"For want of a little wine, the Normans are doubled over, busy wiping their own arses," added the first man who spoke.

"Where are our soldiers when such an opportunity arises?" asked the jowled man next to him.

"If the Norman swine had brought less wine across, they might have been tied to their privies sooner—perhaps on the day of the big battle. A curse on the provisioner!" Ridley shouted.

Edan and Fergus joined the chorus of laughter and hoorahs that followed the bawdy joking.

"It is said that Harold Godwineson's old mother sent a messenger to Duke William offering to buy back Harold's body for its weight in gold. Have you heard anything about this?" said the thin man.

"Na, I have not," replied Ridley.

Another man, unheard from until now, moved forward, twisting his forelock. "I heard it that Harold was sorely wounded, but his Danish wife Edith chose a body at random to be buried by Duke William and spirited him away."

"I have not heard this either," said Ridley.

"The woman in the cloak!" Edan murmured to Fergus. "Remember the woman hunting Harold's body as we took Father from the battlefield?" Meanwhile he hoped the latter rumor about Harold was true. This Edith in the cloak. Who was she? Had she truly spirited him away?

"Aye, I remember. Mayhap this fellow has a kernel of truth," Fergus replied.

Could either of these things be true? Edan mused. If Harold lived, hope was still alive. Yet if the Witan voted, wouldn't they have to follow the rules of succession Ridley had shared?

"They say Duke William stayed on in Dover to refortify. Where will he go next?" asked the young woman. The conversation turned to strategy. What could be keeping William from moving on London itself? Were his soldiers too depleted? Or had so many young Norman nobles scattered over England to take personal booty that William's main army had shrunk?

When trade finished, Ridley prepared fowl on a spit over the fire, with fresh bread, cheese and ale. Edan savored the hot chicken and lamented over when they would eat so well again. If Ridley were kind, he would send some food along to get them a couple days on their journey.

Licking his fingers, Edan asked, "Do you think there is any truth to what the villagers heard of Harold?"

"It is too soon to know. Rumors are flying now. If he does live, he will lie low for a bit."

"How many days until we reach Bala?" asked Fergus.

"Maybe two, then you will have to get someone to take you to the uncle's household north of Bala, across a mountain from Betws y Coed (Betus uh Coyd), or send a messenger with word you are near."

"How would we pay a messenger?" asked Fergus.

Ridley chuckled. "Have Uncle Kadeg do so."

They talked of the massive mountain, Cadair Idris, a landmark in Kadeg's territory of Gwynedd, and the masses of wild and barren rock around it. Ridley drew a picture in the dirt. "This creature is the Red Dragon, the Cymru national symbol since the days of King Arthur," Ridley stated. "Each petty king may also carry his own colors but all Welshmen fight under the Red Dragon."

"They don't fight under Harold's Dragon?" Edan asked.

"Na, they're a breed apart, they are. Remember, their ancestors are the Old Britons and Celts," Ridley replied. He paused, punctuated the air with one finger, saying, "Ah!"

With a jingle and a whirl of his cape, he rose and drew something bulky from the wagon's back. "Here are two sheepskins to wear. The cold can be bitter in the high crags where you go."

Surprised, Edan was speechless for once. Lamely, he said,

"Many thanks, Ridley."

"Once you are away, mayhap you will think of me from time to time. I will be in the north the rest of the winter. In the spring I will retrace my path to the Wessex coast. If the need should arise, inquiry in the villages should locate me."

Edan had not expected to see Ridley again, but felt some weight of responsibility lift at the offer. "If Fergus and I make enemies in Gwynedd, we will come after you with all speed," he replied. Would it be better if they were continuing with Ridley to the north? The loss of the pedlar's wit, knowledge and company would leave an empty space. Ridley reached out and hugged both boys. "Godspeed to you both."

Fergus wet his lips, as if to speak, a look of sudden apprehension shadowing his face, but said nothing. Was Fergus afraid? Edan's own demons clawed at his stomach.

28 October 1066

When the clear, frosty morning came, Edan and Fergus were off. Packets of food bulged in their waist pouches, Edan's firebox held embers again, cudgels filled their hands, and the new sheepskins lay warm against their chests.

By noon they had followed the river valley to a more remote one where there was no clear going save along the streamside, traveling in deep forest. In late afternoon they munched meat pies without stopping to rest, except to drink. Now and again where the forest thinned, they caught glimpses of the surrounding hilltops, white with fresh snow, and there were more behind those. The air had the feel of snow and the bite of cold.

Toward dusk Edan heard wolves howling up near snowline. As dark drew in, he heard sounds in the underbrush and saw a shadow slipping away between trees. Wolves made his skin crawl. He was glad to see torch lights at a village bridge. The hour being late, the gates were closed. Edan built a blazing fire nearby from the embers in his firebox. After they ate good bread and cheese, they curled up about the fire to sleep. Glad of the sheepskin against the cold, Edan pulled the mantle over the lower half of his face. No wolves came to threaten them that night.

29 October 1066

In the morning Edan stared up at row after row of ascending mountains behind the village. The granite rose in steep-walled cliffs, furthermost peaks obscured by cloud. A zigzag, narrow goat track clung to the steep walls.

"Must we go up there?" Fergus asked, his breath making clouds from his mouth.

"There is no other path and it appears to head north as Ridley said," Edan answered, rubbing his hands together against the cold. They ate bread and cheese, drank from an ice-encrusted stream, and gathered their belongings.

Several rods up the incline, the track became so precipitous there was often only the length of Edan's foot as trail width. The path switchbacked often, the view swinging back and forth in dizzying fashion. He didn't dare look over the side to the depths below. The higher they went, the sheerer the drops.

"A few days of this and I will be toughened to begin warrior training under Uncle Kadeg," Edan said.

Fergus grunted, "Sa," and kept climbing.

As the climb became steeper, their lungs complained. Red-faced and panting, every few steps they had to stop to catch their breath. They learned to slow their pace. This enabled them to stop less frequently yet cover more ground.

Behind him Edan heard the scrape of Fergus's shoe on the fine gravel of the path as he slipped. Fierce scrabbling followed, accompanied by a yelp. Edan whirled. Fergus clung to the rocks along the path, his lower half hanging over the drop.

"Edan, help me!" he panted.

Bracing himself and grabbing a sturdy bush, Edan reached down to grab Fergus's arm. The firebox slid from his pouch, bounced once with a sharp clang and disappeared. "What else!" Edan exclaimed.

"Edan," Fergus breathed. "Now."

Edan reached down again, securing Fergus enough for him to

swing one leg upward onto the path, then the other. Fergus lay there, panting and shaking.

"You're all right now, Fergus," Edan reassured, though his own heart raced.

"The curse of the Old Ones on this path," Fergus gritted out between spasms of shaking. "Even under St. Witold's care, I thought I was dead."

"We just have to slow down and be more careful," Edan said. What if Fergus had plunged over the edge and not just the embers? What would he have done then? He tried to put it out of his mind. He reached down to give Fergus a hand up. When he was on his feet again, Fergus cautiously climbed again behind Edan, staying as far from the outside edge of the path as he could on feet that were several sizes larger than Edan's.

In late morning, under graying skies, a strong wind began to blow through the valley. This was truly an inhospitable place.

A fierce rainstorm boiled up from behind a hill to the north. Lightning flashed and thunder echoed off one peak then another. The hair prickled on the backs of their necks, but there was no shelter. Edan told himself, *one bolt of lightning and all their suffering would end.* He lifted his face to the downpour as if the force of the water itself would make the whole nightmare of Hastings and its troubled aftermath go away. Before the rain passed, they were terrified and soaked. The track had become slick and even more treacherous.

Edan turned to talk to Fergus, to keep from dwelling on their freezing hands and feet, or on falling off the slippery track. "You know, I keep thinking about what we would be doing at home if Duke William hadn't come. Harvest and apple-picking would be nearly done, and we would be spending hours riding, wrestling, hunting…" Saliva ran in his mouth at the thought of the crunchy red apples in Father's orchard. He could almost feel the skin smooth under his fingers after shining it on the front of his tunic, taste the sweet juice seeping into his tongue.

"By the Black Dog's hairy toes, only wolves and wild men must pass this way," interrupted Fergus as he clung to a bush when his foot slipped again, nearly pitching him off the path.

"Aye, and perhaps some sheep or goats," replied Edan, growing silent once more to better concentrate on the track.

Goat-like themselves, Edan and Fergus scaled the sides of the deep defile, clutching at protruding rocks and bushes to steady their progress. Following this path resembled when Edan had been caught in the flood swollen rivers at the village mill and at the Severn, but there was no choice but to go on. He had to go where the river or path took him.

Several times Edan caught Fergus looking over his shoulder and making the devil horn sign against evil behind his back. The eerie rock formations must have turned Fergus's mind to the spirit world again. Hours passed as they climbed, putting one foot mechanically in front of the other. Planting their cudgels ahead, then pulling themselves even. When his legs were shaky and weak with the effort of climbing, Edan knew they must rest before someone fell. "Let's eat," he suggested.

"Thought you'd never say that," Fergus grumbled and plopped down on the nearest rock. They ate jerky and cheese with stiff, cold fingers. In a few minutes, the rest and food having helped, they were underway again. The first few steps were stiff as they could scarcely feel their feet. If only they hadn't frozen. They needed to reach the warmth of a village soon as they could no longer build a fire to warm themselves or cook any food—if they had any.

Near dusk they descended yet another wild gorge into a stream-fed valley with trees.

"I smell smoke…and food," observed Fergus, visibly relieved to be out of the rocky highland and back among people.

"Bala must be near," said Edan, peering into the misty air and flexing his cold-stiffened fingers, more than relieved. Would they be welcomed in this clannish village?

Chapter Twelve

29 Oct 1066

Before long, the muddy, rain-swollen tributary Edan and Fergus followed joined a larger one. Clambering over stream tumbled rocks, they descended the drainage. At its bottom they came to a small settlement nestled amid trees. The natural curve of the stream made a moat around its front, while on the back side a sheer cliff provided protection. Inside the settlement, steep defensive earthworks had been built, crowned by palisades.

"They must expect the Normans," Fergus observed, eyeing the elaborate fortifications.

"Aye." Stamping his feet against the cold, Edan hailed the gate. A burly man appeared at the top of the palisade and squinted down.

Edan called out, "We seek lodging for the night and news of the whereabouts of my uncle, Kadeg of Caer Bannog."

The man grunted a reply and disappeared. With a creak, the gates swung open to reveal the muddy main street of the village. It was little more than an alley. An inn lay just inside the gate, a low building, roughly built of stone. The surrounding structures were wattle huts, daubed with mud. The inn roof was newly thatched with reeds held down by a rope net weighted with stones. A heavy curtain of skins hung across the door. Peat smoke curled from its chimney, mingling with the smells of supper cooking.

"Why so much protection for such a small village?" Edan said.

"We haven't seen many villages at all. They can't depend on help from neighbors," Fergus pointed out.

A few hungry looking dogs skulked about. The boys entered the gate, and abruptly the burly man from the palisade appeared beside them as if he'd flown down from the heights.

He held his hand out for the toll. Edan dropped a silver penny from Ridley's pay into the grimy palm. He saw the drawn scar of an old wound across the back of the man's hand as he put the coin in his scrip. The gatekeeper said something in what Edan thought must be Welsh and pointed toward the inn. With a bold-eyed stare, the gatekeeper turned away to resume his vigil.

The boys slogged along the muddy street to the inn. Edan looked over his shoulder to see that the gatekeeper indeed returned to his post. Something about the man made him uneasy. He held onto the pouch at his belt which contained the rest of their coins, so they wouldn't jingle. No sense tempting fate. The skin of his other hand turned white with his grip on his cudgel.

They heard voices as they neared the inn. Pushing the skins aside, they went in. Everyone looked up, and talk hushed. Edan hesitated, uncertain what to say.

An elfin man rousted energetically around the room picking up used trenchers and talking, ordering the serving maid to the kitchen for more ale. He bore himself as the man in charge.

Edan said, "You be the innkeeper?"

A nod from the little man.

"I be Edan, nephew of Kadeg of Caer Bannog. I was told to ask for him here."

The little man cleared his throat, Adam's apple bobbing. "Indeed. You and your friend are welcome. My name be Alun. I'll tell you the way to Kadeg when the meal's done." He made a welcoming gesture with one hand. "Come in. Don't stand there in the draught. Supper's cooking."

Relief ran through Edan. The man had replied in the Anglo- Saxon tongue. Some people in these parts spoke both dialects.

"Is my uncle well?"

"Praise be to all the saints, he is well and he is at home in his fortress." He bustled away toward the kitchen.

Fortress? Edan wondered at that choice of terms, while he

looked about. *What should he say next?* Anything he said would be heard by all in the small room. Some half-dozen men could be seen in the smoky interior. With their curiosity sated, talk resumed. The newcomers were no longer the focus of all eyes.

Edan exhaled slowly and took a place at a rough table near the fire. Fergus followed holding his hands out to savor the warmth.

"By my own frozen backside, I'm afraid to bend my fingers. They might snap off," Fergus said.

Edan chuckled. "Aye, and my toes might join your fingers."

Soon, thawed a bit, they took off their mantles and sheepskins and spread them out over the bench to dry. The pain Edan felt in his feet let him know he could at least still feel them.

When Alun arrived with a trencher to share, Fergus attacked the meal of greasy blood sausage, pottage, and bread with his fingers, his waist dagger and a smacking of lips. "I was in grave danger of starvation when we arrived. Now I am saved." He rolled his eyes at the ceiling.

Edan grinned at his friend's enjoyment and filled his belly at the same pace. To the accompaniment of cups thumping nearby tables and rough voices calling for more gwyn and ale, talk turned to Duke William. Fortunately, some men spoke in Saxon. The boys listened attentively as they toasted themselves next to the fire.

It seemed the Norman army had marched to Canterbury, while Edan and Fergus had journeyed to Bala. It, too, had surrendered without a fight. This Edith, widow of old King Edward, king before Harold, ruled as dowager queen here, retaining her title and estate. Edith inherited a large garrison to defend Canterbury. *Why hadn't she done so? Did it have anything to do with her husband having been cousin to Duke William?* Edan's anger smoldered. Any brave Saxon soldiers who remained alive must not serve at Canterbury.

When the pace of service slowed, the little innkeeper returned to the boys. "You may sleep under the loft steps. There's straw, and it'll stay some'at warm from the fire here. I'll send me boy, Dyfan, with you in the morn to show you to Kadeg."

The fire burned low. The drinkers had gone home or settled to sleep in the loft above. Edan and Fergus nodded before the fire, dry and warm at last, barely noticing the diminishing clatter from the kitchen, too exhausted to move. Alun emerged from the kitchen with a tallow candle and led them to the small space beneath the stairs.

They nestled into the straw, covered by their mantles. "Fergus, what think you of Alun's description of Uncle Kadeg's house as a fortress? Does that mean its a fortified castle?"

"I wondered at that. He sounds like a borderlord," Fergus mumbled, half-asleep.

"I wonder if he has a wife and children or lives in the fortress with his army?" Edan said.

He got no reply. Fergus slept.

Despite a long, hard day of travel, Edan's mind flashed from one topic to the other. Tomorrow his life of the past fortnight would come to an end. He would be in the household of a relative to whom he would be beholden. Would he be welcomed or cast out? From past experience, he knew that his mouth might get him into trouble.

At length, the sound of animals munching hay on the opposite side of the wall lulled him with its monotony.

At dawn, Alun appeared with his candle. Edan awoke on edge. The outcome of going to Kadeg was beyond his control.

Out in the public room, the fire blazed and food waited on a table. Alun chattered cheerfully. His son, Dyfan, already eating, appeared near Edan's age with a long shock of black hair and close-set gray eyes. Short and wiry like his father, he moved with that same energy as he gathered what he needed for his journey. He spoke intelligible Saxon dialect.

As they exited the gate, Edan looked for the gatekeeper. He sat atop a perch protected by a palisade. Even from that distance, his eyes seemed to bore into them. Uncomfortable but relieved, Edan was reminded of Ridley's admonition of knowing a man through his eyes. In this case, he was not sure what he saw. A strong protector, a crafty opportunist, or a murderous spy. They left the village behind to travel a twisting, steep valley with plunging ravines and rushing boulder-filled streams.

Edan could contain his curiosity no longer. "The gatekeeper, is he a former soldier? He seems more protective than those at other villages we've visited."

"Innis was a soldier, a housecarl under your uncle. In a battle he fought next to your uncle. One of Harold's men broke through and wounded Kadeg. Innis did not protect his lord well enough. He left the fortress. Now he is obsessed with protecting our village."

Edan nodded understanding. The man suffered humiliation. His curiosity turned to his uncle. "What sort of man is Kadeg? Have you met him?"

Dyfan turned to look at Edan. "Ye don't know yer own uncle?" he said. His high-set brows in a perpetual position of surprise rose even higher.

"After my mother married my father, they moved to Wessex. She went back to visit but never took us children…or Father, so no, I haven't met him," said Edan and for the first time asked himself why.

Dyfan appeared to digest that information but didn't reply to it. "Me own father used to be with Kadeg as a young man. He speaks high of him."

"Have you ever seen him?" Edan prodded.

"He came through our village with his men when he joined Llewellyn ap Gryfyd in battle against Harold two years ago. He be a tall man with fearsome eyes," Dyfan said.

Edan gave a small shiver. *Twice now Dyfan said his uncle fought against Harold.* Fergus shot Edan a look but said nothing. *Who merited Kadeg's allegiance now?* "Is he against Duke William?" Edan asked, anxious for the answer.

"Men are gathering by Kadeg now to discuss alliances," Dyfan replied enigmatically.

Uncle Kadeg sounded formidable. *Could he be bothered in times like these with a Saxon stripling like himself, relative or not?* He had counted on Kadeg for his fostering. Somehow he had envisioned a kindly uncle, not a warlord who had fought against the English.

Questions gnawed at Edan as they traveled. *Would Kadeg now fight with the English to repel Duke William or fight only to save his fiefdom in Gwynedd? If accepted and trained in the arts of war, would Edan help Kadeg fight neighboring rivals and never have the opportunity to help oust Duke William?*

Dyfan continued to chatter about the battle between Cymru's famous leader, Llewelyn ap Gryfyd, apparently from a long line of Llewelyns, and Harold. Edan normally would have hung on every word of battle tactics, feats of heroism, and politics that influenced alliances. Today, each tale made him more unsettled. His heart beat faster than the altitude made necessary. Be calm, he told himself as apprehension threatened to overwhelm his relief at coming to journey's end.

Half-listening to the drone of Dyfan and Fergus's voices, he concentrated on the track, the landmarks around him, the approximate distances. They might need to retrace their steps in a hurry and catch up to Ridley.

They climbed ever higher, low-lying clouds blanketing tops of nearby mountains. Mist descended, and the peaks were lost from view in moving caterpillars of fog.

In late afternoon snow began, a few flakes at first, then in earnest. The three progressed slowly, slipping and sliding, into the craggy heart of the granite peaks, all landmarks lost in the driving snow.

An occasional "By all the fleas in England" or "By the wolf's tooth" let Edan know Fergus had not slipped off the steep path behind him.

Snowflakes as large as coins drove horizontally across his vision. His fingers were stiff as icicles. The woolen mantle swathed over his head and across his lower face and upper torso protected all but his eyes and upper cheeks against the driving wind and snow. Ice built up on his lashes had to be brushed away every few steps.

Dyfan plodded steadily ahead, seemingly sure of his route.

"Dyfan, how much further?" Edan shouted into the howling gale. Wind shoved the words back down his throat.

Somehow Dyfan heard. "We are nearly to a crossroad where we head up a pass to Kadeg's. Help me watch for a tree snag with a marker sign."

A fall of fist-sized rocks cascaded down from above. Some scattered in the path, the rest plunged over the side, bouncing down, down. "What was that? Is someone above us?" Edan yelled, reaching back to stop Fergus.

"No, that was just a rockfall. It happens all the time up here. When it rains or snows, the dirt and rocks loosen."

"The mother of all mischief…" Fergus gasped.

Edan turned to look at Fergus. Both eyed the slope above. *What if the rocks had been larger or had not hit in front of them?*

Edan rubbed his hands together and stamped his feet to speed circulation. If they did not reach shelter soon, their hands and feet would be frozen. He could no longer build a fire after the loss of his embers yesterday, not that he'd seen much wood. They must keep moving as fast as possible.

Dyfan had walked on around a curve, out of sight. Edan heard his voice. He hurried ahead. The snag loomed out of the blizzard on the side of the path. A new path diverged up a gash in the cliff.

As soon as they entered the gash, the wind lessened but the snow grew deeper. Drifts reached to their knees. The incline grew steeper, and all of them panted as they climbed. Edan felt his right foot go out from under him. He flopped onto his side and slipped backwards. His feet hit Fergus. Edan heard a grunt as the bigger boy fell heavily.

"There's nothing to grab!" Fergus yelled.

Edan heard scratching sounds below as Fergus sought to slow his slide. He felt Fergus grab his ankles.

Ice particles slid under his tunic, smeared up his back, sending new chill through his body.

"Help us!" Edan yelled.

Both continued to slide back down the gash, on their stomachs. There was no rock, no bush to grab to stop their slide. Visions of the two of them sliding all the way back down the gash and shooting out into boundless sky whirled through his mind. *Are we going to die together?*

From above Dyfan shouted, "Roll on your back. Dig in your heels."

Edan rolled and dug frantically with his heels. One heel caught, slowing his descent. Then the other heel caught. He came to a stop, heart pounding as if to burst from his chest.

Below, the scratching sounds of Fergus sliding on the snow ceased. He, too, had found a way to stop himself.

Edan lay there panting. He heard Dyfan scrambling down.

"Are you hurt?" Dyfan called out.

"I don't think so. Fergus, how about you?"

"By all the ice on this crusted mountain! I don't think anything is broken."

Dyfan slid down next to them. "Can you go on?" he asked. Concern showed on his face.

"Aye, we can go on," Edan replied.

"It is only a short distance now," Dyfan reassured.

Edan rose cautiously to his feet. Each step was secured before he took the next. Progress slowed to a crawl. Blinded by the swirling snow, his senses turned inward. So cold that it felt as if he sunk through time itself. So cold he knew only that they had reached the top of the gash once more and continued across a windswept ridge.

Dyfan instructed them to hold onto one another. The combined weight helped hold them onto the crag against the wind. How Dyfan could find his way in this, Edan could not fathom. He could not feel his feet or hands. His cheeks stung. Were the others this cold? Dyfan's "We're almost there" seemed long ago.

A harsh cry burst from the whiteness. They were surrounded by several bundled figures brandishing spears. Ice-encrusted features made them all look alike.

"I be Dyfan, son of Alun, from Bala," Dyfan slurred some words in Welsh through cold lips. "This is Edan, nephew of Kadeg, and a friend."

Edan heard names Alun, Bala, his own name and Kadeg. The name, Alun, appeared familiar to the warriors. The leader grunted acceptance, turned and led them forward into the storm.

They must indeed be close if these sentries were out on patrol. Edan hoped this was true because it would take a hundred years to thaw himself.

Chapter Thirteen

30 Oct.1066

An enormous gate clanked, winch chains rattled. A black passage yawned. Edan stumbled forward among the close-packed sentries on feet that ached worse than ten toothaches. Inside, the small party moved across the common area to a large stone building almost invisible in the swirling snow.

A heavy door opened. Edan saw torches placed along the dark walls flicker in the draft. The men filed into a cavernous hall furnished with two long tables and benches the length of the room. Along one wall an enormous fireplace lit the dimness. The cold diminished. Edan heard a great baritone laugh, another voice replying—then silence. Dark figures seated about the warmth rose to see the newcomers. Edan peered through snow-crusted eyelashes.

One of the sentries removed the cudgel from his frozen fingers. No weapons allowed on strangers.

One man stood taller than the rest. All were only silhouettes between Edan and the light. He could not see faces. Someone spoke in Welsh. The leader of the sentries replied, apparently explaining the new arrivals.

Frustrated, Edan could only guess at what was being said. If Uncle Kadeg only spoke Welsh, how could he communicate with him? Mother had never spoken Welsh around her children, except the use of an epithet when nettled.

The fire flared as one of the men threw on more fuel. Warmth hit Edan's half-frozen cheeks.

Someone said in Anglo-Saxon, "Come here."

The flames dazzled Edan's eyes. The three boys stepped toward the voice. All Edan saw was the tall shadowy figure he supposed to be Uncle Kadeg, watching him, eyes dark smudges in an expressionless face. Wolfhounds rose and crept forward, hackles raised until the same voice barked, "Stay." The hounds turned tail back to the corner by the hearth.

As Edan approached, the tall figure turned to allow the boys access to the circle of men surrounding the fire. Light fell on his face, and for the first time Edan saw him plainly. Perhaps in his mid-thirties, he was not as young as Edan had supposed. There were lines at the corners of his eyes, extraordinary light gray eyes, beneath heavy black brows. A neatly trimmed black beard fringed his chin. Dark hair hung loose over his shoulders. He wore an elegant leather tunic over a woolen shirt with gaitered warm leggings below but few adornments, only copper arm rings.

"I am Kadeg. Which of you three is Edan?" he asked, his face still expressionless, his eyes boring into those of the boys.

Edan blinked in the glare of firelight. "I be Edan. My mother sent me to you after Harold lost the battle at Hastings and Father was killed. Our village was overrun by Normans. She sent my friend, Fergus, with me because she thought we'd be safer." Made stupid by the cold, Edan could think of nothing else to say. His legs wobbled with fatigue and he fought the feeling, forcing himself to stand erect.

Silence lay thick in the room. Only the crackling flames and the clank of a sentry's sword broke the quiet. Kadeg looked Edan up and down for what seemed like minutes with a piercing gaze. One hand played with his copper arm rings. For Edan, his towering presence stretched to the rafters, filled the room. The men around him listened like foxes at a rabbit den.

Edan heard Kadeg take a breath to speak. "How old are you?"

"Thirteen, sir. Almost fourteen."

"You've had your fostering then?"

Edan looked to see the expected surprise on Kadeg's face at mention of his age. Most men thought him eleven or twelve. It did not come. Just the same, he could feel the flush rising in his face.

"No, sir. Father was away at battle." He paused, feeling he must defend this oversight. "He said I was a late bloomer and needed another year to grow, but then…he was killed."

Kadeg motioned him closer to the fire, leaving Fergus and Dyfan with the sentries.

Edan obeyed.

"What has your mother told you of me?" His tone was cold.

"Only that you are her older brother, a warrior, and that you live in Cymru."

Kadeg stroked his dark beard, then stared into the fire. During that time Edan glanced around at the other men near Kadeg. Mature men of warrior type, lean and strong. His eyes returned to one, lightly built and young but already tall. The young man's color was high, and his breath came harsh and rapid, as Fergus's did when he wrestled Edan. The look on his face was unreadable. Edan looked again at Kadeg.

The piercing gray eyes came back to him. His hand returned to the arm rings, twisting and fingering. "You may not be full-grown, but it is time to make a warrior of you. You aren't afraid of cold iron are you?" Sarcasm dripped from the last sentence.

The accusation rankled, but Edan met the numbing gaze. "No, sir. I would be proud to learn from you and then to serve you," Edan said holding his tongue with effort. He felt his exhilaration rise. His hope might be realized after all.

"Your father's death didn't deter you from your duty?"

"No, sir."

Suddenly Kadeg pushed up his arm rings in a violent gesture. "By the dragon, let's hope you have your father's courage without his stubbornness. If so, we'll make a decent warrior of you."

What did Kadeg mean, his stubbornness? Had he disliked my father? Edan's heart sank. Living here might be harder than on the road dodging Normans.

Kadeg stared briefly at Edan, then with an impatient breath turned to the sentries who had brought the boys to him and said in Welsh, "Send Cerdic to pour a hot bath for this lad. It's a late supper we'll have when everyone is ready." He then translated for Edan.

The circle of men closed about Kadeg as Edan, Fergus and Dyfan were escorted out of the hall. His mind as numb as his body, Edan followed the servant upstairs to bedrooms where hot water soon steamed in a tub. Edan's body thawed in just a few minutes in the hot water. Cerdic bathed Edan himself, scrubbing, oiling and drying him. Talking all the while, in a high reedy voice, the stocky servant stood over him until he was clothed in a clean tunic of white wool.

Cerdic said in Anglo-Saxon, "Corpus bones, you flea-ridden clod. You will have the little beasties hopping all over the master's chamber." He clucked his tongue and glanced at the floor as if he expected an army of fleas to be hopping about. He directed the boy who helped with the hot water to gather all the clothes and take them to be washed. Holding them at arm's length, the boy started for the door.

"Wait," Edan said.

He rummaged in the clothes, pulled his scrip from them, and attached it to his new belt.

Cerdic's brows raised in curiosity, but he did not ask. "At least you're clean now. Hungry? Time to get down to the hall for supper," he rattled on.

"I could eat a carthorse," Edan replied.

Cerdic shot him a look, then grinned. "You handled yourself well in front of the master. He'll be good to his word. He's a strict taskmaster but fair." He turned, picked up a container of white powder and sprinkled it about the floor of the chamber.

Long before they reached the hall, the smell of food came to meet them, then the clank of ale cups as the men emptied their trenchers with their fingers or an occasional knife.

Platters of fried gamebirds, breads, cheeses and tureens of soup loaded the tables. Fergus and Dyfan sat at the end of a long table far from Kadeg as they had come late. Edan joined them and thought he had never eaten anything so good.

"By God's sweet breath, this is heavenly and hot," Dyfan breathed as he took the first two bites.

"Marry, and I give thanks to the gods we are here to eat it," Fergus said solemnly. "A while ago I wouldn't have given much for our chances to survive."

"How could you ever tell where the path was, Dyfan?" Edan asked in awe.

"I just know the mountain, where things are even if I can't see them. But I, too, am glad we arrived."

Conversation stopped as the boys dug into the shared trenchers. When plates of honeycakes and dried fruit were passed, Edan was too full to even take any.

Servants entered the room with bowls of fresh water and towels and waited while the diners rinsed and dried. Across the room Edan spied the same young man who had been so agitated when they arrived. As if by signal, he looked up and their eyes met. He stared hard at Edan then turned to talk to the warrior at his side. After the cleansing, the servants cleared tables. The men gathered again in groups about the fire.

Kadeg rose and left the room alone. Cerdic followed. Cerdic must be Kadeg's personal servant.

A short time later, Cerdic returned. He went to Dyfan and Fergus, saying something into their ears.

Dyfan stretched and rose from his bench. "I'm going to leave you now. Morning will come soon enough, and I must make the journey back to Bala. Father can't spare me for long."

Edan stood and reached out for Dyfan's shoulder. "God's blessing on you for guiding us here. Without you we'd be lying stiff in some snowdrift."

Dyfan shrugged. "Me father has promised an errand to this fortress for a long time—the time finally came. Now I've seen it. It's a wonderful defense for Gwynedd."

Edan dug in his scrip for the rest of his coin. "This is all we have to pay you for your trouble."

Dyfan waved it off. "Keep your coin. Kadeg will make it good with me father. He doesn't stay beholden to anyone for long."

"Godspeed back to Bala tomorrow." Edan felt a pang of regret Dyfan could not stay. He owed him his life. "Watch that spot where

Fergus and I slid almost to the brink of nothingness," he cautioned. "May the blessing of St.Dunstan go with you."

As Dyfan left for servants' quarters, Cerdic reappeared. "Fergus, go with Dyfan. Come along," he motioned to Edan.

Edan looked after Fergus who seemed confused, then back to Cerdic, who shook his head. Why was Fergus being taken away?

Games had begun among the men—chess, knucklebones, and dice. Edan heard teasing voices, bets wagered around the room as he left with Cerdic.

Kadeg was not playing games when they got to his room. He sat at a table littered with maps and writing materials, with his chair tilted back. He sat staring into the brazier which warmed the room.

"The boy, sir."

"Thank you, Cerdic."

"Sir." Cerdic bowed slightly and went, the door falling closed behind him.

Kadeg turned to face Edan. He nodded toward a stool.

Edan pulled the stool closer and sat.

"I see they found something for you to wear. You'll grow into it. Did you get supper?"

His cheeks warm from the perceived size reference, Edan wondered that Kadeg hadn't seen him in the hall. "Yes, sir."

"And you're warmed now? Pull the stool nearer the fire if you feel the need."

"I'm warm now."

"You appear to have courage and intelligence since you found your way here, dodging Normans and thieves." Kadeg said this as if the thought followed upon food and warmth. "Your mother, did the Normans harm her?"

"The Normans beat her, but she said she was alright." Edan stopped and passed a hand over his eyes. "She seemed to have a plan." Edan stopped. Had he said too much? Kadeg listening attentively, shot his arm rings again. A frown took over his face.

"She would. Always she was the quickest of us children. Did you know there were more of us? Another brother, Camlach.

"No."

"The oldest. He was killed when your mother still lived here. After your mother, our mother had no more."

Edan noted a long, narrow white scar from Kadeg's right temple down into his hairline by the ear. Was that the wound the gatekeeper, Innis, could not protect against?

Kadeg leaned forward in his chair resting his elbows on the table. His deep eyes bored into Edan. "Edan, son of Rowena, princess of Gwynedd, and the Saxon warrior, Selwyn."

Hearing his lineage recited as if he should know it, Edan started at the word princess. His eyes widened. Why had he not known that? Then Kadeg was a prince. What would life be like in the wealthy house of a prince?

"You seem surprised. How is it you know so little of your own lineage?" He waved a hand dismissively and proceeded to give Edan more information. "Your mother took Father at his word. As a girl, she was headstrong and would marry whom she pleased. When Selwyn fought battles in a Saxon alliance against other Saxons at our father's side and she laid eyes upon him—well, she chose. Her choice did not please our father. He favored a petty king's son. She married Selwyn anyway and ran off to Wessex. Father disowned her. Our mother sympathized. I could do nothing. When Mother grew ill years later, your mother returned to nurse her. After she recovered, your mother left."

The mystery of Mother's solitary visits was explained. Father had not been welcome, nor Mother either for any length of time. He noted to ask Cerdic what a petty king was.

"But she came more than once…" Edan faltered.

"She came again when Mother died. She has not returned. It must have been hard for her to send you to me, but she sent you to me, not to her father. Father is still very much alive."

Edan nearly fell off his stool. His grandfather lived!

Mother had never mentioned him. Had he been in the hall this evening? Did the old man know the son of his disowned daughter had come to Kadeg?

They talked for hours. Kadeg wanted details of the battle, Norman behavior, tactics of how they won the battle. Anything to give him intelligence on Duke William's strength and battle techniques. Edan told of the bluffs, the faked retreat, the sudden reversal and surprise to the Saxon troops. He told of the fighting from the backs of their horses, the riders using leathers for their feet.

When he finished, Kadeg said, "Harold fought this battle differently than any other he led. He was only on defense. It was almost as if he knew he was doomed."

A memory of a courier arriving in their yard before the troops went to battle flashed into Edan's mind. The shocked, pale face of Harold after he read the message. Had that affected the battle?

Cerdic came in once and restoked the brazier. Finally, fatigue made Edan stumble over his words.

Kadeg sat back. His intensity faded. He became aware of Edan's stumbling words. He peered at Edan.

"You are tired. Get a good night's rest. Your training will begin tomorrow. When I can, I will send a message to your mother that you arrived. Oh, and your companion will be trained as your man-servant. We have no one else to spare for you."

"But Fergus is my friend not my servant," Edan blurted.

Kadeg gave him a look that fair peeled the flesh from his bones. "You forget yourself," he said.

Edan cursed himself. He had done the very thing he swore to himself he would not do, let his mouth get him into trouble.

"Cerdic," Kadeg called out. "Take Edan to his room. He looks half-dead for lack of sleep."

Cerdic reappeared so fast he must have been standing outside the door. Following him down the drafty corridor, Edan continued to chastise himself for daring to argue Kadeg's last remark. *How could he have on his first night here? But Fergus is my friend not my servant!* Yet if he truly was of rank, would he be allowed to be friends with Fergus?

So upset was he, the luxury of his bedchamber went almost unnoticed. A big bed lay covered over with woolen blankets and pillows stuffed with fleece. Sheepskins concealed much of the floor, thick curtains draped the walls, and a brazier warmed the chamber. He could only think, *where is Fergus sleeping?*

In a fatigued stupor, Edan took off his new clothes, folded them, and fell into bed. The blankets smelled of cedar, and servants' voices came soft from the corridor.

Even disturbing thoughts of Fergus could not prevent Edan from sliding into the comforting world of sleep. For the first time in a fortnight, someone else had the responsibility for his safety.

Chapter Fourteen

31 Oct 1066

Edan awoke next morning to footsteps in his room. The curtain had been drawn back, letting in a chill, gray day. From the window slit he could see that snow blanketed the landscape. His cudgel leaned against a chest in the corner. Today he would put it aside for real weapons.

Cerdic placed a tray with breakfast on the bed, brown bread and honey with dried figs. As he laid out Edan's clothes, he said, "Good morn, lad. It is time to meet the chieftains and petty kings. Kadeg is out with his men already, drilling in the bailey. He wants you to watch, so get dressed and I will take you there."

Remembering Kadeg's mention last night of petty kings, Edan asked, "What is a petty king?"

Cerdic's brows rose. "I guess you could say he's a chieftain who wants to be a king. He ignores his feudal rights and asserts himself as if he were a king."

Edan puzzled this for a moment then bolted the bread and honey and pushed his plate aside. Even though he hurried, questions came tumbling out. "Cerdic, does Kadeg have a wife?"

"Na, he hasn't now. She died of the milk sickness many years ago."

"Does he have children?" Edan persisted, pulling a clean tunic over his head.

"Aye, he does, five of 'em. You've already seen one of 'em in the hall when you arrived. Ardel. He's a little older than you. The rest are girls except the little 'un." Cerdic's small black eyes twinkled. His plain, reddish face creased in a grin.

"Oh." Could the oldest son be the young man who stared so at Edan? "Do you know where my friend Fergus spent the night?"

Cerdic saw Edan struggling with the unfamiliar sheepskin leggings and assisted with the wrapping.

"In the servants'—quarters--with the rest--of us," Cerdic panted from his bent-over position. "Now no more questions. You sound like a flock of hens with a fox in the coop." He straightened, laughed and patted Edan on the shoulder.

Edan grinned. No more questions. As he watched Cerdic work, he dreaded the days ahead when Fergus must serve him. He must find something to say to save their friendship.

As soon as Edan stood dressed, Cerdic came from a rack next the brazier with his sheepskin overshirt, newly washed. A short, rust-colored cloak topped the clothes. On his way from the room, Edan grabbed up a few figs and popped them into his mouth.

Cerdic led Edan briskly through the corridors despite his grain sack belly, by the empty hall, and out into the bailey. Thick, formidable stone walls enclosed the fortress. Nestled at the base of the wall across the open yard were the stables and armory. Pens of sheep, cattle, and pigs adjoined the stable. Chickens pecked about at random. Soldiers drilled under their sergeants, puffs of steam billowing from each face. Kadeg and his fellow petty kings and chieftains observed, talking among themselves. Edan almost asked how many petty kings there were among the chieftains but decided now was not the time.

Kadeg's penetrating, gray eyes shifted to Cerdic leading Edan around the end of the drills. He motioned Edan to join him. Cerdic returned to the manor house.

"Enough!" Kadeg shouted. The sergeants halted the drill and reassembled the soldiers in small groups to practice skills on the small flat area outside the walls.

Edan tried to estimate how many fighting men were in the fortress, perhaps 300 he thought. Thoughts of his loose tongue the previous evening caused his steps to falter as he hurried across the open ground to Kadeg's side. A quick glance told him nothing of the man's mood.

"Good morning, lad." Kadeg's tone sounded neutral, not angry.

Mayhap he had a short memory of last night's slip of the tongue concerning Fergus's servant role. "It is time you met some of my neighbors and allies. This shaggy beast is Bleddyn of Llangollen…" A large man with black hair down his back and a long black beard to mid-chest nodded to Edan. "The one next him is Glyndwr…" Edan noted a slighter, older man with a serious demeanor, temples streaked with gray. He paid heed to each of the leaders in turn trying to memorize names and connect to faces.

"Now it is time to get you into some fighting gear, lad." He turned to his companions. "If you will excuse me for a time, we'll get the armorer busy on some trappings for my nephew." He nodded at the other men and led Edan toward the stable.

Whatever anger Kadeg felt, at least it had not affected the fostering. Next time that Edan disagreed with his uncle, he must hold his tongue. He huffed a small sigh of relief.

At one end, a smithy fire radiated welcome heat. Sounds of metal clanging on metal filled the air.

When they entered, Edan saw two small-statured dark men with broad shoulders and muscled forearms hard at work fashioning various pieces of armor—chain mail hauberks, coifs, helmets. Briefly, his mind questioned the men's diminutive size and almost primitive appearance. The busy ring of hammers of others working at shields and all sorts of weapons—swords, lances, mace drew him back to his surroundings. He watched one armorer as he heated a sword blade in the forge flame until the glowing metal took on exactly the right color, iridescent in the flame-light that flooded the place. In one swift move he plunged the blade into a trough of cool water. Edan heard the furious hiss and smelled the steam that rose. The process repeated three times until the temper made a strong blade that would not fail a man in battle.

Edan's head swiveled, taking in everything. At the sight of Kadeg, the chief armorer scuttled over. He proceeded to measure every part of Edan's body—head, shoulders, waist, length of torso, width of chest, legs. Kadeg ordered the length and weight of broadsword he thought Edan could handle. Excitement rose within Edan.

From there, they moved to the stable where Kadeg had a groom bring out a smallish, chestnut stallion.

"Dinas is a young stallion but level-headed. You two should be a good match."

Edan's heart beat faster as he looked over the splendid animal. The horse pawed the ground and tossed his head. His big brown eyes looked intelligent.

"Saddle him, and we'll see how the two get along."

The groom nodded and set about his task. Edan's stomach clenched when the groom tightened the girth strap and all was ready. Doubt and fear itched like a flea in the waist of his breeches. He did not want to say he had never ridden a war stallion, only his little horse not much bigger than a pony.

With trembling fingers, he grabbed the reins in his left hand as the groom gave him a leg up onto the stallion's back.

The horse snorted as Edan landed in the leather saddle. It pranced a few steps before he took up slack in the reins. He settled himself before giving the horse a signal with his knees. It moved out smartly at a brisk walk. Edan took it around the edge of the bailey, the crunch of its hooves on snow and the creak of leather loud in his ears.

When Edan thought he had the feel of the horse's mouth, he urged it into a trot. Dinas had a smooth, non-jolting gait. As they passed by Kadeg, Edan saw a keen look on his face, assessing. It was time to go faster. He squeezed his knees against Dinas' ribs. The horse leaped forward as if charging into battle. Edan had to haul him up. Dinas laid his ears back and gave several stiff-legged jolts putting Edan high off his back before settling into a smooth canter. Edan's breath came shallow and fast. He mouthed a prayer, thankful for the high pommel and cantle which secured his seat on the military saddle. He knew his legs gripped too tight and tried to relax.

This horse loved to run. He'd have to be careful or the horse could run away with him. Especially if he were around other horses moving fast.

Kadeg called out, "Take him into a hand gallop."

Edan did not want to do this, but now he must. His legs tightened again, and he urged the horse forward. Dinas leaped into a gallop, snorting with each stride, neck arched, pulling at the bit to go faster. The reins cut into Edan's hands as he returned the pull. He clung like a burr, though he knew he rode high. The snowy ground caused Dinas to slip. As he started to go down, Edan felt his body thrown forward with nothing to stop his progress. The breath flew from his chest as he hit the frozen ground. The horse recovered and galloped on.

Gasping for that first breath of air into empty lungs, Edan heard titters of boyish laughter. When he could raise his head, he saw two dark-haired boys near his own age in battle gear, standing with a third brown-haired boy whose face carried a look of concern. Quick anger flared from his humiliation, and Edan wished he could spit in the sneering faces of the two dark-haired boys.

Everyone waited for Edan to get up under his own power. His jubilant mood had disappeared with his seat in the saddle. He crawled to his feet and walked unsteadily toward Uncle Kadeg who held the reins of Dinas and motioned him forward to remount. *This time he must stay on.*

After mid day, a few hunting parties formed to shoot birds nearby. Several more, surrounded by hounds, packed to hunt for two days or more for bigger game. Edan was assigned to a bird hunting group. As they rode from the fortress on small, agile horses, leaving the war stallions behind, Edan saw the fortress was situated well on a crag commanding a river valley. It was approachable only by the ridgetop Dyfan had led them across yesterday. The promontory which held the fort jutted out from a circle of rocky hills which provided a natural hollow where horses could graze in summer. All about the little valley mountains towered, white with snow. If Kadeg and his men dug themselves in with ample supplies, any army would be hard put to flush them out.

When they clattered back into the fortress, torches already burned. The horses, along with the day's kill, were handed to grooms and the men trooped into the hall. Smells of horse and sweat mingled with the odor of beef pies as Edan moved by the fire with the other men. Kadeg and Ardel sat together surrounded by several of the petty kings and chieftains Edan had met earlier. Neither had joined the afternoon hunt but had remained with the other petty kings, talking of alliances. Edan craved knowledge of their words. His future depended on Kadeg's choice of alliances.

He noticed All Hallow's preparations around the fortress. While they had been out hunting, servants hung hazel branches over windows and doorways to ward off evil. Great mounds of sticks were piled in the common for evening bonfires where prayers would be offered to the gods. Edan's memory of the treeless ridge made him wonder about the origin of the sticks.

Tonight more men gathered in the hall than the previous night. Among them were the boys he had seen when he was thrown from Dinas. Avoiding the sneers of the older boys, Edan sat next to the slender boy with a long, fox-like nose and coarse brown hair worn free.

"I be Edan. I arrived yesterday for my fostering."

"I bid you welcome," the long-nosed boy said politely. "I be Owain. That makes four of us being fostered. I've been here two months only so am not far ahead of you. The other two, Elphin and Lleu, are sitting together next Glyndwr…or do you know anyone yet?"

"No, please go on. Tell me who everyone is." So the two dark-haired boys were fosterlings, too, as well as Owain and he. Edan forced himself to be polite. No one mentioned his fall, but his humiliation still stung.

By the time supper lay on the tables, Owain had introduced Edan to the other fostered boys and increased Edan's knowledge of the occupants of the fortress, where the chieftains were from or how the fostering happened. Owain promised a tour of the house after the meal. Edan gathered that fosterlings must have more privileges than soldiers within Kadeg's fortress.

When the others gathered for games, Owain led Edan from the hall and mounted the stairs. Turning the opposite way from the men's quarters they traveled a corridor hung with colorful tapestries. The first depicted a wizard standing before a palace on an island surrounded by a lake. Across the corridor, a second showed the battle of the trees—mighty oaks pitted against ash and hawthorns. Another showed a white-haired old man carrying an infant from a castle. Such strange pictures.

The sound of women's voices from a large room at the end of the hall distracted him from the wallhangings. Fragrances of apricot and honeysuckle wafted in the air.

"This is the solarium where the women and children are," Owain explained. This is the family quarters.

Edan glanced in to see several youngsters and their nurses. The older girls wove and did needlework, as his own sisters did. Or used to do. Thoughts of home flooded his mind. Brusquely, he pushed them away. He must put them behind him. Curious to see Uncle Kadeg's family, he studied the faces of the children through tear-blurred eyes.

"The oldest is Bryn, only a year younger than we are. She is at the loom. Heulwen and Olwen are just children doing needlework."

Bryn, a slender girl with large eyes, looked up from her work to stare at the boys. She reminded Edan of his sister, Moira. All of them were cousins, so the resemblance was not unexpected. Even across the room she showed promise of becoming a beauty. Her hair, a red gold, streamed long and unbound over a green houserobe. She looked down again, demurely.

A small boy burst from his nurse toward them. "Come on with you now," his nurse chided. "Tis only the foster boys."

All heads turned to Edan and Owain. A flush of heat swept through Edan's veins, ending in his cheeks.

Pouting, the child returned to his nurse.

"That's Gareth." Owain moved on, Edan stepping on his heels in his haste to leave the doorway.

"How did you ever get to know Kadeg's children? They never eat in the hall with the men," Edan questioned.

"I know. Kadeg does not think the men's coarse talk is suitable for women and children's ears. The longer you are here, you will see the girls occasionally, out riding and playing games."

"What is the older brother, Ardel, like?"

"I don't know him well. He doesn't spend time with us fostered boys. He fancies himself a man to associate with the warriors. But he hasn't reached his majority yet." He let the remark hang without further explanation.

"How old is he?" Edan prompted.

"Fifteen, almost sixteen."

So far, Owain made no mention of Kadeg's father, Edan's grandfather. "Does Kadeg's father live here? My uncle mentioned he was still alive."

Owain hesitated. "He lives here. Physically Gwion is still strong, but he…he has some strange ideas."

"Are you saying he's mad?" Edan asked.

"Not exactly, but he's in his own world much of the time. Those tapestries in the corridor by the solarium are his doing. It's as if he has gone to live in the past of myth and legend. Even Caer Bannog is a legendary name."

Edan wondered what that meant. "Have you met him?"

"Once when Kadeg decided his father was in the right…mood…he brought him from his chamber to be among the men in the hall. He told stories of the old days before history began, stories depicted on the tapestries."

Edan wanted very much to meet his mysterious grandfather, a man who had forbade his mother to marry his father, cast his mother from his household. A man who had been a great warrior and now told stories of the old times. Surely he could not be completely mad.

The rest of the tour went quickly. They ended in the kitchen where the servants now ate. Fergus sat among those clustered about a big table, eating beef pies and drinking ale. Edan wanted a word with Fergus, but Fergus averted his eyes and talked with Cerdic. With a sigh, Edan turned and followed Owain back to the hall for games. A harper accompanied the evening activities.

Afterward, all the occupants of the fortress gathered in the bailey, and the bonfires were lit. Around the fires rings of people formed, with faces made grotesque by flickering shadows. The crackle of flames and crash of burning sticks rekindled a mood in Edan. He remembered the whir of lances, torches on the battlefield, shadowed faces, burned villages, an evil invader that attacked innocents. A coldness swept over him despite the fire.

A voice rang out. A priest uttered Christian prayers in Latin against the evil spirits about in the world on this night when all rules were suspended, the air was charged with magical powers, and the passages to the underworld and to the evil powers were open. This was a crack between seasons through which primeval magic entered. Transformation spells could be performed… He stopped himself. Despite knowing the beliefs about evil were pagan, old Celtic beliefs about Samhain, the mood of the evening sent shivers through him, and Edan found himself alert for signs of evil, an owl call, or a hex sign. He chided himself. *How many times had he berated Fergus for such fears? Yet what soul passing alone by a dark wood could tell himself with conviction there was nothing to fear?*

When Edan could no longer keep his eyes open, he found his way to his room. He had just climbed into bed when he heard footsteps move outside his door. Someone rapped softly. "Come in," Edan called.

It was Fergus. He carried wood for the brazier.

Edan sat up and threw the blankets back. Fergus moved to the brazier and restoked. He kept his head down, his eyes on the floor. He said nothing.

"Fergus?" Edan said. "I didn't want this. Uncle Kadeg decided. I don't want it to change things between us."

There was a wariness in Fergus's demeanor. He spoke at last without looking at Edan. "I know all that. Cerdic told me." After the long silence the words hissed like water onto a hot stone.

"What is wrong then?" Why didn't Fergus understand?

"Nothing." He shut his mouth on the word and looked aside, like someone unfairly treated. Suddenly he whirled. "Nothing, master," he spat, eyes sparking with anger.

Edan raised both hands in front of him to ward off Fergus's anger. "Look, I don't want a servant, but Kadeg says everyone here has to provide some service, whether military or in the kitchen or chambers. It's his house, so we have to obey. It won't be forever."

That last sentence startled Fergus out of his resentment. "Why?"

So that was it. Betrayal, being put down—these were not the issues. The length of time in servitude bothered him. He understood that he was stuck here for the rest of his life, as a servant. "Fostering is only about a year. Then either I'll be sent home, or I'll be with the rest of the men in the garrison quarters. You should be able to go home then. Mayhap we can travel together."

His brows drew together considering this last. "By the boar's rancid breath, I had not thought of that."

"We can make this an adventure. I'll be working, too, learning a new task just like you. We can still talk like we always have. You can fill me in on household gossip." Edan rose from the bed and walked over to stand face to face with Fergus. "And I'll tell you everything I learn, so you can know it, too."

Fergus looked disconcerted and slightly ashamed.

"We're better off than if we were at home," Edan offered.

Fergus looked up at last. "You're right about that. We'd be hungry for sure," he said grudgingly.

"We can talk about Duke William and how we are going to run him out of England. We can no longer expect the world to be fair now that Duke William has come. We have to take what the gods send and while here, what Kadeg sends," Edan said. His own words surprised him. *When had he come to these conclusions?*

Fergus stood a moment stiffly, stuck out a toe to nudge the fresh clothes he'd brought into a neater pile.

"Aye, we must accept what Kadeg gives. But what if you go off to fight against Duke William and leave me behind? What then?"

Chapter Fifteen

2 Nov 1066

Two days later when Kadeg handed the two-pound sword to him, Edan could think of nothing else but the burnished, deadly beauty of the blade, the hilt twined with gold and silver wires that fit so perfectly into his hand, the pommel encasing his grip. He barely heard Kadeg's words as he watched light ripple on the gray iron and wondered if he should name it.

"You have progressed quickly, Edan. You do yourself honor. Use this with temperance." Kadeg's voice interrupted Edan's thoughts as his uncle motioned one of his sergeants forward.

The fosterlings had nicknamed the sergeant, The Turtle, for the forward posture of his head and almost no neck. When he wore his armor, his head truly imitated that of a turtle peeking from its shell. Otherwise, the name did not fit. The man moved with lightning speed despite his awkward appearance.

Holding the new broadsword, the Turtle made Edan practice the leaps and ducks he needed to escape an opponent with a wooden sword. "Faster, lad, faster. Twist to avoid downward slashes that can take off an arm."

Panting with effort, Edan ducked, twisted and leaped back. He had gotten good enough to avoid two out of every three slashes. It was that third one he had to work on or be armless, another reason besides humiliation to excel.

"Now, lad, I'll aim backhand strokes at your knees. You must leap over my slash. Let's try."

Edan saw the Turtle's stroke begin. He leaped. The sword

swished beneath him.

"Good, lad, again."

By afternoon, even though Edan had practiced with a small wooden sword from early childhood, his tired arms denied that he had. Near the end of practice, the Turtle handed him the new broadsword. Caught at the ebb of his strength, he ached everywhere and longed to flop onto the snow and mud churned ground instead. Gathering himself, he reached for the shining blade. The iron nestled in his hand, the weight just right.

A short time later, horses thundered across the bridge into the fortress, shattering the routine. The clatter of arms and the glint of colored pennants flowed into the common. Excited voices rang like swordplay in the cold air.

The leader rode forward. Voices hushed. Grateful for the interruption, Edan stared at the swarthy look and black eyes he had come to recognize in the small-statured men of Gwynedd.

Kadeg emerged from the hall to greet the dark leader. The men conversed in Welsh. Owain stood next to Edan. "What do they say?"

Owain responded, "Kadeg said,'By the gods, it is you, Riwallon. I had given you up.'

Riwallon replied,'Tis me for sure. Sickness kept us from you until now.'"

"If he has been ill, his ruddy cheeks and robust actions do not show it. He must mend quickly."

"Come in by the fire and we will catch you up on news," Owain parroted, ignoring Edan's comments on the leader's health.

With an assessing glance at the assembled troops, the leader dismounted and the two disappeared inside the fortress leaving Riwallon's men to find their way to the soldiers' quarters.

Questions raced through Edan's mind. Was this another petty king to advise Gwynedd's alliances?

"Do you know who that was?" Owain asked.

His thoughts disturbed, Edan shook his head.

"Prince Riwallon. He and Prince Bleddyn are the most powerful in attendance here. I'm sure Kadeg was worried when he didn't show up earlier."

Did Prince translate to petty king? Edan wondered. Instead he asked, "Are you saying these two and Kadeg will make the final decision on alliances?"

"Aye, though they will listen to all the others. Many experienced fighting men are here. I am sharp set to know if these men will ally with Saxon men of the north."

Owain's words echoed Edan's growing concern. "What do you think they will do?"

"I do not know. It will be a difficult decision."

Edan could not tell Owain's passion toward one side or the other.

Could he trust Owain with expressing his own feelings? He did not know. Adhering to Ridley's caution, he asked only, "Will they decide soon? It is not too late to mount an offensive yet this season."

"It depends on how many allies they can gather and whether all agree on one action."

Edan's hope continued that these men could join the fighting men of Northumbria before William could declare himself King and instead, put the Aethling, Edgar, on the throne. Or as rumor suggested, Harold, if he still lived. Ridley's explanation of succession crowded into his mind. *No. It would have to be Edgar.*

The cold air and brief inactivity had stiffened Edan's tired body. When the Turtle said, "Let's call it enough for today," Edan sighed with relief.

Owain and the others nodded agreement, and the foster boys headed for the armory to put up their weapons.

At dinner, between bites of shepherd's pie, as he and Owain shared a trencher, Edan shot glances at Kadeg and the men at his table. Even now they appeared to be scheming, their heads close, talking animatedly. If only he could be at that table listening.

Frustrated, he tucked into his food. He ate but a few bites before his concentration returned to Kadeg's table. Someone pounded a fist on the table, spilling wine, and shouted. His hunger all but forgotten, he watched the men's expressions, every nuance of hand gesture or nod of head. As quickly as anger flared, talk calmed again and men returned to their wine. *Could Riwallon be trusted even if he agreed to an alliance with the men of Cymru and with the northern earls and petty kings?* Mistrust grew in Edan as he noticed again the man's calculating eyes.

Making himself attend to his food, Edan forced down a few mouthfuls, but the spinning thoughts in his head made his stomach flutter. Edan worried Kadeg would decide not to support the English and support William.

After the meal, Edan played a game of chess with the other fosterlings. His concentration and the exertion of the day had left him fatigued. The hour grew late, and he wanted to go to bed. He prayed they were all equally tired, but none left the hall. At last he got up from his bench grimacing slightly. Owain grinned. "A few aches and pains, aye? We all did at first." The others nodded in sympathy.

"See you on the morrow," Edan said, heartened by the signs of acceptance from the small group of fosterlings. Still, he tried not to shorten his stride or limp as he left.

He had just dropped onto his bed thinking of names for his sword—"swine-eater" or "windtamer" or… A rap sounded at the door.

"Enter."

Fergus's tousled head appeared. He hadn't spoken much when he brought breakfast or wood or clothes the last two days. Edan ached for Fergus to get over his anger.

Edan watched while Fergus put wood in the brazier and laid out clean clothes for the next day. Before leaving, he looked at Edan and seemed about to speak. Instead, he turned and closed the door after himself with unneeded force.

Sinking down onto the bed, Edan felt more exhausted than ever. What would make Fergus come around?

It seemed as if only minutes had passed when Edan startled awake. There was a thumping upon the door. Having fallen asleep on top of the bedcovers, he staggered up and shuffled to the door.

He opened it and faced Fergus. The corridor was silent. The torch outside his room guttered. The hour seemed late.

"What's the matter?"

"I come to get you," Fergus said softly.

"What for?"

"You'll see. You're still dressed, so come on."

Fergus set off at a good pace down the corridor, his soft leather boots whispering along the stones. After a moment's hesitation, Edan sleepily followed. They saw no one in the halls as they walked. It soon became apparent to Edan that they were going to the kitchen.

The cavernous room stood empty. The floors had been swept clean, although coals still smoldered in the immense hearth. The room remained warm, and the aroma of cooked meat lingered in the air. Eerie shadows flickered over the hanging pots and the foodstuffs for morning that cluttered tables. With no one here, the dark spaces seemed ominous. A squeak and a scuttling announced the presence of mice.

Fergus turned and put his finger to his lips, but motioned Edan to follow. He disappeared into the pantry. Sweet fragrances of baked honey and cinnamon overwhelmed Edan's senses. They were surrounded by shelves of sweet figs, spices, flour, crocks of pickled vegetables and more things than Edan could name. By now he was wide awake. Fergus moved to one of a series of cloth-covered platters and lifted a corner of the cloth.

He turned to Edan. "Here, take one."

Edan moved closer and saw his favorite dessert, honeycakes. He reached for one. Fergus followed his lead. "Thought you might like a sweet to tickle your belly," he said.

Edan knew then that his friend tried to put things right between them. He bit into the sweet cake and let the sugary flavor sink into his tongue as he chewed. He smiled at Fergus in the dim light. A glint of teeth signaled that Fergus smiled back.

Each had eaten two cakes when a scuffling sound in the kitchen caused them both to stiffen. That was no mouse. Fergus grabbed Edan's arm and pulled him deeper into the pantry behind some large barrels. They crouched and listened.

They heard the rustle of cloth, the patter of light feet and the scuff of bigger feet. A muffled giggle. Whispers.

"Did anyone see you come?" a male voice demanded.

"Not a one of 'em, Master Ardel. They was all sleepin'," replied a soft female voice with a brogue Edan did not recognize.

Edan squeezed Fergus's arm at the mention of Ardel's name. Fergus placed a hand over Edan's to signify he had heard.

"Are you sure, Ceridwen, that Father wasn't about?" Ardel insisted with an urgent tone.

"No. I saw no light under his door, no light in the hall."

Another giggle and several rustles of clothing.

"Stop," Ceridwen said in a strangled voice.

Kissing sounds and heavy breathing followed.

So Ardel met some girl here in the kitchen at night. *Why would Ardel be afraid of his father finding him with a girl?* Dallying with servant girls by sons of nobility was not uncommon. Kadeg would pick a wife for Ardel in the future to strengthen alliances or prosperity.

Suddenly, a sharp whistle came from without the kitchen. An alarmed scramble followed. The light feet fled. The heavier ones departed in another direction.

Fergus choked back laughter. Edan did the same until he realized someone was probably coming. Mayhap the whistler was a lookout Ardel had posted for his tryst. If caught, he and Fergus would be the ones in trouble for sneaking about in the middle of the night, stealing from the kitchen, not the lovers. He could never use mean-spirited information about Ardel to get himself out of trouble with Kadeg.

Fergus put his finger to his lips again.

More footsteps outside the pantry. Had someone returned? A shadow fell across the doorway. Edan held his breath. Were they to be caught after all? A small figure slid into the pantry and made for the shelf containing the cloth-covered platters. Picking up a cloth corner, the visitor snatched up some cakes and left. Edan exhaled slowly knowing it wasn't Ardel.

Edan and Fergus sprang up and looked out the door in time to see a green houserobe and a flash of coppery hair disappear into the corridor light footsteps echoing off the stones.

"Bryn," whispered Edan, "come down for a tit-bit like us. I thought we had been caught out."

"Was it she who whistled?" whispered Fergus.

"I don't know. I bet Kadeg would not be happy to know that his daughter roamed the fortress at night even with Ardel's knowledge," Edan whispered back.

"The people we serve always forget about us being around. They think no one sees them do the things they do."

"Did you know Ardel would come? Or was it a surprise to you as well?" Fergus *had* let him in on fortress doings as he had promised, even if it were a small thing like an early sweet or a secret tryst.

"I've seen him about in the corridors at night but never with this girl," Fergus replied.

They waited a while longer. When no one else came, Edan said in a hushed voice, "I'll keep my end of the bargain, too. I'll bring a weapon to my room each night, and when you come to stoke the brazier, I'll show you how to use it and tell you what I've been taught."

Fergus nodded agreement, looking thoughtfully at the doorway where Bryn had disappeared. "Mother of mischief," he whispered, "if she whistled, was it to warn him or trick him?"

"Trick him?" Edan hadn't thought of that. "Do you suppose Bryn knew what her brother was up to and played a prank on him? If she knew something that would make her father angry with Ardel, would she use it to her advantage? But if she was in league with her brother and served as lookout, she could still use it to her advantage later."

"In a household as large as this, there are many secrets," Fergus murmured, wiggling his eyebrows.

"How can you know *many* secrets in only three days? What else is going on?" Edan demanded in a fierce whisper.

Chapter Sixteen

2 Nov 1066

His head filled with kitchen gossip, Edan crept through the shadowy corridors back to his room, jumping at every whisper of torch flame or sudden snore from the rooms he passed. His moving shadow on the stone walls towered like an evil companion. He let out a sigh as he turned into his own corridor, when something, human or spirit, snagged his collar from behind and held him tight. Edan's heart tried to pummel its way out of his chest.

A voice snarled in his ear, "Whistle a tune for me, you skulking little spy."

Edan twisted just enough to see Ardel's angry face. By deus, at least the grip was human. His cousin must have hidden after he fled the kitchen to see who had whistled.

"The chapel, I was in the chapel praying," Edan blurted. "Why do you call me a spy?"

"Shut up and keep your voice down." Ardel's quiet whisper held deadly menace. "Don't deny it you sneak. Why else would you be about in the fortress at this hour?"

"I couldn't sleep after all the talk of evil spirits these last days, so I slipped down to the chapel for another prayer."

Ardel snorted a soft laugh. "Sure you did, you pious little wretch."

A flicker of uncertainty in Ardel's eyes gave Edan hope for an instant. Maybe he would survive this yet.

Ardel's hand still gripped his collar. Without warning Ardel spun and slammed him to the wall. Hard stones tore into Edan as his head crashed back. Small points of light danced before his eyes. His knees buckled.

"Don't ever let me catch you sneaking about spying on me again," Ardel hissed into Edan's face. "Or I'll cut off your pretty ears." He flicked a fingernail against one ear.

Edan's breath caught. *What did Ardel plan to do?*

Ardel glared a while longer, released his grip, and skulked off.

Letting out his breath, Edan wiggled his shoulders to remove the feel of the stones against them. He stood shaking awhile before he could make his feet move. When he stepped into his room, he flattened himself against the door, leaned his head back, and closed his eyes. Despite the chill air, sweat trickled down his ribs. His legs trembled and his hands shook.

When his heartbeat returned to normal, he undressed and leapt into a cold bed, glad out of all measure that he came out of his encounter without worse harm. He longed to talk to Fergus.

3 Nov 1066

Near dawn when Fergus arrived to stoke the brazier and deliver breakfast, Edan lay exhausted but sleepless.

Fergus had a big grin on his freckled face as he said, "I'd like to have seen the look on Ardel's face when he heard the whistle." He put the breakfast tray on the edge of the bed and bustled about the room stoking the brazier, laying out fresh clothes, and opening the curtain. With a dramatic flourish, he inhaled fresh air.

Edan enjoyed having Fergus be himself again. He roused and sat up, every muscle protesting the previous day's efforts.

"I saw the look on his face shortly after, and it wasn't pleasant."

Fergus's grin faded. "By the dragon's scaly toes! He saw you?"

"That he did and grabbed my collar from behind and threatened me for being a sneak and spying on him. He thinks it was me whistled and broke up his tryst with the girl."

Fergus frowned and looked down at the fire, poking it with a stick. "Clodpole! How come he didn't see his sister instead! Wait, there's another small stair down to the kitchen from the solarium. She would have used that." He looked up. "What did you say to him?"

Edan grimaced. "I told him I'd been having trouble sleeping and went down to the chapel to pray."

"Did he believe you?"

"I don't think so, but he seemed to have a little doubt after I denied spying on him."

"Him coming after you like that tells us the answer to one question—his sister wasn't in on the tryst as a lookout."

"If it was her, it must have been a prank. And it wasn't a friend of Ardel's, or he wouldn't search for someone else. Why is it so important that Ardel meeting a girl should be such a secret?"

Fergus shrugged.

Edan reached for his clean tunic. A spasm of pain shot across his shoulders."Ow."

"Here, let me help you get the tunic over your head."

Fergus helped Edan get dressed as his arms were so sore he could scarce lift them over his head. Edan prayed they would do another activity today other than swordplay.

Edan's pains were to persist for many days. Each new weapon's awkward use caused new aches and bruises. Even as he thought his arm would fall off, the Turtle ordered him to swing the battle axe at a target time after time. Then came the lance, finally a mace. Fergus got some balm from somewhere and massaged Edan's arms each night.

The fosterlings rode every day that the weather allowed. They wrestled and ran and jumped. Eventually, the aches and pains were behind Edan, and he felt stronger every day.

November progressed with winds that chilled to the bone. Edan avoided Ardel as much as possible. Once they came face to face in the entrance to the hall. Behind his easy grin and those probing green eyes lurked something indefinable which gave Edan renewed apprehension. Ardel put a hand to his sword before moving off. A chill ran up Edan's spine. Here was an enemy of whom to be wary.

At night Edan taught Fergus the skills of weaponry, while Fergus gave the fortress gossip.

"You've heard nothing of Kadeg's intent?" Edan asked Fergus one November night.

"Not a word as to whether they attack William or not," he replied. As the days passed, Edan slid into a calm acceptance of fortress routine. News would come in its own time.

9 Dec 1066

It came in December when a mist covered the surrounding peaks. The air was still in the common. Edan rode Dinas in the common when the horse suddenly threw his head up, ears pricked, apparently hearing sounds outside the fortress. Edan listened. Hoofbeats drew closer until a horn blew, sign of someone's arrival.

Winches ground bringing up the gate. A lone figure rode a pony across the bridge, something bulky strapped over his shoulder.

"A minstrel!" shouted Owain in a great excitement. "There will be more than harping tonight!"

The other fosterlings joined in. "Look he has a lute."

"Maybe he has news of Duke William."

"Maybe he knows the poems of Taliesin."

"Who is Taliesin?" Edan asked Owain.

"Only the most famous poet in Cymru, but he died centuries ago."

Edan grew excited, too. He had never heard a minstrel, as none had ever come to his father's manor. He heard they sang songs from all parts of the country and sometimes even from other lands. The minstrel would have the latest news as well. During the rest of the day, a buzz of excitement grew within the fortress walls.

After the evening meal of roast lamb, venison, and upland dove, the sharp-featured little minstrel set up on a stool before the fire. A low buzz of conversation among the men anticipated the entertainment. Haze hung in the air before finding its way out the smoke hole. The mingled odors of dry rushes, many bodies, and the recent meal created a friendly warmth.

Just as the minstrel placed the six-stringed lute across his lap to begin, the buzz of voices hushed at the arrival of another member of the family. Like a fresh meadow breeze Bryn swept in, dressed in blue velvet, her hair piled partly atop her head, the rest cascading down her back. Kadeg accompanied her and led her to the front row, where Bleddyn and Riwallon sat, and admonished the men to speak gentle with a lady in attendance.

The first time that Edan had seen her in the hall, he could not help but stare. While he focused on the back of Bryn's head, hoping she would turn at least a profile to his gaze, the musician tuned his instrument and began to pluck strings. Tonight Edan sat closer to her than that first glimpse of her across the solarium. What went on in the head of this girl who dared to trick her older brother? If he looked into his cousin's eyes, could he read them? Ridley had said one could read a man's intentions in his eyes… but a woman?

The words of the "Ballad of Roland" rang out. The minstrel had a pleasant tenor voice, and the music-starved occupants of the fortress hung with rapt pleasure on every word. Bryn never turned to look behind. She listened and talked with Bleddyn. The minstrel next played the much recounted ballad of Arthur of Britain—more a tale set to music than a ballad. Some of the soldiers hummed the tune in accompaniment.

Owain whispered, "Notice the princes sitting next to Bryn. Mayhap Kadeg is planning a match with one of their sons. Bryn is of marriageable age."

Edan gave Owain a quick look. This put a new twist on the alliances being formed. Could this involve Ardel, too? Would he marry one of their daughters?

Restless, Edan scanned the room as the minstrel sang "Havelock the Dane." Servants came and went filling ale cups. He spotted Ardel near the back of the room, next to a wide-bodied old man with a long gray beard, who kept time to the music and mouthed words. Edan had never seen him in the hall before.

Edan poked Owain. "Who is the bearded man next Ardel in the back of the hall?"

"That is Gwion, your grandfather."

Edan stared at Owain.

Edan turned again to watch the old man who flung his arms in a great excitement. Edan saw Kadeg leave his place and go to where the old man sat. He bent over and said something to Ardel after which the two helped the old man to his feet and moved toward the door with him. He hung back, his head turned toward the minstrel in obvious distress.

Leaning over, Owain said, "This has happened before. He got too excited, shouting and ranting. They took him away before he embarrassed himself."

Edan noticed that before the ballad ended they returned without the old man.

A brawny knight at the end of the table who had obviously caught the ale-server each time she passed, spoke loudly, "Give us the 'Ballad of the Unicorn' next." The minstrel nodded and kept playing his present tune.

After a half dozen songs, Bryn joined the minstrel, placed a psaltery across her lap and strummed its strings for one song, a romantic little ditty. She sang along with it in a high sweet voice. Edan thought she sang and played well for someone so young. The men in the hall applauded her loudly and shouted for more, but the minstrel took a break. He stood and held his arms over his head.

"I am Hafgar. News, I have news to tell you of Duke William."

When Hafgar began to talk, Kadeg escorted Bryn from the hall. This time Edan viewed her face not the back of her head. As she passed by, something drew her gaze to where Edan sat. Her gaze rested briefly upon his face, then she turned ahead once more, her skirt swishing over the stones, and exited the hall.

The last time Edan heard news of Duke William, the Norman army was in Dover. Eager to hear the latest, he turned his attention back to the minstrel.

"One-third of William's army stays on in Dover recovering from their illness," Hafgar began. "The other two-thirds who took Canterbury also fell sick, including William, so they rested at Broken Tower." The little musician mimed a coarse bodily function which brought loud laughter.

What good news. Edan squirmed in his seat with eagerness to act. Attack them now while they are sick. Wipe them out before they take London. He looked at the other princes' faces as they heard this news. No excitement showed. Had they already possessed this news of William?

Hafgar continued. "At November's end, William became impatient with London holding out. The Witan Gemot selected 13-year old Edgar Aethling and proclaimed him king. They promised to fight for him. When William heard this, he began devastating the villages around London."

He paced about excitedly, waving one arm then the other.

Edan listened intently. The Witan had selected Edgar after all. He leaned over to whisper to Owain. "Will Kadeg support Edgar?"

"I would guess he will discuss it with the other chieftains. They must present a united front."

A low rumble of discontent and anger rose amidst the men. A knight shouted, "Has Edgar been crowned?" Another, "How many men has William?"

"I do not know about Edgar. Estimates run around 5000 men for William," Hafgar answered.

"Only 5,000? We can raise twice that."

Kadeg quieted the men for the minstrel had more.

"Next he massed his troops and marched to the Thames, crossed in two places and razed the countryside." Waving both arms with clenched fists, Hafgar leaped onto a table.

More shouts of anger and disbelief rang out.

"Then came the first defector from London to William at Wallingford," Hafgar shouted and paused for dramatic effect, one finger pointed upward.

"Who was he?" shouted the men.

"Stigand, Archbishop of Canterbury."

"Traitor!" shouted the men.

The minstrel hushed them, moved his hands in a downward motion, and continued, "Last I heard William marched north, skirting London, still not attacking. Stigand said Sheriff Esgar of London tried to rally men against William, then he claimed Edgar couldn't be crowned because the bishops had doubts. Old bishops who didn't understand the import of acting quickly and delayed Edgar's coronation. Some say the Sheriff later was bribed by William with the promise of power and gold, so he would urge Londoners to submit."

More angry voices. Someone shouted, "Has London submitted yet?"

"Not that I know," replied Hafgar.

The hall became frenzied. Men shouted, "When do we fight? When do we fight?"

Edan realized the men had revealed their allegiance at last. They had decided to fight for England, try to oust William. Now he began to feel part of the men of Cymru. He threw back his shoulders and shouted with the rest. He was ready to mount Dinas in the company of Kadeg's men and ride straight for London.

Kadeg stood and came before the assembled men. He held up a hand for quiet.

"I don't like to wait any more than you!" Kadeg shouted, his voice husky with tension. "This is our land and we must take it back, but we must not fail as there may be no second chance.

"We fight when we are ready to fight and when we can win," he said. "William may get crowned in the meantime, but it is winter. No more troops can sail across the Narrow Sea to William's aid until spring. He cannot leave. His military position is weak with little hope of reinforcement, no retreat, no food unless he captures it, and no winter quarters. We may have lost one army, but we have enormous reserves if we have time to gather them. If we march against him in early spring, we can gather a greater force and try to consolidate our leadership with the northern earldoms."

After a long pause, as the men turned these ideas over, slowly they nodded their heads.

Edan's respect for Kadeg swelled his chest.

It seemed to Edan that Kadeg's outburst relieved his uncle somewhat from all the serious considerations which had weighed heavily on him. His posture appeared straighter, his manner more energized.

Hafgar rose from his stool and placed his instrument in a cloth. Someone gave him an ale horn to wet his throat. The gathering dispersed, some into small groups to talk, others leaving the hall.

Chapter Seventeen

Too keyed up to sleep, Edan paced restlessly in his room, waiting for Fergus to come with wood for the brazier. He could not wait to discuss the news of William. When the expected rap on the door occurred, Edan yanked it open. It was not Fergus.

Edan's mouth hung agape. A brown-haired girl of about his age stood there. She curtsied.

"Miss Bryn wishes to meet with you. I'm Maeve, her maid. Come with me to the chapel." The words came out as if she'd memorized them.

Should he go? This meeting broke the rules. Boys his age did not fraternize with unchaperoned girls even if they were cousins. Still he managed to nod. He followed the girl through the corridors, seeing no one, and arrived at the chapel. *Did she want to become friends? They were cousins after all.* Or could she want to play another prank? His mind spun with possibilities.

Maeve pulled the heavy wooden door open and entered, looking back once to see that he followed. On the altar two large candles burned. Edan saw a shadowed figure in a front pew. She turned at the sound of the door but remained seated.

Maeve led Edan to stand in front of Bryn, who motioned him to take a seat beside her and waved the maid to the back of the chapel to guard the door. Bryn's green eyes fastened upon Edan.

"It was good of you to come so quick for what must seem to you a strange summons," she whispered.

Face to face, Edan was tongue-tied by her daring, stranger that she was. He felt in awe of such a headstrong girl. "What is it you wish of me?" he whispered at last.

She fingered her chin. "Help with Ardel. His fate may rest with us."

Edan tensed, her words bringing back the unwanted memory of Ardel's hands shoving him into the hard stone, the snarling words. His eagerness to know Bryn's wishes faded a notch. "How so?" he replied through stiff lips.

A mouse scuttled across the altar. Bryn jumped. Her hand flew to her mouth, but she did not scream. She looked over her shoulder, then leaned closer and whispered, "I saw you and your friend go to the kitchen that night. I was on the way myself when I heard you coming. I hid. Before I could leave, I heard someone else, Ardel and a girl. I followed to the kitchen and saw them together—a lover's meeting. She is no servant in this house. I wonder who she is and how she got here because Ardel must have spirited her in which makes it more serious. When she spoke, I heard a brogue from the north. I whistled to break it off. Any relationship must be broken because I overheard Father's promise of marriage for him." She stopped her headlong explanation and considered her next words.

Did she know Fergus and he hid in the pantry? Edan caught her spirit of unease. A shiver ran over his body.

"I need to find out who she is. She may wreck Father's plans for Ardel to marry Riwallon's niece. That union next year is necessary to Father's alliances."

What does she know of Kadeg's alliances? She's just a girl. "How can *I* help? I don't know her, where she stays or where she came from."

"Ardel doesn't know I whistled. He thinks it was you. He's afraid you'll tell Father, who would be furious. I saw you come out the kitchen, and Ardel follow you from a hiding place. So, I followed, too, and saw what happened. Obviously, you kept the information to yourself. I respect that. As a result, I trust you to help me."

So she *did* know he hid there. Warmed by the words of praise, whether she said them in earnest or to convince him to help, Edan was flattered.

She continued, "I know you don't know this girl, but you can help. I've gone to the kitchen every night since Ardel met her there, and they've never come again. I need to find out where they now meet or even if she's still here. If she's gonc, mayhap I'm worrying over nothing. Ardel can be a lackwit sometimes, but he is my brother. Still, I don't want to tell Father if I don't have to. Ardel would hate me for it."

She sounded much older than twelve. She seemed more deserving of Kadeg's favor than Ardel, except she was a girl. Beneath her poise lay a fierce spirit. Edan hesitated, searching for words. She protected her older brother. He could not protect his own older sister, Moira, from the Normans. A lump formed in his throat. He swallowed hard.

Any help he gave Bryn would avail him nothing. Yet he wanted to help this spirited cousin. "I'll help, but how? I heard him call her Ceridwen if that helps."

"You will?" A quick lift entered her voice. She went on quickly. "Her name might help. Maeve watched the chapel, while I watched the kitchen. So the kitchen and the chapel are not the trysting places nor the cellar. I also had Maeve's sister watch Ardel's room and the main hall. No girl came to his room. I can't go out to the stables, the armory or the soldier's quarters nor can my maid. Could you and your friend, Fergus, somehow search those areas to see if there is a place where someone could hide?"

"You do not wish me to tell Owain, so I could have more help?"

"No, I want to keep this in the family. Other families have other motives." A glimmer of a smile.

Didn't she trust Owain's family motives? "I'll preserve your secret quest then, except for Fergus. Together we should be able to winkle out this wench whoever she is. Where could Ardel have met this Ceridwen to bring her here in the first place?"

Bryn looked at the flickering candle flames and remained silent a long time, thinking.

Finally, she said, "Ardel did ride north to Northumbria with father in September to speak with a petty king there. Other allies of this man met there also. Some could have brought their women if they stayed for a social occasion afterward. But, if a young girl went missing, a search would be on. How could he have snuck her in?"

How could Bryn be so upset about Ardel breaking rules when she also met him on the sly? "If she were from a family in Northumbria, would that be so bad? Kadeg hopes for alliances there, too."

"True, but Ardel is promised to Riwallon's niece and to break that honor would put Kadeg and Riwallon at odds just when they need to be together." Bryn shifted and looked back at Maeve. She pressed her lips together in a thin line. "I am promised to Bledynn's son in the spring when I turn thirteen. After that I will no longer be here to save Ardel from his own folly. Next year he will marry also."

Edan's hands tightened on the edge of the pew. Bryn married and gone from here? He found he wanted to be friends with this cousin, who seemed to have a finger on the pulse of fortress events and who decided to talk. She reminded him of the sisters he had left behind, yet she would leave so soon. *Was he destined to never have a family home again?*

Bryn drew a long breath, rising to face the back of the church where Maeve stood guarding the door. Edan rose next to her. She stood nearly as tall as he.

"If I do this for you, will you do something for me?"

Her eyes turned back to Edan's, wide and questioning.

"Take me to meet my grandfather."

She put out a hand to touch Edan's sleeve then withdrew it. "He has become somewhat simple after a fit he suffered. The left side of his body is weakened and his face sags, but he still understands when you talk to him. He remembers only things from the far past. After he meets you, he will probably forget who you are. He doesn't know me half the time. But yes, tomorrow evening I'll take you to him."

Chapter Eighteen

10 Dec 1066

The next morning dawned cold and clear. A thousand, no ten thousand diamonds sparkled on the white blanket that lay over the fortress. A hoary beard of icicles hung from the roofs of the stable and armory. Fresh snow squeaked underfoot as Edan walked across the bailey to join the other fosterlings, chill air stinging his cheeks.

Sword practice had barely begun when the minstrel took his leave along with Riwallon and his men. Most likely, the musician would accompany them to Riwallon's caer to play and be glad of the protection on his journey.

All morning Edan poked into nooks and crannies of the armory when he had an excuse to be there. Excuses like his sword felt dull or he needed an adjustment in his mail shirt. Any small, private storage areas he saw were so filled with metals for weapons-making that they seemed unlikely meeting places. He dared not be too bold about his search and cause questions.

Toward breaktime he asked Owain, "I've never seen the soldiers' quarters. Could I see where you and the other foster boys sleep?"

Seeming pleased that Edan showed an interest, Owain grinned. "You want to see how the others live who aren't privileged to live in the fortress?"

"I never lived in such a grand place before, so I'm not accustomed. It would be all the same to me if I slept in quarters with you." Another part of his mind knew he would miss his warm brazier.

Rush pallets filled each open-doored cell. Personal items decorated each man's space. A central area appeared to be used for playing chess, shooting dice. A central privy outdoors served all the men. *No private hides here*, Edan thought. Tomorrow he would check the stable when he rode Dinas.

In mid-afternoon, a messenger came up from Bala. To Edan's surprise, Kadeg came to him with a letter.

"You may stop practice and read it," Kadeg said.

Edan broke the seal and unrolled it. Writing in his mother's fine hand filled the page.

Dearest Edan, *23 Nov 1066*

Kadeg sent word you had come to him and that he would foster you. He said he told you of our family, the rift between my father and me.

I am glad he bid you welcome. My heart is sore wounded by your absence, yet it is best for you. You would not be safe here.

Moira has been taken in marriage by the son of a Norman landowner, a liege of Robert of Mortain who now holds our land.

Edan stopped reading and looked up at the fortress walls. A blurriness fogged his eyes, and he couldn't read. *Moira married to a Norman? She had eyes for Ralf, the son of the thane of Guestling. Had he been killed?* Then he remembered. Even if Ralf lived, no Saxon-born would be holding property. All were under control of the Norman conquerors. Moira had no choice.

"We buried Father in the chapel cemetery. The priest said the prayers. I miss your Father terribly. Your little sisters are safe with me. And now you wonder where I am. I am in Chichester, new wife of Robert Bremule. He is pledged to Bishop Odo, half-brother of Duke William. This is a different Robert than Robert of Mortain, also a half- brother of Duke William, who took over Herstmonceux. I had hoped I would not have to do this, but there was no place for me and your sisters against the Normans, only as part of the new life."

Sudden anger flared in Edan. He crumpled the letter into a wad.

Kadeg's eyebrows shot up, but he said nothing of Edan's actions. He asked, "How is my sister?"

"She is healthy and…" words failed him. *Was she happy also? How could she! It had been only two months since Father died.* "She married a Norman!" He spat the words as if to get a bad taste from his mouth. He visualized the hall at Herstmonceux, his father's chair, a strange brown-headed man sitting in it, smiling at his mother and his sisters. His mother stooping to caress the man's shoulder. Before his mind could stop his mouth, he said, "How could she!"

A shocked look came over Kadeg's face.

"And my sister did, too!" Edan blurted. A scream rose in his throat. Before the sound escaped, he ran from the common into the stable. Smells of manure and sweet hay filled his nose. He rushed past startled grooms and let himself into Dinas' stall. The stallion whickered a greeting, turned his head, and looked at his master with curious eyes. Edan crept to the front by the manger and turned his back to all who walked by. The warmth of the horse's big body comforted him. He tangled his fingers in the horse's long mane and pulled at snarls, combing with his fingers. The horse continued munching hay.

When the blurriness in his eyes cleared, he straightened the crumpled letter against Dinas' neck. The light was dim, but he could read the words. He skimmed until he found his place.

"Tell Kadeg, Duke William builds a stone castle near Hastings at the shore of the Narrow Sea. Other new Norman landowners are also building castles. Our old village suffers under Robert, but I asked Cecil to get this letter to you.

Rumors fly that Duke William will soon storm London and be crowned King. He has been bitterly opposed but only with words. He has watched and waited for English armies to come from the forests but none have come.

I wish I knew—is Kadeg with the English or not? I want to think armies be coming to overthrow the Normans. I fear for my country.

It seems the old archbishops and the Witan Gemot are timid and have been bluffed. If they surrender, and no army comes, England is lost forever to Norman rule.

I hope you understand what I have done and what I've encouraged Moira to do. If not now, in time.

I love you dearly and wish I could fly to your side, but my place is here.

Lovingly,
Mother

He could not understand. She said she missed Father, yet she married again. "That does not make sense," he murmured. She married a Norman, but she wanted the Saxons to rise up and conquer them. Nothing made sense. He wanted to reply, but how could he? She had given him no way. Mayhap it would be too dangerous. He smoothed the letter, folded it flat and slipped it inside his tunic.

He gave Dinas a last pat and turned to leave the stall. He nearly knocked over a groom carrying a feed bucket. The boy was about his size with dark hair wisping out from under his cap. Enormous brown eyes went wide with surprise. He gave a high yelp and jumped back, spilling the bucket. Immediately, he dropped to his knees and scrabbled about on the ground, scooping feed back into the bucket. His bare feet were wrapped in muddy canvas.

"Pardon, sir. I'm so clumsy," he mumbled.

Edan glanced at the slender figure clad in dull homespuns. "It's all right. I startled you coming out of the stall so sudden."

The groom finished scraping up the spill with his hands and moved on to an end stall to feed the horse there.

Edan shook his head at the retreating figure. He imagined he smelled a faint fragrance. Could it be fragrance from the sweet meadow hay?

He left the stalls and returned to practice in the common.

"Is something wrong?" Owain's long, thin face wore a look of compassionate concern.

"A letter came from my mother. I guess news from home was

just too much for me. I'm alright now."

Swordplay resumed, but Edan's mind wandered elsewhere.

By supper's end Edan had calmed. He told Kadeg of the Normans building castles. He shared his mother's conclusion that the Archbishop wavered in giving up London, and her theory that if no one opposed William immediately, Saxon rule was lost. He knew Kadeg felt the same as his mother after last night's speech following the minstrel's entertainment. Kadeg already knew the rest.

After the recital of news, he made one remark that gave Edan pause. "My sister always could see ahead. No matter her lingering feelings for your father, she has remarried to give your sisters a future in this new regime."

Too full of remembering to absorb this, Edan excused himself.

Edan had expected to find his grandfather, Gwion, attended when Maeve led him to his room that evening. Would the old man remember Edan's mother, his exiled daughter, Rowena? What would he say to her son if he did?

Good to her word, Bryn waited for him. "Remember what I told you," she admonished. "His fit left him with a sagging face and a crippled arm and leg. Don't stare."

Grateful for her dependable actions, he followed her as she opened the heavy door to their grandfather's space.

The old man kept his own chamber, unattended. A large bed sat against one wall, sheepskins on the floor by it. His sword lay across its hanger behind the bed. A faint odor of incense wafted from the other side of the chamber. A bronze tripod, higher than Edan's head, held triple torches, mouthing tongues of flame.

An apprehensive quiet settled over the room before the old man, dressed in a blue houserobe, looked up from where he sat in a chair by the brazier. Chill blue eyes under a frowning bar of wild white brows bored into Edan. The old man still possessed a formidable warrior's face.

Bryn moved forward, and Edan followed.

"Good evening, grandfather. I brought someone with me tonight to meet you. This is another of your grandsons, Edan. He is here to be fostered."

"By the snake," the old man boomed from his twisted mouth. "A grandson, eh? Come here, let me see you. Red hair and all. You look like one of our clan." His strong voice still possessed an arrogance and pride.

Even after Bryn's warning, Edan was startled at the effects of the fit on his grandfather's left cheek and mouth. He tried to look at the luxurious white mane of hair, the brows, anything but the crooked mouth and sagging cheek.

Bryn cleared her throat to remind Edan of her warning. "Edan fosters here with my father."

Edan studied Gwion's face, while he waited for the angry reaction he feared would come. Nothing happened. Lines around his eyes, creases across the old man's forehead made him look in his late fifties. Gwion appeared not to remember where this mysterious other grandson came from or even remember to ask. Relief washed through Edan. *What did the old man remember?*

Edan stepped toward the hand his grandfather extended. It gripped his shoulder firmly and drew him closer. This was the good hand. The other lay in his lap, broad but with an old man's veins distended and knotted on it. Even so he gave off a restless energy. He released Edan's shoulder, reached for a goblet of wine on a small table next to him and swallowed some.

"How old are you, lad?"

"Near fourteen, sir." Was it uncertainty or fear that made his voice quaver?

The old man stared at Edan in rigid silence. At last his brow cleared, and his mouth relaxed into something like a smile. "You look much like my oldest son, Camlach."

Would he remember Camlach died, then remember his daughter, Rowena, and that he was angry with her?

"If you become as good a warrior as he, you'll make me proud."

Edan had no way of knowing where the old man's thoughts would jump next.

Bryn said, "I came to hear a story from you, grandfather. I know Edan would love to hear it, too."

Edan glanced at her, grateful to her for guiding the conversation in another direction.

"Oh you did, eh. Let's see—Merlin? No. Taliesen?" He paused. "Another night. How about the "Enchanter's Fosterling" in honor of Edan here." He settled himself, took another swig of wine. Bryn and Edan sat on a rug in front of him.

"A long time ago the rich mountain lands of Gwynedd, in northern Cymru, lay under the protection of two wizards, Math and Gwydion. The story begins at Caer Dathyl, Math's mountain fortress, with Gwydion's sister, Arianrod, a sorceress in her own right.

Arianrod came to Caer Dathyl to serve as Math's handmaiden. On the day she arrived, she gave birth to two sons. She abandoned them and fled to her own palace by the sea.

One infant leaped into the water and disappeared, but Gwydion caught up the other and decided to be father to the child. He saw to it the boy was well cared for, and he protected the boy with charms. As the years passed, the boy grew strong and healthy. When he was four, it came time for his naming. In Gwynedd at that time, only a mother could name her child, so Gwydion set off with the child for Arianrod's palace…"

As Gwion's words filled his ears, Edan remembered Owain's mention of Gwion's choice of a mythical name for his fortress. The old man seemed to dwell in the world of myth. The tapestries depicted other mythical figures from the past. For someone with little apparent memory of the present, how could he remember so much detail from the past? Edan had feared a wild-eyed, babbling old man. Instead Gwion seemed sane and talked sensibly as long as he talked of the past.

The tale wound on, and Edan found it fascinating. Bryn, of course, knew the story but seemed to enjoy listening to it again and being with her grandfather. Once she glanced over to Edan with a questioning look in her eyes. He smiled in return. She relaxed and immersed herself in the fosterling's life and the battle between the two wizards and Arianrod over the fosterling's fate.

11-19 Dec 1066

So it was that in the nights that followed, whenever Gwion was willing, Bryn and and Edan gathered in his chamber to listen to the myths of old. He had hot mulled wine brought for them. The old man welcomed their coming and had a new story each time. Even Bryn heard new ones as the old man's bag of stories emptied. When the tales ended, he told stories of his travels or his battles to keep them in his company. On other nights he took the two of them to his window slit and showed them the stars, told their names and their powers and how warriors could use them for a map on their travels. He never talked of any present events. Gradually, Edan learned more of the language of Cymru from Bryn and Gwion on these enjoyable evenings. Gaining his grandfather took away some of the sting of his mother and Moira's marriages to Normans. The cold December days passed, and somehow the ache of his grandfather's banishment of his mother faded. But Edan was aware a part of him cried out for the lack of something in him that he was not even sure had a name.

The last week before Christmas Bleddyn and his men departed for their own hall, leaving the fortress much quieter.

20 Dec 1066

The day had been dark and overcast, fraught with mist, the common ankle deep in wet mud. Dinas had not been out of his stall in four days and was eager. He grabbed the bit in his teeth, tried to gallop despite the heavy going. One foot went from under him. He slipped and fell, straining his leg. Edan jumped to the side and rolled away, unhurt. Grooms led Dinas away and treated him.

Edan worried all day about his horse. When the dice came out and games began after supper, restless, he excused himself to check on Dinas. Holding a torch high in the pitch blackness, he stumbled across frozen footprints to the stable. Once inside, air scented by the smell of sweet grass and warm horseflesh met his nose. The only sounds were the chewing of horses and an occasional nose-clearing snort.

Edan moved softly over the straw to stand in Dinas' stall. The horse stood square on all four legs, with no favoring of the injured one. He moved closer, speaking soft to let Dinas know he was coming. He put his hand on the horse's warm flank and sidled in next to him. He bent down to look close at the swollen leg. He ran his fingers down the leg below the hock. The leg twitched at his touch, but Dinas did not take his foot off the ground.

"Good. Likely, you will be alright in a day or two," he murmured to the horse. In response Dinas' nostrils fluttered in a soft nicker. Still, Edan massaged the leg with his fingers.

His thoughts moved to Ceridwen as he worked. No dropped head-band or lace handkerchiefs. No footprints of a girl's slipper anywhere. He had combed armory, barracks, stable, and all he had found was a crust of bread not yet carried off by rats in the straw-littered passageway of the stable.

At the other end of the throughway he heard low voices, a male voice, a familiar, young male voice. Ardel! Then came a female voice. That brogue again. He straightened and snuffed the torch in dirt under the manger. He knelt to listen. Which way were they coming?

He must not be caught by Ardel a second time! His ears tingled at the memory of the older boy's threat. He scrunched his body deep under the manger, pulled straw over him, and hardly dared to breathe. He knew he counted for nothing in this household. If Ardel wanted to do worse than cut off his ears, no one here would know. Fergus would be a very small voice asking his whereabouts. Mayhap Bryn would notice his absence.

"Only two days until you leave, Ceridwen. What shall I do without you?" Ardel said.

"I don't know if I can bear to leave. When will I see you again?" came the reply.

Only two days? Bryn's request jumped into Edan's mind. He must see this girl, discover her identity for Bryn. But he dare not get caught. He crept from under the manger on his hands and knees. A dim light shone at the end of the stall. They must have a torch. If he could just find a crack in the boards to peer through. One movement at a time he crept closer to the end of the stall, making sure the straw did not rustle.

A crack two boards from the bottom allowed a thin sliver of light. He bent and put his eye to the crack. The two lovers sat in a pile of loose hay in the throughway between stalls. Ardel had his arm flung over the girl's shoulders. A horse snorted somewhere, and she jumped. She turned her head in Edan's direction. Those big brown eyes in the too small face. Where had he seen this girl?

The groom who spilled the feed! He *had* seen her before and didn't know it. She'd disguised herself this whole time. That's how she escaped discovery.

"Remember my message?" Ardel asked.

"Yes, I tell Edric you will join him after the new year," she said. Suddenly she giggled and burrowed into the hay, Ardel kissing her neck.

Edan scooted backwards until he knelt under the manger again. Who was Edric? He wanted to rush out of the stable and straight to Bryn with his newfound information. Maybe she could make sense of it. Only two days to figure it out before the girl somehow left for this Edric.

Why would Ardel join Edric after Christmas? Wouldn't he stay here with his father and go into battle against William in the spring?

At this moment, Bryn's concern over Ardel seemed justified.

Chapter Nineteen

20 Dec 1066

After the couple left the stable, Edan charged across the uneven, frozen ground to the hall, his unlit torch clutched in one hand. He let himself in, the heavy wooden door creaking in the cold, and slid the torch into its rack.

Smoke from the fire in the hall filtered into the corridor, scenting the air. Edan scurried toward the kitchen, grateful for the emptiness. No one must delay him. Bryn must hear what he had discovered. She would surely know what it was that must be done.

His feet firm under him, he strode forward. A flash of movement ahead. Someone descended the small stair from the solar. The brown hair and swishing skirt that emerged into the corridor belonged to Bryn's handmaid.

She hesitated when she heard footsteps.

"Maeve, wait," Edan said in an undertone. In a few strides he stood at her side. Her eyebrows raised in question, she waited for him to speak.

"Tell Bryn I found Ceridwen tonight." Edan's voice dropped to a whisper. "I need to talk to her. I'll wait here for her answer."

Without a word Maeve lifted her skirts and scampered back up the stair.

Edan leaned against the stones. His heart still beat fast from his hurried traverse of the bailey and the excitement of finding Ceridwen. As his heartbeat slowed, he paced a small circle in the corridor.

At last, Maeve returned, her small feet pattering down the stair. Her face flushed with excitement, she whispered, "Go to the chapel again. I must go to the kitchen on an errand." In an instant she disappeared down the corridor toward the clatter of pots and murmur of voices that was the kitchen.

How fortunate to have run into Maeve here, without other curious eyes and ears about. Edan straightened his shoulders and hastened back the way he had come, putting down the urge to run.

When he reached the hall, Owain emerged on his way to quarters.

"How was Dinas?" he asked.

"Better I think. I stayed awhile and rubbed his leg. In a day or two he should be alright."

"I'm happy to hear that. Now I am headed to sleep. I feel a chill coming on and hope a good night's rest wards it off."

Edan looked behind him to see that no one watched, strode down the corridor to the end, and turned to the damp, cold passage that led to the chapel. A twisted rush torch sat in its bracket by the door. He pulled the latch which slid smooth as butter, opened the door and slipped into the chapel. He stood for a few moments letting his eyes adjust to a place full of shadows. Two faint candles burned at the front of the nave. His eyes strained to see if anyone sat in the front pew.

A creak sounded behind him. The carved wooden door opened. In the torchlight he saw the shimmer of Bryn's hair framing her excited face. She gave a start to see someone there before her. Recovering her poise, she sidled through the door to stand beside him.

"Is it true? You found her? Where?" Her words came tumbling out in tense whispers.

"Aye, she was in the stable dressed as a groom, in tryst with Ardel," he whispered back.

"So that is how she kept away from us. Go on—go on!" she murmured impatiently.

"They talked about her departure in two days. And when she leaves, Ardel is sending a message with her for someone named Edric. He said 'tell Edric I will join him after the new year.'"

Bryn made no immediate reply. She must be trying to find reason behind these actions. At last she began. "Edric has been an ally of Father's. He's from Powys, south of here. He did not join Riwallon and Bleddyn and the others this past autumn when they met here. I'm not sure what all this means yet, but I will ask some questions. If Ceridwen is from Edric's household, he may have another alliance planned and uses this girl to draw Ardel into it, and through him, Father. Edric has been a trusted ally. Ardel fostered there."

Even though he could not see her face in the shadows, Edan could hear the worried tone in her voice.

"I will ask Maeve and her sister to listen for news of departures from the fortress in two days or any news of Edric and make it seem not too meddlesome. I'll keep you informed through Maeve." A rustle of her skirt, a crack of light from the open door, then darkness and silence.

Edan stood in the chill room. Somewhere outside the fortress, men plotted. Was it against Duke William or against Kadeg and his alliance? Shadowy images of men whispering with heads together, of weapons being readied, of troops gathering multiplied and swirled before his eyes in the dim candlelit nave. The chapel seemed to fill with enough murderous intent to give him the screaming willies. Edan found it difficult to breathe.

For the second time in his life, the desire to strike out at an enemy burned in Edan. Unconsciously, his hand went to his dagger and loosed it in its sheath. But was Ardel the potential traitor, or Edric? If men of Cymru and Saxons fought among themselves for power, no English alliance would ever grow big enough to defeat William.

Edan closed his eyes against these worrisome images. When he opened them again, only the guttering candles filled his vision. With a tremulous sigh, Edan left the chapel and trod the cold stone to his room.

21 Dec 1066

Edan grew more anxious with every passing minute but somehow endured the next day with no word from Bryn, no hint that anything changed. In the stables he had not seen the disguised groom again. He wasn't sure his face would not betray his knowledge of her if they came face to face.

That night he lay in bed, impatient for Fergus to come stoke the brazier. At least he could talk to someone.

A faint rap sounded at the door.

"Enter."

Fergus shut the door behind him. Walking to the brazier he set down his armload of wood. A piece at a time, he stoked the fire. "There, that should hold til morn."

When he turned to face Edan, the eager expression on his face told Edan there was news.

"What is it?" Edan sat up and flung his legs over the side of the bed.

"Maeve told me someone leaves the fortress morning after next." He stood, eyes glinting, enjoying his role as bearer of news.

"Aye, who?" Edan could barely contain himself. "And must I crack the side of your pate to hurry your words?"

Fergus grinned. "The two fosterlings, Elphin and Lleu, return home for Christmastide. By the grace of the Old Ones, there will be that much more of the cook's special treats for the rest of us."

No mention had been made in daily practice that these two departed soon. Edan stared. "Will they have escort?"

"That Bryn does not yet know. You may be in a position to hear something yourself, she said."

"Aye. I will read with you for a while now, but weapons practice must wait for tomorrow."

Fergus's face fell as he struggled with his disappointment at a short evening, then regained his good humor. They practiced for an hour before Edan said, "Enough." Fergus did well and could read a few words plus write his name now. He also picked up the language of Cymru in the kitchen as Edan did on the practice field each day.

When the door had shut on him, Edan went across the room and knelt by the fire. He absently fingered his father's cross beneath his tunic. He waited in the quietness for his mind to calm. He had not thought to ask Fergus if he knew where Elphin and Lleu called home. If it were far, then grooms and soldiers might well accompany them in these uncertain times.

Beside him a log crumbled and fell into the center of the fire. He started in surprise. He realized he could do no more tonight. Padding to bed, he settled his wool sleep gown around him, burrowed into the covers and fell asleep.

22 Dec 1066

Morning came, dry and with heavy frost. Clouds hung low and dark. Except for the early snow in October when Edan arrived, the rest of winter had been late. The earth had been frost-bound since, but very little snow had fallen. Just the bone-chilling cold, day after day. Enough to keep a body from gaining weight just from shivering it off.

At a break in practice at arms Edan asked the others of holiday plans thinking some may leave the fortress.

"I go tomorrow, home to Powys for Christmastide. I've finished my fostering and will wait for word in the spring to join Kadeg's forces to march against William," said Elphin self-importantly.

"I, too," said Lleu. "I hope it doesn't snow and delay us," he added, eyeing the sullen sky.

"I will stay here," said Owain. "It is too long a journey in winter to Caer'narvon for Christmas feasting and back to finish my fostering. I shall stay here until spring."

Edan asked Elphin, "Does anyone accompany you on the long journey through the wilds?" He remembered his own journey over the rocky paths, the wolves, and the Normans close at his heels.

"When I came, my Father's men brought me. This time Lleu and I and our grooms go," Elphin explained.

Edan's mind sped to the mention of grooms and Powys. Bryn had said Edric lived in Powys.

"Your grooms came with you all these months?" Edan pretended surprise. As he spoke, he did not shift his eyes from Elphin. Ceridwen had indeed disguised herself well to remain undetected this long if she had come with them.

Elphin looked at Edan a moment in silence. A quick flash of some emotion, maybe doubt, maybe fear, rested in his eyes before his gaze flicked away. He replied, "But of course. Someone had to attend us and our horses we brought. Who better than our own, so we did not become a burden to Prince Kadeg."

Just that brief pause before the answer made Edan suspicious of how much the boys knew and what their motives might be. Had they been sent here to spy on Kadeg in the guise of fostering with an ally's young warriors? Again Ridley the pedlar's words came to him. "A man's intentions are in his eyes." These two had been thick together during the time Edan had been here, not companionable with Owain or Edan except in the hall. After all these weeks of comradeship in practice of arms, a chasm opened between them the size of the gully leading up from Bala. Owain, he knew, had not brought his own horse or his own groom. However, he was not even sure of Owain's loyalties since Bryn brought spying to his attention and implied every family's loyalty was suspect.

At the next meal he would pass on this latest piece of information to Fergus who would get it to Bryn through Maeve.

23 Dec 1066

Edan peered down from a window slit. In the bailey below four horses stood saddled, breath steaming in the early chill.

Would Ardel dare show himself to bid them all farewell?

Bryn's words from last night still rang in his ears. "Elphin and Lleu and their grooms may all be spies. It is time I ask questions of Father about Edric's loyalty. Depending upon his answers, I will ask if he or any of our family is to meet with him soon. If he asks why I want to know, I will say I have heard talk in the kitchen among the servants that a strange groom, maybe a girl, works in the stable and she has claimed a tie to Edric's household."

Leaning against the stone with his gaze riveted below, Edan would love to have been a mouse in the corner to overhear such a conversation between Bryn and her father.

At that moment, Elphin and Lleu strode from the hall, Kadeg with them. Edan dashed from his room, down the stairs and out the door. Owain appeared from the soldier's quarters. Both said their farewells. Though they had been good company in practice, Edan could not put the thought they might be spies out of his mind.

Their breath clouded the frosty air. Kadeg seemed in good spirits, clapped them on the shoulder and wished them Godspeed. Two grooms appeared, helped the boys mount, then clambered aboard their own ponies. For all that his eyes strained to see, Edan could not tell if one groom was the girl, Ceridwen. The foursome approached the gate, the chains rattled, and the entrance opened to them.

Ardel had not shown himself.

Had Bryn been able to talk to Kadeg before this leave-taking or not? If Bryn had not reached her father, it would be two or three more days before there was any news as Kadeg prepared to leave with a hunt party, the packed horses standing ready with hounds milling around their feet.

Chapter Twenty

Christmastide 1066

In the winter days after the departure of the more experienced fosterlings, and Kadeg's return, Bryn sent word to Edan. She had told her father of the suspicious groom, Ceridwen, and her possible connection with Edric; however, Kadeg had given her no further information. She did not know what he planned to do with the news that he may have had a spy in his household. Would he do nothing because the spy was a girl? Edan found this non-action disappointing after their earnest search and discovery. He had been eager to see the look on Ardel's smug face when punishment was given.

When Kadeg returned from hunting, nothing changed. Ardel engaged in his normal activities. Even so, Edan often woke in the night from a terrifying nightmare where Ardel crept after him through the fortress corridors, a long knife in his hand and a horrible grimace on his features.

Before long, Christmastide cooking filled the fortress with tantalizing smells. The hall's tables groaned with holiday foods, like stuffed piglet with nuts, cheeses, eggs, breads and venison en frumenty and his favorite, blackmanger, containing chopped chicken with rice, almonds, and sugar. Sweets like yule dolls, humble pie, puddings, and possets made even the hardest of warriors smile. Music from the harpers, storytelling by visiting gleemen, dancing and games filled the days. Grandfather Gwion made several appearances in the hall throughout the festivities. Yet for all the gaiety, Edan missed the holly and mistletoe of his father's Christmas hall and his own family as it had been.

During the long dark nights afterward, snow piled high against the fortress walls, and winter began in earnest. Those within pulled their woolen mantles close about them just to walk the corridors. After drifts grew high and treacherous, no one came or went outdoors. Frost held the ground as cold and hard as a battle sword. The fortress sat in a place cut off from every other world and existed on its own stores. A great loneliness loomed beyond its walls.

January 1067

While bleak weather howled outside, Edan fretted out the month of January. Weapons practice came to a halt. He and Owain played countless games of chess and listened to the soldiers of the fortress become more restless as the weeks rolled by. He and Bryn spent some evenings huddled about grandfather's brazier listening to stories of his youth. He waited for his cousin, Ardel, to leave for Edric's as he had promised the girl, Ceridwen. Instead, everyone hunched close about the fires when they were indoors, scorching one side or the other.

At January's end, the sun shone warm. Stable thatch icicles dripped cold tears. After three days of this, drifts outside the walls shrunk to passable depth. Men ventured out on horseback to pack paths. Since the fortress contained many mouths to feed, talk of hunting began.

On the morning of the fourth day, Kadeg stood before an assemblage of men in the common assigning them to hunt. Some groups would go on day trips for fowl, others would go further in search of the little red deer prevalent in nearby valleys. Eager for another activity, Edan listened for his own name. Several assigned hunt parties already packed supplies of foodstuffs on their horses. The men cavorted in high spirits after their imprisonment by the weather and had quivers of fresh fledged arrows, taut bow strings and sharpened lancepoints. Now these weapons were attached to saddles or slung across the hunter's shoulders.

Hounds scampered between men and horses, yelping their eagerness.

"Ardel, you are to lead one party to the east to the lower wooded valleys for roe," Kadeg directed.

Edan waited, his eyes on Kadeg's face. He heard the low murmur of voices, the drip of the melt, the low of cattle in the stable, and under it a quietness of anticipation.

"Wiermund, Brand..." his gaze swept the men and stopped, fastening on Edan.

Edan's breath caught. No, not with Ardel!

"...and Edan will go with Ardel."

No, I must not, Edan's mind protested. Keeping quiet never came easily to him, but he could not refuse nor could he give any reason not to go, let alone the real reason. He longed to let Fergus know that he rode with Ardel, so someone would know where he had gone besides Owain and Kadeg. He forced his gaze up against the intolerable weight that seemed to bear it down. "Aye," he said, and his voice sounded hoarse and heavy in his own ears.

The next minutes blurred as he set about packing bannock cakes and dried meat into a pouch upon his horse. This time it was not Dinas but one of the smaller horses used in hunting. Before he knew it, they were underway. The others talked, while Edan rode in silence. For him, only the wind sounded in his ears as it swept up the desolate valley. He turned once to see the fortress, a black speck in the distance, and fear engulfed him like the waves of a dark sea.

Talk ceased as the terrain grew steep. Edan held himself tense and bent a little as though to ease the ache of a wound, knees gripping firm against his mount to keep his balance. The path grew unfamiliar and narrower as they passed the furthest point he had ever hunted away from the fortress.

His numb brain unlocked, and he began to think. These men were not close with Ardel. As long as they were together, in his mind, he remained safe from his tormentor. If they split up to hunt, he was in peril.

The new scenery drew him in, as they left behind the short grass and stones, now covered with snow, the little blue sheep in the byres of outlying shepherds, and the mist-shrouded, snowy peak of Cadair Idris. With sudden twists and ascents, they came into rocky, wild passes, eagles spiraling high overhead. They descended to half-frozen streams in valley bottoms, making their way to the lower, wooded valleys.

On the eve of the first day, they reached a barren valley with sparse set, bare-limbed oaks. The track dipped to skirt the alder-grown fringes of an ice-crusted lakeshore. Mist hung over the open water in the lake's center, creeping up the glens of the far mountainsides already blue with twilight. The horses crunched over matted heather and bog myrtle between patches of snow.

As they dismounted and gathered fuel for a fire, the mist became dense whiteness that wreathed around them. Soon the reek of smoke, the tang of horse droppings, and the smell of cooking food filled the air. Edan filled his belly, but an emptiness remained within him. Ardel bided his time, acted pleasant, but Edan became uneasy when the older boy's gaze fell upon him. So far they had seen no game to shoot, no occasion to separate.

The fire burned low. The mist had turned to dense fog that shut out everything within a lance length of the firepit. An eerie wail sounded a short distance away.

"Wolves," said Wiermund, throwing another log on the fire. "I take the first watch to keep the fire high."

The rest of them lay close by the fire and wrapped their mantles about them. With company, Edan relaxed and fell asleep until his turn at watch.

Morning brought clear skies, a warm sun. Little freshets of melted snow ran everywhere, trickling and gurgling. After they chewed down some dried, smoked meat, the party splashed out of the valley and pushed onward toward forest lands.

Edan's defenses lulled by the excitement of the hunt, Ardel's dark humours were almost forgotten in the time out of the fortress and the presence of the other men. He was not ready for the sudden stirring next to him, the rapid thump of feet, then, like a snow squall, a deer herd swept past before anyone could launch an arrow.

Edan's heart thudded in his chest at the sudden passage.

"Wiermund, Brand, go left," Ardel commanded. "Edan and I will go right and flush them to open ground in the meadow we just passed through."

The other men took off at a trot. Edan woodenly followed Ardel, alone with him at last. The terror had come to pass. They rode hard through trees, swerving and keeping within the sound of the deer's passage. Ardel never slowed, never turned, his eyes focused on the deer. Wiermund and Brand reached the meadow first, and stood ready, arrows nocked when Ardel and Edan burst into the meadow. When the deer spotted the hunters, the herd split apart, some back into the trees, the rest racing across the meadow. Arrows flew, and two deer fell.

"Follow the ones in the open," ordered Ardel. "Then cast back along tree edge for sign of the others. We will meet back here in the meadow." The rest of the animals wheeled into the trees and soon were gone. Minutes later Ardel and Edan returned, their horses blowing from the chase. Wiermund and Brand had wasted no time stringing up the game, bleeding them out. The next hours were spent skinning and quartering. Edan had helped his own father twice before but worked slowly compared to the others, due to his lack of previous experience.

That afternoon they crossed the track of wild boar. Ardel halted, put up a hand to signal silence. The older men walked beside their horses laden with the quartered deer. Ardel motioned them to stay and waved Edan ahead with him. Edan's hand turned white as he clutched his horse's reins. His heart lurched. They rode, gazes riveted on the cloven footprints heading for the shallows of a stream. They crossed into dense forest that choked the valley's far side. A silent magpie flew down to drink from one of the puddles left in the tracks. Their horses splashed through the icy stream, where, on the opposite bank, tracks in the damp earth led them onward. The distant alarm call of a jay and a tuft of hair on a low-hanging thorn branch told of the boar's passage. It was not a tall forest but a dark one with dense tangles of yew and holly, gray-misted and brown-shadowed. Ardel and Edan moved with light swiftness in a twilight world. As long as they moved, Edan's safety seemed certain.

Ardel paused for an instant. Snorts and pawing sounds came from the brittle shrubbery ahead. A little cold thrill swept Edan's heart and left his body in one swift shudder. They circled wide as to come upwind on the pigs. In thick alder next to a stream, they came upon the boar and his sows. The bristled head of the old boar swung from side to side. The grunts turned to squeals of rage, menace in every paw of its hooves. It stood for a long moment tensed to charge, savage red eyes blazing. Without further warning, it lunged forward.

Ardel and Edan rode at it with spears poised. Ardel loosed his spear. The boar squealed, but whirled to charge his tormentor. The sudden move tore the spear from Ardel's hand, the stuck weapon bouncing at its shoulder. The boar's tusks swung at Ardel's horse. It whirled away. Edan's nostrils widened. His hand clenched on his spear shaft. His arm drew back. Little tremors ran through his body, like Kadeg's hounds at the kill. He thrust at the boar's shoulder. The spear stuck deep just behind the first. He let it go. The boar ran a few steps, staggered and fell, grunting in anger one last time. He had killed it!

Ardel spurred forward, leapt from his horse and wielded his battle axe upon the boar's head to be certain of its death. The body jerked with each blow. Abruptly, Ardel whirled and glared at Edan.

Surprised, Edan did not think to rein his horse around. Ardel's green eyes were hard with hate. His open mouth twisted in savage triumph. "I warned you once about spying on me. This time you went too far," he growled between clenched teeth.

A moment's deadly silence passed. Edan knew then Kadeg had confronted Ardel about Ceridwen.

Ardel, whitening about the lips, gave a hideous yell and charged. His red hair swept back in rapid passage and his fierce eyes welded onto Edan's memory. Full of the boar's blood and hair, the blunt end of the axe bit into Edan's upper leg as he whirled his mount.

Metal hit bone. Fiery pain took his breath away.

What a rogue! He tried to bash my leg off!

Somehow he managed to stay on his horse. He just rode as his mount plunged into the forest. Behind him he heard Ardel shout to the other men beyond the thicket, "Come. Take care of the boar. See if you can spear a sow as well. I must chase Edan. The boar frightened him." He laughed a cruel laugh.

Edan slashed through dense undergrowth and deeper forest. He stole a quick glance down at the red stain spreading across his leg. What would have happened had he not whirled and run? *Would Ardel have killed him?* Roots rapped under his horse's hooves. He lay low on his horse's neck to avoid sweeping branches. Presently, he clung to the mane as he grew faint from pain. Save for his horse's thudding strides, no sound of pursuit came to his ears. The trees stood quiet. No breeze fluttered the dead leaves. If any deer, boar or wolves were abroad, Edan did not see them.

When the blowing horse stumbled, it slowed of its own accord. It came to a path and followed. Ahead, a gap in the boughs showed the gray-blue sky of late afternoon. A twist in the path took them into deeper gloom. The horse slowed to a walk. Edan hardly noticed. All his energy went into staying on the horse. His whole awareness centered on his pain.

Darkness fell. Starlight flickered between stark branches. An owl cried, away to his right. From somewhere ahead, another answered. The sounds screamed into his ears like a war cry. The horse, half asleep as he walked, shied at the unexpected cry. The breath exploded from Edan's chest when he landed onto ground hardened by frost. The horse lurched into a gallop and disappeared into the forest. Edan lay for a moment half-stunned. The taste of blood lay on his tongue and jagged lights flashed before his eyes.

"By St. Dunstan, now who can help me?" he whispered. He fumbled at the neck of his tunic for the cross which lay beneath and dragged it out. He cradled it in his hand.

Soon he heard the trickle of water nearby. Dragging himself toward the sound, he drank from its ice-crusted coolness and splashed some over his face. Revived a bit, he struggled to his knees and tried to stand. He had only his mantle. His food had been in a bag tied to his saddle. He needed to hide. He took a step. An unbearable stab of pain came from his leg. He slid downward into a black fog.

When Edan woke, small, dark hill men knelt all around him in a circle, their eyes gleaming at the edge of firelight like so many wolves. The eyes began to move, to swim about the fire. He closed his eyes against the dizziness.

His leg ached. He reached for it and felt a poultice. He heard a sound and opened his eyes again. One of the men moved forward to the fire and scooped some liquid from a pot into a bowl. He supported Edan and held it to Edan's lips. The hot broth warmed him as he sipped. The other men grunted and nodded, but Edan only heard them vaguely and a long way off. His head fell back, and his eyes closed.

After that, there was a time of darkness and confusion. When he woke again, the same face leaned over his. The bowl again touched his lips. A fire burned in his eyesight, while another burned in his leg. Sometimes the confusion thinned like receding fog, and there were faces. He tried to remember, but the thoughts slipped away from him.

One day Edan opened his eyes and saw clearly. He lay in a cave. He saw the slanting beam of afternoon sun striking through a smoke hole in the cavetop, showing a ladder. He lay on piled ferns, under a deerskin. He heard small rhythmic sounds that meant someone sharpened a weapon. The skin tickled his chin, and he tried to thrust it down. To his surprise he barely had the strength to raise his hand to his chin. The pain in his leg had lessened, replaced by a stiffness.

The little man's eyes met his. He showed a gap of broken teeth. He spoke a strange slurred mix of Welsh and something else. Edan understood well enough. "You will mend. We caught your horse. It is lame, but it will recover." He fed Edan with broth from the familiar bowl.

He saw hunters hacking meat from a quartered kill. He had heard of these dark men of the Wild Forest and wild hill country. Had he come that far? They were descendants of the tribesmen before the Saxons, the Romans, the Celts. They lived like homeless wolves—small, dark-haired with leathery, lined faces like old wood. They wore tanned skins and coarse woven cloth breeches of brown, green and murrey. His eyes drooped. All that he cared for was sleep.

The household rising to work the next morning roused him. A pony whinnied outside, and someone came clambering down into the cave, the man who tended him. Edan looked up at him. "How long have I slept?"

"Three days you have not been among us," the little man replied.

"How came you to find me?"

"Aiee, you lay in the forest as dead. One of our hunters found you."

Memory came back to Edan as he listened, ideas that had hovered at the fringe of his memory. The hunter throwing him over a pony, walking it to the cave, hearing men in pursuit, the hunter hiding, the little man tending him. Without conscious thought, his fingers moved to his scrip and cradled the small wooden shape from home.

In the days to come Edan saw their clubs, knives, stone axes from a time gone by. He grew familiar with the fortified hilltop they called their own. They were seen by none except by choice, small families living a furtive life outside the crowded parts of England. He shared their fare of roast hare, black bread and drank their honey mead. Several families shared their food with him. The women managed to make him a warm fur cloak to wear over his worn mantle. He ate porridge, flat cakes, and dined on hen and venison. Their larder seemed to hold foods as good as Kadeg's kitchen despite their poverty. He remembered tales of food left at the old shrines that disappeared. Some of their food must come from the offerings to the old gods.

The children seemed fascinated by his red hair, strange speech, and the fact he was so much taller than their clan members.

His ear became tuned to their speech. Now he could pick out more than the Welsh of Gwynedd. Edan began to understand some words of their dialect. He saw them worship at their small shrine with its polished stone, like Galt's in the deep wood where he and Fergus had left the wounded knight.

Llyd, the little shaman who tended him, gave him news. "Duke William was crowned King on Christmas Day in London. The Normans hang close to their fires during the cold months. All will be quiet until Spring."

Edan fretted at his own weakness and inability to do anything. Finally, he remembered Kadeg's words about William. "If he is crowned King before forces are gathered against him, it does not matter. We can still kill him in battle." He began to think of what lay ahead as he made his way about with a crutch. Llyd nodded encouragingly every time he changed the poultice and placed his Fingers of Power, his healing touch, on the wound. The wound had drained and scabbed over, a jagged, many-forked wound where the flesh had been bashed and ripped. He knew he would bear this scar the rest of his life.

He had not left the cave except to sit outside on one or two warm days. He helped sharpen their chipped weapons and worked at curing hides, rubbing on herbs and salt and working in goose grease to soften them. He watched the women dying the coarse cloth from which they made breeches. Saw them crush mountain plants they had gathered and boil them to make the dyes of brown, green, and murrey. He helped wherever he could to repay the little clan. The people showed kindness to him and never asked how he had been wounded or why he had been chased. Since they seemed to be aware of all that took place in the surrounding forest, mayhap they already knew. In fact, as he saw strange Hill men come and go every few days, bringing news from all across England, Edan realized these Hill men trafficked in information within their clan. The last men who came exchanged silver coins with the head man for information they sold to men of Powys. It appeared they sold news to whoever would pay for it.

April 1067

As days passed, the weather warmed, a thaw began, and he knew the worst of winter had fled. What would he do when he recovered enough to travel? He had no idea what Ardel had told Kadeg when he returned with the hunt party. Would Fergus suspect Ardel's story and think Ardel had done something to him? Poor Fergus. He must be confused and worried. And what did Bryn and Owain think? He remembered Ardel's shout to the others as he rode away. "Edan is frightened," followed by the derisive laugh. Yes, he could imagine what Ardel had said, imagine him taking credit for the boar kill as well leaving Edan's name out of mention.

Edan could not bear the soldier's leers, the cruel jibes, the shame of being called a coward when he was not. Even if Owain and Fergus did not believe Ardel's words. Even if Bryn stood by their friendship. With sinking heart, he remembered Bryn might be gone by now, married to Bleddyn's son. A sense of loss flooded over him. Where else should he go? "If ever you need me, I shall spend the winter in the North." Ridley's words crept into his mind. Would he still be there? Should he ask the Hill Men to help him find his way to North and ask of Ridley's whereabouts?

As soon as weather permitted, he left the cave to limp weakly about. Each day he grew stronger. Every third day Llyd pointed the Fingers of Power at the wound in his leg, driving new life into it. He dressed the wound with salves that smelled of comfrey and yarrow and that little flower Edan's mother used to gather—pink centaury. The wound healed, leaving a puckered purple scar on his thigh.

Within a month he could limp with his crutch out of sight of the cave. Llyd set a small boy the task of accompanying him. By the time some buds showed on the blackthorn and the alders that fringed a nearby stream dropped their dark catkins, true spring was underway. He ranged further, the crutch left behind with the small boy. He limped still but could walk miles now and knew he would be able to ride. It was nearly time to ask Llyd to set him on his way. To Northumbria? He'd rather face half a dozen of Fergus's dreaded red-eyed black dogs than go back to the fortress near Ardel. Yet, he agonized, *if I don't go back, what of Fergus? I can not leave him there.* Mayhap Kadeg would even expel Fergus from the fortress now that he was not there.

Chapter Twenty-One

April 1067

Edan thrust out of the cave and hurried across a wide stretch of beaten earth one early morn. Halfway to the valley below, he stepped onto a game trail that took him to where a stream formed a pool above a gushing weir. Fish darted in its shadowed depths. He almost stopped to fish but continued on. With a nose full of the damp earth, last year's yellowed fern and rotting wood, a wanderlust filled him.

Afternoon found him far from the cave in a dense wood of oaks and chestnut that hung like a thick cloak on the shoulders of low hills. He heard sounds, not animal sounds or bird calls, but voices. Hoofbeats thudded accompaniment on the mossy forest floor.

"I never change my mind," said a stubborn voice.

"Russet is a warm color for winter," a softer voice reasoned.

"But winter is nearly gone," the first voice stated.

Edan smothered laughter. The headstrong mood of the one woman reminded him of the times Moira would argue with Mother over clothes as these two did. He slipped behind a broad oak and looked down the hill. Two women rode along a narrow track. The two, one young and one older, remained unaware that they were watched, though Edan stood quite close. The younger rode a flighty little chestnut mare with a light hand. Her companion sat like a bundle on a heavy-footed gray horse.

Edan kept his distance and let his curiosity lead him on. Shadows masked their features as they picked their way across a shallow ford. When they came even with his hiding place, the women emerged into sunlight. The young woman turned out to be a girl in a rich blue gown, slender and upright in her saddle. She was gimsy enough from this distance, her dark hair loose down her back. Large dark eyes took in the surroundings. Cheeks pink from exercise, her whole manner seemed energetic. The older woman wore a drab homespun tunic and kirtle that told Edan she must be a nurse or maid. He wondered if the dark haired girl rode every day. Leaning forward, he watched as the two rode on until the wood opened into a clearing where a small village surrounded a manor house. They crossed a bridge guarded by sentries and disappeared into the common of the village. So far away now he could see no detail of the men by the bridge, what weapons they had or what clothes they wore. An ache started in the back of his throat as he viewed this scene so like his own village.

He looked for signs of Norman troops but could see none. Were the sentries to sound the alarm against Normans?

The thought occurred to him that perhaps he could meet this girl if he came earlier tomorrow. If he kept away from the village, the sentries would not matter. He craved conversation with his own kind after the long recovery with the Hill People.

The next day Edan arrived earlier and settled himself along the track to await the passage of the girl and her nurse. He could have ridden but chose to walk to keep strengthening his leg. The day had dawned clear and fresh, so he hoped the women would ride after being cooped up for months by winter weather.

He sat against the same oak inhaling the perfume of the wildthorn which bloomed in a white haze along the track and listening to the thrushes' chorus to spring.

It proved to be a long wait. A sunbeam broke through the budding foliage overhead and crept across the opposite tree trunk, marking the passage of time. Magpies fluttered and called, as they fetched sticks for their bulky nests high in the treetops. Edan chewed a strip of dried meat, not really hungry but fidgety.

At last the thud of hooves on damp earth came to his ears. The lilt of girlish laughter joined the birdsong. Edan came to full attention beside his backrest and peered down upon the riders below. He had a quick glimpse of a determined, intelligent face.

At that moment a stag burst from the copse alongside the horses causing the little chestnut mare to rear, then snorting with fear, leap forward into a swift gallop.

"Mother of all mischief," Edan muttered while he admired the rider, who clung tenaciously to the horse. The mare had the bit in her teeth. No amount of restraint slowed her flight.

The nurse watched in horror as the mare bore her charge away. Helpless to chase the fleet horse, she sat and screamed. Her horse, upset by the actions of its companion and its rider's screams, sidestepped and pranced. The nurse, surprised by this sudden action, slid sideways before toppling to the dirt.

Edan burst from his observation spot and ran down to the track. He didn't know what he would do, but he couldn't just sit and watch. Could he think of something to say to the woman that wouldn't frighten her as she sat next to her nervous horse?

"I be Edan," he panted. "Let me use your horse to help your charge." Meanwhile, he gestured toward her horse and pointed after the runaway.

The woman gave one high shriek, and her hand flew to her mouth before her eyes focused on him and his words or gestures registered. She sat frozen, unable to speak or act, obviously torn between fright at Edan's appearance and concern for her charge. At last she managed to nod. Edan helped her up and settled her next to a large oak. Racing back to the stolid gray, he gathered its reins and leaped to its back. He had not ridden since his injury. His injured leg lacked the power of the other, but it seemed strong enough. He kicked the gray. The old horse grunted, not having been treated so in recent memory. Its head flew up, and it lumbered forward into a gallop.

The mare and her rider were out of sight. Edan could not even hear hoofbeats. He leaned to stare at the muddy track. The oval prints were clear in the soft ground and led straight down the track. He doubted the horse would veer into the dense wooded areas off to the side. After its fear faded and it galloped itself into a sweat, it would slow. If only the girl were a good enough rider to stick to its back like a cockle burr until that happened.

Wheezing and puffing, the old cob carried Edan forward at a steady pace. They crossed a small stream, climbed a hill, descended and leveled out again. Despite the cob's steadiness, Edan's injured leg lost its grip three times.

At last, Edan spied the mare ahead. The girl remained astride, her hair windblown into wild tangles, her clothes spattered with mud. Obstinate to the end, she still sawed the reins to no avail. White foam flecked the horse's sweat-darkened flanks.

At his approach, Edan saw the girl turn her head to see who came. She laid her cheek on the horse's damp neck and talked to it, then pulled hard one last time. The mare ignored it. Edan came alongside and reached over with his left arm to grab the reins. His injured leg failed him.

I ride like a weakling!

He grabbed at the gray's neck to steady himself against the jerk of each galloping stride.

After three strides, he grabbed the saddle and reins with one hand and reached out again to clutch the mare's reins close under her chin. He almost fell flat on his face a second time. Only his hand clenched on the edge of the saddle saved him. A few shortened lunges and they halted, both horses blowing and snorting. The chestnut nuzzled her gray companion. It took the out-of-breath girl a moment to gather herself.

She lifted her chin with a defiant air, though her lips trembled and her dark eyes were huge with fear. One hand flicked from the reins toward her waist, then back when the mare pranced a step to the side. Edan wondered if she had a dagger. Her display of spirit was admirable.

"I be Edan. I wish you no harm. On the contrary, I borrowed your nurse's horse to come after you in case you were hurt." He let go the mare's bridle. Her eyes widened at his words, but she did not speak. Gradually, her rapid breaths slowed. She had the horse under control again. "But I see my services were not needed. You took care of yourself."

Giving her a chance to resume her dignity, Edan reined the gray around as if to return. "I must return your woman's horse as I promised. Do you go back now? If so, may we ride together?"

"Most certain." She turned the mare to ride alongside.

Edan studied her face. The wind and exertion had rouged her cheeks and put a sparkle in her black eyes. Her lips were full, her nose strongly bridged but slender. The eyes were alert under expressive black brows. Her voice had an unknown lilt to it. Like Ceridwen with her brogue that Edan could not place.

She laughed shakily. "May the god smile upon you for coming to my aid. I'm afraid my manners are amiss that I did not thank you. I am Merane."

"You are most welcome, Merane," Edan smiled. "You did not need my assistance. You had your horse all but stopped when I caught up to you."

She made a small mocking nod of acknowledgment. Her smile bloomed. "Do you live close to my village?"

"I be staying with friends nearby. It happened I took a walk in the forest today and witnessed your trouble."

"I'm afraid Dove has more energy than common sense after confinement all winter. The past few days are the first we've been out in months."

"Most horses unused for a while behave this way," Edan agreed, remembering Dinas.

They passed the time in simple conversation until Merane spied her nurse ahead in the road. The woman's agitated movements told of her anxiety over Merane and her fright over what punishment she might suffer for allowing danger to befall her mistress.

"Can't we hide from her and ride awhile?" Edan asked.

Merane shook her head. "She has seen us already. And it is time for my lessons with the tutor." She screwed up her face in a frown. "Latin and history."

The horses reached the nurse, and Edan sprang down.

"I am fine, Odette," Merane soothed. "Dove ran herself out, then Edan came along on Jolie. He accompanied me back. He stays with friends nearby."

The woman, close to tears still, looked puzzled but accepted Edan's help to remount. She placed one foot in his laced fingers, and he heaved up. Sprawling against the old gray's side, she managed to get aboard and settle herself. Her red cheeks spoke of her effort.

"Perchance you will be in the woods some other day when we go out to ride," Merane said with a shy smile before the two rode off toward the village.

"I should like that," Edan replied.

She looked back once. Edan still stood in the track. He waved before climbing the bank for the long return walk, his injured leg stiff from his efforts. He massaged the old wound as he walked.

He waited a day and returned to the track in late morning. He listened to the rustlings and bird calls in the wood around him, but no hoofbeats came down the track. He watched bees move among the wildthorn blooms below him, mayhap from the beeskep in Merane's village. Another sound began in the distance, a foreign sound, someone beating upon metal. He straightened and gazed down the track. Just then a team of horses hove into sight around a bend, drawing a wagon covered with pots.

Ridley? His heart thudded faster in his chest. It was! He recognized the dun-colored team he had tended and helped hitch to the wagon so many times. The wagon drew closer. Now Edan could see its driver, the red cap upon his head, the frizzy hair escaping from beneath in all directions. The crimson mantle flowed over the wagon seat, covering the stout, muscular body Edan knew lay hidden. A gladness welled within him that had been long absent. He descended to the track waving both arms over his head and ran after the wagon.

"Ho, lad, be that you, Edan?" Ridley's voice boomed out as he peered behind.

"Aye," Edan shouted back. He managed to run toward the wagon limping only slightly.

"Where is Fergus?"

At mention of Fergus's name, Edan experienced a stab of worry.

"He is with Kadeg at the fortress. It is a long story."

"Come up here on the seat by me and start this long tale." Ridley screwed his body around and gave Edan a hand up. "Well lad, over the winter, Kadeg's cook put some meat on your bones," he observed. "What do you in these woods all alone and far from the fortress with Normans all about?"

Edan's stomach tightened. "Normans? I have seen none these past months. Where have you seen them?"

"North, almost to Northumbria. All through this area."

In Merane's village? She had said nothing. He turned to Ridley. "Let me start at the beginning. All was good at the fortress as I left. Kadeg fosters me. I learned much over the winter. Kadeg makes Fergus work as my servant." Edan frowned. "Both he and I are unhappy about that, but it won't be forever."

"Go on," prompted Ridley.

"In the cold month after Christmastide I went on the hunt with three men, one of whom was Ardel, Kadeg's oldest son. We had a disagreement earlier…no, he thought we did and chose the time out of the fort to make things even between us."

Ridley listened, silent as Edan spoke, flicking the switch over the backs of his horses from time to time.

"You think the boy attacked you to kill you?" Ridley asked after Edan finished his tale.

"I know not, yet his look said 'aye.' I rode hard to get away. I must have fainted from pain at last, and some hunters from the Hill People found me and took me to their cave. They helped me mend. I have been with them for three moons at least."

"Gods and fiends! Are you going back to the fortress with that viper in the nest?" Ridley's eyes blackened with anger. "He'd stick a knife in your ribs faster than a frog could catch a fly."

"I know not what to do. I am well enough to travel, and I have my horse still. I could go back. I miss Fergus terribly and wonder if he is all right or if Kadeg put him out when I did not return. What story Ardel told when he arrived is one thing that keeps me here. He may have told his father things that were untrue. One thing, if I wait long enough, Ardel himself could be gone and married. He is betrothed to Riwallon's niece, and they were to marry this spring. Still, I may not be welcome any longer if Ardel said certain things."

Ridley grunted, and his brows drew together as he concentrated.

What did Ridley know that could help? Edan wondered.

"Did you spend a quiet winter in the North?" Edan asked, breaking a long silence.

"Aye. I stayed as warm as a tick in a rug." He pinched his belly. "And you can see I had plenty to eat." He laughed. "I have not been on the road long. Few pots are gone from my wagon."

Had he made these pots over the winter? Ridley somehow did not seem to want to talk of such things. Or about where he stayed.

"Have you heard Duke William was crowned King in December?" Edan asked.

Ridley nodded. "Aye. Archbishop Stigand had to crown him."

"Why did the fool do that?"

Ridley snorted. "Do it or lose his head! Soon after, William left his army here under his regents and sailed back to Normandy. Only the god knows when he will return."

"Now would be the time for our soldiers to attack!" Edan burst in.

"Is Kadeg of the same mind?" Ridley looked hard at Edan.

"He is. Alliances have been made with Welsh petty kings and chieftains and maybe some others. I don't know the extent of his promises myself." Ardel's words concerning Edric crowded into Edan's mind.

"Do they plan to take up arms against William?" Ridley's eyes fastened on Edan's.

"They do, but I do not know when. Do you know of any men in the north who have the same mind?"

"They all fear the yoke of the Normans, but no one man has committed to the task of going against William."

While they talked, the wagon had drawn close to Merane's village. Ridley pulled to a halt. "Do you go back to the Dark Ones tonight?" he asked.

"Aye, I do. Are you stopping at this village for the night?"

"I should have one day's work here before I go on to Buxton. I shall camp outside the village here in the wood. Bide you with the Hill Men another night. Come to me tomorrow night. I will think on your problem and try to help you. Keep your eyes open for Normans." Ridley wagged his finger.

Edan jumped down from the wagon and lifted his hand in farewell. It grew late. He could wait no longer today for Merane, or he would be overtaken by owl-hoot time. All the way back to the cave his mind churned with thoughts of the fortress, Fergus, Merane, and what he should do.

Chapter Twenty-Two

30 April 1067

Up before cock-crow the next day, Edan descended on horseback through a wooded valley close to the track where he first met Merane. As if he had called her, she rode with her nurse through an overhang of budding oak and chestnut.

Edan stood motionless in a bed of fern, fearful she would vanish. *Had he conjured her from a dream that moment?* He could not move though his body seemed to walk to meet them. What was the matter with him? She saw him then, and a smile lit her face. In the mix of light and shadow of the moving boughs, she came closer. She wore no cloak and hood, a sweep of black hair loose over her shoulders.

"Merane, what do you here off the track?" At least he could speak.

"Exploring the grove, looking for flowers," she replied pertly, quieting Dove who tossed her head impatiently at being stopped.

"I thought you must soon be out riding again, despite your Latin lessons. Is Dove behaving herself?"

"When Father heard she ran away, he had the head groom ride her to re-teach her manners. She is much better now," Merane patted the mare's neck.

Odette sat stolid on the gray, mute, waiting.

"May I ride a way with you?"

Merane smiled. "We would enjoy your company, but this path is too narrow. Let us go back to the track."

Reaching the soft track, Merane turned away from the village to ride in the direction of Dove's runaway, Edan alongside. Odette rode behind, a sharp eye on the two.

Merane watched Edan with something in her expression that had not been there before. At last she spoke. "How goes the spring plant at the village where you stay?"

Edan's blood ran faster in his veins. *How should he reply to this?* In recent weeks he had been in no other village, but he knew how it must be at home…or was it home anymore…in Herstmonceux. The glimpse he had of her village, the fallow plow strips, no men in the fields. They should have been turned by now. *What was wrong?*

"They turn the plow strips for barley. The kale garth…" he began.

Her eyes widened. "It *is* time for that?" she broke in.

"Aye." He looked at her. Did she not know? Had she recently come to this place?

"We have had hunger and sickness among the villeins in our village." A kind of uncertainty filled her eyes. She opened her mouth as if to speak, then closed her lips and turned her head to the blackthorn along the track. She raised one hand to push the hair back from her brow.

She spoke to the trees, her gaze directed from him. "There are few who have the strength to do field work. I fear for this coming year's crops."

"How do the animals fare? Was there meat to last the winter?" Edan asked. *Villeins? Was that a word these northerners used instead of crofters?* He recalled more of the village scene as they talked. He could not remember any oxen or milch cows grazing in the garth. Something ailed her village.

"The oxen had to be butchered for food. And all the swine." She paused and looked down. "Father knows not what to do."

Edan stared hard. "There will be no spring crops without oxen to plow. No more pigs to farrow if all are killed. How will your village eat?"

He realized Merane's narrow face and slender form were thin. The horses were thin. Somehow Odette retained her squareness.

"Let's talk of happier things. Soon the trees will be green, flowers will bloom, the apple trees will be white," she said with determined spirit. Her chin came up. She looked at Edan and smiled, her good spirits back in evidence. "Is that your horse? You did not ride before but walked."

"This horse belongs to the place where I stay. How are your Latin and history lessons?"

"They go well. Mayhap I will see you out riding soon again?" Merane asked.

"Aye, I'm not sure…I mean…" He did not want to tell her that he did not know his plans. "I will try to ride this way soon."

Conversation stayed with trivial matters as he rode a league with them, then reluctantly turned and rode back to meet Ridley as he had arranged the day before, his mind full of Merane's face, his own stumbling words, and Merane's village.

The pedlar rested by his wagon in a clump of hawthorn, the horses unharnessed and tethered. His camp lay out of sound and sight of the village.

"Good day, Ridley. I pray you had good business yesterday."

Ridley raised an arm in welcome. "Aye, the place needed pots and had many dulled swords. I could have used you to turn my sharpening stone."

"I have not forgotten the way of it these past months," Edan said. "And neither have my calloused hands."

Ridley smiled. "Sit you down."

Edan dismounted stiffly, rubbing his thigh, and tied his horse. He squatted on one knee across from Ridley who munched a bannock cake.

Ridley tossed a cake to Edan. "Do you know the state of yonder village?" he began.

"I have heard there be sickness and hunger," Edan said slowly, holding the bannock without interest.

"Aye. The livestock has all been eaten as has the seed grain and all the foodstuffs laid away. It is on the edge of starvation." Ridley stopped and glared out from under his brows. "It is as we feared last autumn, the soldiering Normans know not the way of farmers and have destroyed the villages they occupy. A goodly number of villagers died over the winter."

Edan drew a sharp breath. He felt as if someone had kicked him in the stomach. "Normans?"

"You didn't know?" Ridley's brows shot up. "They crossed the

Severn close behind us last autumn and took villages northward until winter shut them in."

Edan's memory thrust out images. Merane, Odette, Jolie—French names. Villeins. Her father not knowing what to do for the village. The man wasn't the thane or a farmer but a Norman noble! *How could he have been such a clodpole!* She must have thought *him* a Norman, a follower of William—no, she should have known as soon as he opened his mouth, but then she spoke the Saxon dialect.

"What is it, lad?" Ridley asked. "You look as though you'd seen the ghost of your own father."

Edan stood there feeling foolish and not a little angry. Had she deliberately deceived him or had he just been too dull to realize the truth? "I met someone from this village, we talked in the Saxon tongue. I assumed…I mean I had no idea Normans took this village, except no animals were in the fields and no earth had been turned this spring." A strange expression, almost of disbelief, came over Ridley's face. Had the pedlar wondered about Edan's own loyalty to his Saxon roots?

As if he had come to a decision, Ridley's expression softened. "Sa,that is it then. I had forgotten you had not had the benefit of my gossip-mongering, and you've had more important things on your mind of late. Normans occupy all the area hereabouts over to the east coast and all of the south. They are on the move this spring after laying up for the winter."

In his mind Edan thanked the protection of the saints. He had been lucky not to have run into any of the Normans in his wanderings away from the Hill Men. What if a band of them rode out of this village and came along the road while he sat here with Ridley?

A vision of Merane, the spirited black eyes, the flow of ebony hair filled his mind. He had found a friend, but she was a Norman. His mind spat the name. His face flushed with anger. What a halfwit and fool he had been.

"Where is your mind, lad?" Ridley's voice cut the vision short.

"I'm sorry. I was so surprised by your words. Are the Normans headed further north or into Cymry?" He took a bite of bannock cake at last.

"Not yet." Ridley's mouth set in a grim line.

"Do they have the main army in London still?"

"Aye." Ridley paused. Carefully he began again. "In the North where I wintered, the chieftains and petty kings hosted and talked of a battle in spring. Did Kadeg talk of the same?"

"He did. He has allied with Riwallon and Bleddyn and more, but I do not know who exactly. I heard mention of Edric." Edan left it hang, hoping Ridley would carry it on. He took another bite of bannock cake.

"Ah, Edric the Wild. So he has decided to rise against the Normans and ally himself. Well, he can't defend Hereford alone, and he wouldn't mind fighting alongside the Devil himself, as long as the Normans can be ousted. Surely it will be soon. Those from the North will rise soon as well. I want to be clear of the battlefield and far south beforehand. And what of yourself?"

"I trained hard all fall and winter until the wound I told you of. I had planned to fight with Kadeg in the spring. Now, I don't know if I would be welcome if I return. And I may return too late."

"Those in Northumbria are waiting for word William is back from Normandy where he spent the winter. You have a little time."

"Do you think I should go back? Could I not come with you?" Edan looked into Ridley's eyes.

The pedlar stared back, but a veil dropped over his gaze. "Na, na, that would not be safe for you." Edan leaned forward. He screwed up his courage. "Ridley, do you have family in Northumbria or do you stay with a chieftain there?"

"Both." The brief answer only. He volunteered no more while staring steadily at Edan.

"Are your loyalties with Northumbria's chieftains then?"

"Aye."

"Then why do you go among the Normans with your wagon instead of fighting with your countrymen? We all fight for the same thing, to oust William." Edan held his breath for the reply.

"It is not as simple as that, lad. Where I must go is not safe with

Normans everywhere. They are no longer blinded by their success, but now their noses are tuned to rumors of revolt like a fox vixen to a mouse run."

Edan digested that as he exhaled softly. "I could deliver messages for you back to the north."

A flicker of movement around Ridley's lips. "Na, lad, go back to Kadeg. I have thoughts to share that never visited me until this morn." He paused to gather his reasons. "Your place is with your uncle, surrounded by the strength of his fighting men and his fortress. It is in my heart that Kadeg will look out for you."

Yesterday the pedlar seemed fearful for his safety at Kadeg's. Today he advised him to go back. Why the change of attitude? More sure than ever that Ridley indeed performed duties as a spy for the northern chieftains, Edan reluctantly nodded.

"If all goes well, I will pass this way again in the autumn. By then, mayhap the tides of power will flow in another direction." Ridley shrugged and got to his feet, the bell on his cap jingling. "We can but take what the god sends." He walked to the horses and began to hitch them. Edan jumped to his feet and helped.

"When you return to the fortress, do not tell Kadeg of your wound and how you got it. Do not force him to make choices. Instead suffer any teasing and tell Fergus and any friends you have made of what happened. The word will eventually reach Kadeg's ears, and it will not have come from your mouth," Ridley said, threading the reins back through the harness and up to the driver's seat of the wagon. "If Kadeg's son is still in the fortress and not married off, avoid his presence until he does leave or the whole fortress rides out to battle."

"Aye, that makes sense. Many thanks for the advice. May the god protect you on your journey."

"And you also, if you go to battle."

Ridley rolled off down the road, clanging his way south.

Edan stood and watched, more than physically alone. Ridley had given him more information today than at any other time. Trust between them had survived his absence and his ignorance that Merane's village had passed to Norman rule. His anger flared again with the thought of Merane, replaced by images of Fergus's face. He missed him terribly. What must Fergus think now that he had been gone so long?

Wind came up so that the forest roared like the sea as he made his way back to Llyd and the Hill Men. His horse snorted with alarm at the wind-driven noises, its ears flicked back and forth. It shied its way through a patch of waving fern and last year's swirling leaves. Somehow Edan stayed mounted.

By dusk the wind dropped, and the trees were still. Edan flung his mantle about him and went out of the cave after the evening meal. Outside the moon rose high, and there in the north, the Bear shone brilliant. His blood ran steady in his body. He felt light and free now that he had followed Ridley's advice and made the decision to go. He already looked forward to seeing Fergus. Sucking in great breaths of damp night air, he stood for a few moments outside the cave.

It was time to ask Llyd to set him on his way. When he re-entered the cave, the clan sat around the fire, each busy at some task, the children playing at throw stones. Edan and Llyd sat a little apart from them and talked.

"Can your people take me to a track that leads back to Kadeg's fortress at Caer Bannog?"

Llyd threw a gnawed bone over his shoulder, wiped his mouth, and met Edan's eyes straight on. "I do not ask your business, but tell me this much, did the wound you suffer happen there?"

"Na, somewhere else." How much should he tell? He remembered Ridley's words as he and Fergus sat about the wagon last autumn, 'Don't tell a man too much until you know which way the wind blows,' and kept it simple. "You have healed me. It is time to go."

"Is there somewhere else you can go?"

Surprised at this probing question after no questions, Edan said, "There is a man called Ridley, a pedlar. I do not know who he lodges with, but I journeyed with him to Gwynedd last Fall of the Leaf. He went on to the North for the winter and told me as we parted that I could call upon him if I ever had need."

Llyd nodded. "I know such a man. His wagon came from the north two days hence."

Edan's eyes widened. How did these people know of Ridley? These people knew of whence he came, Kadeg's fortress, the news of Normans, and now Ridley. How? Did they also know where he took his walks?

"Did you tell the pedlar, of your wound?"

The question startled him. "Aye, I did."

Llyd nodded in a knowing manner. "Many years he has come through our lands. If he said return to the fortress, then go. We know of each other's journeys and can get messages to each other if need be."

Was Llyd suggesting Ridley could be trusted further than his own relatives at the fortress? "Why did you ask me if I was wounded at the fortress and if there was someplace else I could go?"

Llyd sat silent for a while gathering his thoughts. "When a man saves another's life, he holds that life in his hands and becomes concerned for his welfare. You have become like one of us these past weeks, and I would warn you of danger if I see it in your future. Ridley has such knowledge as well. If he feels it is safe for you to return, I agree."

Edan wavered a moment longer before he said, "I go to the fortress tomorrow. You have healed me, and I would not be a burden. Thank you for the caution, and I will watch out for my safety. Always I will remember your kindness."

The next morning Edan set off with Llyd's son, Hob, seated double on his horse. They moved swiftly. They traveled two days before the boy announced they neared a track he could follow back to the fortress. He paused on a ridge and pointed to a valley below. Beyond a small meadow, a track split the forest.

"I leave you here," Hob said. He spat at the ground. "You will be safe. Already the word spreads among our people to watch over you."

Edan slipped the last coin from his scrip into Hob's brown, leathery hand. "If you ever need to trade for something, this may help. I shall be always grateful for your father's healing."

The boy nodded.

The way he showed Edan was easy to follow by the secret signs he told. The first one, an old shrine next to a dead, hollowed out tree. An arrow had been cut into the stone and obscured by shrubbery. A faint path led west to a stream where a small, moss-covered cairn marked safe crossing. Again the path led west over a forested ridge to a knob of stone. At its foot, another ancient shrine with its arrow, north this time. And so it went, until afternoon, Edan stood on the track he'd traveled with Ardel. Leaving the Hill People after being with families again left him melancholy. Uprooted yet again, he felt a sense of loss. He fed his horse from what the Hill Men had given him. He knew he was within a day of Kadeg's fortress. Would he find Ardel there when he returned? His stomach tightened. The hunger that gnawed his belly faded, despite his eagerness to be with Fergus again.

Chapter Twenty-Three

2 May 1067

During the day's ride since he bid farewell to Hob, Edan had decided on the story of his absence. As he neared his destination, a creeping chill settled in his stomach and spread outward, to overtake the rest of his body bit by bit to the ends of his fingers and toes. His horse lunged up the last steep, rock shelf to the spine of the ridge, returning his attention to the terrain.

To the northwest the black immensity of Cadair Idris dominated the horizon in the late afternoon. Blue-misted lesser mountains laddered upward to it. To the south across the barren upland, Kadeg's fortress bristled on its promontory at the entry to the heart of Gwyndd. Fingers of snow splayed into every crevice from the ridge to gorges below. Vegetation lay matted, only recently shed of its white cloak.

Sentries waited behind a rock formation ahead, Edan knew. He slowed his horse in anticipation. Moments later two armed soldiers appeared as if they sprang from the ground. His horse snorted and bolted to the side, stiff-legged.

"Steady, old man," Edan soothed.

"What word do you bring me?" shouted a soldier.

"It is a long road from Caer Bannog to the sea." Edan knew him and shouted, "Tyrnon is that you? Edan here."

The man did not reply immediately and said something to his rugged companion.

"Come ahead, Edan."

When he came abreast, Tyrnon said, "We never thought to set eyes on the likes of you again." His eyes bored into Edan's own. No judgment could be seen within them. Edan wondered again what the men of the fortress had been told.

"Nor was I sure I'd live to return to the fortress," Edan replied, raising his arm to them as he passed.

The stone walls ahead seemed to grow from the ground, taller and taller, as he approached. The gate stood open. Inside, he could see soldiers in the common at their daily exercises, the Turtle shouting orders. He never thought he would be glad to see Turtle, but at this moment he found comfort in familiar surroundings.

He heard a shout. A figure broke away from a group in front of the armorer's and ran toward him.

"Edan!" Owain stopped by Edan's knee and looked up. "By the magic of the Old Wizards! We thought you were dead. What happened to you?"

"I was lost and injured. When I recovered, I came back."

By then grooms, armorers and smiths crowded around, asking questions, but Turtle kept the soldiers at work. Someone ran to the hall to tell Kadeg. Anxious, Edan scanned the men for Ardel, but he was nowhere to be seen. He dismounted and a groom took his horse.

A mumble of voices came from inside as Kadeg appeared. He strode rapidly across the common to where Edan stood surrounded.

"Edan, lad, we took you for dead. Come into the hall and tell me what has happened." Kadeg's face did not show anger, or disgust, only surprise. Cerdic, his cheeks ruddier than usual, his black eyes sparking, followed, a broad smile upon his face.

Edan vividly aware that his future depended upon what he said next turned to follow Kadeg indoors.

"Well?" Kadeg said, striding along.

It seemed to Edan, Kadeg's face was nothing but eyes and behind the eyes the coming judgment. They burned into him, and he found himself caught and held by those eyes. He raised his chin, his mouth curved into a smile. He might as well put a brave face on what he was about to say.

"I rode at the boar Ardel speared, thinking to be near if the kill was not safely made. But my horse took fright when he smelled the blood and heard the squeal of the dying boar. He bolted and ran into the forest, bit clenched in his teeth. I could not stop him. He ran far, and we were in strange country. Suddenly a limb hit me, and I was knocked senseless. When I woke, my leg was injured."

The bright, piercing gaze remained upon Edan as they entered the hall and sat in chairs by the hearthfire. Cerdic hurried off to prepare a bath and clean clothes, chattering about food.

"Go on."

"I lay there and saw the horse close by, but I could not mount. I heard a stream run and dragged myself to it and drank. I don't remember more until I felt myself carried. A hunter of the Hill Men found me and took me to his clan's cave where their shaman healed me. They were very kind. It took me a long time to heal. They led me back to a place I recognized and set me on the path to the fortress." Every nerve on stretch, Edan waited for Kadeg's reaction.

Something flickered far back in Kadeg's eyes. Edan noticed the gray at his temple had grown more prominent these last months. A long silence stretched before he replied. "So, you had a dangerous time and survived it. I find your tale a stirring one. I did not know if you yet lived."

"Did Ardel and the others not tell you what happened when they returned without me?" Somehow he dared to ask. He wanted to know what Ardel had told his father.

"I would hear it from yourself, Edan." For a moment a hush fell over the conversation, then Kadeg broke it. "Ardel told of the boar frightening you."

So, Ardel had continued the lie he'd shouted for the benefit of the other hunters. Now Kadeg must choose the truth. Edan wanted to say, "If you do not believe me, see the wound," then drop his breeks and show the angry scar. Instead, he said, "If I were frightened and ran, I would be too ashamed to return, so perhaps Ardel misunderstood the way of it."

Kadeg looked at him a moment longer, then threw back his head and laughed deep in his throat. "By the dragon's forked tail, welcome back, Edan. In the days to come you will have opportunity to test your courage. Go now with Cerdic to clean the stink of the Hill Men from your person."

Words that Kadeg spoke the first night he had come to the fortress surged into Edan's mind. "Before I go, could I ask why Grandfather thought my father less than courageous?"

The mirth faded from Kadeg's face. "Selwyn wanted to scout the best place for an upcoming battle, study the enemy's past strategies. Father thought he stalled, afraid to join battle." Rubbing his chin contemplatively, he continued. "As for myself, I fought at his side in several skirmishes and never saw a lack of courage when battle enjoined. Mayhap Father wanted Selwyn to be more like himself, charging headlong into a fray, or thought no one was good enough for Rowena." He shrugged.

When Edan reached his old room, a steaming wooden tub stood waiting and next to it, Fergus. His freckled face broke into a grin. He clasped Edan tight around the shoulder.

"By the grace of the Old Ones, it is you come home again."

"And I wondered if I'd ever see this rockpile while I yet lived, not to mention your freckled face." Edan hugged Fergus to him, surprised to see he had grown as tall as his friend during his absence.

"Come on now, into the tub with you before all the heat is gone." Cerdic plucked his clothes away much as he had last autumn and held them away like filthy rags.

Before he knew it, Edan sat mother-naked in the tub like he had that first night in the fortress.

"This time you've brought beasties from the Hill Men back to us." Cerdic grimaced, clucked and scolded as he scrubbed. Something out of place or unclean caused him discomfort equal to a sharp stone in his boot.

When he came to the scar on Edan's thigh, Cerdic asked, "What manner of wound was this?"

Fergus looked sharp at Edan.

"I came off my horse. Somehow my leg must have whacked against something that pierced it. I don't remember much, until I woke up in the Hill Men's cave. The wound had gone bad, and I had a fever."

Cerdic shook his head still examining the scar. "Tch, tch, those little men do have healing skills or you...well, it's a good thing they found you. If I didn't know better, I'd say this looks more like a battle wound. You must have fallen into the sharpest pile of rocks in the land."

Fergus still stared at him. Edan gave a slight head shake when Cerdic bent to get more soap.

"I could soak here for the rest of the night, uhmm." He leaned back and slid down to let the water lap under his chin.

Cerdic leaned away and wagged his finger. "I must get down to the hall. There's clean clothes on your bed. Fergus will help you finish up. Don't be long. The meal is ready in the hall." With a grunt he heaved his round body up fussing with discarded clothing, tidying bath items and sprinkling fleabane over the floor before his exit.

Fergus rounded on Edan. "What really happened?"

"The four of us, Weirmund, Brand, Ardel and I, were hunting for boar. Ardel and I went ahead. The other two stayed behind in a thicket holding the horses laden with venison. The boar charged. Ardel's lance struck it in the shoulder, but it didn't go down. I threw mine and killed it. Ardel wanted to make sure it was dead and grabbed his mace to strike it in the head." Edan stopped, remembering his shock.

"And then?"

"After, he turned and came for me, saying I had spied on him a second time and snitched to Kadeg, but we both know it wasn't me told Kadeg. He got one blow in with the mace and gashed my leg. I whirled my horse and ran. He called out after me for the others to hear that I was afraid of the boar."

Fergus's face contorted in anger. "Aye, I heard the story Ardel told when he returned. I knew it wasn't so. That murderous son of a horse's arse! Now that I've seen the scar, I wonder if he'd have killed you if you hadn't run away."

"Where is Ardel? I looked for him when I came into the fortress."

"He came back from the hunt for maybe a fortnight before leaving again with a small band of soldiers. I heard nothing of where he went. He's been gone all these weeks."

Edan frowned. "Could he have gone to Edric?"

Fergus shrugged.

"Is Bryn still here?"

"Aye, the marriage is next month."

The bath water seemed suddenly cold. Bryn, his closest cousin, would be gone so soon. Edan clambered out, and dried, while Fergus slipped one of his clean tunics over him, the arms newly short at his wrists, and helped with breeks and boots. They hurried to the hall for the meal and the questions Edan knew he must continue to answer as he had for Owain, Kadeg and Cerdic. What must he tell Bryn? That story or the truth as he told Fergus?

On his way to Grandfather Gwion's that evening for stories, Edan came upon Bryn, already seated on a chair outside their grandfather's room with her chin propped between her fists. Maeve had sent word through Fergus that Bryn wished to meet him here. He was very near before she saw him at all, his shadow blending into the darkness of the corridor. Her gaze flicked back to the stones at her feet.

His mouth was open to tell her what had happened before they met with the old grandfather, then suddenly, he could not. He didn't know why. Mayhap because Ardel was her brother after all. Instead he knelt down next to her.

At last Bryn looked sideways at Edan. "I thought of many ways to tell Father about Ardel, but giving myself as the source was the only way. I don't know how Ardel thought it was you told him," she said as though they had been talking of Ardel and Ceridwen all the while. She seemed to know his thoughts.

She knew that Ardel had acted against him without his telling her. Taking a deep breath, Edan burst out with what he had been about to say when he first saw her seated there. "You placed no blame when you told your father. Ardel is the one who decided to blame. Since he despises me, his first thought was of me. You must not feel guilty.

I am back, and he is away. Now you will soon be away, too. Let us enjoy the time we have."

Bryn didn't move, only some indescribable feeling flickered in her eyes. "Maeve said Fergus saw a great wound on your leg. That it was Ardel who gave it to you."

"Ardel was misguided. It is no one's fault. Please, don't blame yourself." He just knew it had been Fergus who spread the word. Ridley had been right; his friends would spread the word. He would not have to tell on Ardel. Eventually, word would reach Kadeg's ear.

"I want to tell Father that Ardel aimed to do you great harm. He should know."

"Please do not. Then he must make a choice I do not want to force on him. He has been very kind to me. It is best to leave things as they are."

Bryn stared at him. "But Ardel might do you greater harm," she protested, her eyes wide with alarm.

Edan shook his head. "He might either way."

As Bryn sat watching him in surprise, he got to his feet. "We will go see Grandfather now." Without another word, he took her by the hand and lifted her to her feet, crossed the hall and rapped on the old man's door. With a flicker of a smile, Bryn squeezed the hand that held hers.

15 May 1067

In the days that followed Edan resumed wargames. Sprigs of green showed in the brown mat upon the hillsides, and the wild geese flew north. Over the winter he had gained new-found strength and agility. Military maneuvers came more easily to him. Too soon the day came for Bryn to ride out to her groom.

Kadeg and Edan, and this time, Fergus, with Kadeg's band of housecarls accompanied Bryn and her maid, Maeve, and several horses laden with goods, including casks of Bride Ale, to Bleddyn's hall. The younger sisters and little Gareth were left behind.

Edan stared out at the hummocked crests of ridge, the receding hills, and the overpowering bulk of Cadair Idris. He noticed every cleft, every clump of mossy campion leaves before lifting his gaze again to the hugeness and emptiness of the high country. His thoughts turned to Merane. The smile, the high bridged nose, the flowing black hair, her slender form. Had she grown thinner with food too scarce? Angrily, he thrust away her image and any thoughts of her. After all, she was a Norman.

On the evening of the fourth day, they came down to a gray lake-shore in the twilight to the sound of little wavelets lapping in.

On the shore rose a great hall full of firelight and torchlight, men and hounds and a roar of voices. Grooms appeared to take the horses of their little band.

Edan heard the voices going to and fro. Then a tall, fair woman came forth. "Where is Bryn? I am Edlyn, mother of the groom. Give her to me to make ready for the wedding."

Other women followed and crowded around her exclaiming and enveloped Bryn and Maeve. The mass of them flowed back into the hall amid excited laughter.

The men came close behind. Once inside, Edan saw a long firelit hall. The rooftree rose into the dark overhead beyond the drifting smoke. Everywhere men crowded the benches, with their legs outstretched, some hounds curled up here and there, while others stood, tongues lolling, to greet the newcomers. He smelled the sweet fresh fragrance of the fern deep floor and the odor of roasted meat. He hoped some remained.

At last the dark and hairy Bleddyn was visible in a chair by the hearth, a harper across from him strumming to the gathered guests. He motioned Kadeg and Edan forward, the soldier escort given places among the other men on the benches. Food was brought and space made for them nearer the hearth. Kadeg spoke with Bleddyn. Curious, Edan and Fergus searched faces for a young man who looked like Bleddyn, a young man who would be his son and groom to Bryn. Fergus joked about how hairy he would be. Edan wanted to like him and be happy for Bryn. Two or three dark young men lounged on the benches nearby. The bridegroom could be any of them. Edan gave up the guessing game, and side by side with Fergus attacked the roast hare which had been brought to the table. Women moved throughout the hall filling the ale horns. Determined to enjoy himself, he reached for another piece of roast hare when a clamor arose outside.

Staring at the entrance, he saw a giant of a man, blond and bareheaded, come striding into the hall, sword clanking, followed by a sizeable number of his housecarls, including Ardel. Edan's throat tightened, and he laid the roast hare, uneaten, back on the trencher. *Would he even be safe here among the wedding party?*

Abruptly his attention turned to the charismatic man who had caught the interest of the hall. Was this man with such presence, Edric the Wild? Why was he attending Bryn's wedding?

Fergus's hot breath filled his left ear. "The young stallion dares to strut at his sister's wedding."

Ardel's glance fell on his Father. Kadeg nodded a greeting. A look of shock came over Ardel's face as his gaze slid sideways to take in Edan, a look that transformed to menace before he gained control of it and he set about greeting his host. A faint sense of relief seeped through Edan when Ardel turned away. Given the occasion, surely Ardel would not dare try any further assault on him. Memories of their last meeting crowded in. Anxiety overtook the brief sense of relief. The wedding party would only last a few days. The rest of his life stretched before him. Who knew when Ardel would enter into it on intimate terms again?

Chapter Twenty-Four

18 May 1067

Bleddyn's hall bulged under the press of men. With the smoky torchlight, the food and ale, talk and laughter, the place grew uncomfortably warm.

Edan sat beside Kadeg, his back straight, the excitement of the occasion filling him. Slightly dizzy from the closeness of the room, he eyed the throng, noting the men who were there. He and Fergus judged by their looks and with whom they sat, whether they were friends of the Saxon cause to oust King William. No one looked hostile or reluctant to be there, but to whom did their allegiance lay—Bleddyn, Kadeg, Riwallon, who also had just arrived, Edric the Wild, or the Saxon cause in general? He heard snatches of the Cymrian tongue and Anglo-Saxon dialect.

A movement near the front caught Edan's attention. Edric stood up and took a spot next to Bleddyn. The boys watched the man carefully as he pounded a table to gain attention and began to speak.

"My lords, you all know why we are met here. Kadeg's lovely daughter is to be married during this time of feasting, but also we meet to discuss reports of King William's forces. You have seen and heard of the Norman host that occupies the land. They are as fly eggs in a dung hill."

A rising growl of murmurs threatened to drown his words. He flung up a hand to quell it. "Friends, hear me out. You know much of the island lies under Norman yoke. We must decide how to stand forth to meet our foes in arms and perhaps die as did our fellow Saxons at Hastings after which our women and babes will be thralled or slain. Or do we make terms with this Red Norman King?"

A fierce clamor of denial rang through the hall.

"The power of our enemies which has been massing must be broken and driven back before their reinforcements arrive. But more important than this, we can see what unity can do and what we might suffer with lack of it. Singly, what hope would we have? But with one leader and one plan, we can thrust our lances into the heart of King William's army. We can emerge as a new kingdom with its own laws, its own gods. With the right King, I believe this will come about. This island may again have an English King and a Cymrian King, along with its Scottish King."

Edan sensed rather than saw Kadeg stiffen next to him. Was it the talk of the "right King?" Or a separate Cymrian King? When Edric finished, a heavy silence lay over the hall. Looking about the room to see the effect of these words upon the listeners, Edan saw Riwallon watching with a strange kind of eagerness upon his face. Unease set Edan's fingers drumming atop one knee. How would these kingships affect Kadeg and the alliance?

After a draught of ale, Edric began to speak again. The men remained solemn and intent. He told of dead King Harold's teenage sons by his Danish wife who fled to Ireland for sanctuary and other alliances about which Edan had heard nothing until now. News that Kadeg, and mayhap some others, had not been privy to unless they had bought news from the Hill Men as he knew Edric had done. Edan did not know what to think. Fergus looked at him with raised brows and an expression of surprise. He watched the reactions of the other men as they listened.

"...they think they have our country conquered with the putting up of their fine stone-built castles and the dungeons they be building below ground. Plump as fall pigs on acorns, they sit not worrying that their larders are empty and no one plants the fallow fields for the next winter. Every fool knows they will be in need of food soon and will be raiding to get it. We know the people are barely alive as it is. A raid on food would finish them. Their line of defense rests in Herefordshire. That is where we will fight them. Their main mass of troops remains in London. Only regents remain in charge, while William tends to his French affairs."

Ridley had mentioned Herefordshire. He had already known of the place of the coming battle. How? The Hillmen? Looking about, he saw the light of battle gleam in men's eyes. They seemed willing to follow this man. For the first time since last October, hope sprouted in angry men. This seemed different than the vengeful feeling he witnessed in Kadeg's hall.

"For one, I do not want to have to speak with honey-smeared tongue to Norman conquerors. Let us raid the frontier of the Normans and see how much we can take back before the regents bring troops against us."

Bleddyn looked broodingly at the chieftains and warriors who filled his hall. In the silence that followed Edric's words, he stroked his beard for a time. He got to his feet and spoke to the throng. "That which we lack in numbers must be made up in guile. The quick raid, the retreat. Even when the regents arrive with more troops, as they surely will, we can pare their numbers and have a place to fall back to while they are stretched thin on their border. This is a time for cool heads."

One of the chieftains rose from the crowd. "We have had hard dealings before. Let us seek aid from Scotland."

"Scotland is torn with troubles and has no aid to give." Bleddyn's voice went harsh.

Edan had not seen Bleddyn take leadership before. Did all these princes plot to be the next Cymrian King? Who did they have in mind to replace King William if he could be defeated? He glanced sidways at Kadeg, who sat silent, watchful. Did Kadeg have aspirations, too? Edan could not wait to discuss all this with Fergus when they were alone.

The deception in Bleddyn's plan appealed strongly to the whole of the assembly. They began hot and urgent counsels among themselves as to how this strategy would begin and how it would be played out.

20 May 1067

In the days that followed, feasting and games preceded the day when Bleddyn's son, Phelan, would take Bryn from her father. The young man was not the dark soul Edan had seen next the hairy Bleddyn that first night but a well-made, brown-haired lad who resembled his mother. Edan decided Phelan was a fair match for his cousin after all, and he seemed pleasant enough during the games when he competed against the other young men.

One afternoon Bryn pointed out Ardel's betrothed to Edan, a brown-haired girl with light gray eyes tinted amber. She appeared about Bryn's age. As Edan watched her over the wedding feast days, she showed signs of willfulness. Mayhap Ardel would meet his match in days to come.

When the day of the wedding arrived, Bryn appeared in a pale silken gown with a heavy silver-gilt bridal crown upon her head, her hair cascading in a molten gleam down her back, and the women brought her out to Phelan and his groomsmen in the hall. Bleddyn set her hand and Phelan's together. The Christian priest of Bleddyn's chapel spoke the marriage words. Edan watched Bryn's face, flushed and smiling during the proceedings, seemingly happy at Kadeg's choice of her groom. He determined to be happy for her and dismiss the loneliness that rose up from his belly.

The rest of the day was spent listening to harpers and feasting. The younger warriors wrestled, raced and competed at war games and returned to the tables for more fruits, venison, silver char, boiled vegetables, and platters of bannock cakes and cheeses. Plum tarts and puddings tempted the sweet tooth. Edan and Fergus abandoned themselves to the gaiety and enjoyed the time away from the fortress.

When the day waned and darkness fell, the great wedding host sat in Bleddyn's hall or gathered about fires that burned before it. The women went to and fro between the hall and the fires refilling the horns with the stronger than usual traditional Bride Ale that Bryn had brewed and brought along.

Presently, someone called for the harper to play a certain song. He sang of another wedding as his hand rhythmically strummed the harp strings. The tune ached with the nostalgia of happy times and laid a spell of stillness over the revelers. The light of the flames flickered on their faces from the fire's extended tawny reach.

As the last notes died away, the women busied themselves with the ale jars once more.

3 June 1067

This late afternoon, not a breath of air moved. Edan sprawled atop a ridge next Owain who had arrived two weeks ago for the wedding with a band of men from Caernarvon. Since the wedding, all the clans' warriors had remained, except Edric's, and more had arrived, including men from Bala with Alun, the fosterlings Elfin and Lleu with their fathers from Powys, waiting for the battle everyone knew came soon. The lake below shimmered in the heat, and Edan's tunic stuck to him between the shoulders. Far to the north, an ominous tumble of dark clouds edged in pink and purple massed along the shoulders of the hills.

"A storm comes," Owain said, twisting a blade of grass around his thumb.

Edan rested his chin in his cupped hands, elbows deep in the fell grass and looked at the lake below swimming in the haze. The stillness of everything around, no lark song, no call of plover told of the coming weather. He looked overhead to see if a hawk's shadow had quieted the smaller birds. None in sight.

"That is not all. A different storm brews tomorrow," he replied, sure it was somehow meant that it should be so; the physical stormburst would herald the imminent battle. The whole world changed. Bryn married. Ardel would soon. Now a battle after which life would change for better or for worse.

"Have you ever seen a man slain in battle?" Owain asked.

Edan replied slowly. "Aye, too many. For so long I have wanted to slay Normans after my Father died. Now that the time is upon me, the blazing anger is gone."

Owain nodded. "I, too, feel no anger. Sadness, I guess because of all that is lost when battles occur."

Clouds crept over the last afternoon light. The sunset took on an angry pallor, lower cloud edges ragged gray with slashes of rain floating earthward. A breath of air stirred the grasses, and the low rumble of thunder echoed across the ridges.

"Listen to the sound of hammer on anvil, beating sword edges for battle," Edan said.

Owain did not reply but nodded slowly.

A few drops of moisture pelted onto their sweat-streaked faces and sent them scurrying off the height to the shelter of the hall.

The storm broke soon after with a crashing, tree-rending chaos that flung itself against the earth until the whole world seemed to be shaken by the rumble of thunder and the fork of lightning. By midnight, the only sound was the steady hiss of rain upon the thatch above their heads. Edan lay awake, too restless to sleep, thinking of the day to come.

4 June 1067

Somewhere out in the near dawn an owl called. With a little shiver, Edan rose up with the rest and donned his chainmail shirt, gathered his weaponry. He would serve as Kadeg's lance bearer in this first battle of his life.

Word came yesterday that the Normans were on the move from their frontier, marching north from London, still on the English side of the border. A regent's troop had arrived to shore up the defenses after the Welsh princes' raids over the border the past two weeks, where a few villages had been retaken. Those raids which were intended to soften the target mayhap instead caused the call up of reinforcements? Edan saw men exchange nervous glances. Had Edric waited too long? The Norman troop progress slowed with the need to post archers along their backside to guard their supply lines. With every mile they traveled, Bleddyn's and Edric's small war parties skirmished about them, harassing their flanks. Yesterday they put up defenses in Hereford to await the coming battle.

While he ate a bannock cake which grated dry as sawdust in his throat, Edan relived the one raid he participated in with Bleddyn's men. The small band of twenty had found a place near a river to secret themselves until Normans came to ford the river. Edan's breath had caught when he saw such numbers of fortified Normans in one place. His head swirled with flashbacks of that first battle—the sounds, smells and sights. His body trembled. Hopefully, no one had time to focus on fellow warriors.

Bleddyn had waited until a good number of Normans were in the water, into the deepest part before he gave the word. Twenty men let fly a volley to those in the water. As soon as one volley flew toward its quarry, arrows were nocked with a second volley. The bow string creased Edan's cheek as he drew the fletchings of the arrow to his lips. His arm trembled as he held the bow taut and loosed. Breathless with shock, he saw his target go down with the second shot, scream as he clutched his chest. He had never before killed a man and his stomach heaved. This was not the same as hitting one of the Turtle's targets. For a moment he thought he might vomit, but Bleddyn called for another volley.

Normans grunted and fell. The river became a splashing, churning chaos as some tried to continue across, while others retreated into their own ranks. While confusion reigned in the Norman ranks, Bleddyn waved one arm. All twenty raiders retreated, mounted, and galloped away at top speed. Edan looked over his shoulder to see if they were pursued, but no one had burst from the Norman ranks. The raiders made for the nearest track where their hoofprints mingled with hundreds of others. Only when they were well away did Edan's breathing slow.

Another image filled his mind. Edric leaning against the door of the hall last night, drenched and weary, come home from a raid in the midst of the storm. "We diminished their ranks and made them nervous before we left," he said. "They are a great host still, but the ravens will have good feeding from the Severn to Hereford."

As a member of Edric's raiding party, Ardel was absent from Bleddyn's hall until last night as well. The brief time he spent in the hall, he ignored Edan. Bryn's new husband, Phelan, stayed behind to be with his bride, otherwise he would have gone with the raiders.

When all had been readied for battle, Edan saw a runner arrive. He brought word that the Normans broke camp. Many months had passed since the War Hosts last met at Hastings. Now a feeling of excitement filled the warriors. The clatter of arms, the jink of mail, the stamping of horses filled the air. Ardel took up the Red Dragon pennon and rode between Edric and Bleddyn. Riwallon and Kadeg fell in behind, all followed by their housecarls. Edan nudged Dinas in at Kadeg's flank with his bundle of lances. His sword hung ready in its sheath at his side. He turned to give Fergus one last look. Fergus raised his fist, his face a grim mask. Edan knew he wanted to come, but Kadeg had not allowed it since Fergus had no formal arms training.

Owain rode forward to Edan. "God be with you, Edan."

"And with you, Owain." Solemn, Edan turned forward to follow Kadeg, their War Host bunching in behind. He tried not to think thoughts that might jinx his friend. Soon Owain disappeared into the rear guard of horses and men.

Somewhere a lark sang into the misty early morning. Like any other morning. Didn't it know today was different? A rain-scented breeze ushered them southward toward their Norman foe. Edan's stomach churned around the bannock he had eaten. The long-awaited battle crowded upon him.

In late morning a distant shouting came on the wind. They topped a rise to see the Norman army in full view, advancing across an open field, a swarm of deadly hornets ready to sting with arrows and lances. The distant thunder of many hooves and marching feet and the challenge of trumpets swelled as the War Hosts drew nearer each other. Those in the rear of each army slipped and slid in the clinging mire churned by those who had gone before. A line of archers skirmished before the advance lancers, knelt to shoot, ran and reformed—so like the tactics at Hastings.

The close-massed ranks of the main hosts narrowed the distance. Pale sun struck glints on helmet and lance of the advancing enemy. Edan's throat tightened. He could barely swallow. With one hand he checked Swine-eater, his sword, which hung at his waist. It was loose in its scabbard, easily drawn. His grip on the lances tightened until his knuckles shone white, yet his hands shook.

Looking ahead, he saw a tall figure on a gray stallion at the head of the Norman warriors. He remembered that figure on that horse helping Duke William remount in that other battle, helping him remove his helm to prove to his men he still lived.

Riwallon, Kadeg and the other leaders halted and dismounted as by custom, while some men remained to hold the horses as their riders marched forward to battle. Edan found his insides knotted so tightly he nearly fell when he dismounted. He handed Dinas to a holder and joined the others sworn to protect Kadeg's life.

Edan's legs trembled as he made long strides to keep up with Kadeg and his loyal housecarls, lances clattering in his clasp. For the first few steps, he could not feel his legs working. Somehow the warriors were so exposed without the horses. Around him came the clink of armor and the thud of feet. At first, there was something other-worldly in the noise, then men found their voices, shouts blended as they began to run forward and became a wild bellow. In the running their fury grew. An enormous rush of energy swept through Edan and pushed him forward. He had seen the advantage the Normans had while mounted.

"Do not forget what you've been taught," Kadeg's voice came at his elbow as they approached engagement.

The roar of battle swept through the ranks when Norman and West Country and Saxon warriors came together, the shout and the weapon-ring, the thunder of the Norman horses' hooves. A great tide of men and horses spilled into Edan's vision accompanied by colorful flames of pennons streaming over.

Misted sunrays glinted from raised axe-head and helm. From the corner of his eye Edan saw the Norman gray stallion plunge forward, striking out with its hooves. The shouts became screams, a deafening roar of sound. Warriors jostled him. Edan tried to concentrate on keeping a lance ready for Kadeg while his eyes darted in all directions that he not be cut down.

A wild outcry from the rear of the Normans signaled an attack from their rear, which threw them into temporary confusion. That would be Bleddyn's and Edric's bands of men on horseback. Still, the gray rider's housecarls spurred their horses at the mass of West-country men, tearing great holes in their ranks. Edan saw the ranks around him fall back and regroup, in a constant ebb and flow.

On and on, the hails of arrows, the flails of axes and lance thrusts continued. Victory or defeat hung in the balance. All around Edan now, a nightmare of yells, blood smeared faces, close sword-play and back stabbing dirks, trampling hooves, tossing manes, and horses' screams. A mind-numbing chaos that threatened to crush not just the body but all thought.

Somewhere close, another horse reared and grunted as Riwallon's men with dirks ran low among the horses' legs and stabbed upward into their vulnerable bellies. Now the death screams of stricken horses, the Norman warriors who trampled the wounded and hacked at their enemy panicked Edan. He suffocated in the close quarters and looked desperately from one side to the other.

A Norman horse fell against Kadeg, but he staggered clear. A gray stallion filled Edan's vision, rearing on its hind legs, front hooves thrashing. It scattered warriors and clipped Kadeg's shoulder. His weapon flew from his hand. Beneath the helm of the gray's rider, Edan saw the fierce amber eyes, a contorted face. He steeled himself and ran forward with a new lance for Kadeg only to see another Norman warrior head straight at him. Kadeg's housecarls ringed around, leaving Edan to confront the warrior. Dropping the lances at his feet, he drew Swine-eater. The point of Edan's sword sliced up at the man's chin, splitting a gash in his nose. The man howled in anguish, blood gushing from his face. Edan yanked his sword back, stunned that he had inflicted this wound. Another warrior came at him, shield-smacked him and sliced at his head. He ducked and whirled to parry the attack. He warmed to the work but kept the lances close to his feet. When he had a break, he grabbed the lances and closed the distance between himself and Kadeg.

The fire of battle kindled in Edan. He no longer moved in tentative fashion. His sword seemed to flash in his hand at Kadeg's side.

Strength flowed through his sword arm. Vividly aware of Kadeg's shoulder against his, they fought off that warrior and another. Then the housecarls closed ranks around them once more. *Was that how it would have been in that other battle if he had fought at his father's side? No. Then, he had no skills and strength.*

Slowly, the main body of Cymrians and allies recruited by Edric was forced back by the Norman cavalry and sheer numbers of Norman warriors. Back and back, keen blades blunted, until they reached the horseholders. Edan's arms were limp ropes, and his legs only just supported him. The men of Cymru's arms cramped and turned to slow-motion. Too many of their original number had gone down. The battle line had been reduced to a wavering line of barley stalks. They could only mount their horses and leave the field in bewildered retreat.

When Edan looked at the carnage around him, it took his breath away. The horrors and rising stench turned his stomach. He leaned forward by Dinas's shoulder and lost his breakfast.

The sun backlit the clouded sky, turning it to gray-red glowing coals. Behind them, the Normans already stripped the dead. Edan heard the cries as they killed the deserted wounded. The shock and numbness he experienced after Hastings returned. Groups of Edric's War Host commandeered some of the horses for a few fallen warriors removed in time to be taken away.

The screams, the tumult that seemed to pierce the heavens still rang in Edan's ears as he rode blindly behind Kadeg and the tattered remnants of a War Host that had ridden out proudly so short a time ago. At last he thought to look at who rode around him. Riwallon, Kadeg, and a few of each clan's men and himself followed. What of Owain? How many of their number had been lost this day? Would it have made a difference if some of the men of the northern kingdoms had joined them?

His first true battle behind him, a swelling sickness returned to Edan's gut when he saw how few were left.

Chapter Twenty-Five

4 June 1067

Amid the buzz of flies, Edan, Kadeg and the others, who scoured the edge of the battlefield for their own, watched Owain's father lead the horse closer still. Someone hung from the saddle. Edan's breath caught. In the gloom of late afternoon, he could see blood on Owain's long, foxlike nose where it had run down from a chest wound. His coarse brown hair hung straight from his head giving him an astonished look. Edan saw the bloody hand, the dark-crusted sword.

One of the men stopped the father's progress, touched Owain's neck for a heartbeat. When Edan saw the man shake his head, the very air went out of him. Arriving next to Kadeg, Owain's father lifted his son down as though he had merely fallen and needed comfort. He clasped the body to his chest, sobbing into the boy's back. Kadeg put a hand on the man's shoulder.

Edan could no longer watch. He had gone through fear and come out the other side into a place where it was bleak and cold. Voices buzzed around him. His whole world drained away from him. He walked toward Owain and touched his cold hand in farewell, the hand that still held his sword.

They lifted him again over the horse for his father to take away. The voices faded as Edan, turning, slogged through the mud, blurred eyes fixed on a distant point where some still held horses.

The big battle to free the island and keep the Normans out of Cymru had failed. He understood for the first time what that meant. England would never throw off the Norman yoke.

At length they returned to Bleddyn's hall. All through the night torches burned, to light the tending of wounded by the field surgeon and Bleddyn's wife, Edlyn, and her women. From the shadows came soft sobs of women who had lost their men. Edan saw Bryn move about with the other women, her lips set in a grim line. The moans of the wounded rended Edan's heart.

Wind rose sometime in the night making the torch flames flutter. Rain came again as it had the previous night but not in such gusty chaos. A fine rain whispered sadly at the membrane of the windows and onto the roof thatch. All through the night battered warriors kept watch with drawn swords.

5 June 1067

In the morning when the torches guttered, the dead were laid in the burying place behind the hall. The silence of the fells gathered them in. Rain-mist continued to fall, silvering hair and cloaks, while Bleddyn's priest recited Christian prayers over the heathery sods laid back over the new inhabitants of the glen. The harper strummed the lament for the fallen.

The wild, sad cadences set Edan's tears rolling. He could not stop the remembrances of Owain, showing him the fortress the first night, telling him all the names of the men, the concern over Dinas' injury, the talk of Roman Christmas customs, all the days practicing together at arms. The boy's good-natured camaraderie and thoughtfulness of others was gone forever. And for what? The loss of Owain, piled onto the losses of his own father, family and home made his sadness close to unbearable.

Soon stones were mounded over the graves and crosses erected at the graveheads. He stood long with bowed head before he turned away, the last to leave. Drained and numbed, he could scarce put one foot before the other.

6 June 1067

A day later Edan sat in a clump of birch overlooking the lake. Since no Normans had trailed them from the battlefield, the various leaders made plans to return to their own halls.

Word came that Edric's band had been pinned on the other side of the Norman forces who marched back to Winchester after their victory and that he fled back into Cymru, Ardel with him. Kadeg would not stay here any longer.

Edan mulled his choices. Return to the fortress with Kadeg, a home with Bryn and Owain gone and mayhap Ardel with a new bride before the month was out. The bloodlust for battle gone, his mind emptied. Where had the anger gone? Fostering was finished.

His face turned toward the lake. Watching gulls wheel in, he did not hear footsteps approach over the grass.

"Are you going home with Father?"

Startled, he jerked around to face Bryn. She sat down beside him, pulling her knees up and clasping her arms around them. She pulled one arm away to draw something from a pouch and extended a bannock cake to him.

He took it. After a moment he replied, "So much has happened so fast—Owain and all the rest, losing the battle, the wounded and dead. Today, here we sit, eating, watching gulls, dreading tomorrow." He broke off a small piece of cake and absently chewed it.

"Men are still hungry and bannocks are still plentiful. Many of the wounded will recover."

"Somehow it doesn't seem right for everything to go on just as it was," Edan said angrily.

Bryn smiled a tight smile. "Nothing will ever be quite the same, I know." She looked out over the lake as puffy white clouds gathered. She watched people moving around the hall. "The new tomorrow will be an adventure, just like all the past days have been."

Edan changed the subject. "I like Phelan. He seems honest and kind. Are you happy?"

"Yes, I am lucky to have been matched with Phelan. I have good company here among the women. I only hope all this warring will soon be over so life gets back to normal. So men can raise grain and hay, shear sheep. Women can grow herbs and gardens, and watch children play."

They sat for awhile in silence, while the day faded. A gull cried out from the lake.

"I came to tell you that I am sorry Owain is gone. He was loyal and good. And that I found out about Ceridwen."

Edan looked at her, eyes questioning.

"She came from Powys and is back there now. Ardel met her last year as I suspected. They planned to meet at Edric's because they fancied each other. It was a convenient meeting for Ardel as Edric had allied with Father, Bleddyn and Riwallon. Ardel could go there as emissary from Father. However, Father had no idea such a girl dwelt in his own fortress and grew furious when I told him, but decided to let Ardel end their relationship as his marriage draws near. I had no idea Ardel would try to injure you, thinking you snitched to father."

The guilt-ridden look on her face caused Edan to put up one hand to stop her apology. "As I told you before, don't blame yourself. Ardel made his own choice…and I survived. What I don't understand is how the girl, Ceridwen, disappeared all those months and no one wondered where she was. Was she not a spy?"

"I heard nothing about spying. It must have been as simple as she liked Ardel." She grimaced, sheepish over her fears. "She and a cousin plotted the whole thing, telling her family she wanted to visit a cousin in Edric's household. He had no knowledge of it. Therefore, everyone except the cousin thought she had a lengthy visit in Edric's household."

"What a flibbertigibbet! She nearly caused much trouble with people suspecting her of breaking alliances. Your suspicions of the trouble she could cause were true even if her motives were different."

"She got into trouble when Edric caught her out. Or I would not have known what happened. The women here knew she got caught and sent home in disgrace." A look of satisfaction took over Bryn's face. "Served her right."

Edan grinned for the first time in days. "Thank you for telling me that. I'm sure her father will marry her off soon, before she gets into more mischief."

"Another thing. I talked to Ardel myself after the wedding. I wanted to know why he injured you, and I promised not to tell Father. He seemed shocked I knew. I assured him I had not learned of it from you but from others. He was reluctant to talk of it, but finally admitted he was jealous of you, a Saxon, in the home of a Cymrian and his father treating you like a son. Especially after hearing grandfather rail against your father and Saxons in general all his life. Then when he thought you told on him, he lost all reason.

"I admitted I had been the one told Father and I should have told him earlier. It might have prevented him attacking you. He understands now. His anger has faded."

"Thank you for doing that, Bryn. That talk must have been hard."

She shrugged. "It had to be done." She rose from the grass, brushing away bits of grass blades. "I must go help the women with the wounded. A little fresh air has helped. Whatever you decide, to go with Father or go on your own, godspeed. Try to send word to me of what you do."

For a moment he didn't speak. Bryn suffered, too. Why had he never thought of that? His emotions held him. He looked Bryn in the eyes. "I was angry when Father died, when the Normans came. After all the battles and defeats that anger has no place to go. It is useless. This last battle…I thought…well, I have to find another way to make a difference."

"When you find it, you will know," Bryn murmured. She raised one arm in farewell and walked through the birches, descended the hill. Edan watched her until she reached the hall. With a sigh he lay back, hands folded beneath his head and stared at the wind-driven shapes of the clouds scudding out of the north.

The air grew cool enough to drive Edan from the hill before the shadows began. He sought out Fergus, where he watched the smith at work before his forge. Fergus glanced up at Edan's approach.

"Are you ready to leave this place tomorrow?" Edan asked.

Fergus looked startled, then seemed to realize it was time. "Aye, but go where? Back to the fortress?"

"Na, my fostering is over. Like I said last autumn, when the training is past, we will leave."

"I can not think Herstmonceux could be home any longer. It would be dangerous for you there, nor would it ever be the same for me."

"We should start anew then?" He felt tears rise at Fergus's offer to never go home again to see his parents, instead staying by his side. He blinked them back.

"Aye, we should."

"All I want now is life somewhere without war."

"Aye, me too, but where?"

"Let us ride out from here to the north, to villages where we might still find life without war."

Fergus nodded, his brown cowlick bobbing. "Aye, onward together." He put up a hand which Edan clasped with one of his own.

7 June 1067

Kadeg put food into a pouch tied onto his saddle. His men all around readied their mounts. Edan tied his supplies onto Dinas.

The night before, Kadeg had listened without questioning, while Edan explained his desire to channel his anger into something worthwhile. Kadeg did not try to persuade Edan from his plan.

"Is there anything I can do to help you?" Kadeg had said at last.

"Can I borrow Dinas?"

"Aye. He is yours in loyalty regardless. If you need sanctuary or decide to return to fortress life, you will always be welcome. Bryn thinks highly of you. I commend your courage in battle as you fought by my side. Don't forget Ardel's wedding feast next month. Godspeed in your endeavor."

Edan couldn't seem to get enough air. He had been prepared to argue his case. Kadeg had praised him for his courage, a worry that had hung over his head since Gwion had suggested his father Selwyn lacked courage. Kadeg's words were no lickspittle tribute. Edan knew Father had not lacked courage, and now he was truly his father's son. "I thank you," he said at last. "If the Normans come into Cymru, I will hear of it and come fight by your side." He owed Kadeg that.

Kadeg intensified his gaze over Edan's long pause, then acknowledged with a nod.

The morning sun warm on Edan's shoulders, they all mounted.

He turned Dinas north followed by Fergus, while Kadeg and his men rode west.

The woods were silent except for the shriek of a curlew and the thud of their horses' hooves.

Fergus could keep quiet no longer. "Now that we have left the fortress life, where do we go?"

"How would you like to go back to a crofter's life in a village a bit north of here?"

Fergus's face scrunched into a mixture of concentration and disbelief. "How will we do that without getting skewered? Normans hold much of the north."

"I have an idea. If it works, we will have a new home."

Fergus stared, doubtful of Edan's ability to make this come true.

Edan surprised himself when he decided to turn Dinas toward Merane's village. What was it about her that drew him? She is Norman, he told himself. Yet, she had been friendly to him. Was it because she did not know he was Saxon? He argued back and forth with himself as he rode, trying to make sense of why he wanted to return. Mayhap he could help his Saxon people in Merane's village in a way that he could not do on the battlefield.

10 June 1067

Lying in wait in the oak grove with Fergus, ferns up to their horses' bellies, Edan again envisioned Owain lying pale and still, his young life ended. His death had become a strong reason to find other ways than warfare to reclaim some of the old life. Vaguely, he noticed bluebells among the ferns and heard the song of a lark.

With a flutter of anticipation, he saw two horses, one chestnut, one gray, appear around a bend in the track and proceed toward him.

The horses had slicked off since he last visited here and had fattened on summer grass. As they drew closer, he saw Merane's long, dark hair glistening in the sun. Odette rode beside her, talking animatedly expressing with one hand, the other on the reins.

"Wait here for me, Fergus."

He nudged Dinas in the ribs. The horse moved smoothly through the ferns until he reached the bank along the road. The little stallion jumped down with a grunt and turned toward the approaching horses, his ears pricked. He uttered a shrill whinny. Edan tightened the reins and smiled. "You like the looks of Dove, eh?"

Within a few steps, Merane recognized him and called out, "Is that you, Edan?"

As he rode nearer, he worried that his plan would not work.

Silhouetted by sunlight streaming between the full-leafed blackthorn, Merane put Dove into a canter. She pulled up when she reached him and she smiled as if she had seen a long-lost friend.

That was something he had hoped for. She hadn't forgotten him. He nodded to her and to Odette, who trotted the old gray to catch up.

"It gladdens me to see you again. Dove looks well-fed. How does your village now?"

Merane smiled, reminding Edan of all the times her smiling face had appeared in his mind these past weeks. Although her long hair was tangled and her face was still thin, he thought she looked beautiful.

"Where have you been since I saw you last? At home or still visiting?" Her words were slightly breathless.

"At home and visiting in a different place." He wasn't about to mention fighting a battle against Normans or wonder where home really was.

"You are well-travelled. Come, ride along with us."

"It would pleasure me to do so." He swung a prancing Dinas alongside Dove.

"You asked about my village. Two men using horses have managed to plow a few acres for some barley. Not enough for the whole village for next winter. The kale-garth is going, and there will be orchard fruits later. Father still needs help. It is no better at other villages around."

Edan frowned. "Have many people died?"

Merane's eyes glistened. She ducked her head. "Yes, they have."

He looked away, not sure how to begin. Turning back to Merane, he studied her expression for a moment. His mouth felt suddenly dry.

"I have an idea that might help your village. Would you listen?"

"Of course." Merane's eyes sparked with interest.

"I have seen many villages these past months overrun by soldiers. These soldiers are not farmers. They do not know that slaughtering oxen to eat keeps the farmer from planting the crops that allow the village to survive. Somewhere, your village must get at least two yoke of oxen if it is to survive this next winter, and quickly. The farmers must get a share of what they raise; it can't all go to the soldiers and your father. The moot system the villages used before the soldiers came worked well. If your father would go back to that, your village could survive."

Edan felt pressure in his throat, while he waited for her reply. She rode in silence. Finally, she looked over at him, her eyes intense.

"Yes, I will tell Father. I will convince him to let you try."

"So you know—I am not Norman. Will your Father imprison me, make me thrall?" Edan had trouble breathing as he waited for her reply.

Surprise, then understanding reflected in Merane's eyes. "Now I realize why you never came into the village." Her forehead wrinkled in concentration. "I don't know what Father will do, with all the soldiers there." She paused. "I know. I'll get Father to come riding with me, so he won't have to do anything to keep up appearances. You can explain your plan, and no one else will know."

Edan sighed a deep breath. "I appreciate your help."

"We are desperate for help. My father is a fool if he does not listen and take your advice." Her cheeks flushed pink.

When Edan returned to the bank where Fergus waited, he knew Fergus was angry. Ruddy spots of color on his cheeks, the downward slant of brows, the thin pressed line of his mouth told of words to come. He was barely close enough to hear when the torrent of words began.

"You addle-pated nincompoop! You'll get us skewered for sure. You chase a pretty face—a Norman face! You said we would live in a farm village and farm as our families always did. You did not say it would be a Norman-held village and we would be thrall..." his tirade sputtered as he stopped for breath.

Edan jumped in. "We will not be thrall. We will be free to go or stay. There are Saxons here, our own people. I am trying to help them survive and make a better life. I was hoping for help from you. The girl is our entrance and protection."

The two argued for the rest of the afternoon, ate in silence from their rations with Fergus brooding as he had done last autumn at the fortress when Kadeg made him a servant. As they lay down to sleep under the stars like they had done on their journey last October, Edan hoped Fergus would decide by morning to stay here. He could not let this threaten their friendship. Where else could they go? North to Scotland?

Chapter Twenty-Six

11 June 1067

By morning Fergus had calmed and agreed to give the experiment a try if Merane's father could be persuaded. He hid, while Edan again waited by the path. Edan stayed out of sight until he assured himself no Norman patrol approached to capture him. He watched a dragonfly hover over blooms along the track. The hot sun had lifted the mist from the grass long before. Already it sat higher than it had yesterday when Merane and Odette rode out. Were they coming?

The sound of voices caught his attention. Down the track came Merane and her father. Edan stared at the man as they drew closer. What kind of man was he? Today, Edan waited for Merane's signal, waited for signs of other Normans and a trap.

Coming even with the big oak, Merane called out. "Edan, come and meet my father."

Edan mustered his courage and kneed Dinas forward, descending the bank. The two riders stopped, waiting for his appearance.

Edan assessed Merane's father. Nervous movements and a figure verging on corpulence suggested a man out of his element. A man around forty years, Edan thought. The expression upon his face as he sat watching Edan approach, suggested a prideful man reluctant to accept help.

"Edan, I am Geraud. My daughter has told me of you and your plan," he said in French.

Merane chimed in. "He listened to your idea."

The florid-faced Norman's wary, dark eyes measured Edan. "I

have questions about this moot system of yours."

Edan cocked his head and looked deep into Geraud's eyes, searching for his motives. In rudimentary French he said, "Aye, I expected that. Ask anything you wish."

"First, what village are you from? What experience have you with farming?" Geraud tucked a long strand of dark hair behind one ear.

"My people are from Herstmonceux, a small village near the coast of the Narrow Sea." He saw Merane's eyes grow big. "I was at the battle between King William and King Harold and saw my father fall." He had decided to omit that his father was thane. "My father planted his own fields and oversaw all the other farms. He saw that all had enough ground, enough animals to do the work and enough to eat. He settled arguments, punished petty crimes. Always there was enough grain, enough animals, enough food, and reasonable order within the village. My mother served as healer and taught my sisters…I worked alongside my father…"

Conscious of both pairs of eyes on him, Edan's stomach tensed.

Geraud gazed intently at him as he digested the words Edan spoke. Seeming to swallow his pride, he smiled bitterly when Edan concluded. "How do I know these villagers will work for me? Who will teach my wife of herbs and healing? What evidence can a mere lad give that this plan might work here in my village?"

Edan's throat all but closed. He swallowed hard and began his defense. "I know of some herbs, and some village women may know some others."

"Teach me," offered Merane. "I will teach Mother."

"If I agree to this," Geraud said, "I believe it is best that only my family knows the truth. You will be explained as a relative come from the south. My troops need know nothing. You can tell me what I must do for my villagers." He pulled his horse around. "I will function as…what do you call it?"

"Thane," replied Edan. "You and I can go north to find oxen to plow and pigs to raise for meat at harvest fairs." Edan swallowed down his emotions. *This would not be easy. Geraud wanted all control and, if he refused to try certain things, the whole plan could fail.*

And would this reduce his own anger?

"In fact, come with me now. Let us start this remedy today."

Merane smiled at Edan, nodding at him to come.

Geraud led the way back toward his village. *My villagers*, Edan scoffed inwardly. With a moment's hesitation, he followed. He had to trust his safety to Merane and Geraud. He had to trust a Norman's word. And trust that the man would listen to a lad's knowledge of farming to save the village, not be mired in his own pride.

"I have a friend with me who wishes to help. May I bring him along with us?"

Geraud's astonishment evidenced itself in his open mouth. Gathering his wits, he clamped his mouth shut before mumbling his assent.

Motioning Fergus from the wood, Edan waited until he caught up. Fergus looked wary and uncomfortable, but he had promised to come if Geraud agreed.

18 Oct 1067

Edan wielded his wooden rake and surveyed the neat piles of cured grass that would feed the livestock in Merane's village. Onny, the Saxon farmer who helped make this stack, worked hard despite his crippled arm. Edan no longer noticed Onny's handicap or the large brown mole on his left cheek, only his cheerful presence and hard work.

With the help of Geraud's housecarls, the slain villagers were replaced, and the work had been done. He wiped his forearm across his sweaty brow. Surveying the fields with satisfaction, he noted the barley threshed and winnowed, the hard-worked oxen which grazed alongside a few sheep and lambs, and a few goats. The sow that Geraud had bought at a northern market and her half-grown litter of ten fattened on acorns in the nearby wood.

The summer had flown by filled with hard labor. After the first week, when Fergus saw Edan's plan would work and they were not to be skewered, he threw himself into the everyday tasks as had the other men of the village. Fergus lived with a family who had lost a son when the village fell to the Normans, while Edan stayed with

Onny's young family who needed the extra pair of hands to enlarge their harvest share.

In the beginning he encountered blank faces among the few village men who remained. Gradually, the expressions had turned to cautious hope with each successful venture back into the old moot ways. True, Edan could not see it ever going all the way back to the way it was. But, if this village could be brought to self-sustenance, it was a step forward. And Merane would not starve. By luck, Edan had stumbled across Geraud Bouvier, who preferred the life of gentleman farmer as opposed to that of conqueror, one of a handful of adventurous families who had followed the soldiery from Normandy.

"The fodder work will be finished tomorrow, aye?" said Onny, while they drove the loaded cart to the hay garth. The small-statured, dark-haired young man had joked and laughed as he toiled hard at his side all day. Only three or four years older than Edan, he had yet to grow a full beard.

"Aye, and a nice lot of it there is. With the late planting, we were lucky to have no early frost."

"We all be thankful to you. This winter will be better than the last. I never thought a year ago I'd say 'I thank 'ee' to a Norman as I will say to the Lord Geraud."

Edan nodded. "Nor did I." He reminded himself he had done nothing but convince Geraud to let the Saxon farmers do what they had always done.

Talk stopped as they pitched hay onto the sizeable stack. When they finished, his tousled curls chaff-covered, Onny nodded and said, "Enjoy your meal at Geraud's table." He strode off toward his cottage and his wife's dinner.

Edan knew the young farmer would play with his two small children until their bedtime. He looked back again at the haystacks, the harvested fields, the mill grinding the barley into flour. Each night he fell onto his pallet within Onny's loft tired to the bone, yet happy because he and the village were productive. Responsibility weighed on him, and he frowned at the empty, harvested gardens. Would the village have enough to survive the next winter? The two yoke of oxen Geraud had purchased, all he could find, did yeoman duty but could not do the work of eight. Crops were only half the harvest of pre-Norman times, but he knew the women had been hard at work all week making cider and ale. At least the morale would be higher as the villagers had hope again.

"Edan!" Geraud's voice boomed. "A word with you, lad."

Edan turned. Geraud strode toward him. Behind him, some women in the common stirred kettles of soap, the smell of lye strong in the air. The Norman had settled into the role of "thane" remarkably well. Merane's mother, Angelique, had taken on the wife's role of herb collector and medicine dispenser to the village. Merane helped with this duty and in the vegetable garden. Their family's role as conquerors had changed. No talk of building a stone castle with dungeons to house dissenters had occurred here as in so many other conquered places. These peasants were too busy rebuilding their lives.

"The hay field looks finished. Good work. In fact that is what I want to talk about with you." Geraud stepped to the bench before the hall, gazing at Edan. "Sit here. This year's harvest is almost done. Soon it will be time for plowing and sowing the winter wheat and rye, and the slaughter of a few of the pigs." He paused to gather the words he wanted.

Geraud spoke as if the ideas were all his own, had not been taught to him by Edan. Still, he seemed to believe in them.

"I have been thinking you need to have an audience with King William. Someone needs to explain this moot system of yours. If other villages go back to this, the hunger and starvation would lessen."

An audience with the King! He must be daft. Edan's mind revolted at the thought. A tight knot formed in his gut, his pleasure at having convinced Geraud of the worth of the Old ways overshadowed. He could not be in the presence of this man who had killed his father, who had made nomads and outlaws of his people, who had killed and starved thousands.

"If you could explain how this has helped my village, it would be a chance to improve life for all my countrymen in this new land."

The knot in Edan's stomach grew tighter. *Were his own country-*

men Geraud's main concern? Did he not care about the villagers after all, except as people who grew his food?

"What do you think, lad?" Geraud's florid, dark-complected face held a questioning enthusiasm.

Edan struggled to find the right words. "What would you have me say to convince him? I speak a little of your language after being with you these past few months, but I am not fluent. Wouldn't it be better if you went? The King would surely be more apt to listen to his own countryman."

"I am needed here for the fall moot, handling the village complaints and parsing out the harvest in accord with your Saxon system. Going off to London for weeks would lose us the advances we have made in the trust of the villagers. And in all truth, my gout has worsened, and I do not think I could or should ride that far. Would you go if I send you to a friend of mine at court who could help you with the French?" Geraud had mounted a canny argument.

"Let me think on this. This plan would be good for the country if I could convince the King to try it in other places," Edan said carefully. *Why would the King care if every Saxon citizen died? The Normans would not have to fight to secure the rest of the country. They could bring French farmers in to work the land.*

"Good enough, lad. Think hard on it." With that he heaved himself up and entered the hall with a limp. His gout was worse. Edan continued to sit, watching puffy gray clouds scud in from the north. A storm seemed to be building. The hay had been gotten in just in time.

Although Geraud made a generous offer, Edan feared he would be laughed out of the King's presence for his audacity, if he went at all. *What a foolish idea to argue before the King. On the other hand, he reasoned, what if Geraud's friend had some influence? What if he could help more of his own people through Geraud's offer?* He thought again of the villagers branded and sent to thralldom. Images of the battles, the men and boys who died, his own father, and Owain, floated within his memory. A jolt of pain thrust through his gut. He sat a bit longer.

When he could no longer ignore the smell of food, Edan entered

Geraud's hall to eat his dinner.

That evening after the meal, Merane's mother spun before the fire. She and Geraud exchanged stories of their youth, while Merane and Edan played a game of chess. He had taught her the game when he first came, and she had become an able adversary. Her two little brothers, Auric and Denis, played loudly with wooden swords, scampering around the parents' chairs.

Edan remembered his own sisters running about his parents' chairs as he played chess with Father, while his own mother spun. Suddenly anger flooded his mind. Anger at the Normans who had taken his home and life away.

"Check," announced Merane.

Edan's attention returned to the board. How had that happened? He made his move out of check.

Merane's brows drew together in concentration. Her slender fingers moved her bishop but remained on the piece, uncertain.

A moment here and there and life in this village seemed almost like he remembered it before the Hastings battle. Somehow he knew he must go to King William and try to gain back some of the old system for all England. Everyone deserved to share in his good fortune. This was a chance to save some of his people.

After he left Geraud's hall, Edan sought out Fergus to tell him of his decision. He found his friend helping his host family with chores talking with their comely daughter.

"Hallo, friend," called Edan.

"Aye, and a good day it's been in the hay fields," Fergus replied.

"Come with me a moment," Edan asked.

Fergus followed him to a nearby orchard with a quizzical look.

"Geraud asked me today to go to King William and ask to have all the villages go back to the moot system. I doubt he'll listen, but I must try for the sake of our people," Edan explained.

Fergus snorted. "The King will laugh you out of court."

"Mayhap he will, but I must try. Would you like to come with me?"

"Na, I am needed here, not on a fool's errand."

"Would care for my sword then?" Had the time spent with his

host's cheery blond daughter anything to do with Fergus's decision to stay behind?

Fergus's face lit up. "Will I? Of course, I would be honored to have its care. When will you return?"

"I do not know how long this will take. Geraud sends a soldier with me, Roger. This could be over quickly, or I may have to stay somewhere to oversee the moot system if by some chance he should agree to try it. Take care while I am gone and watch to see Geraud does not return to being lord rather than thane." He handed Fergus his sword.

Fergus nodded and inspected Swine-eater with admiration. He looked at Edan with serious eyes. "May St. Dunstan go with you and protect you on your journey."

20 Oct 1067

Two days later after a storm cleared, Edan guided Dinas from the village gate, bound south for Winchester, a letter from Geraud in his tunic to assure his safe passage and one of Geraud's soldiers, Roger, to protect and speak for him. Fergus had settled in so well, he seemed content to stay behind and keep an eye on Swine-eater. Edan waved at Merane, Fergus and the rest gathered before the hall to watch his departure. Riding over the bridge, Edan acknowledged two soldiers, then he was into the fields. This being a small village, about 200 rods of cleared land surrounded the cottages. The thane and eighteen families had dwelled here before the Normans. Now Geraud's family and ten families lived here. Nearly half the village had died in the fight to keep their village or had starved. Only 52 people dwelt here, counting soldiers. He was anxious to see if other villages on his way had suffered similar fates. If so, he knew what he intended to say to the King.

They rode slowly southward on the cobbled Roman road as their horses wore no shoes. Edan remembered another blacksmith and his family from Seven Oaks who, a year ago, searched for a new village. Too bad he could not have come this way. The village smith here had died in defense of his home, or the horses would have shoes.

On the second day they passed a burned-out village where no one dwelt. A smell of wild mint wafted on the breeze mellowing the charcoal odor.

By the end of the day Edan saw several villages, much reduced in numbers, which he made no move to enter. They had no reason to stop and were better off to camp in the forest.

On the fourth day Edan's soldier companion, who had said little on their journey, as he had few Saxon words at his disposal, looked pale and slumped as he rode. By noon his lips were clenched into a thin line. Edan stole concerned glances at the man at frequent intervals. Finally, Roger pulled his horse to a halt.

"I cannot go on. My belly is on fire with pain," he gasped. His feet slid free of his stirrups, and he slowly dismounted. He tried to walk to the side of the track. Before he took three steps, his body slumped to the ground.

Edan had no idea what was wrong. He dismounted from Dinas and hurried to Roger's side. The man breathed unevenly, and his skin had a sheen of sweat despite the cool day. One hand clutched at his belly. His body curled, protecting his stomach. Edan grabbed him under the arms and dragged him under a tree. He mounted Dinas and rode at a gallop to the next occupied village less than a league down the track. In his rudimentary French he explained he needed help to get his sick companion to the village.

By late afternoon he had gotten Roger to the mistress of the village who said the young soldier was too ill to continue. She promised to take care of him and send word back to Geraud. Edan's position put him halfway between Merane's village and Winchester. Should he return or continue? He had no weapon, no companion. However, Galt was closer than either of the other places. He could go there. He wanted to see the old hermit again, so Edan set out to the south.

24 Oct 1067

At the end of the week he approached the area where he and Fergus had first met Ridley. He knew he was close to the forest of the hermit, Galt. Of a sudden, he felt a desire to be with Galt, a need he didn't understand. Late harebells lined the grassy sward along the track. Bees buzzed industriously among the flowers. He searched for the spot to enter the woods. Where was the notch on the tree? It had been a big oak. Finally he saw it. He entered the woods, Dinas swishing belly deep through yellowing ferns and wild thyme. Somewhere a thrush sang accompaniment as they made their way along an overgrown path. Edan strained to see the notches on trees that signaled the way.

Trees grew larger and sunlight dimmer as the forest deepened. Uncertainty flooded over him. Should he have tried to find Galt? What if he became lost? He saw it then, a spear-cast away, a notch at head-height on the trunk of a mature oak. Breathing a sigh of relief, he sat back and let Dinas pick his way. Up and down two hills, through a bog, and on through the enormous trees. By late afternoon he recognized his surroundings, the ancient stonework, the high creeper-covered walls, the small ruined chapel.

He urged Dinas ahead over the mossy ground. The horse's ears pricked forward, his gait grew stiff and expectant, little snorts betraying his sense of the spirits about. Did the owl still live in the chapel? At the edge of the outer wall stood Galt's hut. He saw no activity. Behind him a dog barked. He jerked his head around to see the old man and his dog in the path.

"Peace to you, keeper of the shrine," Edan said.

The old man walked closer. "I have been out gathering herbs. Come to my fire and share supper, traveler." His white beard appeared longer than ever.

"I would be pleased to share supper with you."

The old hermit peered at him. His eyes lit up in recognition. "The young lad from Herstmonceux. Where is your friend?"

"My friend, Fergus, is at a village in the north where I will return when I am done with this errand. I am on my way to see the Norman king on behalf of my people. Half the country starves."

The old man shook his shaggy white mane. "Aye, my sister's village among them. There was naught I could do, and I had your wounded knight to tend. A fortnight later I slipped in to see my sister. She survived, but her husband and nearly every man in the place had been slain." The old man's voice grew hard. "I helped tend the wounded with my herbs and told the women I would check on them now and then." His eyes grew vacant and his voice trailed off.

"How did the knight fare? Did he live?"

Galt's gaze jerked back to Edan's. "Aye, he did. And he wanted to know who had saved him. I told him two lads from Herstmonceux who were on the run themselves. It turned out he was from Mesewelle, King Harold's home, one of Harold's housecarls. Niland was indeed his name, but he worried about a friend, Oren. The two of them had taken on the charge of Harold's three sons. Niland and Oren left the battle before the end to tend their promise, but Niland was wounded and lost track of Oren. When he grew strong enough, he rode west to dispatch his duty."

Edan asked, "I heard Harold's boys got to Ireland, raised a small army and came back to England to battle King William."

"Aye, they did, so Niland must have been successful. They remain a danger to King William." He wagged a forefinger in emphasis.

"What of Harold's wife?" Could she be the woman he saw at the end of the battle searching for Harold's body?

"His wife, Edith Swanhols, the mother of his children, girls as well as boys, is alive and in hiding according to Niland."

If Fergus had not discovered Niland, he may have died before he could complete his mission. Maybe the spirit of this old shrine had strengthened the knight and nourished a flame that could still scorch the reign of King William.

"Did Niland say anything about the end of the battle when King Harold was killed? Who stood by him?" Edan's throat tightened. He both dreaded and wanted an answer.

"Only that Harold did not seem like himself. Like he fought in a trance, defensive. Niland said always before he fought as the aggressor. Mayhap it had to do with a message from Duke William before the battle. It contained a message from the Italian pope that Harold had been excommunicated from the church."

Edan remembered the message that came for King Harold in the road by their village. How his face registered shock, his skin turned pale. Why had the Pope sent such a message? *What a blow that must have been to Harold. Could that explain Harold's choice not to fight in his normal way? Had he felt God controlled his fate and had already rendered a judgment?*

Galt moved toward his hut. When he reached the fire, he stirred the stewpot. "This spring I planted a bigger garden and I have a larder full for the coming cold. I've food to share with you. Tie up your horse and let us eat. That snare you left caught me a fat hare this morn."

When the meal finished, Edan caught him up with events, and he explained what he planned to propose to the king.

Galt nodded. "You must do what you feel is right. Serve no other man's ideals. If it is your desire to speak for the moot way, not just within the Norman Geraud's village, then speak with all your heart. Then let us hope the man has some common sense in his head," he said with strong feeling. Brieg lay next to Galt, his grizzled muzzle across the old man's knee where he sat cross-legged by the fire. He raised his head and cocked it at his master when he heard the loud tone of his voice. Satisfied nothing was amiss, he lowered his head once more.

Stars shone overhead, and the air grew chill when the two said good night. The hermit went to his hut, and Edan curled up by the fire. Meeting with Galt had calmed him. He had wondered so long about so many things and now realized that was part of what he was looking for—-Galt's calmness, his lack of a political stake in any event, his objectivity. Everyone else he knew vied for one faction or another. Galt's life remained the same whether Norman or Saxon ruled the land. His vow had been to tend the shrine all his days.

In this new peace, this new calm, Edan planned his words to King William whom he hoped to confront within a few days' time. This would be his vow to carry out, help his people through restoring the old ways like Galt held true to his vow.

Chapter Twenty-Seven

2 Nov 1067 (All Souls Day)

On a damp, cold day in early November, Edan wound his way through forest and village southward from Galt's forest, entered Winchester proper, and fought through milling throngs. He had never seen so many people. The seat of the royal court drew all kinds. A band of Norman knights forced through the crowd, the horses pushing everyone aside up against buildings.

"Norman swill," yelled a merchant whose vegetable cart had been upended. He pitched a split cabbage after the riders, falling far short of them.

In his head Edan repeated the name Geraud had given him as he asked directions to the house he sought. Shivering with the cold wetness, he came to a broad thoroughfare where merchants had set their stalls and hawked their wares. He saw cutpurses working the crowd, a deft slice of their dirks freeing the purses of the monied, and thanked the gods he rode high above on Dinas's back. As the light of day faded, he came upon the correct street filled with fine houses. He found the house of fitzOsbern to be the finest one. He gave Dinas over to a groom to be stabled. A heavy haze settled over the city as its citizens kindled peat fires for evening meals, and fog crept in from the low places.

An elderly, French-speaking servant let him into the hall and bade him sit by the fire. A few knights sat about a long table telling tales and draining their ale cups as he warmed himself. No one paid him any attention.

Shortly, the same manservant returned with his tall, well-built master. In his thirties, the nobleman seemed in good humor, a friendly expression upon his face.

"Good eveningtide, lad. What is it you wish to speak with me about?" A look of curiosity filled his eyes.

"I be Edan. I have come from Geraud Bouvier," Edan replied in halting French. "He said William fitzOsbern is a friend and would help. He has tried some of the old Saxon ways to lift his village out of starvation this past summer and bade me come tell you of this circumstance. He wishes for you to set me an audience with King William to explain the use of this practice on other Norman holdings. Will you help?" he finished, breathless from concentrating so hard on his French.

William fitzOsbern's eyebrows jerked up in surprise at the words. He put one hand on his hip and looked at Edan closely. "Geraud, eh? How does he up north on the frontier?"

Edan noted the mannerism of fitzOsbern's hand on hip. Was that how courtly men behaved? "Geraud is well, as is his family, but the village fared poorly until he tried the old moot system."

From the man's expression Edan could not tell what the man thought of Geraud or Geraud's request.

"I wondered how he fared after the flare-up in Herefordshire in late spring." His eyes bored into Edan's. He let the statement hang, still not replying to Edan's request.

Edan wanted to look away but did not. If he only knew I was there in Herefordshire, part of the flare-up, he thought. *I can not look away or I look guilty.* Was this veiled way how people of the court made social conversation and found out what they wanted to know? Ridley had hinted of high ranking nobles considering political effects of all decisions. For the first time he wondered how Ridley had learned of such things as a pedlar. Edan guessed he hadn't always been one. He hinted broadly that he dealt in information—mayhap he *was* a spy. He tried to gaze into fitz Osbern's eyes again, but light from the fire was too dim. He waited, anxious for the man's decision.

FitzOsbern stroked his chin before speaking again. "I will think about your request until King William returns from Normandy. You may lodge here meanwhile." He motioned to the servant who stood near the door. "Get this lad some food and show him a place to sleep." After he had given the order, he turned on his heel and left the room.

Edan huffed. He'll think about my request? For how long?

Edan followed the servant to the noisy kitchen where a roomful of staff crowded around a large wooden table, eating with good appetite.

"Lad, I am called Tudwal. Cook will get you food. After, I will show you a place to sleep."

Edan nodded and found a place on a stool by the great cook fire. At Tudwal's direction a serving maid got Edan a trencher of food. Conversation continued as if he had not come. Edan strained to understand the rapid French.

"Aye, and you should have heard her tell of the King's religious brother. No one would think he was a man of the cloth." The speaker raised his brows and pantomimed the king's brother by grabbing the maid next to him and planting a kiss on her mouth.

She shrieked and turned pink. "Be off with you!" she sputtered. The whole table-full erupted in raucous laughter.

"Who told you?"

"One of the ladies in waiting at the court."

"Tsk. Tsk. Bishop Odo should be ashamed," said a plump, motherly woman who seemed to be in charge.

She must be cook, thought Edan.

"He must have a woman in every town. Mayhap a child in every one, too." More laughter.

"I only know of one son," said the man who had pantomimed the lecherous bishop.

"Well, girls, keep your skirts tight around your ankles if he comes here to see our master," pronounced the plump woman.

"And if you cross him, watch your head, too," added the pantomimer.

Gossip ceased as the sound of a woman's skirt swished along the corridor. A well-dressed woman, a bit plump, hurried into the kitchen and motioned to cook. The motherly woman rose from the table and joined her mistress. Edan heard talk of amounts of meats and vegetables to be bought. This must be fitzOsbern's wife. Talk of the court and its members continued through the dessert after the mistress left. Afterward, everyone went to the crowded chapel for the priest's prayers on All Souls Day. At a late hour, Tudwal showed Edan a pallet on which to sleep in the attic where all the servants had a cubby. The house did not quiet until even later. When he did fall asleep, he dreamed of a fierce man in charge of one of the new stone dungeons the servants had described, flogging and torturing whole villages of people. He awoke in a sweat, heart beating madly in his chest.

"Am I a complete lackwit?" Edan muttered. "What am I doing here?" The vow he had made to himself in Galt's wood seemed impossible under Norman tyranny.

A week went by. He had explored the whole of Winchester by now and knew all the servants' names. Each day he expected word from fitzOsbern, but none came. A second week, then a third passed. Edan thought his host had forgotten his request. The weather had become so rainy and cold that any thoughts he had of returning, task undone, to Geraud, became impractical. To pass the time, he spent much of each morning grooming Dinas and caring for his saddle, restless and more unsure of his task. At last, in the first week of December, fitzOsbern summoned him to say he had an audience next week.

12 Dec 1067

William fitz Osbern smirked but spoke with his courtier's smoothness, "Well, lad, are you ready for your audience with the King?" He stood, one arm crooked, eyebrow raised, outside the guarded entrance of the King's chamber.

Edan straightened his shoulders, jutted his chin. Never mind that his legs trembled and he felt as if he had run all the way from fitzOsbern's manor house to court instead of riding Dinas. He fixed his gaze on the tall, double doors ahead. "Aye, sir, I am ready."

"Ah," fitzOsbern sighed, "then let's get on with it."

They passed through the merchants and petitioners who waited their turn in the corridor. As the sentries opened the doors, Edan saw several men across the large room, courtiers and servants. Men conferred in small groups, low-voiced and serious.

Heads turned as the two went through, and Edan heard whispers run through the groups like the rush of wind before the rain. Men who apparently knew fitzOsbern stepped forward with a wink for him and a stare for Edan. FitzOsbern did not introduce Edan but walked closer to where the auburn-haired King sat surrounded by this crowd of armed and jeweled lords.

Edan scanned the faces. There were none he knew, only Norman lords of lands taken from his people. His eyes strained to find the eyes of King William, remembering Ridley's comment about reading a man's intent through his eyes. Anger and hate for this man who had killed his father, the former king and so many of his people fueled his courage.

They were nearly to the chair. Edan's gaze was caught by a tall man next to the King's chair with the look of the King but younger, a man he felt he should recognize. Those chill amber eyes bored into him from the formidable, hard face. Where had he seen this man?

William fitzOsbern paused. Edan halted abruptly. His gaze returned to the King who stopped talking and looked at his steward. "Good day, William, who have you brought with you this day?"

The coarse, commanding voice caused Edan's breath to catch in his throat. Coming from under frowning brows, the hard, dark-eyed gaze pinioned him. A drawn look under the eyes of the King told of the burdens of the conqueror. Even though he was seated, his breadth of shoulder, arrogance, and warrior demeanor dominated the room.

"This lad has a proposition for you. He is come from Geraud Bouvier on the northern frontier. At his behest, I have brought the boy to you." FitzOsbern bowed his head slightly and stepped back leaving Edan alone before the king.

William pulled his robe about his knees as if in a draft. Edan could not help but watch the man's every move as a rabbit watches a coiled serpent. He cleared his throat to speak and willed his knees to stay steady.

"Your majesty, if it please you, I would tell you of what has taken place in Geraud Bouvier's village." He waited. The King nodded.

"Last year was one of starvation. Many souls perished from lack of food. They had no oxen to till the fields to plant grain to sustain the village." He stopped, swallowed and continued in his basic French, careful to use no words of blame, only the facts. "This spring Geraud brought in two yoke of oxen, some cows, a few sheep and goats, and a farrowing sow. Now the hay garth is stocked, barley is being ground to flour in the mill, there is fresh milk and cheese, and the women brew cider and ale. In short, if the oxen in each village are replaced and some of the old Saxon farm system returned to the villages, the starving could stop…" Edan paused under the stony look, his courage draining away.

"Go on, boy," King William demanded.

"The farmers must have animals to do the work and be able to keep some of the food for themselves as well as contribute to their lord's table and feed his soldiers."

Edan saw a brief flicker in his eyes before the lids veiled them. Was it anger? Disdain? He could not tell what the King thought. He continued, "If everyone is well fed, you will have less need of stone castles to protect your lords from their villagers who as much as anything are merely hungry if they revolt against their masters. I would like your permission to try this system in other villages." Edan bowed his head and waited for the King's reply.

"Why should I care if a few peasants starve?" the King retorted.

"Because sir, they grow the food for your lords. If no one is there, your lords will starve."

"You think I can not solve this problem? I can bring Norman farmers across," he flashed, his voice rising. "Or I could fix yokes about the necks of the peasants then they wouldn't need oxen."

"And their cows, sheep, goats, pigs, and chickens?" Edan replied, anger rising in kind toward this man who had taken everything but his life from him. Before he could check himself, he blurted, "The animals that sustain us are equally important. We can not eat them all—some must be left to increase."

In an intense moment of apprehension, Edan's voice would no longer work. Had he said too much already? Fear crowded out the remnants of his courage. He watched the King's face turn dark-mottled. King William breathed through flared nostrils. A tic jerked the left corner of his mouth. The knuckles on the back of his hand whitened as he gripped the arm of his chair until Edan feared the wood would splinter. Like a man in a corner, the king seemed to struggle with indifference, with how he appeared to his courtiers who stood listening, and with what a king should do to keep his power unchallenged.

The king stood to see fitzOsbern. "This young pup has yet to grow beard hair, yet he thinks to advise a King?" He snorted in disgust. Edan could not see fitzOsbern behind him, but he heard derisive titters from the courtiers. His knees quaked at the imposing height of the king.

Edan felt a flush run across his skin, rise up his neck, and rush across his face. What would the King decide? Would he send Edan to one of his new dungeons for his impertinence?

William let go the chair and pounded the arm with his fist. Unschooled anger crept into his voice. "Conquered peasants do not try to tell the King what he must do."

Edan felt the angry stare upon him. William shifted in his chair in apparent discomfort. He looked to the side and motioned. "A goblet."

A servant scuttled forward with a goblet of wine, pressed it into the King's hand and hurried away. Did he stall for time to think what he must do? As Edan waited, his flush faded. His hands shook and his fingers turned icy cold. Seeing his father's killer in the flesh as he toyed with people's fates reopened the half-healed wounds of Edan's grief. Bitter emotions caught flame inside him.

William took a draught then stared in rigid silence. The tic twitched once more. At last his frown cleared, and his face relaxed. "You may try your magnificent healing on Bishop Odo's lands," he said, sarcasm dripping from his words but his tone under control once more.

The tall man next to his chair turned to the King, a disbelieving look upon his face; his wild, amber eyes flashed.

So the tall, formidable man was Odo, Catholic Bishop of Bayeux, the King's half-brother, the very subject of gossip the previous evening. According to the kitchen staff, his reputation for callous treatment of the conquered rivaled or exceeded that of the King. Edan's spirits sank. The man nodded assent yet obviously had an unwilling spirit. The courtiers around whispered in surprise at this act of benevolence toward the conquered.

"The Bishop will take you to one of his villages forthwith." King William raised a hand in dismissal.

Edan bowed and turned with a stumble to rejoin fitzOsbern. *The filthy, murderous hypocrite!* He gave permission for Edan to help only to impress his courtiers. He could not wait to leave King William's presence. At that moment, a jester in a red cap with a jangling bell came rolling forward, dressed in tights, tunic and pointed shoes. He somersaulted to their feet.

Edan watched with open mouth. The frizzy red hair sticking out from the cap could belong to no other man. The jester looked up at him. Ridley's eyes met Edan's with a knowing look and an almost imperceptible shake of the head. He did not speak. Scampering around them, he dropped into a handstand and walked toward the King. Titters of laughter broke out. All eyes followed the jester.

Edan's heart and mind raced. *What was Ridley doing here? A jester?* Somehow he must find out.

His audience over, he walked toward the double doors, behind fitzOsbern. As he left the hall, he turned back to hear Ridley telling court jokes to the King.

That evening Edan stuffed himself with delicious lamb stew in fitzOsbern's kitchen. Who knew when he would eat so well again?

Edan had just cleaned the bottom of his trencher and prepared to eat the bread when a small man entered the kitchen from the stable area.

"I have a message for the boy, Edan," he announced.

Edan nearly fell from his stool.

Tudwal said, "Here he sits, my good sir."

In a bow-legged gait the dark little man strutted to Edan's bench like a rooster and handed him a rolled letter. "I'll wait for a reply," he said.

Tudwal got a horn of ale for the messenger, while Edan stepped to the hearth for firelight to read his letter. Who knew he was here save Geraud? Had something happened to Merane or Fergus? With trembling fingers he broke the unfamiliar seal and unrolled the paper.

"Send word with my messenger if you can meet in the stable behind fitz Osbern's at midnight. R."

Ridley!

Edan turned to the messenger enjoying his ale. He nodded to him. The little man's eyes took in the message. He drained his horn and thanked Tudwal for the generosity of the house and departed.

Curious stares greeted Edan as he tossed the message into the fireplace before he resumed his seat at the table. Knowing the servants' love of gossip, he dared not say anything about the real message. Instead he said, "Details of what I must do before I leave tomorrow." Turning to cook he asked, "Are you sharing the apple cobbler I smelled this afternoon or did the master of the house consume it all?"

Hildy, a plump, motherly woman, smiled, her red cheeks dimpled. "Of course you may have some, lad. And you leaving tomorrow just as I was putting some meat on your bones." She heaved herself up, put the dish of cobbler on the table and ladled out a portion to everyone.

Talk turned to courtly affairs. The King's recent return from Normandy, the strengthening of his liason with the Pope after his victory, the rewarding of his vassals for their support. Then something that affected England more directly.

"Has anyone a thought of what the Saxon political hostages will do now that they returned to England with the King and were set free?" asked fitzOsbern's manservant.

Edan listened carefully. Here was important news. Who were they? He stopped chewing his bread.

Tudwal replied, " No, but if I were King William I would keep a sharp eye on the young northern earls Morcar and Edwin, the man Waltheof, and old Bishop Stigand now that they are back. Don't count out the aethling Edgar either despite his tender years." He wagged a finger at no one in particular. "He has powerful friends even though he is still here at court."

Edan drew a sharp breath. Edgar is here at court? Which one had he been? And the young northern earls, too?

The young earls and the aethling are just boys. No wonder the earls in the north had sent no war host to help Kadeg and the others in Herefordshire. The earls had been prisoners.

"And what of Bishop Stigand?" asked the manservant.

"He doesn't have the courage to oppose even if he wanted." Tudwal waved a liver-spotted hand dismissively.

"Speaking of enemies of the King, what of Harold's brats?" asked the groom, grabbing for another chunk of cobbler with cook's big spoon.

"I've heard nothing of them since their weak attempt last summer in the south," Tudwal reached for his mug, "when they fled back to Ireland their tails between their legs."

"I for one would love to be a flea in this lad Edan's coat as he goes to Odo's castle to see what goes on there." Hildy rolled her eyes suggestively.

"Aye, and you'd be the plumpest flea in his hem," laughed the groom slapping his knee.

Hildy picked up a spoon and whacked the table in his direction, then laughed good-naturedly.

Tudwal said, "Odo has plenty of Saxons ready for that new dungeon of his. Pity on any rebel he catches."

Edan felt the blood drain out of his face. He would enter the viper's den tomorrow according to these servants.

"Not only that, to my mind Bishop Odo has higher ambitions than bishop and regent. Mark my words," Tudwal added.

Eventually the meal ended, the dishes were cleared, and the servants were sent with bath water, wine and various subtleties to the rooms of fitzOsbern's family. Edan went to his own pallet in the servants' attic to wait impatiently for church bells tolling the midnight hour.

Ridley waited for him when Edan slipped into the silent stable. He had even found Dinas' stall and stood by the little stallion, his cloak damp from the rain falling outside.

At Ridley's look of relief, Edan ran forward and found himself hugging the secretive pedlar/jester.

"By the faith, what's this now, lad?" Ridley said, then hugged Edan against his barrel chest. "All is well," he soothed. "I heard your presentation today in court. You accounted well for yourself. I admit I was as surprised to see you as you probably were to see me. Now I must warn you of Odo before you go under his care in the morn. Since he is co-regent, he has been given the choicest Saxon land, and most of all, has high political ambition. He has been made Earl of Kent and is privy to King Williams's plans. He may allow you to try your plan but watch your back." He wagged his forefinger at Edan. "You are in more danger if you succeed."

"What would he do if I succeed?" Edan whispered, aware not only of the political problems of his plan but suddenly its dangers. King William and Bishop Odo did not want the Saxons to regain any strength or hope.

"He will quash any sign of Saxon success, lad. If you save lives, you must not do it by any grand measure."

"Many thanks for the warning, Ridley. I knew coming here that my plan had slim chance to succeed, but my Norman patron, Geraud Bouvier, insisted I come. Despite my doubts, I hoped to save a few of our people. Too many starve."

"How did you get yourself hooked up with the Normans after hearing you and Fergus rail so against them? Where is Fergus?"

"It's a long story. I went back to the fortress as you suggested. Ardel was not a problem after all. I joined with Kadeg in arms for the battle at Herefordshire. After, I decided that battles of arms were not my answer to these new times. I was fortunate enough to meet a Norman girl, Merane, whose father would try the old way. Fergus waits with them for my return."

"Aye, and is she a pretty lass?" Ridley said with a twinkle in his eye. In an instant his face turned solemn. "Lad, it could be you are right," he sighed, "yet there are those of us who have not given up the route of arms."

Edan leaned closer. Was Ridley about to admit involvement?

"I parked my pedlar's wagon and put on the jester's guise to get myself close to the decision-makers. When you play the fool, some men forget to hold their tongues." He waggled his bushy, red brows and chuckled. "I can keep a finger on the pulse of the court. And pass on what I know through messengers like the one come to you this night."

Edan nodded. He had recognized one of the little, dark Hill men in the messenger.

"The King greatly fears what is happening in Northumbria under the Danelaw on his frontier. His own spies have let him know of the unrest and the strength that remains there, not only among the Saxons in England but also in Scandinavia which has close ties to Northumbria. I do not believe he will push the frontier further to the north at this time. He has too many other wildfires to quench. Edric in Cymru, Malcolm in Scotland, the hostages he brought back from Normandy who will soon be back among their followers now that they are released, and Harold's boys in Ireland, to name a few. Even among his own ranks there are those with ambition to take his prize from him. He picks up enemies as a dog picks up fleas."

Edan listened and worried more now that kitchen gossip had been confirmed by Ridley as truth. He wondered which faction Ridley held loyalty to.

"Who do you pass messages to, Ridley?"

"Ah now, that I cannot tell you, for your protection as well as mine. But you already know I spend time in the North, sometimes north of Hadrian's Wall. Let's just say that soon events will happen that will tell you more." Solemn-eyed, Ridley stood silent a moment. "If you get into trouble with Odo, ask in the village of Ashford for Caw. He will get word to me."

"You would help me against Odo…" Edan began.

"Tush. Tis the least I can do for patriots of England. Soon I leave for the North again, but word will reach me still. Take care until we meet again."

Also certain of their shared destiny, somehow Edan knew they would meet again as he watched Ridley draw his cloak about him and step into the cold December rain, his breath blooming into a cloud of fog.

His thoughts dwelt on Ridley's words, "I spend time in the North, sometimes north of Hadrian's Wall." For the first time he had said more than just North. Did he have business for Malcolm, King of Scotland? He had said something would happen soon that would reveal more.

Chapter Twenty-Eight

13 Dec 1067

Edan watched from the second floor window of fitz Osbern's house in Winchester. Cantering down the street came a band of men, a tall man on a gray stallion in the lead. Edan caught his breath sharply.

He remembered the gray stallion and its rider in the battle at Hastings, fighting fiercely at then Duke William's side. That rider bringing William a new mount when his was killed beneath him, pulling the helmet from William's head as his men were about to retreat to prove their leader still lived, and killing so many Saxons at Hastings. And again at the battle in Herefordshire where Owain fell. Odo played a vital role in raising his half-brother to the throne, and now Odo was come for him.

He grabbed up his few belongings and raced down the stairs to say his farewell to fitzOsbern.

"Thank you, sire, for your help and your hospitality. You are indeed a friend to Geraud Bouvier."

"Give him my greetings when you next see him," said fitzOsbern. A quick nod, and he turned away to his breakfast.

Tudwal stood by the door. "Godspeed, lad," he said and clasped his shoulder briefly.

"Thanks be to you as well, Tudwal. You have been very kind to me."

A groom already stood in the street with Dinas next to the armed group of Normans.

For two days they rode through narrow tracks in the brooding forest, closer to the sea and Edan's own village. He could not help but think of Herstmonceux, the King's castle being raised near there, and his sisters and his mother nearby. Yet he had no excuse to go there and see them. Bishop Odo took him to Dover and his castle.

Edan's shock when he saw Odo astride the big gray stallion lingered. The coldness of his behavior on the ride had helped sustain the shock. Edan's own battle memories of the warrior Odo fueled anger which in turn fueled his courage. Despite his religious responsibilities, Odo was every bit as much a warrior as his half-brother, King William. Could a warrior such as he have a cleric's compassion for his fellow man?

A party of ten, they camped at night and dined upon wild fowl the men shot in late afternoon. The men were polite to Edan but sought no conversation.

Edan's first glimpse of Dover seen through a curtain of sleet brought a wave of sadness, bordering on physical pain. He was only 13 or 14 leagues from Herstmonceux.

Pulling his mantle closer, Edan crouched lower over Dinas's neck. Not long now and they would find shelter in the castle. The horses' big hooves splashed mud and cold water up onto their bellies and the legs of their riders. They quickened their pace sensing the end of their journey.

A short time later the streets of the town led them to the castle moat and bridge. A quick hallo and blast of trumpet and the horses' hooves thundered into the castle, chains rattling behind them as the drawbridge raised.

After a flurry of activity, the horses were led away, and Edan found himself in the hall before a roaring fire. Dozens of men with short-cropped hair and military dress milled about. Odo moved from group to group. Edan settled on a bench close to the fire and set about warming himself.

He watched Odo working his way among his men, observed the natural leadership, the expressions on the faces. Was he sharing court gossip? Everyone seemed attentive.

Servants appeared with ale and food for the evening meal,

smoked ham and pottage. Edan could not help wonder at the source of the meat and who went without, so this hall of Normans was well fed. He did not take a second helping.

His mind filled with his plan for whatever village Odo set before him. *What would the man be willing to provide to help the village get started as Geraud had done?* A tightness began in his stomach. The small supper he had eaten lay like a hunk of iron in his gut. *What if this plan didn't work? Or worked too well? Would Odo let him go back to Geraud, or would he be punished? Or worse?* Ridley's warning pounded in his mind. The walls seemed to grow closer, while the heat from the fire and the press of men made him light-headed. He rose from the bench, threaded his way among men to the drafty corridor. *Could he slip out unseen and escape this castle, return north?* Drawing a deep breath, then another, he leaned back against the cold stone. His heart raced. He stood there until two maids came with pitchers of ale, their stares rousing him. *No, he could not.* He left the chill corridor and returned to the hall.

15 Dec 1067

The next morning dawned foggy and chill, a thin layer of sleet upon the ground. They had risen early, eaten and set out at first light. Odo and the same men from the previous two days' journey led Edan to the village where he would spend the next few months. Which one would it be?

A sense of dread crept over Edan as they rode into the ruins of a small village inland from Hythe, just as the gray skies let loose with a drizzle. The thane's manor was in ashes. Not one ox, sheep, pig, goat or chicken could be seen. Half the wattle and daub cottages lay in ruins. A tattered group of villagers, perhaps fifteen or so, mostly women and children, except for two old men, timidly came from their hearths to greet the visitors. Edan looked into hopeless, beaten eyes.

Odo spoke to the gathering. "I will send two yoke of oxen, two crates of chickens, six sheep, two goats and two pigs. They will arrive within a fortnight. This lad here will stay with you and heal this village." With a cold smile he held out a plump sack of grain to

Edan. "This should make bread for a time."

With that he whirled the gray stallion about and galloped from the village flanked by his men.

Edan sat on Dinas's back shivering and watched the riders disappear across the fallow fields into the forest. Slowly, he turned to the villagers. The dark eyes watching him were unreadable. No uneducated Norman lord resided here. These people knew as much as he did. What could he do to help them survive until spring? The weight of the grain sack across his right leg was not nearly enough. Of the animals promised, only the goat and the chickens would produce anything they could eat. For the first year, the animals must be saved to work or provide wool, milk and cheese or eggs, yet if it came to starvation... He had a sinking feeling that all the villages around were in the same dire state. No help would come in this area so heavily devastated. Only desperation would allow these people to trust a mere lad such as himself to help their situation.

Jutting his chin, he said, "I be Edan. Tell me your names."

A hollow-cheeked young woman, two young children hidden in the folds of her skirt and another older girl by her side, spoke, "I be Wenda. My husband, the miller, died defending our village. This woman, Bess, is my sister, with her two lads. Her husband died, too." She pointed to a gaunt, older man with a useless arm. "Ulfer is our father."

Wenda turned. "She is Blythe." A younger woman nodded, a babe in her arms, too small to have been from her husband who died over a year ago, and a toddler. A Norman-fathered babe, Edan realized. "And that one is Neva." Another older woman with two girls of ten and twelve nodded. All had been introduced but one elderly man who now spoke for himself.

"Calder be my name. All my family is gone, my wife, my sons, their wives, their children. I have nothing left to lose. I welcome you here and will help as best I can, but we have little to work with. At least, we now have a pinch of hope. Even your horse can be put to work. The grain you hold in that sack will be well used."

Wenda looked skyward. "We'll all catch our death if we stand here in the rain. Come into my cottage."

Everyone surged in. Two small benches before the fire filled quickly, the rest sat around the table or stood. The peat fire smoked along, warming the interior.

Calder spoke. "The grain from the Normans will get us through until they return with the animals. If they bring us more, we have three or four months to get by before Spring and the new growing season. The milk and eggs will help. Next summer we can shear the sheep for wool. The oxen can plow in spring, but what will we plant?"

Ignoring the question, Edan asked, "Have you been snaring fowl and hares?"

Calder nodded. "We would shoot pigeons, squirrels, or deer, but King William has made it against the law to have a bow and arrows. Any Saxon peasant caught will spend time in Norman dungeons for the offense. But we have gotten by with slingshots and stones, as well as our snares."

"Is there a stream close where you can fish?" Edan asked.

Two small boys, perhaps seven or so, listened to the discussion. One said, "We been fishing every day and catching some."

Wenda added, "Our orchard survived. We women have made cider and a bit of honey mead and dried apples. All of us have gone nutting and have a good supply of acorns, chestnuts and hazelnuts. We have root crops and kale from the garden. We have a little honey from the beeskep and a little salt, dried berries and currants."

Calder broke in, "We would trade with another village, but all the villages around are just as needy as we and we have nothing to trade."

Edan nodded and stood silent for a time. The villagers had already done what they could to survive. If Odo kept his word, the promised livestock would help. There would be butter, milk and cheese. Mayhap enough cheese to trade. He had seen stacked wood and peat for fires. But what they really needed was grain and seed for the spring plant.

Edan knew little news filtered into villages like this, isolated from the larger ones. No moots, no market and no pedlars. How far away were any villages with a surplus of anything where grain could be had? The beginning of an idea came to him. He would wait for Odo's animals, before he made his plan.

"Let us continue as you have until the Normans return. If they bring no grain, I must try to get a small supply and some seed for planting barley or oats. Get containers and we will divide the grain we have."

Everyone nodded and made their way to their own cottages. Edan realized then only four cottages were usable. He shivered at the thought of how long it would take to fix one of the partially destroyed ones for himself. The women returned, and the grain was divided according to the number of mouths to feed in each cottage. When they had gone, Calder said, "Don't worry, lad, you don't have to stay in a ruined cottage. I have plenty of room and welcome the company. You can help us hunt and repair broken items. The gods know there are plenty of those. Do you play checkers? I haven't had a partner all these months since the conqueror came."

For the first time since he left fitzOsbern's with the blessing of the kitchen staff, Edan felt warmth of feeling on his behalf. The relief which followed cheered him.

30 Dec 1067

Two weeks passed quickly with all the hunting necessary to feed sixteen people. No one mentioned the Christmastide season. One evening while Edan played checkers with Calder, he discovered Ulfer had been the village tinker until the Normans came. "With one arm useless, he can do little of his old trade. He can help a bit with the children and do a few light chores."

"What were you before the battle?"

"I was the bee keeper. The old hives were smashed and raided. I built new boxes and managed to recapture some bees. This spring I will capture more.

"What we really need," Calder continued, "are a couple of young men to help the women take up the plowing and planting in the spring." He looked pointedly at Edan.

"I'm afraid I can't help with that," Edan replied, with a mirthless laugh. He could feel a blush rising in his cheeks after Calder implied young men were needed to be husband to Wenda or Bess or Blythe. "Most villages suffer the same need." Somehow these words made him think of Merane far to the north. Did she wonder at how long he had been away? Did she miss him? Often he thought of her face, her voice, her gaiety. When would he be free to return?

Calder nodded. "I know, I know."

In the days after Edan arrived, mud changed to frozen ground and Odo's men did not return with the promised livestock or more grain.

As Edan sat in Calder's hut, repairing broken items, a plan formed in his mind, a plan to help the village. He shared it with Calder who grew excited at the prospect.

1 Jan 1068

On the beginning of the new year, Edan prepared Dinas for a trip. He packed dried apples and nuts in a bag but would take no more from the meager stores.

Every village he came to on his ride south he assessed, as to how many people, how thin they were and asked for any news. The villages all resembled the village he had been sent to heal. He rode on to Herstmonceux. He had to see for himself. All through the two days he rode, his emotions raged and waned. Would his family still be alive? Would the villagers he knew still be there? How would it be to see his Father's grave? These and a hundred other questions filled his mind.

Edan approached Cecil's hut from the forest side and tied Dinas in the trees. Smoke rose lazily from the chimney. He hoped the woodcutter still dwelt here. As he approached, two dogs ran forward, Cecil's Bear and Toby, barking to announce him.

"Toby," Edan said softly to himself. "Cecil must still be here."

Toby began whining and jumping about. With a creak of wood in the frosty air, the door opened and Cecil's tousled head appeared. For a moment he stared before looking furtively toward the village.

"By the whiskers of St. Dunstan, it be Edan. Come, lad, get in here where it's warm."

Edan sprang forward to the doorway. The forester's wide grin made him feel at home again. Cecil clasped Edan to his chest, then held him away. His ragged brown tunic told of hard times or a bachelor's inattention. Edan's throat tightened. A thrall collar rested around Cecil's neck. At least the Norman who held this village had not branded as in Swindon.

"You have been away overlong," he said.

"I thank you for your food and the letter from Mother," Edan returned. "And I thank you for still living here."

Cecil chuckled and looked at him kindly. "You have grown toward manhood in your absence. Tell me of your adventures since you and Fergus went away." A sudden flicker of fear crossed his face. "Fergus is alright?"

"Aye, Fergus is well. He stays at a northern village where he has enough food to eat. He is just not involved in this task I have set out for myself."

"Fergus's people are well, too. Tell him when you see him."

"Now to the adventures…" When Edan finished the telling, early winter darkness had fallen. Cecil bustled about boiling some kale and onions with a dab of smoked venison.

Edan raised his eyebrows when the forester dropped the meat into the pot. Cecil looked back with a steady gaze. "I may wear the thrall to keep my life, but no Norman king tells me what I can eat. And if I am caught, I pay the price."

Toby stood and thrust his nose into Edan's hand. Edan grinned. There was something about being back with Cecil, a feeling of sanctuary.

"What have you done these past months since the Normans came?" Edan asked as he scratched Toby's head and fondled his ears.

"I helped your mother say the last prayers for your father and all the others slain, and then I took up my axe and got to work again. Now your sister, Moira, and her man live in the thane's house, and the villagers have gone back to the fields. Your mother and your little sisters, Regan and Cara, is gone to Chichester with her new husband."

"Moira, here?" Edan said, surprised.

"Aye, and have you come home to stay?"

Edan shook his head. “No, only to beg for a couple sacks of grain to get the remnants of a village through until spring.” He couldn’t find it in his heart to tell Cecil the part about doing the saving under the banner of the Normans. “I shall ask Moira tomorrow.”

“You will have hard shrift to get Moira to part with any grain. There is little to spare.”

“Did the menfolk who hid from the invaders ever come back to the village?” Edan asked.

Cecil shook his head. “Na, they could not stand the thought of wearing the thrall collar. They leave gifts of meat now and then at my door to be distributed to the people of the village. They roam in bands of outlaws and steal from the Normans who travel the roads.” Cecil smiled a sad smile. “I think they watch their wives and children from the trees. A painful choice they’ve made.” He stood to ladle the stew into trenchers for the two of them.

“A merchant came through on his way to Lewes yesterday with word of Exeter refusing the Normans and trying to form a resistance group among neighboring villages.”

Despite his choice to farm instead of fight, Edan’s hope surged, then diminished. One town would not be enough. He had seen what it would take to defeat the Norman troops.

4 Jan 1068

In the morning, over ground white with frost, they tramped deep into the forest to a hidden rocky place. Under pewter skies they halted among forest shadows, and Edan found himself looking down at a long, narrow hummock of turf piled with stones. The cross was simple with Father’s name and the year. Cecil stood, patient, to one side.

For a long time he stared down at the grave. The smell of the wood filled his nose and the frigid breeze tugged at his hair. Father had loved this rock outcropping with its spring. He was glad for him that he would from now on always be close to it.

He ran over in his mind the good times they had passed together, Father’s understanding, willingness to teach, and the security he offered. He regretted it had been taken from him so soon, but he had come to accept it.

At last he knelt beside the grave and tidied it before he put his clenched fist over his heart. "You are with God now my Father. May you be at peace."

He rose and, taking a deep breath, turned away from the grave of Selwyn, who had fought bravely at King Harold's side until all had fallen. What had become of the sword? He turned to ask Cecil and saw him standing there with a long object wrapped in cloth. While he knelt at his father's grave, Cecil had retrieved a hidden item. He held it out to Edan.

"It is time for you to have your father's sword. You may not return again, and you've now been trained to use it."

Edan took the bundle and opened it. The one-handed sword still possessed a dull gleam, its extended hilt and wire-wrapped grip ended with a decorative pommel. The two-edged blade broad and strong. He rewrapped it, held it to his chest and wondered if like Yoghan in Galt's tale he could still make a difference for the Saxon people with or without this weapon. By God's grace, he wanted so to make a difference.

Still, this was a leave-taking. Though he had mourned Father and he would always be part of Edan, it was time to move on.

Chapter Twenty-Nine

5 Jan 1068

Later that morning, Edan walked beside Cecil's woodcart, dressed as any other villager. Once inside the gate, the familiar kale plots barren in midwinter, the familiar thatched cottages spouting smoke, his parents' house, all created a feeling he had never left. Chickens scratched in the common, and by the stable stood his old pony, dozing, one hip dropped. At the same time, he felt like a ghost, walking unseen among all these people he knew well, who seemed not to see him.

Cecil took him to a cottage at the end of the row where a young woman had given birth a day ago. He said Moira would be there with hot ale laced with feverfew and nutmeg to bring forth the new mother's milk. According to Cecil, Moira had taken their mother's place as mistress of the village.

The two unloaded wood into a scant stack by the cottage. As they finished, Edan heard the cottage door open. A young woman in a gown of green wool emerged, carrying a closely bundled child of less than a year. His breath caught in his throat. He couldn't see her face clearly in the shadow of her red-gold hair. A quiet expectancy settled over him.

She looked up, and the blood drained from her face. Frozen in place, she stood looking at him. The babe looked up and stared at him also with round blue eyes.

For that long moment it became clear to Edan that Moira did not believe what she saw. The time since they were last together had turned him from little more than a boy into a lean, hard, near-man, with red-gold hair tied back in a thong, a frown line creased between his brows, wind-burnt skin, and a longing in his eyes.

Edan saw not the pouty young girl he had left but a grown woman, her child on her arm, so much of the teasing laughter that had been in her face, gone. She wore fine wool clothes of the nobility. His gaze took in these changes and the child.

Moira's lips barely moved. "Edan?"

His heart pounded. "Aye," he said, "how are you, Moira?"

She made a gesture toward the child, as though somehow that answered his question.

"Does he belong to the Normans who came the night Father died?" he asked through shut teeth.

She nodded. "You knew what happened then?"

"Aye, I guessed. I've dreamt I heard you crying for help. And I wanted to come to you, Mother, Regan and Cara and slay the invaders. I've dreamt of that all this time." He heard a strange plaintive sound in his voice that seemed to belong to someone else.

"Isn't it always this way? After the men fight and die, the women are the spoils of war," she said, as her eyes took on a distant look.

She seemed to grasp hold of the present then. "You must not be found here. You can not stay. Why did you come?"

Edan glanced at Cecil who stood by, wordless, his hair sticking out in six directions. "I come to beg two bags of grain—no matter barley, oats or wheat. The village I stay in is starving."

Moira was silent. Then she said, "Come to the mill now with the woodcart. There is room for something under your load away from the gaze of the sentries."

"Come, Selwyn, it is time for food." She leaned over the babe and spoke gently. She turned and walked toward the thane's house.

For a moment, Edan could not move. Moira had named her babe after Father. She ran the village the way it had always been run—the Saxon way, yet now under the watchful eye of the Normans.

Cecil said, "Let us unload more of this wood among the cottages and make our way toward the mill."

At the mill Cecil passed the time of day with Alric the miller.

Edan slouched in the seat of the woodcart, drumming his fingers on the seat. Except for Cecil and Moira, no one had recognized him. In the distance he saw Gildas, who had helped him escape, and Fergus's mother but dared make no contact. A familiar ache came into the back of his throat. He could imagine, if Fergus were here, the look they would exchange. Then Fergus would shake his head, mayhap with the same ache in his throat.

A short time later Moira returned down the path, this time without the babe. She said, "Load two bags, one of wheat, one of barley into Cecil's cart."

Alric looked surprised. "Aye, m'lady."

When he had loaded the bags, from under her cloak Moira brought a package of smoked meat and a large cheese. Alric's eyes brightened, and he quickly took the offerings and hurried into the mill, his silence bought.

Another bundle appeared from her cloak. "Here is food for your journey and Father's chess pieces. I'm sorry one piece is missing."

Edan took the bundle. He opened his scrip and took out the missing piece he had kept all these months and held it before her. Moira had not forgotten their childhood. "Now the set is complete," he mumbled. They stood looking at each other.

"How are Mother, Regan and Cara?"

Moira shrugged. "Mother is making a new life, making the best of her situation. Regan is nearly thirteen, and Mother is making a match for her. Cara is ten and loving horses."

Edan's eyebrows shot up in surprise. Somehow he had forgotten his sisters were older now, too. Even Moira would be eighteen.

"Mother gets to court with her husband and meets many eligible young men to make a fine match for Regan."

Court? Had Mother and her new husband been there when he had his audience with King William? He almost staggered.

"Come with me," Edan said, impulsively. "I'll take you to Uncle Kadeg in Cymru."

"…and leave my babe?"

This thought gave Edan pause. He had not considered the babe.

"Bring him, too."

"The child of a Norman?"

Edan looked down. "I will know only that the babe is yours," he said slowly and looked up again.

She stepped closer. "It isn't that I wouldn't like to come with you, but there is more than the babe."

"What?"

"Selwyn's father is my husband."

Edan's hands clenched into fists. "You mean you care for a Norman now—too much to leave."

She nodded, her eyes bright with tears. "Not only that. I can't leave our land. Try to forgive me."

Suddenly, Edan began to understand what Mother had said in her letter. "Someday I hope you understand what I have done..." Mayhap it would be the women like his mother and Moira who would conquer the Normans. Saxons far outnumbered Normans in the villages. If children were given Saxon names, raised in the old ways, and inherited the Norman holdings when their fathers died, all could eventually return to the Saxon way.

The thoughts he had pressed to the back of his mind came piercing through. He hadn't quite believed everything of the old life was gone forever. Among those images came Merane's face, a Norman face, the long slender nose, the dark hair, the laughing eyes. In a toneless voice, he said, "I am indebted to you, Moira, and I do forgive you."

"Godspeed, Edan. Think of me sometimes."

"And the god keep you, Moira." Edan felt a small, harsh sound escape his throat and turned away. He heard Cecil turn the cart and come alongside him.

6 April 1068

When Edan emerged from Calder's hut this warm morning, a new and tender green tinted the fields about the village, a contrast to the freshly turned dark earth. Two young men who tired of the lonely life had come from the outlaw band at Cecil's urging and chosen two of the younger women, Blythe and Wenda, as wives, then threw themselves with fervor into the farm work. Everyone seemed to be in good spirits despite the scant food and hard work distributed among so few.

That afternoon Wenda's boys ran into the village carrying a bundle. When they opened it, a clutch of duck eggs gleamed in the sun. This treat boosted morale further as more would be sure to come.

However, for the past week a restlessness had filled Edan and a sense that he needed to move on. Ridley's warning about Odo was never far from his mind especially now that the village had survived the winter, just. He could do nothing more here. The time had come to return to Merane and Fergus. That night he shared Ridley's warning with Calder.

"Since the village has survived, be ready to leave whenever I give you a signal. I don't trust the Normans to be true to their word. Once they gave the impression to the Norman courtiers of helping, you were of no consequence. Keep Dinas in the wood ready to leave at a moment's notice," Calder responded.

Edan realized Calder had already thought about this possibility. He felt better after this plan was in place.

8 April 1068

Two mornings later the thunder of hooves before dawn still surprised him. Shaking the muzziness of sleep from his head, Edan slipped from the cottage at Calder's urgent warning. Still fastening his mantle, he grabbed his bundle and slipped from the cottages to the fields. He had just crouched into tall grass when horses snorted to a stop in the village. He heard the clank of weaponry. To his wonder grass rustled to his right and left as the other villagers fled also. Calder had indeed been wise and made more plans than he had shared but perhaps had sacrificed himself by staying.

A harsh voice called out, "Send Odo's emissary forth!"

Edan shivered. Calder had known. The old man's voice rang out, "The boy ran off soon after the Bishop brought him. We've barely found enough to eat to still be alive."

Crude laughter.

Edan prayed Calder was believable.

The harsh voice again. "Search the cottages."

Edan's stomach cartwheeled. Would the soldiers destroy the village when they didn't find him? Or would they be angry when they didn't find anyone but Calder and kill him?

He crawled through the grasses on his belly toward the forest as did all the others. He must get to Dinas. He could not wait to see what happened. *If Calder should be sacrificed, it must count for something.* Once again he turned away from all that was familiar.

A dense white mist had formed in the fields overnight, salt from the sea tasting on his lips. Dampness seeped into his clothes. A spasm of shivers raced over his body.

Abruptly, the ground dipped beneath his feet, and he found himself in a little hollow which held a stand of thick oaks. To his right, a couple of spear throws away, Dinas should be tied.

Moments later he sat astride the chestnut stallion and quietly picked his way deeper into the forest, north toward Caw who Ridley had promised would help.

Behind him, he heard shouts. Then the crash of horses charging through brush. Had someone seen him? His heart did a jig in his chest. His heels dug into Dinas's ribs. He felt the horse gather itself before it lunged forward, swerving around trees, leaping deadfall.

What Bishop Odo had done was against all Christian teaching. Edan's fear turned to anger as he rode. He had only been trying to help his fellow countrymen in a Christian way, not attack King William. Why was it so important to Bishop Odo to make sure Edan failed to help even one village?

For the next few moments, Edan heard only the cracking of sticks and deep breaths of his horse. He approached a stream, full with rain from the previous day. The little stallion, feeling Edan's heels, stretched his stride, leapt the water, and continued at a sure gallop on the far side.

Edan came to the track he knew led to Ashford. From then on, the journey went straight and smooth, like the track for horse racing he had witnessed so long ago at the Lewes Fair. Stones littering the pathway rapped under the chestnut's hooves as he hurled himself forward. Edan lay flat on his neck to avoid low branches. Presently, the track climbed, and he came into a section of low hills. Concerned for Dinas's strength, he pulled the horse down to a slow canter. The trees hung still in the mist. If deer or fox were about in this early morning, Edan never saw them.

His mind turned back to the village he left this morning. He couldn't shake the guilt that anything Odo's men did would rest on his own head for going there to raise the villagers' hopes. How had Odo known the village prospered? Had he sent spies to peer at them from afar? He shook his head, chastising himself. Ridley had been correct all along. Somehow he knew that, yet he hadn't wanted to believe the warning.

Suddenly, Dinas stumbled over a root, lurched and pitched half down. Flung clear, Edan sailed over the horse's shoulders onto the turf. He lay for a minute unable to get his breath, while Dinas scrambled to his feet and stood trembling.

Edan raised his knees to his chest and at last could gasp in a breath of air. Slowly, silence drifted back. A brush of soft wind through the trees cleared the mist. Carried on the wind, the noise of hooves floated to his ears. Could he be away in time, leaving the soldiers to find nothing but another set of hoofprints among dozens? Edan shook the dizziness from his head and got to his feet. He grabbed the reins, flung himself onto Dinas's back and dug in his heels. Dinas hurled himself forward once more.

Almost immediately, Edan smelled smoke; a village lay ahead. Knowing his pursuit closed on him, he slowed Dinas to a trot and moved into the trees. He could see men in the fields, but Norman guards stood by the gates. A sense of foreboding came over him. What bad luck to have gotten to his destination, then mayhap be caught by Odo's men before he could find Caw.

He chewed on dry bread and cheese from his food bag, while he wracked his brain for an idea. His foot tapped restlessly. He could use the mill to gain entry as he had once before, but he would need to wait for darkness.

What if there were a woodcutter's cottage like Cecil's outside the village? He moved around the perimeter of the fields. At that moment, Dinas threw his head up and pricked his ears. Edan heard a party of men galloping toward the village. Odo's men! Lucky that he had moved to the opposite side of the fields in search of safe entry.

He watched the men pull up by the guards, before riding into the village. From this distance, he heard no words but guessed the soldiers asked about a youth who had ridden this way in the last hour. He decided to stay where he was and see if the soldiers went back the way they had come or continued on.

As he sat, a figure moved from the village into the fields, pausing to look behind, an axe over his shoulder. Edan could not tell if it was boy or man, but his interest increased. The figure drew closer to the edge of the wood where Edan sat.

With one last look back, the short, dark-haired man slipped into the wood only a spearcast away. Edan sat very still, one hand tight and high on Dinas's nostrils in case he chose to greet the newcomer. The man turned left, eyes to the ground, then right toward Edan, apparently searching for sign of someone's passage.

Holding his breath, Edan waited for the man to look up and see him. One more probe into the trees then back out, almost at Edan's feet. The man's black eyes narrowed as they met Edan's, full of urgency. His narrow, brown face showed no expression.

Chapter Thirty

8 April 1068

"Be you Edan?" he asked in a gravel-edged whisper.

Surprised to hear a stranger call him by name, Edan managed to nod and let his breath out in a sigh.

"I be Caw," he said, looking Edan in the eye. "Odo's soldiers came into the village asking if a young red-haired lad rode through today. I kept an eye out for you after I got word from our friend. Since you did not come into the village, I thought you might be close by waiting."

"Aye, I saw no easy way to contact you, and they were hard at my flanks." Edan liked what he saw in this calm, decisive man's face.

"We need to be away before they search for you around the edge of the fields." Urgency sharpened his soft words.

"Where can we go?"

"Follow me," Caw said and set off at a jog trot.

Edan mounted Dinas and followed. The little man held a fast pace, moving like a wild animal, paused to listen, looking over his shoulder. At times Caw followed game trails, at other times he did not but appeared to know where he was. By dark they were at least three leagues farther toward what destination Edan knew not. Still he felt safer in Caw's presence.

Caw paused and ducked behind a large tree. He popped into sight again and motioned Edan forward.

"Tie the horse in here. The trees make a natural garth for him."

Caw found water from a spring and grass for Dinas which he cut with his dagger.

They both ate the rest of Edan's bread and cheese before they crawled under a nearby fallen tree to sleep. Settling in among fallen acorns, Edan found too many thoughts alive in his mind. He rolled over and scooped out an arm's sweep of the hard, round nuts. He squirmed into a new place.

"Where are you taking me?" Edan asked.

"North, away from the king's men." With that, Caw turned over, his back to Edan, conversation over.

An owl hooted nearby, another answered. Those few calming words allowed Edan to relax. He remembered nothing else until dawn when he heard Caw moving.

9 April 1068

"This day we will travel to the edge of Odo's lands. By tomorrow we should be…" he broke off and listened, intent. Moments later Edan heard the sound of hooves, many hooves, and the chink of weaponry.

Caw's eyes signaled silence. Edan ran through the gray dawn to pinch his fingers high over Dinas's nostrils to prevent a betraying whinny. The stallion gave him an affectionate nudge with his guarded nose. Caw ghosted closer to the sounds to see who passed.

Sometime later Caw reappeared beside Edan, so suddenly that Edan jumped. "A large troop of the King's men rides west---something must have happened." Caw climbed up behind Edan, and they set off northward. He gave direction to Guildford. After a league passed, Caw surprised Edan by saying, "I know a man in Guildford who will have the latest news, though I hadn't wanted to go nearer to London. Those who follow you may not be our only danger." To Edan's own ears, his belly growled like an ox bellow with hunger as they rode. Caw fastened his axe to Edan's saddle alongside the sword.

Big silver-lined clouds scudded over a moon riding high when they reached Guildford long after dark. Caw left Edan in a wood and crept toward the village, looking over his shoulder at intervals. Soon Edan saw his silhouette glide up the ditch of the moat and become a dark figure racing the moon shadow across the common to the thatched cottages.

Edan half dozed against a tree. Just then Caw touched him. His muscles tensed. His heart leaped to a faster pace. According to the moon's position, an hour had passed.

"My friend says the King goes to Exeter to teach a small force of local rebels a lesson. We dare not stumble into the King's path in his present mood."

So there are still men who would rebel, Edan thought. Caw's words echoed in his ears. Battle at Exeter. A small force. Why did the rebels not realize they must join forces? Words from Ridley emerged from his memory, "tribalism." The men would not join together because each wanted to lead, and no one would give up power to one man.

"If we ride hard this night, we might catch up to a group of friendly men and join their numbers northward."

Edan heard the decision in his voice and climbed onto Dinas and held a hand down to Caw to be pulled on behind. Caw seemed driven to reach a destination by a certain time. Edan remembered the rest of the night as a blur of dark tracks, shadowed villages and Dinas's snorting breaths as he trotted and cantered steadily northwest. His stomach gnawed on his backbone. Dinas had to be starving as well with all his hard work. He reached down and patted the sweated neck. Edan caught himself dozing off and on near dawn but awakened to a fierce whisper when Caw's keen hearing picked up voices. They rode into cover and waited. A party of men moving fast in the near darkness slowed and stopped. Bits and weapons clanked. Edan held his breath hoping his stomach did not growl.

11 April 1068

Two days later near the eve of a cloudy, gusty day, Caw led Edan into the blackened rubble of a deserted village. In the ruins of the small chapel next to the former thane's house lay remnants of a recent campfire. Caw poked a finger into the blackened coals and nodded. "Still hot," he muttered. "They are not far ahead."

"Who is?" Edan asked.

"The group of friendly men," Caw replied in a distracted way, as he looked over his shoulder.

Edan wondered, who is friendly?

A scrabble on a broken wall caused Edan to whirl, his heart pounding. Caw tensed. A half-wild calico cat crouched there staring beyond the ruin. Something startled it besides their presence. Nothing else stirred in this decayed place, yet Caw continued to stare outward like the cat. An image flashed into Edan's head. Did the village he fled look like this one after Odo's men finished?

Behind Edan hooves sounded on the bridge into the village. The calico cat streaked down the wall with tail bristling. Shouts sounded. Edan's fatigue and hunger evaporated like fog under a hot sun.

"Tracks here. Fresh." French words.

Another voice, "How many?"

"Several---perhaps half a dozen." A clank of weapons.

A cold, knife-edged fear sliced through Edan. His gaze flew to Caw, who jerked his head to the left. For one brief moment, Edan hesitated, his hand still on Dinas's reins, then put one hand on the horse's nostrils. Caw melted behind the broken wall, Edan and Dinas on his heels. They moved on silent feet through the darkening village, behind ruined byres and out into fields.

Edan heard another shout, "Here's coals from a recent fire."

Already men were where he and Caw stood only moments before. By the mischief of thieves and fools! What next? His feet rustled through the grasses of the orchard into a fallow field. How long would it take for the men to track them?

Edan heard the sound of moving water and saw the shadow of a ruined mill ahead. They would have to swim for it. Caw stepped into the swirling water with no backward glance. Edan followed with Dinas. The second step plunged him into water up to his waist before Dinas lunged forward with a splash dragging him after.

"Over there," a voice shouted from the orchard. "A splash. They're in the water."

"Probably ducks landing," replied another voice in a tone of disbelief.

Edan heard a horse gallop toward them across the fallow field.

He swam hard beside his horse careful to keep away from the thrashing hooves. He saw Caw close to the steep bank on the opposite side, his wet black head gleaming. The bank too high, Caw floated downstream in search of a spot to climb out.

An arrow whistled by Edan's ear and splashed into the water. "May the curse of the plague be on you," he muttered to his pursuers as his heart leaped, paused, then hammered a rapid pace in his chest. He stroked forward after Caw who now clung to an overhanging branch and dragged himself out of the water.

Someone shouted behind him, "There's still two in the water."

Still two? Were there more men here? Had these soldiers mistaken Caw and him for someone else or part of a larger group?

Another arrow whistled past. Dinas grunted and shook his head. Edan tensed. Had Dinas been hit? The horse kept swimming, then his feet hit bottom. He lunged in slow motion through shoulder deep water toward the bank. Edan clung to the saddle with one hand, his feet scrabbling in knee-deep water.

A bulky figure appeared near the bush on the bank where Caw had disappeared. Not Caw. Who then? Edan peered into the near darkness. Indecision filled him. Who was it? He had no time to waste.

"Here, lad," a voice whispered hoarsely. "Come out of there." The man reached forward with one hand. "You're among friends."

What was it Caw had said? "A group of friendly men is near."

Edan slogged through water to grasp the offered hand and was yanked into the shelter of the shrubbery, Dinas following. Arrows pelted into the bushes around him.

He could hear men shouting on the opposite shore behind him as the armed men came together, then splashes as they urged their mounts into the water.

He clambered onto Dinas. The gusty wind which had been from the southwest all afternoon, suddenly turned and came out of the north. He shivered and looked overhead to see angry black-edged clouds churning, running before the wind. Thunder rumbled and lightning flashed. Bushes rattled and twigs hurtled through the air. With the chaos and the darkness it was not easy riding. Edan found himself in the midst of a group of five mounted men, Caw on behind the bulky man, whose cloak billowed and flapped about the smaller man's head.

The horses, what with the storm and the tension of their riders, were white-eyed and jumpy as they crashed through the forest. A small bough tore loose from a tree in front of the lead horse, a light gray. It stopped, planting its feet and reared straight into the air until Edan was sure it would go over backwards, its rider with it. The slight figure on its back lashed it between the ears with the ends of its reins. At last it came down, trembling and prancing.

While marveling at the rider's skill, Edan heard the bulky man exclaim, "By the god, dig in your heels and go!"

That voice. Ridley! Friendly man indeed. His spirits lifted, encouraged by his friend's presence.

At their rear, crashing sounds told of their pursuers. Before Edan could think further, all five plunged forward again, cloaks billowing around them. They had scarce gone two arrow flights when the rain burst upon them. Their faces streaming with wet they pushed forward, the horses wet and miserable, their heads drooping and tails clamped tight to their rumps.

The sound of running water overtook that of rain and any hoof-thunder of pursuit. The little group paused on the banks of a stream where the first of the armed men crashed into them in the darkness between lightning flashes. He heard Ridley shout, "Gods and fiends!"

Edan's sight filled with uptossed horses' heads, faces grotesque with fury and rain, with open yelling mouths. He heard the hiss and whine of swords being drawn. Ridley and his companions whirled with reactions so quick even the battle-hardened armed men who followed were initially caught off guard. They came together with a jolting shock that vibrated Edan's teeth. The first of their followers was wounded and unhorsed before the rest could gather themselves.

As a forked bolt lit the streambank, Edan saw a big man, a horsed fighter in his prime, slash at the slight figure next to Ridley, who already fought an adversary. The small man could not know someone attacked from behind. Edan drew his father's sword. Unlike the rest of his party, he made the decision to stay on Dinas's back and fight like the Normans. He attacked the man, who left the small man and turned on Edan, his sword whining around his shoulders. How could they fight in such dim light?

Somehow Edan ducked under the whistling blade in the near darkness, parried a blow and lashed out with a blind kick to the man's knee. His sword whipped past Edan's cheek with a hiss. A hot sting and blood ran warm. Another flash of lightning. He saw the contempt in the older man's eyes as he reined away from the blade.

Edan knew he had little experience and was pitted against a larger foe. But he must fight, as all the other men, even Caw with his axe, were engaged with the enemy. This encounter differed from the battle in Hereford where he fought by Kadeg's side. Here he stood on his own. Being killed was a distinct possibility. He reined in the opposite direction coming into the man's side, ramming Dinas into the other horse's flank. The sword bobbled in his adversary's hand. Seeing his chance in the sporadic brilliancy, Edan struck downward, slashed at the man's wrist. The man's sword flew from his hand.

Not deterred, the man reached for his battle axe tied onto the saddle. As he fumbled with the wet lashings, Edan drove into his foe's horse again. In lightning glare, he saw the surprise in the man's eyes as his horse staggered and fell.

The man rolled away and lunged toward his fallen weapon on the grass. Edan rode forward and flung himself onto the man's back, hacking with his sword. Beneath him the bigger man bucked and twisted, knocking Edan sideways with such force he spread-eagled on the muddy ground. Half stunned and winded, he rolled with his sword still in his hand. The man jumped for him again with all the weight of his big frame. His axe just missed, biting deep into the turf as Edan thrashed away. At any moment Edan expected to fall into the noisy stream alongside. He twisted, knelt and jabbed the sword up at the man above him. He felt it meet flesh and felt it twist in his hand as the man grunted and spiraled downward onto it.

Through straggling hair, Edan watched. The man tried to rise and could not. His eyes lost focus, and he tumbled forward onto his face. Edan did not know if he was wounded or dead. When the next flash lit the scene, he pulled his sword and climbed to his knees to look for Dinas. The chestnut stood a little way off, head high and nostrils flared from his efforts and the smell of blood.

Edan staggered to his feet and ran brokenly toward his horse. A red streak on the animal's neck, visible in a blaze of lightning, caught his eye. When he fingered it, Dinas's neck twitched and he flinched away. He remembered the horse's grunt in the stream. An arrow had grazed him. It was only a minor injury.

He realized he heard no more sounds of weaponry. The clash was over. He knew his companions would be wiping their swords clean before sheathing them. Caw knelt to strip the bodies of the Normans. For the first time Edan saw the slight man face to face. A glint of lightning revealed gray eyes that stared into his own, those of a young man. He stood, his brown hair in sodden ringlets, his face pale but determined, with his blood stained sword dangling downward.

Behind him, one of Ridley's two armed companions bound a sword slash in the other's shoulder.

Ridley looked over at Edan. A glare of light exposed a grim smile which played about his mouth. "Well, lad, you just helped save the life of the future King of England if all goes as planned."

A future king? Edan's brain seemed fuzzed with weariness. Who would that be?

"Edgar aethling, meet Edan, late of Herstmonceux," Ridley said.

From the darkness, the slight young man acknowledged the introduction. Edan stood speechless.

"Now is everyone able to ride onward?" Ridley asked.

One of the armed companions and Ridley piled the bodies of the dead, gathered up the Norman horses, letting each rider lead one, while Caw rode the sixth. "We'll leave these at a needful village on our way," said Ridley.

His head swirling with the news of Edgar, Edan realized that the pedlar had been deeply involved in the affairs of England. Was this even Ridley's country? He still knew so little of his friend, but it was obvious now who the Normans had been after and why. The urgency of the journey yet to come was clear. He knew enough about Ridley not to question his exact destination as he would get no answer, but he would lay a bet with Fergus if he were here that the men were headed for Scotland.

A wave of longing washed over Edan. Fergus. It had been half a year since they were together. As the other riders continued north, what would he do? He had promised Fergus he would not leave him alone forever. Now he knew for sure they would never return to Herstmonceux. He remembered Bryn's words after the battle at Hereford. All she wanted was peace so daily living could go on. She felt much as Moira did, and Mother as well. Was that the best choice?

Mayhap Ridley's plan would work, and Edgar aethling would become King someday. Somehow Edan's knowledge that he had been a traitor to the Norman crown not only in this incident but for the past year and a half seemed less important after the fight to save Edgar. He felt more like a patriot tonight.

How much later Edan did not know, the rain lessened. They had left the wood and entered hilly country with copses of bushes and low thorn. They descended a rocky slope and entered a narrow defile running with water. The rain stopped, and the clouds rose higher, racing the wind.

12 April 1068

By dawn they were through the hills into open country again. Edan could begin to see his companions for the first time. Ridley, his wild hair even wilder after the night's flight, seemed in high spirits. His pedlar guise and his jester guise gone---he was himself, a statesman, a spy, and yes, a patriot. No foolish look in his eyes but a clear intelligence. If anyone could help Edgar become king, it was Ridley. Edgar seemed a serious lad with those gray eyes and reserved expression. The other two men were broad-shouldered warriors consumed with their duty to get Edgar away to safety. And Caw, a man of few words anyway, said nothing.

They had slowed enough to have conversation. Edan had one

burning question on his mind. He urged Dinas forward next to Ridley.

"Who were those men who attacked us---King William's or Odo's?" Edan asked.

"My best guess is fitzOsbern's housecarls. Their livery is that color. The others were engaged in putting down the rebels at Exeter. As steward and co-regent, it would be up to fitzOsbern to decide what threatened the crown in King William's and Odo's absence."

As they rode, thoughts whirled in Edan's mind. He had resigned himself to return to Merane's village as soon as Caw got him away from danger, but now? Could he ask Ridley to continue north with him and help put Edgar Aethling on the throne? Just the possibility of it caused the despair that he felt after leaving Calder's village to lessen.

That evening he sought out his friend. When he asked if he could be included in Ridley's plan, Ridley listened with deep attention. At the end, he did not scoff as Edan feared but nodded with approval.

"Well, lad, I be proud of you. Over the months since the invasion you have gained skills, grown into a man. In the years to come I believe Destiny has a place for you," he waggled his forefinger at Edan. His bushy eyebrows hunched over his eyes, he cleared his throat and put out a square, freckled hand to clasp Edan's shoulder. "If you are one of us, there are things you must know. You've wondered about King Harold not leaving the hilltop at Hastings to fight aggressively. We learned of the message he received before the battle from then Duke William about the Pope excommunicating Harold."

Edan remembered Galt's words relayed from Niland.

"The Duke gave grants to churches to cement his relations with the Pope. But William also had Harold's oath of vassalage to him in 1064 when Harold found himself in a tough spot and had to pledge it. Old King Edward then promised William the kingship before witnesses 17 years ago. Harold's old father also had an indiscretion—Alfred Aethling's murder in 1036. All in all, not only the Pope but the whole continent backed William. King Harold's head must have spun when he realized he had all those strikes against him."

"How could he have known about the mood on the continent and William's bribes to the churches and eventually to the Pope?" Edan asked.

Ridley shrugged. "The rest would have been enough.

Also the King's troops are busy squelching rebellion in the south, not only at Exeter but also with Harold's sons, and the Irish allies they made, somewhere in Cornwall.

"King William wants to bring his wife, Matilda, to England to be crowned Queen at Whitsuntide. First, he must make things safe for her."

Edan grinned. All these stumbling blocks for the King. The longer it took William to surmount all his troubles gave Edan immense satisfaction. Ridley had chosen an opportune moment for his plan to get the Aethling to Scotland when the King was busy in several other places.

The next day while Dinas's strides ate the distance toward the north, Edan wondered how the crops had done during his absence from Merane's village. How Merane fared, how Fergus got along. He shook his head in wonder at how much had happened in the last year and a half.

He must seek his own path now in a changed world, like Cecil who had chosen to stay in Herstmonceux even in thrall to be where he wanted, like Mother who'd married a Norman for his sisters' sake, like Moira who'd compromised to find what happiness she could because of her babe.

Was a traitorous life of arms his destiny? Or would some other thing appear on his horizon as Ridley prophesied?

A fly lit on his cheek, and as he reached up to brush it away, he felt a roughness. He fingered his jowls for the new beard hairs that sprouted there. He grinned widely. He had caught up to Fergus in one more thing. Just wait until Fergus heard of his latest adventure, the long version of course. He saw in his friend a crofter born. He was happier in the village than if he were with Ridley's band of men.

As much as he missed everyone in the village, they did not need his presence for a while. For the first time since that terrible day at Hastings, Edan's spirits flew skyward like a young eagle trying its wings, spiraling upward on wind and eager spirit.

Historical Note

The pleasant pastoral life of an England at peace was upended January 5, 1066, with the death of English King Edward. By the late King's deathbed request and a vote of the Witanagemot, a political council who select and advise the king, Harold Godwineson, Earl of Wessex, was elevated to the throne. In his early 40's with a history of being the king's "right hand man" in keeping the peace and the affairs of state in order, he seemed the most logical choice. Harold's own sister was wife of the late King Edward.

However, three other royals felt they had more of a right to the throne than did Godwineson because they possessed bloodlines of primogeniture. The first of these, King Harold Hardraada of Norway, had the support of northern parts of England, many Scandinavian nobles, and Tostig Godwineson, Harold's own brother. The second, King Cnut of Denmark, was desirous of the crown. The third, Duke William of Normandy, also desired the crown and had aid from his half-brothers, Bishop Odo and Robert of Mortain.

These three candidates were foreign-born and rejected by the Witanagemot for that reason despite their royal blood.

The fourth candidate, Edgar aethling, had the most direct line through primogeniture to the kingship, but he was only 13. He would have to co-rule with a regent until the age of majority. So the Witan rejected his candidacy as well.

What no one foresaw was the depth of desire among the discarded candidates to acquire the crown. First to land on England's northern shores to secure a possible kingship was King Harold Hardraada, accompanied by Tostig, timed after the annual fyrd (the national militia) was disbanded. They battled King Harold Godwineson and were defeated and killed. King Harold then had to rush south to Hastings, with only his housecarls and fighters from Wessex and any others he could assemble on the way, to repel an attack by Duke

William which was opportunistically timed to occur when Harold had just battled in the north, his troops depleted and fatigued. Duke William had engaged the support of the Catholic church besides having fresh troops in larger numbers, a demoralizing blow. Ironically, England had 1.5 million troops available in the fyrd, if it had been active.

After the Battle of Hastings in October, 1066, where William was triumphant, he pulled Edgar aethling,13, along with the two surviving Earls, who were also teenagers, 17 and 18, into his court to keep an eye on their activities. During the first year of his reign he took them to Normandy, an effective exile. By doing this, he prevented possible usurping of his crown by young men of the realm, who had armies, while he was consolidating his power. In later years they challenged his power when they reached maturity, but King William was entrenched by then. Edgar fled to Scotland after he was released from his year in court where he enjoyed the support of King Malcolm, who married Edgar's sister. The earls of Mercia and Northumbria fought William and died. King Cnut never pursued the crown on English soil. Harold Godwineson's three sons aligned themselves with a small band of sympathetic Irish fighters and fought William's troops but were defeated and fled to Ireland.

Though he fought many challengers during his reign, William stayed in power until his death in 1087. His Queen, Matilda, died five years before him. He designated his second surviving son, William, to govern England. His first son, Robert, was given Normandy. A third son, Henry, was given money instead of a kingdom to rule. Normans ruled England through many more kingships.

The populace with predominantly Saxon and Scandinavian bloodlines mixed with the native Britons still outnumbered their conquerors who attained all the earldoms and posts of high rank and owned all the land. However, The Normans never owned the hearts and minds of their constituents. The language and customs of the conquered continued to be dominant in England despite the Norman leadership.

Glossary

Armorer-blacksmith who specializes in making armor
Bailey-common area inside a village or castle, enclosed by an outerwall
Barmcake-beer-leavened cake with fruit, like currants
Borderlord-a petty king or chieftain residing on the border of England and Wales
Brazier-a metal container holding burning coals
Breeks-breeches, trousers
Bride Ale-mulled ale served to guests at a wedding
Brogues-coarse leather shoes of untanned leather
Cairn-a pile of stones in conical form as monuments or landmarks
Cob-a short, thickset horse
Coif-thick skullcap of leather worn under a hood of mail or a helmet
Crofters-peasant farmers
Cudgel-stout walking stick, often used as a weapon
Cutpurse-one who cuts purses from belts in order to steal them; a pickpocket
Cymru-Wales, the Welsh
Destriers-French warhorses
Deus-God
Dowager Queen-a king's widow with title or property derived from her dead husband
Fallow fields-left uncultivated or unplanted
Firebox- a metal box to carry fire coals
Fortnight-a time period of two weeks
Fostering-to nurture or train up (in arms or other skill)
Furlong-1/8 mile or forty rods, measure of distance of a furrow in a plowed field in the Middle Ages
Fyrd-national army of England under Saxon rule, a custom which survived for some time into the Norman period
Garth-an enclosed yard or garden
Glen-a narrow, secluded valley
Gout-a disease characterized by swelling and pain in the hands and feet, especially the big toe

Gwyn-an alcoholic drink of the Middle Ages
Hauberk-a protection for the neck, usually of chain mail
Jus sanguinis-by blood, related by blood
Kirtle-a full undergarment worn by peasant women
Knucklebones-an old game played with the knucklebones of a sheep
League-a Celtic measure which equals three miles distance
Libation-liquid poured on a sacrificial victim
Lynch pin-a wooden pin that secured a wooden wheel to its wagon axle
Mail-flexible, interlocked metal chain worked together into protective clothing, as defensive armor, shirts, neck and headwear to protect the wearer
Mantle-cloak
Marshlights-methane gas occurring as a process of decomposition in marshes, producing glowing lights
Milk sickness-a rare disease, caused by eating or drinking the milk products or flesh of cattle that have eaten any of various poison weeds
Monolith-a large, single block of stone used as a monument or marker
Moot system-an early English assembly of freemen to administer justice, decide community problems, elect high officials, etc.
Ogam or Ogham-the written language of the ancient Celts in Ireland circa 4th C A.D.
Pagan-not Christian; heathen
Perry-pear cider
Petty king-tribal or clan chieftain
Pottage-thick soup of boiled vegetables like kale
Poultice-soft, hot, moist mass of mustard or meal or herbs applied to a sore or wound
Provisioner-a man who planned for and supplied food and drink for a large group, such as an army
Psaltery-a stringed, musical instrument
Regent-a person appointed to carry on a government while a king

is out of the country, too young, or mentally or physically unable to do so himself
Rod-a measure of distance equal to 5 ½ yards
Roman road-old, cobbled roads from days of Roman occupation between 700-1000 years earlier than the time of the Norman invasion
Runes-any of the characters of an alphabet used by the ancient Scandinavians and other ancient Germanic peoples
Scrip-a small waist pouch
Shaman-a priest or wizard or conjuror who believes that the workings of good and evil can be influenced only by shamans
Solarium-private quarters of a thane or chieftain and his family
Stone-a medieval measure of weight; fourteen pounds
Succession-a series of heirs to the throne according to royal bloodlines
Thane-a freeman, headman of a village who holds land in return for his fealty (military service) to the earl of his local earldom or to the king
Tinker-a mender of pots and pans
Track-a dirt road between villages
Trencher-a medium-sized, hollowed out, round bread used as a plate
Tunic-a blouselike garment extending to the hips, usually belted at the waist
Waelwulfs-like werewolves, supernatural animals of myth
Wattle and daub huts-huts made of intertwined twigs daubed over with clay and mud
Weir-a dam to back up the water in a stream to regulate its flow, as for a mill, or to create a fish pond
Wench-a country girl or female servant

About the Author

C.E. Ravenschlag is the author of a Young Adult outdoor adventure novel, *Certain Death*, prior to this Young Adult historical, *Traitor to the Crown.*

A graduate of Western Illinois University with a Bachelor's and a Master's in English, C.E. lives in Fort Collins, Colorado. Marriage, teaching, raising three children filled much of C.E.'s life, yet there was always time for outdoor recreation along the way---hiking, climbing 14er's, biking, horseback riding, running in 5K and 10K races, to name a few.

Next, watch for a historical trilogy set in the U.S. southwest.

Made in the USA
Middletown, DE
21 September 2023